MOVING TO LOVE

PJ FIALA

RT
ROLLING
THUNDER

COPYRIGHT

p. cm.

1. Romance—Fiction. 2. Contemporary—Fiction. 3. Romance-Military

eBook:

ISBN: 13: 978-1-942618-18-8

ISBN-10: 1-942618-18-2

Paperback:

ISBN: 978-1-942618-19-5

ISBN-1-942618-19-0

DEDICATION

To my husband, Gene,
who has been a constant support in my life.
Always encouraging me and loving me all the way.
Without you, I am nothing.

To my children,
who have helped shape me into who I am today.
Thanks, guys, you mean the world to me.

And, of course, thank you to all the men and women
who serve in the various branches of the military.
Thank you for your sacrifices and your devotion.
The tagline in my email is:
We are the land of the free, because of the brave.
I believe this wholeheartedly.
Words cannot convey the gratitude I feel for all you do.
Thank you.

1

TIMES LIKE THESE

There were times like these when Joci wanted to burst out laughing; it felt so good. The wind in her face, running through her hair, the sun warming her skin, the roar all around her, seven hundred-plus pounds of pure unadulterated power between her legs—and she was controlling it all. Gliding through traffic with her son, Gunnar, just a few yards in front of her, feeling all the love and joy God made for her—just her. Yes, these were the times Joci enjoyed.

She smiled as they came up behind a car and floated over to the left lane to pass. As she watched, Gunnar, his dark hair pulled into a low ponytail, glided easily past the car, the two little kids in the back seat watched him and smiled at each other. You could tell they were thinking, *Someday I'm going to do that*. Then as Joci pulled up alongside to pass them, they smiled and pointed at her, one of them turning to the adult in the front seat and saying something, which caused the driver to look over at her as she passed him. He smiled at her, and Joci smiled back at the reaction; it happened often. She could almost hear the kids in the back: *Look, Dad, a girl on a motorcycle.*

She easily pulled in front of the car and continued down the highway to their destination. She loved this life, this group of people with whom she had this in common. A few minutes later, Gunnar and Joci put on their turn signals to exit the highway and onto a frontage road, taking them to the parking lot of Rolling Thunder Motorcycles. They navigated past the last few shoppers straggling out at the end of the day.

Gunnar had worked at Rolling Thunder Motorcycles as a mechanic for the past year. He loved working here. He loved the people he worked with; the customers and their bikes; he loved building bikes. Lately, Dog had let him help in the design on some of the custom bikes for which they were known. And well-known they were becoming. Dog built some of the hottest bikes around. He had recently been featured in *Rider* magazine and showcased on several 'biker' shows. His reputation for building beautiful, custom, mechanically-sound bikes was becoming legend.

Joci and Gunnar parked their bikes among a row of other motorcycles and started toward the back doors to the shop.

"Mom, you're going to love this place. I'm excited to introduce you to everyone and show you where I work. You're going to love Dog."

"I'm sure I will, honey. I'm sorry it took me this long to get here," Joci said with a smile.

As they stepped through the back door, the smell of oil and warm engines hit Joci's nostrils. A smile spread across her face as Gunnar turned and looked at her with a grin on his.

"Gunnar, what the fuck took so long?" a man walking around the corner from the front of the building said. He stopped short when he saw Joci walking in behind Gunnar. "Ah, sorry. I didn't know you had someone with you."

Gunnar burst out laughing at the look on his face. "JT, this is my mom, Jocelyn James. Mom, JT—Dog's son."

Joci leaned forward with her hand outstretched to shake JT's hand. JT briefly hesitated, then wrapped his large hand around her smaller one and pumped once. "Nice to meet you."

Joci smirked. "Nice to meet you as well."

JT glanced at Gunnar. "Ah...we're sitting in the conference room upstairs. I just came down to get the article I found on the Internet this morning."

Gunnar looked at his mom and jerked his head toward the door at the front of the garage as he said, "Conference room is this way, Mom."

Joci nodded once and followed behind Gunnar as they made their way through the store and up the stairs. She noted that the store was neat and tidy. There were racks of clothing on one side of the store and parts, accessories, and motorcycles on the other. The store was well-lit and colorful. The logo painted on the wall, though, was boring. Rolling Thunder Motorcycles, Inc. was painted in silver lettering on a white wall with nothing else. No real logo other than the name.

Entering a room off to the right at the top of the stairs, Joci stopped in her tracks as she crossed the threshold. An incredibly handsome man sat at the conference table, which was a large, well-worn oak table littered with beer cans, papers, and miscellaneous food wrappers. About eight other people were either sitting at the table or standing around talking.

As she stood in the doorway, he looked up from his reading and stared at her.

"Dog, this is my mom, Joci. Mom, this is Jeremiah Sheppard, but everyone calls him Dog."

Joci watched as Dog stood to his full height and rounded the table toward her. Well-built, broad shoulders supported the most beautiful head and face Joci had ever seen on a man. Long, blond hair with a few silver streaks and bright green eyes held her attention as he came to a stop in her space. He reached his hand out to shake hers, but Joci stood transfixed as she looked into his eyes.

"Nice to meet you, Joci. Gunnar has told me a lot about you. I appreciate your time helping us plan next year's event."

A blush raced toward Joci's face as she realized he was standing before her with his hand out. Snapping her attention back to matters at hand, Joci's lips trembled into a smile as she touched her palm to his and tightened her grip.

"It's nice to meet you as well. Gunnar has spoken so highly of you, and I'm honored to be asked to help with your event."

As their hands separated, Jeremiah looked over at Gunnar and smiled. Reaching over to pat him on the shoulder, Jeremiah said, "Thanks for coming back tonight and bringing your mom. Let's take a seat."

Joci and Gunnar took chairs to Jeremiah's left as the other employees in the room were introduced to Joci. Deacon, the manager and Jeremiah's right-hand man, sat across the table from Joci along with Ryder, Jeremiah's son, and JT's twin. Janice and Angel, who were clothing sales, and Ricky, who sold parts, rounded out the group. JT walked back into the room with his printed article as idle chitchat and banter flew around. Joci watched Gunnar with pride as he interacted with his fellow employees.

"Okay, listen up. We're going to start out with what didn't work on this year's ride. Come up with solutions and move on to what worked well, then what we can do to make it better," Dog said.

"Oh, I hope you weren't waiting for me," a blonde woman said as she sauntered into the room with exaggerated posture, forcing her large, mostly exposed breasts out for all the world to see.

"Sit the fuck down, LuAnn," Ryder snarled.

LuAnn smirked as she continued into the room. She pulled a folding chair away from the wall and pushed her way between Deacon and Dog. As she sat, she leaned her shoulder into Dog's shoulder and froze as her eyes caught Joci's.

"Who are you?" LuAnn snapped.

"If you would have been here on time, you would have been introduced. This is my mom, Joci," Gunnar scowled.

LuAnn ignored Gunnar's comment and eyed Joci. Joci smiled and held her hand out to shake LuAnn's. LuAnn reached out to shake Joci's hand, barley touching her fingers in the limpest handshake Joci had ever felt.

"All right, what worked?" Jeremiah continued.

Discussion turned to the Veteran's Ride held just two months before. Joci felt LuAnn's stares throughout the meeting but continued doodling on the tablet she had brought with her, taking notes as something of interest caught her attention.

As they started discussing what should be changed, without thinking, Joci blurted out, "You need a logo."

Jeremiah looked at her; everyone else stopped talking.

Taking a deep breath, she continued, "All you have is Rolling Thunder Motorcycles, Inc. painted on the wall. Your advertising and marketing are mostly word of mouth. What you're doing here is great. You need to brand it. Make it yours. When people see your logo, they'll know exactly who it is and what it means."

Jeremiah nodded once, never taking his eyes from Joci's. She felt her face flush at his scrutiny but couldn't stop herself. Looking down at her tablet, she slowly turned it and slid it in front of Jeremiah. He looked at it for a long moment. Joci's heart raced. Not only was he the most good-looking man she had ever laid eyes on, but she could tell the people in this room, Gunnar included, respected and liked this man. She didn't want to overstep her bounds.

"What colors are you thinking?"

Joci's eyes snapped to Jeremiah's as he addressed her. "Black, orange, and yellow. Bold, hot, sexy."

Joci looked down at the tablet she had placed in front of Jeremiah, her face now a bright crimson.

"That's the stupidest thing I've ever heard," LuAnn sneered.

Joci jerked her head up to look at the angry snarl on LuAnn's face. *Stupid?* Joci was far from stupid, and this was her business.

"I think it's a perfect idea. I've been meaning to do something with branding the business, but I simply haven't had the time. This is exactly what you just said: bold, hot, and sexy. I think it's perfect." Jeremiah smiled at Joci, and her heart started beating a wild tempo in her chest.

His smile was breathtaking. Beautiful, straight teeth surrounded by full, shapely lips. His green eyes shone with light flecks of emerald she hadn't noticed before. All of these features alone would be any woman's dream. Put together in this package, Jeremiah was...magnificent.

Joci swallowed and leaned back in her seat as Gunnar said, "Let's see it."

Jeremiah slid the tablet down the center of the table, and everyone leaned forward to take a look at Joci's drawing. "Fuck. That's cool!" JT stated as the others around the table stated their praise. Gunnar nudged his mom, the smile on his face speaking volumes.

LuAnn reached over and put her hand on Jeremiah's arm and rubbed up and down a few times. "Do you think you need that?" she asked quietly. Joci was paying attention. She wondered if Dog and LuAnn were an item. Disappointing, because if there was one man Joci would finally be interested in, it would be Jeremiah.

Jeremiah pulled his arm away as he said, "Yes. We really need it."

We, he said we. Did he mean he and LuAnn or the business? Joci's mind raced as the meeting continued with a new level of excitement. As they were wrapping up the meeting, Jeremiah reiterated what they had discussed, made sure each person knew what he or she needed to do before the next meeting, and started bringing the meeting to a close.

"And finally, Joci. Can you have a color logo for the next meeting? Just let me know what it costs."

"Yes, I can have a color logo. I'll also have the digital files for you. You'll want to add it to your website, invoices, labeling, letterhead, business cards, and actually anything you use for the business. Maybe have a painter come in and paint the walls downstairs." She smiled and shrugged her shoulders.

Jeremiah laughed. "This is going to cost me big, I think." He gathered his papers together, and everyone stood to leave. Jeremiah looked at Joci, "If you want to step down the hall to my office, I'll get you a business card so you have my numbers in case you have questions."

Joci nodded and stood. JT and Angel started throwing away the food wrappers and empty cans as the others walked out.

LuAnn stood and stretched as Jeremiah stood, thrusting her breasts in his direction. Jeremiah looked at Joci and nodded, "Follow me."

Joci traipsed after Jeremiah down the short corridor to his office. He pulled open a desk drawer and took out a business card. Plain white card with silver lettering. Nothing else. B-O-R-I-N-G. *This is going to be fun.* Joci took the card from him and smiled as she looked at it.

"Would you have dinner with me?" Jeremiah asked.

Joci's head snapped up as she met his stare. "I. I...um. I can't. I'm sorry."

With LuAnn hanging all over him and whispering in his ear, why was he asking her out? Joci had no intention of hooking up with another man like that.

"Are you seeing anyone?" He held his breath, his posture rigid.

"Ah, no. No boyfriend. I...just can't." Joci took a step back and started to turn to leave his office.

"Call me if you have any questions, Joci. I'm excited to get this logo implemented. It's something that's been missing for a long time now."

2

MARKETING

Joci nodded once, turned, and walked out the office door. Her palms were sweaty, and her underarms were moist. She could feel her scalp dampen and prickle. His aftershave was still teasing her nostrils as she walked down the stairs to find Gunnar. At the bottom of the stairs, LuAnn stepped in front of her, causing Joci to stop on the bottom step. "Don't get any ideas about him. He's mine. Understand?"

"Really? It didn't seem like he was yours when he asked me out." Joci met LuAnn's stare with one of her own. She hadn't come here to cat fight. Besides, if Jeremiah and LuAnn were an item, he had no business asking her out. She had already been with two cheaters in her life; she wasn't going down that road again.

"You just watch yourself. You come in here with your big fucking ideas," snarled LuAnn, using air quotes. "'You need a logo.' Only I know what he needs, got it?"

Joci's heart hammered. This was one pissed-off woman. "Got it. Now step aside."

Joci pushed past LuAnn and, with shaky legs, headed to the garage to find Gunnar talking with the guys.

"Mom, check it out. Ryder built this fan." They all looked up, and Joci saw four windshields mounted to a ceiling fan motor, making a very cool fan for a bike shop.

"Turn it on, Ryder," someone yelled.

Ryder hit the switch, and the fan began rotating, creating a very nice breeze.

Joci started laughing, "That is so cool. Did you think of that on your own? You're very creative, Ryder."

Ryder blushed and ducked his head a bit.

"Ryder is the shy one, but he's creative as hell," JT stated. "I'm the good-looking one." His smile was contagious, and Joci grinned at him.

Gunnar snorted, "Since you're twins, I don't think there is a 'good-looking one' between you two. The good-looking one would be me."

"You're so full of shit, Gunnar." JT punched him in the arm. Ryder smirked and shook his head. Jeremiah walked into the garage at that moment, and Joci's breath caught. Walking toward them, she could see him fully. She saw the muscles bunch in his thighs as he walked. His broad shoulders and chest stretched the t-shirt he was wearing to its limits. Tall, broad and beautiful, wow. But, clearly a player, not wow.

"What's so funny?"

The boys relayed the conversation, and Jeremiah smirked. "I see you got it working. Looks great; nice job, son." Jeremiah wrapped his arm around Ryder's shoulders and squeezed.

Ryder smiled at his father's praise. Joci noticed a slight bit of pink tinting his face. She looked over at Jeremiah and caught his stare. She blinked a couple of times and took a step back, "I have to get going. Boss man gave me a lot of work to do." She smirked as she waved her notebook.

Everyone laughed as LuAnn popped up behind Jeremiah and wrapped her arms around his waist. "What's so funny?"

Jeremiah squeezed LuAnn's shoulders once and pulled away. "Nice meeting you, Joci."

She looked him in the eye, nodded once, and turned to look at Gunnar. "I'll see you in a couple of days, honey." Joci hugged Gunnar and turned to leave with a wave at everyone. She got on her bike and headed for home, her thoughts running the gamut from Jeremiah to the logo, back to Jeremiah, to the boys, and to Jeremiah again.

W alking into the garage, Jeremiah saw Joci standing with his boys and Gunnar laughing. Her smile was mesmerizing. It was clear where Gunnar's dimples came from. Sweet little body, tight little ass, perfect breasts—everything about her called to him. Smart, talented, beautiful—fuck. She said 'she can't' go out with him. He was going to have to find out what that meant.

Watching her walk to her bike, with the little bling on the pockets of her jeans catching the light, his stomach fluttered. She climbed on, started it up, and pulled away. He felt oddly sad. Looking over, he noticed Gunnar watching him. He nodded to Gunnar and turned to trek back to his office. A couple more things to finish up tonight and he could head home.

Jeremiah sat at his desk, looking over the notes from the meeting, but his mind kept wandering back to the beautiful, sandy-haired, gray-eyed woman he had just met. Sleep wasn't going to come easy tonight.

3

LOGO

Joci clapped her hands together in front of her as she stared at the wall. "That looks fantastic!" Four months had passed since she had designed the logo for Rolling Thunder Motorcycles, Inc. The logo was all black, featuring an inferno motorcycle in the middle and flames shooting off the back of the bike. 'Rolling Thunder' was in orange and yellow on either side of the motorcycle, and 'Motorcycles, Inc.' was painted under the bike. The bold colors and design were stunning.

Jeremiah stood next to her with his arms crossed, staring at it. The painter had just finished an hour ago. Gunnar, JT, Ryder, and the other employees strode in behind them.

"Holy man. That is so fucking cool!" JT exclaimed.

"Very cool. Wow, sexy logo, Mom," Gunnar said.

Others offered their opinions as they admired the painter's handiwork. The shop had closed at noon to allow the painter to finish his work. Since it was a Monday—their slowest day—it didn't matter, and Jeremiah wanted the painter to finish before their meeting tonight.

"Why don't we pull some tables out of the back room and have our meeting down here tonight so we can admire the new logo?" Jeremiah said.

The employees scampered around, locating tables and chairs to set up in the showroom.

"You did a fabulous job with it, Joci. Thank you. This really gets the juices flowing. Know what I mean? Breathes new life into the shop and the ride."

Joci looked over at Jeremiah. "Ah...thank you. That's very nice of you to say." A slight blush tinted her cheeks.

"I mean it. Since you've been coming here and helping us organize the ride, everyone has a renewed sense of what we're doing. I'm fortunate with all these great employees, but something tells me we were just phoning it in. Now...well, just look at their faces. Everyone is stoked. You've added organization, purpose, and cohesiveness to this ride and this business."

Joci turned to face Jeremiah. "Thank you." Her voice was soft but sincere.

Jeremiah smiled at her, causing Joci's heart rate to kick up a few notches. "Have dinner with me."

Joci blinked. Her tongue felt stuck to the top of her mouth. God, she wanted to go out with him so badly. But she couldn't. She wasn't sure what was between Jeremiah and LuAnn and she simply didn't want to get her heart broken again.

"Joci?"

Joci shook her head to set her thoughts straight, "I...ah...I can't, Jeremiah."

"Get the fuck away from me, bitch."

Joci looked over to see Gunnar's face scrunched up, addressing LuAnn.

Joci looked back at Jeremiah. "I don't think Gunnar likes your girl-friend very much. I hope it doesn't cause problems between you two."

Jeremiah opened his mouth to say something, his brow furrowed, and he closed his mouth again. Joci turned and walked over to the tables that had been set up for the meeting. Gunnar pointed to a seat between him and the head of the table, where Jeremiah would sit.

LuAnn watched Joci sit in the chair she wanted to occupy and hissed under her breath, "Bitch, better watch it."

Joci looked at LuAnn and flicked her gaze to Jeremiah, who was walking toward the table. He sat at the head of the table, brows furrowed, and said, "It's time to get started."

The meeting started, though the mood had shifted. Jeremiah was short and edgy. LuAnn was pissy, and any time Joci opened her mouth to contribute, LuAnn scoffed, shut her down, or made a snide comment, so Joci stopped talking altogether. Sensing the mood, everyone else also shut down.

Jeremiah huffed out a gruff, "Let's call it a night. We'll meet back here in four weeks. Thanks, everyone."

There it was again, `I can't,' not 'I won't' or 'I don't want to.' What the fuck did she mean, she can't go out with him? This was frustrating as hell. For the past four months, all he had thought of was Joci. He didn't sleep at night. He was in a perpetual state of hardness in his nether regions. He had gone to The Barn a couple of times thinking he would pick someone up and get his rocks off, but looking around, no one caught his interest like Joci did. Then the girl-friend comment. LuAnn wasn't his girlfriend. What the fuck did that shit mean?

A few days later, Jeremiah was working on a bike in the shop when Gunnar walked in. Gunnar pulled out some tools and walked over to Jeremiah. "What's up, Dog?"

"Hold that for me, Gunnar. I'm going to pull the back tire off and make some adjustments." They worked together a while until Jeremiah couldn't take it anymore.

"What's up with your mom, Gunnar? She doesn't date?"

Gunnar's brows raised. "You interested in my mom, Dog?"

"I've asked her out a couple of times now, but she says she can't. Not *won't* or *doesn't want to*. She says she can't. What the fuck does that mean?"

Gunnar released a loud breath. "Well, my dad really did a number on her. He knocked her up and left. She caught him cheating with her best friend. Later, she found out he had screwed almost everyone she knew, including my mom's Aunt Susan. She was devastated. For years, she never even looked at a man. Then, when I was about thirteen, she started dating again. Cocksucker cheated on her, too. So, she just doesn't want to get hurt again."

Dog watched Gunnar's face. His jaw tightened; his brows furrowed. So, he had to be patient. It explained a lot. They kept working on the bike together in silence, each lost in thought.

"Why does she think LuAnn is my girlfriend?"

"Oh, yeah, I forgot. She asked me if you two dated, and I told her no. But she said LuAnn told her to stay away from you. LuAnn made it seem like you two are in a relationship."

"That explains why she's been so clingy lately." Turning a wrench and hitting his knuckles, Jeremiah swore. "Fuck."

So Jeremiah now had a better idea about what was going on with Joci. He was going to approach her differently from this point forward.

4

LET'S START OVER

"So, I was thinking. If you add this to the Rolling Thunder Motorcycles website, anyone already on the site will be able to click easily on the Veteran's Ride information. We can capture early sign-ups, which should relieve some congestion on ride day. We can have a separate table set up for those who have pre-registered, where they can get their wristbands and swag before we ride." Joci smiled at Jeremiah as she explained her marketing strategy.

"This is amazing, Joci. We've never had this so organized. How have I been able to pull this off before? When I look back on it, I'm almost embarrassed at the state of organized disorganization I had here." Jeremiah looked into her eyes and held her gaze.

Joci's heart was thumping away loudly in her chest. She could hear her heartbeat in her ears, drowning out almost everything else. Everything except Jeremiah's low, soothing voice as it slid over her. Gawd. Her resolve was waning where he was concerned. He had taken great pains to let her know that he was not with LuAnn over the past three and a half months. At the ride meetings, he always made sure LuAnn sat at the opposite end of the table, while Joci sat next to him.

"This is going to be amazing. I bet we have more riders than ever before," Ryder stated, smiling at Joci.

"That's true," JT chimed in. "You should hear all the comments and compliments from customers on the logo. Every day, someone says something about it."

"Oh bullshit, JT. I never hear anyone comment on the fucking logo." LuAnn's snarl hit an all-time low as she leveled her sights on Joci. "It's not like she cured cancer or anything. I'm sick of hearing how great it is." LuAnn jumped up from her seat and walked out.

Ryder smirked as she left and looked at Joci where he smiled brightly. "I think it's fucking *hot!*"

Joci smiled at Ryder and nodded once at his compliment. "Thank you, Ryder."

"Okay, now that we'll have some peace and quiet, let's get down to work." Jeremiah smiled. Chuckles erupted around the room.

Joci lost herself in the meeting. It was enjoyable without LuAnn. She knew she wouldn't be sniped at every time she said something. The others in the room were in high spirits as they threw ideas around and worked out minor details.

"Gunnar, thanks for figuring that out. The parking has been an issue from the beginning. I don't know how you got Mrs. Wilkes to agree to let us use her land, but thanks," Jeremiah said with a smirk on his face.

Gunnar was a nice-looking man, so the women always said. He knew exactly how Gunnar had gotten their neighbor, Mrs. Wilkes, to agree to let them use her land. One big smile from him with those dimples like his mom's and the old lady probably puddled in her undies. Jeremiah had been trying to get her to let them use her land for years now. He had tried buying it, renting it, borrowing it. Nothing. She wanted nothing to do with him or Rolling Thunder. A couple of visits from Gunnar and suddenly, they could use her land, provided they mowed it, kept it neat, and returned it to her in better condition than they got it to begin with.

"No problem, Dog. So, we need some volunteers to go over and start taking care of it. We'll need to mow it and plant a barrier of evergreens. They won't be very big this year, but I thought if we planted them in a row between her house and the field she's letting us use, it'd give her the privacy she's concerned with."

Gunnar's comments were to the group at large but focused on JT and Ryder.

"I don't want that old bag watching me plant trees on her property," JT hissed.

"All she wants is a little eye candy for a day or two. Since when don't you want a woman to look at you?" Gunnar shot back, smiling broadly.

Deacon laughed. "Besides, you're in a dry spell right now anyway. Maybe she'll put out for you, JT."

"Fuck you, Deacon," JT snapped.

"Okay, okay." Jeremiah was laughing at the banter. This was the most enjoyable meeting to date. "April tenth. Let's plan on being over there at eight o'clock sharp and begin working on Mrs. Wilkes' property. Gunnar, you and JT want to go over after the meeting and schmooze with her and let her know we'll have a bunch of shirtless men out on her property beginning then?"

Gunnar smiled at JT and nodded, while JT wrinkled his face.

Jeremiah looked around the room at this group of people. He was a very fortunate man. Though he hadn't enjoyed the company of a good woman as a constant in his life, he had this. Last year, Gunnar joined his shop, and this year, Joci started helping with the ride and marketing. When he first met Gunnar, there was something about him that instantly clicked with Jeremiah. He had hired Gunnar on the spot and had been proven right a number of times. His boys loved Gunnar, and Gunnar loved them back. They went out together, teased, cajoled, and enjoyed each other.

Now he had to get Joci to come completely into the fold. He wanted her to be that constant in his life. He looked forward to days when he would see her. He went to bed most nights thinking of her.

"Okay. Two weeks back here. The ride is less than three months away. Thanks, everyone."

All the staff members got up and started throwing garbage away and filtering out of the room. "Joci, I'd like a word, please."

Joci looked at him, and his breath caught. "How can I help?" She had a little smile on her face, which created those irresistible dimples and his cock jerked in his pants.

Jeremiah looked up and noticed everyone else had left the room. "I want to start over."

Joci's brows furrowed. "Start over?"

Extending his hand, Jeremiah's grin spread across his face. "My name is Jeremiah. I'm single with two grown boys. I work hard, and I'm honest. I ride motorcycles and eat hamburgers and brats. I drink beer, and I love my parents. And you are?"

Joci laughed. *Start over, okay.* She laid her palm against his and looked him in the eye. "Hi. My name is Joci. I'm a single mother with a grown son. I'm a graphic designer and often have my head in my latest project. I'm honest and dependable. I ride motorcycles, eat hamburgers, drink wine coolers, and love my son and my sister. Nice to meet you, Jeremiah."

With their hands still linked together, Jeremiah's eyes never left Joci's.
Great start over.

5

SO, THIS IS HOW IT'S GOING TO GO

J eremiah burst out laughing.

"That's not funny," Joci grumbled.

"Joci, the look on your face is priceless. And, yes, it is funny." Jeremiah grabbed paper toweling from the counter and handed it to her. She had walked into the break room at Rolling Thunder to grab a bottle of water before the meeting when she interrupted a beer fight between Chase, one of the parts guys, and Deacon. She hadn't gotten hit with any beer, or very much anyway, but she squealed as she saw the beer flying, causing Jeremiah and the boys to laugh at her.

She grabbed the toweling from Jeremiah as the guys all muttered "Sorry" and started cleaning up the room.

"Do you always squeal like a little girl?" Jeremiah teased.

"What does that mean? I didn't squeal." Joci feigned irritation, but the smirk on her face gave her away. As she stood here now, even she realized she did squeal like a little girl.

He stepped close. Very close. "I thought it was cute. Actually, I thought it was sexy."

Joci's breath caught in her throat. *He thought she was sexy? Gawd, she thought he was sexy.* Every time she looked at him, her core tightened and tingled. She grew wet and wanting. The past ten months she'd grown to know him. She liked what she saw, physically and on a deeper level.

She loved watching him with the boys. He was a great boss, a great father and more and more, she saw how he was with Gunnar. It took her breath away.

Her voice breathy, all she could say was, "Jeremiah."

J esus. She whispered his name and his dick ached. Ten months. Ten fucking months he had wanted her. Now that he had gotten to know her a little more, he needed her. His body wanted her, but he needed her in his life. She was great with his boys. She laughed and joked with them. Ryder gravitated to her in an inexplicable way. Jeremiah noticed that on meeting nights, Ryder would watch the door for Joci to come in.

He was done waiting. The Veteran's Ride was tomorrow. They were having an afternoon meeting for the core group and again later that evening with all the volunteers. Then, she was going to be his.

"Here's how this is gonna go, Joci. We're going to finish this meeting. Tonight, after we meet with the volunteers, we're going home together. No more of you avoiding me. I want you, Joci, and you want me. I don't want to hear 'you can't' because you sure as hell can. We can. We will."

She looked into his eyes. Her throat was dry, and she didn't think she could speak. Jeremiah reached up and touched her cheek with the back of his fingers, neither of them breaking eye contact. Neither of them wanting to move.

"What the hell is going on here?"

Joci jumped back. *Fucking LuAnn!* What a buzzkill. All those warm, fuzzy feelings flew right out the window when she was around.

"Last time I checked, I didn't have to explain myself to you. Still don't." Jeremiah's snarl caused LuAnn to take a step back.

"Well…I thought we were supposed to be having a meeting, not making out."

Jeremiah looked at Joci, "We'll talk after the meeting. Yeah?"

Hesitating briefly, Joci said, "Yeah." She nodded and turned to walk down the hall to the conference room.

She stepped through the doorway, fighting the urge to turn her head and see what was happening between Jeremiah and LuAnn. Then she felt someone behind her and felt his lips close to her ear say, "Tonight." Oh, lordy. Her stomach flipped, and she became instantly wet. Her breathing felt constricted.

He walked around her and took a seat at the head of the table and looked at her with a smirk on his face. He motioned with his head for her to take the seat next to his and immediately said, "Okay, let's get started. We have a ton of stuff to cover."

Standing to leave, Gunnar looked at his mom. "Mom, you want to ride a little before the meeting tonight? We haven't ridden for a while. I thought I could take you to eat somewhere and then we'll ride over here."

Joci chanced a quick look at Jeremiah. He grinned and nodded slightly. "That sounds like a great idea. But after the meeting, she's mine."

Gunnar looked at his mom, eyes wide, a broad smile spread across his face. "Yeah? Awesome."

Jeremiah's smile grew, "Yeah. Awesome. I'll see you two later. I have a few things to get ready before the meeting tonight."

Joci's face flamed bright red as she watched Jeremiah walk out of the room.

Gunnar snickered. "It's about time, Mom. He's a great guy, and he's been hung up on you for a long time. I'll swing by your house around four-thirty, and we can ride a little before we eat. Good?"

She nodded, "Yeah. Good. I'll see you then, honey."

Joci walked out of the conference room in a daze. What just happened in here? First, Jeremiah told her how it was going to be; then he told Gunnar she was his! *Holy shit!*

6

RIDE MEETING

"Mom, what's taking you so long?"

Joci looked up to see Gunnar waiting for her at the end of the row. Joci had been daydreaming about Jeremiah again and didn't even notice she was just standing there looking lost.

"Sorry. Coming!"

She quickly walked down the row of bikes to Gunnar and, together, they walked to a group of her friends. Joci's best friend, Sandi, and Sandi's husband, Jon, were standing in the group, as well as a few others. Sandi was a beautiful woman, with long, brown hair pulled back in a braid. She was the most vivacious person Joci knew, with a personality that rivaled the sun.

"Hey, there! How are you guys?" Joci asked as she hugged Sandi.

"We're good. I haven't seen you this week. Busy?"

Joci nodded. "You know, getting all the items needed for tomorrow and the tickets and such ready, I had to keep at it so I could finish on time and enjoy tonight."

Joci hugged Jon. "Hey, big guy. How are you?"

Jon was a great-looking man, about six feet tall, short dark brown hair, and laughing blue eyes. Sandi was madly in love with Jon and Jon was madly in love with Sandi. Joci envied their relationship. She had always hoped for a relationship like theirs.

"Doin' good, Joci, but you have to stop being too busy to have lunch with Sandi. She likes her girl time!"

Jon leaned in a little closer to Joci. "She drove me crazy wondering where you were and how you were doing."

Joci laughed. "Sorry, Jon, I promise to keep in better touch with Sandi."

Sandi and Joci had lunch once a week to touch base and catch up. It was something they started doing years ago when the kids were little.

Joci looked at Sandi and hugged her again. "Everything is fine. I'm fine. Gunnar is fine. But, I do need to talk to you. Jeremiah asked me to leave with him tonight."

"Mom...I'm headed over to see the guys." Joci smiled at Gunnar as he started to walk away. With a wave, he was off.

Sandy absently waved at Gunnar, quickly turning back to Joci and said, "Tell me. What did you say? You better have said 'yes' this time."

"Hello, Joci. You look beautiful."

Oh, Gawd! His voice made her shiver. Shit, her body reacted to that man before she could even put a thought to it. Joci slowly turned to see Jeremiah standing next to her and handing her a bottle of water. Taking a deep breath, she looked into his eyes.

"Hi, Jeremiah. Thank you. How are you?"

Jeremiah leaned in close to her ear and whispered, "You look beautiful, Joci."

She looked at Jeremiah and blushed. He chuckled, and her face flamed a bright red. Great!

Sandi said, "Hi, Dog. Looks like we're going to have great weather tomorrow."

Jeremiah looked up at the sky. "It sure does. That means more riders, which means more money for the cause. Gotta love that." They bobbed their heads in agreement.

Joci undid the cap on her bottle of water and took a long drink as he watched her. God, she was beautiful—stubborn as hell, but so beautiful. She took his breath away.

He knew he affected her. He watched her when she was near. He could see the muscles in her neck moving with each exaggerated swallow. When he spoke to her, she licked her lips and looked him in the eye, not blinking. God, if she only knew what that did to him. His cock twitched every time he thought about her. And when he saw her, it had a life of its own; his stomach flipped, and his breathing became unsteady. She had been avoiding the inevitable, though.

This morning, things changed. Jeremiah looked at his watch. He hated walking away from Joci, but he was anxious to get this meeting finished to begin his time with her.

"We better get this show started. If you're ready, come on over to the side of the building."

He nodded at Sandi and Jon, gave Joci a little wink, and walked away. Joci needed to sit down. God, that man affected her whole body, her whole nervous system. Her knees were weak, and she was light-headed. Sandi laughed at her.

"Gawd, Joci, tell me you gave up and decided to go out with that man. He obviously wants you, and you obviously want him." Sandi leaned in a little. "And just think of all the fun you could be having...after hours."

Joci swallowed to moisten her throat. "Sandy, we're going out tonight."

"Finally. For crying out loud, Joci, he's been circling for almost a year." Jumping up and down a couple of times, Sandy shrieked, "I'm so excited!"

Jon shook his head at his lovely wife. Nodding to Joci, he said, "Okay, ladies, let's go hear what's up for tomorrow,"

As they rounded the corner to the side of the building where the pre-ride meeting was being held, there were about one hundred-forty people sitting and standing around waiting for the meeting to start. All the proceeds from tomorrow's ride would go to area veterans who were in need. Medical assistance, work on their homes to make them more user-friendly to a disabled veteran, educational assistance for returning veterans, or any other sort of need that came up.

Jeremiah was a veteran of the Gulf War, and both his sons and all his brothers served in the military. It was with love and pride that he held this ride every year. Last year, they had over seven hundred riders and over twelve hundred people who attended. This year, they expected it to be much more.

Joci loved stuff like this, and she adored this cause. Her own family had served in the military. Both her parents and her sister Jackie's husband, David, were veterans as well.

As Joci, Sandi, and Jon rounded the building to the back parking lot; Joci saw that the stage had been constructed for the festivities tomorrow. Some volunteers had been working on it today.

"Mom, Sandi, Jon...over here!" Gunnar had a spot ready for them at the front table with her sister, Jackie, and brother-in-law, David, and some of their friends. Connor was there as well. Connor was the best friend of Keith, Gunnar's father. When Keith had left, Connor stepped up and helped Joci with Gunnar.

As they approached the table, Jackie and David got up and hugged Joci. She waved at their friends.

"Hi, Connor. How are you? I haven't seen you in a few days."

Connor stood and hugged Joci. "I'm good, Joci. Had a busy few days at work, but everything is fine. You look beautiful as always."

Joci smiled at him. Connor swept his hand to the side and offered her a seat where he had been sitting.

"If I could have your attention, please. I'd like to get this meeting started so we can relax and enjoy the rest of the night. We'll all be working hard tomorrow," Jeremiah spoke into the microphone.

She loved the deep timbre of his voice as it floated over her whole body, covering her like her favorite sweater. It revved up her senses like nothing else in the world. She could almost imagine him whispering in her ear as he made love to her.

She looked up at Jeremiah as he stood at the edge of the stage with a microphone in his hand. He looked perfect up there. He was confident, strong, in control, and sexy, sexy, sexy! He was wearing tight jeans and a black sleeveless shirt that showed off his perfect arms. Both his upper biceps were tattooed in beautiful scroll designs. And in the same scroll pattern, he had dates tattooed on the back of each of his wrists. God, she could look at him all day. He glanced down at her, but he was scowling.

"First of all, I want to thank a few people before we get down to the nitty-gritty. Deacon, once again, the hard work and effort you give to this cause each year astound me. Thank you for so much dedication and time on your part to keep this ball rolling."

Deacon stood up and gave a thumbs up to Dog as the crowd clapped and cheered.

"Gunnar...you have really impressed me with your organizational skills and your ability to think outside of the box. You've helped us solve so many of our issues with space and parking. Thanks, man; we all appreciate it."

Gunnar had a smile from ear to ear. David slapped him on the back, and Joci smiled proudly at her son. He had his dark hair pulled back into a ponytail and his bright, blue eyes twinkled. Gunnar looked over at his mom; she could tell he was very proud of himself. Joci winked at him and clapped louder than anyone else in the crowd. Jackie let out a loud whistle for Gunnar.

"Joci. Thank you for designing the best logo we've ever had and putting together the marketing plan of the century along with the website. In the eight years we've been doing this ride, nothing has come together like it did this year due to your designs and marketing ideas. Because of you, this ride will be the biggest ride we've had to date. Thank you, baby."

The crowd cheered. Joci did a double take. Had she heard right over the cheering? Did he call her 'baby?' God, he had. He called her *baby*! Joci felt someone bump her shoulder and looked at Sandi, whose smile was spread across her face as she gave Joci a thumbs up.

Oh. My. God. Joci thought she would like to just spontaneously combust right now. As she looked around at everyone, she saw Gunnar look at her with a smirk on his face and Jackie looked at her with a smile and a wink. Jon was grinning as well. Connor was frowning at her. Then Joci saw LuAnn.

LuAnn was looking at her like she wanted to kill her. Joci was plain by LuAnn's standards. The men always commented on LuAnn. They positively drooled when she walked by. Over this past year, as Joci was working with the crew on this ride, she heard so many guys saying very crude and rude things about what they would like to do to LuAnn.

As Jeremiah continued to give accolades and started explaining how things would work tomorrow, Joci brought her attention back to him. "Finally, the sign-up crew will sign the bikers and riders in when they get here in the morning. Janice, Ricky, and Joci, you'll be with me at the sign-in table. Break into your crews and organize yourselves for tomorrow. Sign-up crew, meet with me in the store, please."

Joci stood up to start walking into the store, and Sandi swatted Joci on the ass. "Go get him, Joci."

Joci shook her head at her friend and opened the service door in the back by the garage. The store was in the front, but Joci was used to walking through the back. When she came here, she usually walked through the back way so she could say hello to Gunnar and the guys. As soon as Joci walked into the shop, she could smell Jeremiah's after-shave. It was the most delicious spicy scent that had teased her nostrils for the past few months. He was leaning against a wall waiting for her. His arms were crossed over his chest.

Joci stopped in her tracks at the sight of him. Jesus, he was breathtaking. He smiled at her then pushed himself off the wall with his shoulder and walked toward her. With each step, Joci could feel her heart beating faster.

When he stood right in front of her, he reached his hand out and touched her hair. He slid his fingers in her hair at the temple and back until he was cupping her head.

He slowly bent his head down and kissed her lightly on the lips. She moaned at the feel of his lips on hers. A shiver ran through her body, her breathing erratic. He slid his free hand around her waist and pulled her close. That was the undoing of Joci James. She grabbed his shirt on each side of his waist and fisted it in her hands. She hung on, trying not to fall, trying not to let this man consume her. That wasn't going to be easy.

Jeremiah groaned into her mouth and pulled her closer. She smelled amazing, a scent unique to only Joci, fresh and clean with a hint of spice. And she was aroused by him; he could feel her body responding to him. He couldn't wait anymore. He had to take this chance and make her see they could be amazing together.

He slid his hand down to the top of her sweet, little ass and pulled her into the hardness behind his zipper. She let out a little sob at the feel of him pushed against her. He deepened the kiss, his hold on her head kept her in place while he seduced her mouth with his lips and his tongue.

Every time she whimpered or moaned, it spurred him on. He could imagine how she would moan and mewl while he was fucking her. That thought alone almost made him blow in his pants.

Jeremiah broke the kiss and put his forehead against Joci's. Their breathing was ragged and raspy. They were both shaking and hanging on to each other.

Jeremiah said, "We'll go over things with Ricky and Janice so that tomorrow will run smooth. Then, we're leaving...together...and tonight we're going to be together. No more of you avoiding me. I want you, Joci, and you want me."

Jeremiah lifted his head and looked into her eyes. She saw the determination there.

She took a deep breath. "Then what, Jeremiah? We go our separate ways? You fuck me, so I'm out of your system and move on? Is that what?"

Jeremiah's brows furrowed and his eyes became little slits.

"What the hell is that supposed to mean? What kind of man do you think I am? I wouldn't...fuck. Joci, what the hell?"

He took a deep breath to steady himself. He couldn't scare her away. He could feel how close he was to getting her to come home with him.

Lowering his voice, he whispered close to her ear. "I've wanted you since the first minute I saw you. I still remember what you were wearing, what you looked like when you walked in that door. You were wearing jeans with little shiny things on the back pockets that moved around and sparkled when you walked. You were wearing a gray t-shirt with rhinestone hearts on it. I remembered thinking how the gray in the shirt matched your eyes. God, your eyes. I think about looking into them while I'm in you. I think about it over and over. I have feelings for you, Joci. What happens tomorrow is we ride, enjoy the day, meet and greet, and come home."

She took a deep breath. "I'm sorry, Jeremiah. I'm...I...you..." Joci swallowed. "What I'm trying to say is I didn't mean to make you mad."

Joci took another breath and pulled away. Her voice was small and shaky. "I'm scared," she managed to squeak out.

It was so soft Jeremiah could barely hear it, but he did. He let out a deep breath, not even realizing he had been holding it. He closed his eyes a moment and opened them to see her looking at the ground. He put two fingers under her chin and gently raised it so he could see her eyes. His breath caught in his throat when he saw the tears.

He placed both of his hands on either side of her face and brushed the tears away with his thumbs. He very gently kissed each tear track on her cheek.

"I know this is hard for you. I won't hurt you."

"Hey, there you guys are. Are you ready?"

Ricky and Janice stood in the doorway to the store. Ricky worked at Rolling Thunder in parts sales. His short, spiky, blond hair suited him. He had tattoos on both arms, full sleeves, and a set of red lips tattooed on his neck. His blue eyes sparkled, taking in the scene before him.

Jeremiah looked over his shoulder. "Yeah, we'll be right there. Why don't you make sure the computers are booted up so we can run through the software with Joci?"

Ricky looked at Janice and smirked. They turned and walked over to the computers behind the sales counter.

Jeremiah looked back at Joci. "Are you okay?"

Joci gave a weak smile and wiped her eyes with her fingers. Jeremiah grabbed her and hugged her tight. He needed the contact with her. *Poor thing, she was scared out of her wits. Those bastards in her past had done a number on her.*

"All we can do is try, Joci. Not trying is worse than failing. If we don't try to see if we have something together, we'll never know."

He could feel her shaking and tightened his arms around her, holding her in place so she would feel protected. After a few moments, he loosened his hold on her and whispered, "Ready?"

Joci nodded, and Jeremiah stepped back but held on to her hand. Together, they walked to the counter, where Ricky and Janice were waiting for them.

The four of them spent the next hour going over how the sign-in process would work most efficiently.

Ricky and Janice said their goodbyes and Jeremiah told them to go on out; he would lock up behind them.

Jeremiah locked the door then turned to look at Joci. She looked scared shitless. He didn't want to scare her; he wanted to make love to her, to hold her, to smell her, to talk to her. He walked over to stand in front of her and watched her fidgeting with the little purse in her hands. He could see them trembling, and she was biting her bottom lip.

He stepped up to her and looked her in the eye. He placed his thumb on her chin and pulled her bottom lip out of her mouth.

"It's going to be fine, Joci. You look like a scared little lamb heading to slaughter." She nervously let out a little breath and tucked her hair behind her ear.

Her voice was soft and shaky. "I don't do casual sex...can't. With you, I'm afraid it isn't casual."

J oci took a deep breath. Geez, this was harder than she thought. She was drawn to him, had been from the first moment she laid on eyes on him. But, with all the women always throwing themselves at him, she was so damned afraid. Her stomach turned over, making it hard to breathe. Here it was, this moment she had imagined. But now that it was here, she felt almost paralyzed with fear.

"If you hurt me...I just can't go through that." She swallowed the lump in her throat. "I know it seems foolish to you to not even try, but I can't help myself."

Her eyes became bright with tears. Her stupid emotions were all over the board right now, and she knew she was rambling. She was sure she looked sexy as hell with watery eyes, a red nose, and that icky face people make when they're crying. He would be crazy to want her now.

She had thought about Jeremiah for almost a year, dreamed about him, fantasized about him, wanted him, but she held back because of this stupid fear. If they made love tonight, she knew she would fall hard over that cliff. If he walked away after that, she would be devastated. Joci took a step back. She should just go.

In one swift move, Jeremiah grabbed her and pulled her tight to him. His breathing was ragged, and his heart was beating wildly. Seeing her this way broke his heart. He held her tight, stroking her hair and kissing the top of her head every so often. Oh, he loved the scent of her, her hair, her cologne, the lotion she used on her skin.

"When I was younger, casual sex was all I wanted. No ties, no entanglements. But you've been on my mind so much—I haven't been with anyone in months. I've been waiting for you. It isn't casual for me, either. I need you; I want you as well, but...God, Joci..."

Joci looked up at him. She wanted to see into his soul like he always seemed to do to her, to see if he was telling her the truth. They stared at each other for a long time, gauging each other, neither one knowing what to do now. Joci wanted to be with him so badly. Had she been stupid to wait this long? She had no idea he had been waiting for her. Stunned wouldn't even come close to what Joci was feeling about this revelation.

Jeremiah leaned down and kissed her gently on the lips. He licked her lips, and when she didn't open her mouth to allow him access, he nipped her mouth gently.

"Open up for me, Joci. Let me in."

She opened with an escaping sigh. Jeremiah caught that sigh in his mouth and groaned. He turned his head to fit his lips perfectly over hers, pulling her body tightly to his. His tongue dipped into her and slowly swirled around. A little mewling sound escaped Joci's throat, and he nearly came from the sound of it.

Slowly, Joci slid her arms up Jeremiah's chest to his shoulders as she slipped her arms around his neck. Her hand automatically found its way under his hair at the nape and grabbed a handful of it. She had wanted to touch his hair, to tug on it, feel it run through her fingers.

It was soft and felt so good in her hand. She fisted it, and it tightened against his scalp. He groaned and thrust into her. She felt his growing length push against her body and shivered.

Joci dug her other hand into his hair and held on. His hands were suddenly everywhere on her. One hand was on her breast, massaging it. He pinched her nipple through her bra. At first, it hurt and she moaned, but instantly it turned to pleasure and shot right down to her lower belly and pooled around, landing in her core.

God, she needed relief—badly. She abruptly pulled her mouth away from Jeremiah's, and he instantly loathed the loss of her sweet lips against his.

$\sim$

He looked at her, her eyes half-lidded and sexy as hell. She was ready for him. This was the moment, the one he had thought of all day. The time when he needed to get her out of here with him. He needed to be gentle, but firm, without scaring her.

"Okay... Joci...gotta get control, or I'll end up taking you right here with our kids just outside that door..." His smile stretched across his face. "I'll make sure to file that away for later."

He needed to do this right. Nothing was more important than getting this moment right.

"You're shaking, Joci. I don't want you driving like this. I'm going to have the boys bring your bike in the garage and keep it here tonight. You can ride home with me."

He had wanted to pick her up tonight and bring her with him, but when Gunnar asked her to ride with him and have dinner, Jeremiah didn't want to stand in the way.

Joci opened her mouth to protest, but he shook his head no. "Don't say anything. I don't give a fuck what anyone thinks. You're mine tonight; do you understand? From this point on... You. Are. Mine."

7

GETTING TO KNOW YOU

J oci wanted to call Gunnar and tell him they were leaving. Jeremiah was on his phone talking to one of his guys about her bike. Having him tell her they were going to be together tonight was a major turn-on. She hoped like hell she didn't end up with her heart broken again. That would be a loss she didn't think she would be able to recover from.

Joci took a deep breath as she pulled her phone out of her purse. She swiped her finger across Gunnar's picture and tapped the dial icon.

"Hey, Mom, what's up?"

"Gunnar, I'm going home with Jeremiah. I didn't want you to worry. He's having the guys bring my bike into the garage for the night," she said with a quiver in her voice.

"Okay, thanks for letting me know. I'm glad you're giving him a chance."

What do you say to that? "I'll see you tomorrow. I love you."

"I love you, too, Mom. He really is a great guy."

She smiled, "Yes, you've said that…many times. Oh, please tell Sandi and Jackie so they don't worry, okay?"

Joci looked up to see Jeremiah watching her, and her breath caught.

As Jeremiah watched her talk to her son, his mind reeled. She was a beautiful person, inside and out. He had learned so much about her this past year. She was caring and loving and a great mom. She loved her friends and family, and she would do anything for those she cared about. All she asked in return was honesty and fidelity. She had been lied to and cheated on during her past two relationships. She had major trust issues that lingered with her.

He wanted to give her a good life. He had thought of little else while he was waiting for the right time to make his move. She was the kind of woman he'd always wanted to be with. His past relationship with Barbara, his boys' mother, had been pure hell. It hadn't been a relationship; it was casual sex when either of them needed it, and then she had gotten knocked up. She was a biker bitch all the way. Crass, coarse, rough around the edges and too made up, too over the top—too everything. Thinking about it now, he couldn't see how he was even remotely interested in her to begin with. She was nothing he wanted at all.

Jeremiah finished a text and walked over to Joci. "Everything okay?"

She put her phone back in her purse. "Yeah, it's good. How about with you?" Her lips quivered into a smile. "I have to ask one last time, are you sure about…this? Me?"

Jeremiah nodded his head, "I'm very sure. How many times have I asked you out over these past few months? Did you think I asked you out because I didn't want to go out with you?"

"No. I...it's just, you could have any woman you wanted—except maybe Mrs. Wilkes." Joci smirked. Getting more serious, she said, "I'm just...nervous, that's all."

Stepping closer, Jeremiah reached up and tucked a lock of hair behind her ear. Releasing it, he slid his hand to her nape and gently circled his fingers against her neck.

"Mrs. Wilkes is enamored with Gunnar. I'm enamored with you. Let's go."

She took a deep breath and looked into his eyes. Before she could answer, he said, "I just want to spend time with you and get to know you better. I want to share myself with you, and I want you to share yourself with me."

"I know. I'm sorry. I can't change on the drop of a dime. I've lived with this fear and these trust issues for so long; I don't really know anything else."

Jeremiah's green eyes clashed with her gray ones. He wanted to change that for her, for them. He slid his hand to her cheek and rubbed his thumb where a tear had been not long before.

"I want you to come home with me to my house. Since you've eaten dinner already, I thought we could have a glass of wine. We'll be able to sit and talk uninterrupted there."

Joci took a deep breath and smiled. "Okay. I'm... A glass of wine sounds great."

Jeremiah took her hand in his. He felt a shudder run through her and watched her eyes. She never moved her gaze from his.

"I have my truck out back. Let's go."

They walked hand in hand through the store and out to the garage area of the shop. They went out a side door to Jeremiah's truck, virtu-ally unseen, even with all of those people milling about. He opened the passenger door and motioned for her to get in. She looked at him with her head cocked to the side, and he smiled at her.

"Too late to change your mind, Joci. You've let fear keep us apart for a long time. Time to live a little."

8

HOME

Joci climbed into his truck. Jeremiah walked around and got in. He took a long look at her. She peered at him as a smile spread across her face, and he winked. That one wink shot right to her private areas and made her wetter still. If that was even possible.

She was going home with Jeremiah. She could hardly help herself after he kissed her. Oh. My. God. She was going home with Jeremiah.

He started his truck and put it in gear. As he started driving away from the building, he put his right hand on Joci's leg and gave her a little squeeze. Joci looked down at his large hand on her thigh. He had great hands. Big, strong hands and fingers. Her leg looked positively small under it.

After almost a year of thinking about this, dreaming about this, fantasizing about being with him, it was going to happen. It felt dirty, the way they were driving away, knowing what they were going to do—almost like a booty call.

"Hey, what are you thinking about?"

Joci looked up at Jeremiah and sighed.

"I feel like a...a tramp...leaving with you. I've never done anything like this before."

Jeremiah shrugged his shoulders. "I'm sorry. I was going to ask that I swing by and pick you up, but Gunnar wanted to ride and have dinner, and I didn't want to intrude."

"But," Jeremiah continued, "I want to see if we can forge a relationship. I've known that this past year you were scared, so I get that. A few months ago, when we started over, I wanted you to get to know me and know I'm good. I think you want a relationship with me, too. We don't owe anyone an explanation—we're adults."

Joci sighed and looked out the window. He was right, of course. She did want more but was afraid of it. She was afraid of falling for Jeremiah and having him hurt her the way Keith and Derrick had. She wasn't sure she could trust anyone again after that. Trusting Jeremiah was going to be difficult. She saw the way women looked at him, sighed when he walked in the room.

She knew for sure LuAnn would do anything in her power to get Jeremiah. Joci wasn't sure she would be able to hold on to him with that temptation constantly in his path. LuAnn was trashy, but she was pretty and had a great body. She also had large breasts she liked to flaunt at everyone. Joci didn't have large breasts and she sure as hell didn't flaunt the ones she had.

Jeremiah pulled into his driveway and then into his garage. He had a huge Rolling Thunder logo in the back of his garage, painted on the wall. He also had a big workbench and three hot bikes in his garage; Rolling Thunder bikes, of course. Joci looked at the bikes and snickered.

"Nice bikes!"

Jeremiah followed her gaze and smiled. "Thanks. I own a bike shop, you know. These are mine."

He got out of the truck and walked around to the passenger side. He was smiling as he reached in and helped her down. "The yellow one is the first bike I ever designed. I keep her for nostalgia; I hardly ever ride her anymore." He pulled Joci forward with their hands linked together. "Nowadays, there are better parts and components that make bikes more comfortable to ride. But she was my first love, so I keep her."

Walking to the orange bike, he lovingly caressed the handlebars as he said, "This is the first bike the boys helped me build and design. I keep her because of that. It was our first project together. We worked out here in the garage for days and nights, pulling it together when the boys were freshmen in high school. That was about ten years ago or so now." He brushed some dust from the mirror with his hand. "Every once in a while, I hop on her and take her for a ride. The boys do as well. They love this bike. Eventually, I plan on finding a place at Rolling Thunder to put her up and keep her there as the beginning of the Rolling Thunder garage. It was during the build of this bike that we talked about opening a bike shop and building for other people."

Joci loved looking at him when he talked about his sons. His features became soft, and his eyes sparkled with pride and love.

Moving around the orange bike to the black one, he touched the seat and looked at Joci. "Of course, this is the bike I ride now. More comfortable, different frame than the other two bikes, different motor and exhaust—a whole new design I wanted to try out. I wanted to show customers that they can have a bagger and still have it look cool. I love her. She's fun to ride. Comfortable, stylish, classy. I get tons of compliments on her."

Joci didn't miss that he called his bikes *her* and *she*. Interesting, but not uncommon. Lots of people referred to their bikes as *her* and *she*.

He hung onto Joci's hand and started walking to the door of his house. He opened it and stood back to let Joci walk through first. When she stepped inside, she gasped. There were candles burning everywhere. In the kitchen, they covered the counters. She had a view of the living room and saw that they were everywhere in there, as well.

Joci turned and looked at Jeremiah with a question on her face. He gazed back and kissed her lightly on the lips.

"I've been telling my sister-in-law, Staci, about you, and that I wanted to bring you home tonight. I asked her what she thought would be special and romantic. I have to admit, Joci, I really don't know a lot about romance—I'm just a guy. I trust Staci. She helped my mom and me raise the boys, and she's been a fantastic sister to me.

"She's married to my older brother, Dayton. She told me to fill the rooms with candles and have some chilled wine to offer you. She came over here a little while ago and lit the candles for us." Turning toward the refrigerator, Jeremiah said, "I have white wine in the refrigerator and some cheese and sausage as well. Are you hungry or just a glass of wine?"

Joci looked at him with skepticism on her face.

"You went to a lot of trouble," she said, a small smile on her lips.

Jeremiah smirked. "I hoped like hell you would come home with me." His smile grew. "And be a bit impressed."

Jeremiah walked over to the refrigerator and pulled out a bottle of wine, opened it, and poured two glasses.

"You didn't answer my question… Are you hungry?"

Joci shook her head and laid a hand on her tummy.

He handed her a glass, then picked up the other glass in one hand and Joci's hand in the other. He walked her to the living room to sit on the sofa in front of the fireplace, which held about twenty lit candles of different sizes and shapes. It was beautiful. Joci looked at the fireplace and was mesmerized by all the candle flames flickering and winking at her.

"It's very beautiful. Thank you for going to all of the trouble." She sipped her wine and giggled. "Oh, and I am impressed."

She looked at Jeremiah and her breath caught at the expression on his face. He was breathtaking. In the candlelight, he was even more beautiful. A Roman god came to mind—strong, virile, powerful.

She sipped her wine. "The wine is delicious. Did you pick it out?"

Jeremiah smiled at her. "Yes. Staci made me go to the wine store with her this morning and taste several different kinds to see which ones I liked. This particular one is Dayton's favorite." He drank from his glass, then set it on the table. "Tell me about your life with your sister. Gunnar said you lived together while he was little."

Joci smiled at the memories. "Yes, Jackie and I stayed in our parents' house after they died. Jackie had just turned eighteen. We were able to keep the house. There wasn't a lot of money, but enough that we could stay there and live. We both got jobs to buy food and personal things and not have to touch the little bit of money there was. We wanted that money to go to the house, repairs, taxes, utilities.

She continued in a low voice. "Jackie was able to finish college, and I started college. I was still in college when I got pregnant with Gunnar, but we were able to work our schedules out so that I didn't have to hire a babysitter."

She looked into the candlelight, and her memories came flooding back. "Jackie loved Gunnar instantly. She was amazing with him." She turned on the sofa and faced Jeremiah, a giggle escaping her lips. "We would take him to the park and read to him and make sure he didn't feel the stresses of not having a lot of money or not having a dad around. When Jackie met David, her husband, Gunnar was three months old. David immediately helped with Gunnar. He and Jackie fell in love almost instantly, and he was constantly around. He moved in with us after only about a month of them dating."

Jeremiah smiled as he watched Joci recall Gunnar's youth. Her eyes sparkled in the candlelight, her dimples winking at him as she spoke.

"Where was Keith all this time?"

Joci grimaced. "Turns out, Keith didn't want the responsibility of being a dad. I was young, dumb, without parents, and maybe a little too adventurous. I can see things clearly now—long disappearances, late-night phone calls when we were together, a distance of sorts. After Gunnar was born, Keith really backed away and didn't want the responsibility of a child. Thank God Jackie was there to help me. I wouldn't have been able to make it without her."

"When did Keith leave you and Gunnar?"

Joci looked at Jeremiah for a while. "Are you sure you want to hear all of this? It isn't exactly a fun subject."

"Yes, Joci, I want to know about you. More than I already know. I want to know what you like and don't like. I want to know about your life."

Joci took a deep breath.

"Okay, well, after Gunnar was born, I could tell Keith just wasn't interested at all in him. Keith didn't even come to the hospital when I had him—Jackie was with me. And my best friend, Tori."

Joci winced when she mentioned Tori. She leaned forward and picked up her wine, took a drink and another deep breath.

"Anyway, when Gunnar was two months old, I caught Keith in bed with Tori. I had gone over to his apartment to talk with him. I walked in, and they were in bed together. It wasn't like he was the love of my life or anything, but with my best friend? Needless to say, it was over."

Jeremiah slid his hand over on top of Joci's hand. "I'm sorry. That must have sucked."

Joci looked at Jeremiah for a long while, his green eyes never wavering from her gaze—strong, steady, loving. Yes, he was a different kind of man than those she had been around. He genuinely seemed interested in her life. He was a great listener, and he never took his gaze away from her. She was beginning to relax. She took another drink of her wine.

"What about you? Where is JT and Ryder's mother?"

Jeremiah's lip turned up in a scowl, but he never looked away from Joci.

"Not sure. Barbara rides through once a year or so. She didn't want to be a mother. It was an accident when she got pregnant. I was always careful, so when she called me and told me she was pregnant, I thought she was trying to scam me or something. I was in the Marines, had come home on leave, and met her in a bar. I spent time with her while I was home. Then I went back to California where I was stationed when leave was over. I got a phone call a month or two later that she was pregnant. I asked for a paternity test. She was bitchy about it but got one. My brothers Dayton and Thomas made sure she did it right. It turned out the boys were mine."

Joci nodded. "It must have been hard. Good thing you didn't have little girls."

"God, I don't know if I would have been able to raise girls. They would have been tomboys if I had. I don't do girly things."

Joci burst out laughing at the look on his face.

"You would've learned. I learned boy things. As kids, Jackie and I were girly girls. Our dad liked us in dresses and to have pretty things in our hair. Of course, we loved it. But, I had a boy, and Jackie and I learned boy things out of necessity. Then Jackie and David had two boys."

Jeremiah sucked in a breath watching Joci laugh. She was so beautiful it took his breath away. He was in over his head with this one. Feelings like this were new. He felt primal and feral and, at the same time, protective and possessive. He wanted to lock her up in this house and never let her leave. He wanted her naked and in his bed every fucking day. He wanted to spend the rest of his life with her, sitting like this in the evening, talking to her, working like they had been working this past year on the ride or other ventures at the shop. He wanted to wake up every morning with her in his arms, sliding into her, smelling her, tasting her, touching her.

Jeremiah leaned forward and kissed her, gently at first, but Joci whimpered, which revved him up. He broke the kiss and set her wine glass on the coffee table. He turned back to Joci and reached over to touch her hair. He dug his fingers into her hair and ran his hand through it, cupping the back of her head. Jeremiah leaned forward and kissed Joci again, licking her lips and nipping her bottom lip.

"Open up, Joci."

Joci sighed and gave in to the feelings she had, opening her mouth, and letting Jeremiah in. He slid his tongue into her mouth and floated around, tasting every part. He turned his head so his lips fit perfectly over Joci's, wrapping his free arm around her waist and pulled her onto his lap so she straddled him.

Joci raked both her hands into Jeremiah's hair and fisted it in her hands. Feeling her hand grip his hair so tightly, knowing she must be feeling what he was feeling, made Jeremiah throb. Joci leaned forward a little more, so her breasts were touching his chest. She rubbed back and forth, adding friction. Her nipples were so firm she could feel her heartbeat throb in them.

She was wet between her legs. She ground her hips against Jeremiah and felt his hardness against her, causing them both to groan loudly. Jeremiah grabbed her hips in both of his hands, pulled her tight against him and rotated her, so she was grinding against him in just that perfect way. Joci's breathing became ragged. It had been so long since she had been with a man, she wouldn't need much.

"Joci...I want to be in you so damn bad," he groaned out.

Jeremiah wrapped his arms around her, leaned forward, and stood up, taking her with him. He skirted the coffee table and started walking to his bedroom. She hung on to him, nuzzling his ear as they moved down the hall. She breathed his scent in deeply. God, he smelled great. She didn't have words for his scent. She just knew she wanted it on her. She touched his ear with her tongue. He groaned at the feeling.

"Hang on, Joci. It's hard enough walking with a raging hard-on, but with your tongue in my ear, it's damn near impossible."

Joci tightened her hold around Jeremiah's neck and wrapped her legs around him a little tighter.

As they reached the bedroom, Jeremiah walked in the door and kicked it closed with his boot. He walked over to the bed and gently laid Joci on top. He stood up and looked down at her. She was finally here. For ten fucking months, he had lain in this very bed with his cock hard as a rock, wanting and needing her. Only her.

Jeremiah reached over and unzipped Joci's boots and pulled them off one at a time. He pulled her socks off as well. He looked at her left ankle, where she had a beautiful tattoo. It was an intricate little vine with pretty, delicate flowers on it. The vine trailed around her ankle, down the top of her foot and stopped halfway to her toes. He traced the vine with his fingers and then kissed the little flowers. His voice was husky with arousal.

"What's this, Joci?"

9

WHAT'S THIS?

Joci watched him as he traced her tattoo, kissing the flowers. The emotions running through her were tough to process. So many at once. There was no question he was sexy as hell. But, having him touch her, ask her questions about herself and her life, wanting to know about her and now intimately learning about her, this was overwhelming and emotional.

Her chest hitched, and her voice cracked. "It's my family."

Jeremiah raised his eyebrows in question. She swallowed to moisturize her throat.

"We are all bound by a tenuous little vine, which, if not nurtured, can wither and die. The vine is only as strong as the people who take care of it. The flowers are the fruit of that labor of taking care of each other. Each flower is one of the people in my family who help me nurture this vine. The color of the flower is the person's favorite color."

He touched the little white violet on Joci's ankle. He wanted to know who these people were, though he suspected he already knew. But what if she had Keith or someone else on there that he didn't want to know about? He had to ask.

"Who is this?"

"My mom. Her favorite color was white. Even though she isn't here anymore, she gave me the base to start with."

Jeremiah continued around her ankle.

"And this?"

"That's Jackie. She loves orange."

"And who loves blue?" he said, touching a blue flower.

"Gunnar."

Jeremiah smiled. He knew that one.

"And this, who loves dark blue?"

Joci smiled.

"Dean, my nephew."

"And how about yellow?"

"David likes yellow, though he doesn't tell many people because they make fun of him. Apparently, guys aren't supposed to like yellow."

Joci smiled, remembering the time David told her his favorite color was yellow. He made her promise not to make fun of him. But she had told him her idea of the tattoo, and she wanted to make sure she had him correct on it. After all, it was permanent.

"And purple?"

"My nephew, Jacob."

"And this light blue?"

"My dad."

Trailing his finger down the vine to the top of Joci's foot, there wasn't a flower there, just a little bud. The bud was surrounded in green. There were cracks in the green bud, but the color had not started peeking out just yet.

"Why do you just have a bud here and no flower?"

Joci looked into Jeremiah's eyes and swallowed a couple of times. Her eyes were becoming blurry with the threat of tears. He continued to look at her and waited for an answer.

Her voice full of emotion, she said, "That is someone who hasn't been in my life yet. I saved that spot for the one man who loves me completely, doesn't let me down, doesn't betray me, keeps me safe, holds me when I'm sad, shares my happiness, and wants me and no one else."

Jeremiah looked at Joci for a very long time. He looked at the spot on the top of her foot that held a place there for the man of her dreams. He wondered what it would look like to have a beautiful gray flower there, because since he had met her, his new favorite color had become gray, like a stormy night, the color of her eyes. Before that, his favorite color had been blue. He kissed the top of her foot before carefully laying it on the bed.

He slid his hands up her legs until he got to the juncture of her thighs, her very core. He massaged over her sensitive tissues through her jeans with his thumbs, watching her face the whole time. Joci closed her eyes and pushed herself into his thumbs, needing more contact. She heard Jeremiah's breath catch and opened her eyes to look at him. His pupils were dilated, and she could see candlelight flickering in them.

"Lift up for me, Joci."

She sat up and lifted her arms, watching Jeremiah the whole time. As soon as he took her t-shirt off, he gently laid it on the end of the bed, never taking his eyes from hers. Jeremiah looked down at her breasts and hissed a little.

"Jesus, Joci, you're so beautiful."

He ran a finger along the edge of her bra, watching her chest rise and fall as she pulled in ragged breaths.

"I want the rest of your clothes off. Stand up and take your jeans off for me."

His voice was soft, but commanding. Joci was excited that he told her what he wanted. Sexy, demanding, commanding, and it made her wet —well, wetter.

She scooted to the edge of the bed and slid down the side to her very shaky legs. She hesitated and looked at Jeremiah. He nodded slightly, never taking his eyes from hers. His green eyes had turned darker with desire. She hooked her thumbs into the waistband of her jeans and started to shimmy them down her legs. She chanced a look at Jeremiah again. He was watching her every move.

Slowly, Joci slid her jeans to the floor and stepped out of them. He stared at her for a long time, not saying anything, just looking at her.

"Take the rest off...slowly."

Joci's lips curved into a small, shaky smile. She was stripping for Jeremiah! Holy crap. She had never, ever stripped for any man. And he was staring at her with blatant lust and interest. At least for right now, she could imagine that he wanted her and only her.

She hooked her thumbs into the waistband of her panties and slid them down her legs. As she stood back up, she slowly slid her hands along her body in a sensuous motion. She heard his breath catch and felt more emboldened. She seductively reached behind her and unhooked her bra.

Jeremiah rubbed himself through his jeans, the pressure that was building shocked him with its intensity. He didn't remember ever being this hard. It was painful. Over this past year, as he had thought about Joci, he would get hard and stroke himself off. But standing here with her now, watching her strip—fuck, his cock hurt.

Joci sucked in a breath as she watched Jeremiah touch himself. Now, that was sexy as hell.

She let her bra drop to the floor and took a step closer to him, never looking away. It wasn't a hardship; he was amazing to look at. The candlelight danced on his skin, which was beginning to glisten with sweat. She hesitated a moment, but he reached forward and placed her hand on his hard length. The pronounced bulge in his jeans gave her a thrill, sending delightful shivers the length of her spine. The coarse material between them created a friction against her soft palm.

Joci lifted her hand and began unbuttoning his jeans. Slowly, she slid the zipper down, watching his eyes as she did so. She pushed his jeans and boxers down his thighs and let them fall to the floor. He quivered as her fingers brushed his skin. She slowly wrapped her fingers around him and he gently slid her hand up and down with his, setting the pace. He groaned out an unintelligible word as the air whooshed from his lungs, his eyes closing, his head thrown back. She continued manipulating his cock, admiring the firmness under the satiny soft skin.

She pushed his shirt up his body, touching him as she went. He was a good-looking man: hard muscles, ridges, and planes. His tight abdomen narrowed to those glorious hips and thighs. She ran her hands up his chest and rubbed across his nipples. She heard a light breath escape, and feeling bolder, she leaned forward and lightly licked one pebbled disk. Jeremiah sucked in a breath.

She smiled against his skin and licked him again. When she heard him hiss out a breath, she kissed her way across his chest and licked his other nipple. She sucked the hard little peak into her mouth, and at the same time, added pressure with her fingers to the moist little peak she left behind.

Joci looked up at him. He inclined his head urging her to keep going.

She ran her hands down his body, his firm, broad chest, down the ridges of his abdomen and over his hips, purposely ignoring the bobbing penis straining toward her.

Jeremiah reached down and grabbed her hand, needing her to touch him. Again. More.

As soon as she touched him, a loud groan escaped his lips, and she huffed out a breath. He felt so good, soft and hard at the same time. Slowly, with her other hand, she reached down and palmed his balls. He felt good in her hands. His hardness was impressive, while the soft, satiny skin that covered him felt like heaven. As she moved her hands over and around his thick length, it jumped and moved in her hands. He hissed again.

"God, Joci, you're going to unman me. You feel so good."

She licked her lips and started to slide down to her knees when Jeremiah sucked in a breath.

"No, Joci. We'll get to that later, but right now, I have other plans."

In one swift motion, Jeremiah reached down and picked her up, laying her on the bed. He climbed over her and kissed her again. His kiss was insistent, impatient, needing to be in her everywhere. He invaded her mouth with his tongue, his lips.

When he needed a breath, he kissed his way down her jaw, her neck, and to her breasts. When his mouth encased one of her taut peaks, Joci gasped. He pulled it into his mouth and sucked—hard. Oh, that feeling shot right to her pussy, and she thrust her hips upward, seeking something to relieve the need she felt there.

Jeremiah sucked her breast in again, this time, a bit harder, and Joci pushed forward again.

He sucked in the other breast just as hard as the last one and, at the same time, he pinched the nipple he just left. Joci gasped, at the same time pushing her hips forward and grabbing fists of his hair. Jeremiah kissed his way to her pussy and licked along the seam.

He pushed her legs farther apart and spread her open. He licked from the bottom of her pussy to the top. Circling her clit, he repeated the motion when she moaned. Rocking her hips into his mouth, she huffed out a breath and a moan escaped her lips. Jeremiah held her in place as he continued his sweet, sensual assault. Every nerve in her body was now completely trained on her pussy and his mouth. As his tongue glided along her wet folds of skin, she was overcome with desire and need. The flames shot down into her creamy depths and lit a raging fire within her. The only things keeping her from combusting were his tongue and his mouth.

"Come on my face, Joci—I want to taste you," he rasped out.

Joci rocked forward a few more times. Jeremiah continued to lick and suck her. He slid a finger into her channel, and she let out a cry; it felt so damned good. Just one of his fingers would be able to bring her to orgasm.

She tasted amazing; sweet like honey. He wanted her taste on his tongue every day. Each time he added a little more pressure to her clit, he could feel her getting wetter. She groaned and thrust and was so hot and wet. This was the stuff wet dreams were made of.

"You taste so good, Joci. Your tight little pussy is sucking my finger in and holding on so tight. My cock is going to feel amazing inside of you. "

His finger continued sliding in and out of her. He hooked his finger so he massaged her G-spot. Joci panted and quaked.

"Come on, baby. Come for me," Jeremiah coaxed.

She let herself go and gasped as her orgasm hit with force. The instant she came, he pulled his finger out and thrust his tongue inside to taste her. He moaned, sending the vibrations through her body. Joci whimpered. He continued to lap at her through her orgasm. He lifted her hips a little higher and licked inside of her.

Jeremiah moved up her body.

"Now that you're good and wet, I'm coming in."

He breathed in lightly. "Do I need a condom, Joci?"

Joci shook her head no. "I'm on the pill."

Jeremiah furrowed his brows.

"Female thing," she breathed.

He kissed her, lightly alternated licking and nipping her lips. He positioned the head of his cock at her opening, lightly pushing himself in. He continued to keep her occupied as he slowly entered her. He pushed through her opening and stopped just a little ways in.

He pushed in a little farther. She moaned and tightened her hold on his hair. Jeremiah pulled almost all of the way out and pushed in again, a little farther this time. Joci sighed at the feeling. He kissed her neck and nibbled up to her ear.

"I'm coming in all the way now, Joci."

He pulled out until just the head of his cock was in her and slowly pushed himself in all the way. Joci hissed out a breath.

"Can you feel how great that is, Joci? I'm inside of you all the way."

Jeremiah was still for a moment, letting her get used to him. He could feel her pulsing. It was maddening, staying still inside of her, letting her body accommodate his size. She felt unbelievable.

He breathed in her scent. Their scent. It was intoxicating, like the strongest drug. He'd had sex plenty of times over his forty-five years of life. He enjoyed sex. This was different. His cock ached. It hurt, it was so feverishly hard. As soon as he slid inside of Joci, some of the ache subsided. Some of the fire quenched, but he needed more.

He started moving inside of her and Joci let out a breath. Slowly he moved in and out, loving the tight feel of her. She was wet and tight, and his cock loved this feeling. He kissed her again, his tongue mimicking the movements his hips were making. He ground his hips against her clit, and she expelled all the air from her lungs. The feelings were running through him as a train runs along the tracks, hard and fast. His heart was pounding in his ears, in his chest. He was afraid it would beat right out of his body.

She was so wet, hot, and so fucking tight. And the way her body felt against his, her curves accommodating his hardness in every place they touched. It was perfect. She was perfect.

She was his now. End of story. This is the feeling he had waited his whole life for, this belonging to someone and someone belonging to him.

"God, Jeremiah, you feel like heaven."

"Ditto, baby." He kissed her neck, her cheeks, and her forehead. His hands and arms slid just behind her shoulders as he held her in place, all the while moving in and out of her.

He groaned out, "I need you to come again, Joci. Come for me."

Joci shoved her hands in Jeremiah's hair and fisted them tight, making him groan. She started moving her hips faster and grinding into him. She was mewling and moaning. She placed her feet on the bed, her knees in the air so she could push harder.

"Harder, Jeremiah...harder," she breathed.

He groaned louder, the air whooshing from his lungs. He pumped harder, mating with her like an animal. It was primal and feral. He would never have imagined she would be able to tolerate his need for rougher sex. He began to shake, just imagining all the things he would do to her, with her. And this wild mating, mingling with her, was the stuff of his fantasies. His cock was on fire and the pooling heat low in his belly was becoming unbearable. Faster and faster, he pumped into her, ramming his cock into her tight opening, trying to ease the pain.

He panted out, "I need you to come again, Joci...now, come now for me."

He pumped into her a few more times until she cried out his name as her orgasm surged, pushing Jeremiah over the edge. His vision blurred. All he could see were spots. His breathing was ragged and choppy. He felt like he was going to blow apart. When he came, it was explosive.

Unable to move, he rested his forehead on Joci's and waited for his breathing to slow. His thoughts were jumbled, his heart hammering to the beat of a hard rock song. It was as if something otherworldly had come over him. His life just changed in the most profound way. He had never felt such a desire for another person. This was something on another level, and he couldn't explain it.

When Jeremiah thought about it, this past year was the first year that he looked forward to the next day, hoping he would see Joci, or at the very least that he would hear from her. On the days when they had ride meetings, he was the most excited because he knew she would be there. Yes, Jeremiah was in deep with Joci, and after making love to her, he would never live without her in his life. Now to get Joci on the same page.

Joci was very quiet under him. Jeremiah moved to pull himself out of her, but just the thought crushed him. Instead, he tightened his arms around her and rolled over, so she was on top of him. As soon as they had rolled, Joci slid her legs up, so her knees were alongside his flanks and she straddled him, pushing herself all the way down on him.

She looked at him, her eyes wide when she realized he was still hard and becoming harder as she moved. He watched her. He put his hands on her hips and pushed her down further.

"Ride me, Joci."

She smiled at him and began moving her hips, back and forth, slowly. Placing her hands on his chest, she smoothed over the firm muscles bunching and moving as he moved. She looked into his eyes and was struck by the depth of emotions she saw in them. Beyond the beautiful summer green irises, there was true feeling in them. An intensity she had noticed in them recently, but it was more pronounced now.

She picked up the pace and saw a slow smile form on his lips just before his orgasm contorted his face into the beautiful form that only ecstasy created. Overcome with emotions, she collapsed onto Jeremiah's chest, trying to catch her breath. He wrapped his arms around her and held her tight. His thumbs rubbed circles on her back, gently stroking. It was soothing, feeling him hold her and rub her back. She closed her eyes and the tears slid down the side of her face, and onto Jeremiah's chest.

Jeremiah felt the moisture and moved his hands to cup her head. He gently turned her head to look at him, and concern clouded his features.

"God, Joci, are you okay?"

She nodded her head, swallowed a couple of times until she thought she could speak. Jeremiah continued looking at her and wiped the tears away with his thumbs.

"Please tell me you're okay, Joci. I never want to hurt you."

Joci started to sit up, but he held her in place.

"I'm okay...I'm sorry. I didn't mean to start crying. This...it was...sorry."

Joci swallowed again. Her voice was so soft, almost a whisper.

"I'm overwhelmed. I've never felt like this before."

Jeremiah pulled her back down onto his chest and held her tight. He swallowed hard a few times, too. After a few moments, Jeremiah took a deep breath.

"I know what you mean, Joci. That was overwhelming for me, too," his voice cracked.

They lay together for a few minutes, and Jeremiah rolled over, so Joci was at his side. He pulled out of her.

"Stay here. I'll be right back."

Joci watched him roll off the bed and walk to the bathroom. What a beautiful view that was. He had a great ass. He also had a tattoo across his back, from shoulder blade to shoulder blade. She hadn't noticed it before. But then, she had never seen him with his shirt off before. She heard the faucet turn on and water splash a little, and soon he was back with a warm cloth to wipe her up. Joci reached up to grab the cloth, and he stopped her.

"I want to."

He climbed back in bed and pulled her close.

"Is there anything you need, Joci?"

She whispered, "No, thank you. I'm fine."

He wrapped his arms around her tighter and took a deep breath.

She swallowed hard, trying to keep her stupid emotions under control. Her heart was beating so erratically. She leaned up on her elbow and looked down at him. Jeremiah grabbed her and pulled her to him hard, afraid to let go. His voice cracked.

"I know you're scared. I don't want to make your life harder. I want to make it easier."

Joci took a deep, shaky breath. "I'm scared shitless, to be honest, Jeremiah."

He breathed in deep and slowly let it out. "It's been a long fucking year, Joci."

She lay next to him, thinking about all of this. It was inevitable that they would be together, but when she had woken up this morning, she never would have imagined she would be lying here with him tonight, naked and exhausted.

"Do you want to talk?"

Joci leaned up again and giggled. "You want to talk? I thought men didn't like talking after sex."

Jeremiah smiled at her, saying nothing else. His chest was still rising and falling from the exertion; his sexy eyes were still hooded.

Joci chuckled. "You'll need to get me home soon anyway."

Jeremiah snorted. "You are home, Joci. You're staying with me tonight. If you think that was it for tonight, you have another thing coming. As for the days to come, we'll play it by ear—but I want to be with you. Not just when the mood strikes, but all the time. I don't want to sleep alone ever again. I want you in my arms."

Joci cocked her head to the side and looked at Jeremiah. "You don't think this is moving way too fast?"

He leaned up on an elbow and shook his head. "You're kidding, right? I just told you it was a long fucking year. As far as I'm concerned, we're way behind the ball on this."

Joci looked at Jeremiah and her face softened. "I'm sorry. You know this isn't going to be easy. Jeremiah, I see the way women look at you and fawn over you. That's what has kept me away for this year. I've been cheated on and lied to. I have a real trust problem. You might want to walk away right now, so I don't drive you crazy."

"I'm not walking away, Joci. I know you have trust issues. Remember, I'm the one who was trying to get you to go out with me, to spend time with me. I've watched you struggle with your feelings for me and not want to admit them. I wish I could make those fears go away, but I can't. What I *can* do is stick with you and hang on tight. That's exactly what I intend to do. And just so we're clear, I've never had another lover. I've fucked women, but I've never made love to them. I just made love to you. You are my first and last lover."

Joci watched Jeremiah's eyes. She could see the honesty there. He never wavered when he looked at her. He didn't fidget and twitch. He just looked at her like he was trying to convey with his eyes that he was telling the truth. She didn't know what to say to him. She had never made love either. She didn't know that until just now. Now she knew what the fuss was about.

He hugged her tight, and she wrapped her arms around his waist and hugged him back.

10

AFTER THE LOVIN'

Jeremiah and Joci lay back against the headboard. The candles were burning low, and the light wasn't nearly as bright, though it was still very beautiful. He couldn't stop watching her. Her smile caused her dimples to wink. When he saw them, he wanted to sigh. Talking to her felt good. They had similar tastes in music, foods, movies, and family values.

"Joci, tell me about Connor. What's the deal with him?"

Joci looked at him, her brows furrowed. "I take it you don't like Connor."

Jeremiah looked at her for a long time. "Connor's in love with you. I see the way he looks at you. It drives me nuts."

Joci's head jerked back a bit; she shook her head. "I don't think so. He's been there for us. He feels bad about the way Keith treated us— Gunnar and me. He was Keith's best friend. They're still friends and keep in touch. He knew all along that Keith was cheating and told me he tried talking to Keith about it. Connor's been a good friend for a long time now. When I needed help with Gunnar, Connor stepped in for me—for Keith, actually. That's all."

Jeremiah's lips formed a straight line. "He never asked you out or tried to kiss you?"

Joci cocked her head to the side. "Yes, after he divorced, he asked me out. He did kiss me a couple of times, but each time, I told him I wanted to keep it friendly. Eventually, he accepted that."

Jeremiah leaned over and kissed Joci lightly on the lips. "You can't possibly believe that! I would never accept that from you, and I don't think he did either. I see how he looks at you. He loves you. If he makes a move for you, he and I are going to have problems. That may cause a problem with Gunnar, but I'll deal with it."

"He hasn't made a move in all these years, and he's actually introduced me to girlfriends of his."

"I'm just sayin'." Jeremiah twisted to look at her. "Now, what about Keith? Did he leave the area, or does he still live around here? And how do you feel about that?"

Joci shrugged. "He really wasn't the love of my life. What really hurt was when I found out how much he screwed around. Besides screwing Tori and my aunt, he screwed a woman I worked with. Actually, he had been with almost everyone I knew. It's hard to think these women would see me and talk to me and offer me advice and be in the friggin' delivery room with me and the whole time, they were screwing him themselves." She picked at a thread on the comforter, then smoothed it with her hand. The satiny fabric was soft and cool to her touch. She noticed the deep copper color in the waning candlelight. Looking up into his eyes, she continued.

"That's why I don't trust easily. So many people have betrayed me. But even worse was that we had a little boy who wanted and needed a father. Keith left him. He left the area when Gunnar was one or so. Connor told me that he met someone and married her. I hope he treats her better than he treated me. They have two children together, I believe."

"Does he ever see Gunnar or keep in touch with him?"

"Nope. Since the day I found him with Tori, he hasn't made any attempt to touch base with Gunnar." She quickly turned her frown into a smile; this was not a time for sad thoughts.

"I won't betray you, Joci. Never. My father raised us better than that. No one in my family would ever treat anyone so cruelly. I promise you."

She looked into his eyes and saw the sincerity.

"What about you, Jeremiah? Did you ever wonder if you should have done something different with Barbara?"

Jeremiah snorted. "Hell, no. She shows up about once each year, traveling through. She doesn't ride herself, just hangs around looking for a ride. She wears too much makeup, too much jewelry, too much everything. Last year, when she rode through, she asked JT for money, and he told her to take a hike. Not sure if she'll come back this year. She's been married and divorced three times and has two other children: a boy and a girl. Not sure where they are or who they're with. I assume their fathers."

"That must have been hard on you. What about girlfriends?"

Jeremiah looked at Joci, trying to gauge her mood. "No. I dated a few women, but nothing serious. I devoted my time to the boys and, then later, to growing Rolling Thunder."

"I know what you mean. I devoted my life to Gunnar and then to building my marketing and graphic design business. I wouldn't have made it if it hadn't been for my sister, Jackie. Later on, Sandi and I became friends, but it took me a long time to trust her. But she stayed tough and proved she was trustworthy."

They talked a while longer, enjoying the quiet time with each other. Jeremiah's phone chimed. He let out a huff and reached down to the floor to retrieve it out of his jeans pocket. He smirked and texted something back. He looked up and saw Joci watching him.

"Staci wanted to know if you liked the candles. I told her you did. She knew I was nervous."

"Aww, that's really sweet of her."

"She's been like a sister to me. Dayton found himself a great woman. I can't wait for you to meet her." He pecked her on the lips. "Do you want to take a shower?"

Jeremiah swung his feet over the side of the bed and stood. He took her hand, helped her out of bed, and led her to the bathroom. He reached into the shower stall and turned the water on, letting it warm up.

Joci stood watching him. He moved around his house with strength and confidence. His muscles moved and rippled with him. He turned to look at Joci and raised an eyebrow.

Joci smiled. "I love watching you."

Jeremiah smiled at her. "The moment I met you, I knew I needed to be with you. You're stubborn as hell but so beautiful you make my heart race."

Joci furrowed her brow. "I'm not stubborn!"

Now it was Jeremiah's turn to furrow his brow. "Really? You made me wait a fucking year to touch you."

Joci closed the distance between them and ran her palms across his chest, down his stomach, and over his hips.

"I wasn't being stubborn; I was scared. You have women fawning over you all the time. Making comments and dying for you to touch them. I didn't want to go down that road again."

Jeremiah shook his head, "I don't have women fawning over me."

"Seriously, Jeremiah, LuAnn has made it very, very clear that she wants you. She fawns over you, touches you every chance she gets. She's made comments to me that you're waiting for her to be ready to settle down. How can you not know that?"

Jeremiah's head snapped back. His mouth drew down his lips thinned.

"That's not fucking true. LuAnn is the last person on earth I want. If she's made those comments, she's lying. I have never, ever given her any reason to believe there would ever be anything between us." He shook his head, "I'll take care of LuAnn. She better not give you any grief."

He twisted his head from side to side, then looked into her eyes. He took her hand in his and led her toward the shower.

Stepping in, Joci looked around in surprise. The glass block wall had hidden the size of the shower from view. Standing in it now, she felt dwarfed. The deep brown copper tiles had flecks of graphite colored minerals that sparkled in the light. "This is an amazing shower."

Jeremiah chuckled, "Well, I'm too big for a normal shower. The first thing I did when I bought this house was gut the bathroom and build this big shower, so when I washed my hair, I didn't beat the hell out of my elbows."

He held his arms up to show Joci he could stretch out. Joci stepped under the water with him. She reached over to the shelf and grabbed the bottle of body wash. She squirted some into her hand and held it to her nose. Hmm, that's why he smelled so awesome. She rubbed her hands together and placed them on his back. He was so beautiful, chiseled muscles and clear, taut skin; the years had been kind.

She looked at the tattoo on his back. It was beautiful, lettered scroll-work that went from shoulder to shoulder and said Rolling Thunder. Joci touched the tattoo with her fingers. She slowly traced each letter across his back, noticing that his muscles rippled and moved under her fingers. Once she had traced the letters, she laid her palm flat and ran her hand over the whole tattoo.

"It's beautiful."

Jeremiah slowly turned, finding her eyes. He stared at her a long time, the water beating down on them both. Joci reached up and traced the tattoo on his left bicep.

"What does this mean?"

Jeremiah's voice cracked. "It's JT's initials in Vivaldi Script."

Yes, now that she looked closer, she could see it—JTS. Joci slid her hand down to his wrist. "This?"

"His birth date."

Joci traced the tattoo on his right bicep, RMS. "Ryder."

Jeremiah whispered, "Yes."

Joci slid her hands to his right wrist and traced the numbers.

"And this would be his date of birth as well. Twins."

Jeremiah framed Joci's face in his hands. He stared into her eyes for the longest time. The stormy gray irises framed by a deeper gray. Her long thick lashes now wet from the water of the shower and creating the shape of stars around her eyes. Slowly, he leaned down and kissed her lips. He turned his head so they fit together perfectly, and dipped his tongue into her mouth. He explored, wanting to touch every surface of her body. He wanted to crawl inside her and leave an imprint on her that would never disappear. He slid his hand into her hair and cupped the back of her head, holding her in place while he continued to taste her.

She wrapped her arms around his waist, pulling them closer. When Jeremiah needed to breathe, he lifted his head and laid it on top of Joci's. He wrapped his arms around her and squeezed her to him. He already needed her again; he would take his time and enjoy this.

11

PROMISE ME

"You're mine, Joci. No one elses."

She wrapped her arms around him and held him close.

"I don't want any other man, Jeremiah. I need you to want only me. Promise me."

Jeremiah lifted his head to look at her.

"I only want you, Joci. I'm a one-woman man."

They tucked themselves into bed, and both of them fell blissfully asleep in each other's arms.

Jeremiah woke Joci around six a.m. He brought her a cup of coffee and set it on the bedside table. He leaned over and kissed her lightly on the mouth, surprised that she responded so quickly to his kiss. She rolled to her back, pulling him over with her, causing him to groan.

"God, you're an insatiable little woman. How in the hell am I going to keep you satisfied?"

Joci laughed, "I was just thinking the same thing about you. You're the one who started kissing me."

Jeremiah chuckled, "I just brought you some coffee. It's six o'clock. We need to get to the shop in about an hour and a half."

Joci sat up and took the coffee cup in her hand and breathed in the scent. She took a sip. "Mmm, very good. Thank you."

Jeremiah lay on his side, still nude, watching her.

She raked her eyes over his body. "How is it you look great all the time? Geez, you're going to give me a complex," Joci smiled.

He returned her smile. "How is it you look great all the time?"

She shook her head. "I exercise because I have to. I still have a squishy belly from having a very big boy, and if I don't work at it, it doesn't take long to look flabby."

Jeremiah pushed the covers down and looked at her belly.

"I don't think it looks squishy."

He leaned over and kissed her stomach. She had a few stretch marks he hadn't noticed last night. He traced his finger along one of them, and she moved to push his hand away and grab the covers. He stopped her and kissed where he had just traced.

"These don't make you look bad, Joci. They came from having your amazing son. It's part of life."

Joci looked at him. "Men don't get these marks from having kids. They look for women who don't have them."

Jeremiah looked at Joci. "I don't. I don't give a shit about a few little marks on your belly. I care about you, the whole package."

Joci sighed loudly. Jeremiah kept touching her belly and kissing her imperfections. "Did you ever think about having another baby, Joci?"

She looked at Jeremiah. "There was a time I longed for a little girl. My whole adult life was all about boy things. Boy games. Boy clothes. Boy everything. I wanted a pretty little girl to spoil. Now I'm too old."

Jeremiah looked at her with furrowed brows. "No, you're not. Under the right circumstances, it would be great."

"Yes, well, the right circumstances haven't materialized." She smiled.

Joci watched Jeremiah look at her belly.

"Did you ever want another baby?" she whispered.

"I guess I never thought about it. I didn't have anyone in my life I wanted to have a baby with. It would be so different with the right person."

Uh oh, Joci wasn't going there. She had already raised a boy by herself. She wasn't risking having another child she would have to raise by herself. She started sitting up and pulling away when Jeremiah caught her leg.

"Don't get scared. I was just thinking out loud."

Joci didn't want to have this conversation. The women in her family had all gone through early menopause. She hadn't had a regular period in two years. She was on birth control to regulate her periods. Her doctor didn't like putting her on birth control at her age, but it worked for her. However, if it was the beginning of menopause, she was grateful she didn't have the other horrible symptoms yet—hot flashes, mood swings, any of that.

Joci cleared her throat, "We should probably get going."

Jeremiah sat up. "Will you ride with me today, Joci? I know you ride yourself, and I don't want to take anything from you, but I would love it if you would ride with me and be with me today. I want to feel your legs wrapped around me and talk to you while we ride. Will you do that?"

She cocked her head to the side and studied him. She would be able to look around and see all the bikes and signs people had told her she would see.

She smiled. "I would like that."

Jeremiah winked. "I'm anxious for everyone to know we're finally together."

Joci slid off the side of the bed. "I think quite a few people already know after we left last night. I'm sure word was traveling like crazy once we were gone."

She walked to the bathroom and turned on the shower.

She peeked out at Jeremiah, who was watching her walk away. "We'll need to go to my place to get some clean clothes, though."

"No problem. But I want you to pack some things and bring them here. I'll clear out some space in the closet and dresser for you. We can begin that way."

She hesitated a moment before turning and stepping into the shower and under the spray of water to wash her hair. Jeremiah joined her, quickly washed up and then stepped out, giving her the massive shower for herself. She took her time letting the water slide over her body and the fresh scent of his shower soap tickle her nostrils. She giggled thinking that now she would even smell like Jeremiah. Little doubt they were together.

W hen she stepped out, Jeremiah walked into the bathroom.

"I warmed up your coffee. Do you need anything else?" He set the cup on the counter, and the scent of fresh coffee wafted up to her nose.

She smiled, marveling at her good fortune in finding him. He was wearing a pair of faded jeans, which, of course, were incredibly sexy on him. Slung low on his hips, little frays on the belt loops. As her eyes traveled down the length of him, she noticed his fly move a little and the muscles bunched in his thighs. Now that she knew what was underneath, she thought he was even sexier. Her eyes traveled back up to his, and her breath caught at the intensity of his gaze. "You keep looking at me like that, and you'll be bent over the counter in no time."

Joci's cheeks tinted pink, but she smiled at him and shrugged her shoulders.

"You're not the only one who can't get enough."

He leaned over and kissed her forehead. "I have to get out of here, or we'll be late."

He turned to leave, wearing a t-shirt that was the men's version of the shirt that matched hers for the ride today, tucked in his jeans, which showed off his fantastic ass. He had his hair pulled back into a low ponytail. So sexy. "Do you need anything?"

Jeremiah looked at her, surprise on his face. "Not anymore. I have everything I need right here in front of me."

Joci smiled and cocked her head. He chuckled, tapped the tip of her nose and left.

A while later, Joci found Jeremiah in the garage getting the bike ready. When she stepped out of the house, he looked her over, and a loud breath escaped.

"You look beautiful, Joci. I'm a lucky man."

She smirked and shook her head. "Quick stop at my house and then we can be on our way."

She walked over to the bike and looked at what he was doing. "What's up?"

Jeremiah stood. "I put this air pad on the passenger seat for you. Right here is a pump; you can add air by pumping it. You remove air by pushing this button here. I thought it would be more comfortable."

Joci cocked her head to the side. "Thank you. That's thoughtful. I'm sorry to make you go to any trouble."

"No trouble."

He opened the tour pack on the back of the bike, and she put her purse inside.

He leaned down and kissed her then swatted her on the ass. "Are you hungry? I thought we could go eat somewhere after we leave your place."

"Breakfast sounds great."

Jeremiah got on the bike and brought up the kickstand; Joci climbed on behind him. He had removed the backrest behind him so he could lean into her. He always rode alone, detesting the women who milled about looking for a ride. He was so excited for Joci to ride with him today; he couldn't wait to get on the road. They rolled slowly out of the garage. Jeremiah hit the garage door button and off they went.

It was beautiful riding in the morning. The sun was up, and the weather was mild. The temperature today was supposed to be eighty-two degrees; great for May in Wisconsin. Jeremiah took some back roads, loving the curvy, quiet pace. Joci leaned forward and wrapped her arms around his waist and rested her chin on his left shoulder.

At breakfast they talked about the day and how many bikes they thought would join them. Already one hundred and twenty-six bikes had preregistered. That was a new record, and that was because Joci developed the website attached to Rolling Thunder's website for bikers to preregister.

"Next year, we'll have more," Joci said.

He smiled. "I love that you acknowledge you'll be with me next year."

A soft smile touched her lips, the soft, smooth skin glistening from the coffee she sipped and her little pink tongue peeking out to wet it.

He continued. "You'll be meeting my whole family today. They always participate in this ride. We're all veterans, so it's been a family affair since the beginning. My dad and mom will be driving one of the chaser trucks. Dad is in his early seventies and doesn't feel comfortable on a bike in large crowds anymore, though he still rides by himself once in a while."

Jeremiah told her a little about each brother—he had three. Jeremiah was the second son. Dayton, the oldest, was two years older than Jeremiah. Thomas was two years younger than Jeremiah, and then Bryce, who was five years Jeremiah's junior. They were close, but Jeremiah was the only one in the bike business. His siblings all rode motorcycles but worked elsewhere.

When they pulled into the parking lot of Rolling Thunder, a few people were already there. And tongues started wagging as soon as they saw Jeremiah and Joci together. Yup, it was going to be an interesting day.

As soon as they parked and got off the bike, LuAnn walked over. Of course, she was wearing skintight jeans; her Rolling Thunder Veteran's Ride t-shirt pulled tight and knotted to show off her breasts and belly. She wore high-heeled boots, and her bleached blonde hair was a messy do of some sort. And yes, jewelry on every surface she could accessorize. She walked up to Jeremiah and hugged him.

"I'm so happy to see you. Today is going to be a great day. I'll ride with you today."

Jeremiah put his hands on LuAnn's shoulders and set her aside.

"LuAnn, you didn't say good morning to Joci."

LuAnn gave Joci the once-over and snorted, "Hi."

Joci glanced at Jeremiah and raised her brows in an 'I told you so' look.

"Joci's riding with me today."

LuAnn looked at Joci again and then back at Jeremiah.

"Why doesn't she ride her own bike?"

He took a deep breath and put his arm around Joci.

"Because I asked her to ride with me. Joci and I are together, LuAnn."

LuAnn scrunched her face and snapped her fingers. "Well, that won't last long. We all know you love a smorgasbord."

She looked at Joci, gave her the up-and-down once again and strutted off.

Joci took a step back, but Jeremiah squeezed her shoulders and leaned down close to her ear, "I'm sorry. And for the record, that's not true. I don't fuck around like she insinuated."

Joci blew out a breath and opened her mouth to speak but was interrupted.

"Hey, bro!"

Jeremiah turned to see his brother, Dayton, and sister-in-law, Staci, walking toward them. As soon as Dayton and Staci reached them, Jeremiah gave him a slap on the back, then a quick hug. He leaned down and hugged his sister-in-law, then introduced them all.

∾

Joci noticed how very similar they looked right away. Dayton didn't look like a computer geek as she suspected; he looked like Jeremiah with short hair. Same color as Jeremiah's hair, without the sun's highlights in it. Dayton kept his short and cut around the ears and above the collar in the back with a little length on top. His eyes were similar, though not as bright, and his build was similar as well. Dayton leaned down and hugged Joci, and then Staci stepped forward, also giving her a hug.

Staci's long, dark brown hair and bright blue eyes twinkled when she stepped back.

Staci whispered, "Did you like all the candles?"

Joci smiled. "Yes, they were beautiful. Thank you for doing that."

Staci smiled at Joci and then looked at Jeremiah.

"I was happy to do it. We all just want him happy. He was very excited and nervous about making sure you would appreciate it."

Jeremiah gave Staci a slight nod and a grin.

They were chitchatting when Joci heard, "Mom!"

She turned to see Gunnar striding quickly toward them, and then stepped over to hug her son.

"Good morning. Are you ready for today?"

Gunnar nodded and said hello to everyone.

Very soon, all the family members had arrived. Jeremiah's brothers and parents, Thomas and Emily; Joci's sister, Jackie, and her husband, David, came in shortly after. Jeremiah made introductions.

As soon as Jackie and David showed up, Jeremiah put his arm around Joci and stated, "Joci's riding with me today."

His smile stretched across his face.

Jeremiah's brother, Tommy, looked at Joci and shook his head. "Poor Joci. He's a cranky bastard. I hope you can handle it."

Joci giggled. "I know. It's awful."

The brothers began putting up the ribbons that would guide riders to the parking and sign-in areas. The sisters-in-law walked to the tents set up to hold the clothing and Jeremiah's parents strolled to the large tent that had been erected last night for the drinks. The drink stand was being manned by a local veteran's group, and all proceeds would go to that organization, separate from the Rolling Thunder donations from this ride.

The tables for the sign-up area were set up, and Joci and Jeremiah worked on organizing the area with the sign-up sheets, insurance waivers, and wristbands. He swatted her on the ass, and she stifled a squeal.

"What was that for?"

"You're leaning over the table setting out papers, and I couldn't resist. If you don't want me touching it, don't stick it out in front of me."

Joci smirked. She had some local tech school students showing up to keep the data entry rolling along. She set up their laptops, got them booted up, and was ready for them as they arrived. There were a couple of cash drawers at the sign-up table as well.

Jeremiah's family was available to answer questions and direct traffic. They knew the drill, and everyone worked well together. Just before the first bikers started arriving, Jeremiah walked over to Joci and gave her a big hug.

"It looks like we're ready. Do you need anything before the bikers start rolling in?"

She pointed at the drink tent. "I thought I would go and get a bottle of water. Do you want one?"

He smiled. "Yeah, I'll come with you."

They walked around the parking lot and spoke with everyone working at each area. His brothers were standing around in the parking areas waiting for the bikers to roll in. Jeremiah's parents were talking to the guys in the drink tent. When they got to the clothing tent, LuAnn was there shooting daggers at them. Jeremiah didn't pay her any attention. Joci was wary and watched LuAnn to make sure a knife didn't find its way to her back.

Jeremiah's sisters-in-law were working the clothing tent with LuAnn and Angel from Rolling Thunder. LuAnn made some comment that was off color and louder than necessary, and Angie and Erin—Jeremiah's sisters-in-law—looked at Joci, rolled their eyes, then winked at her. So they were aware of LuAnn's interest in Jeremiah as well.

Photographers were also getting set up. Jeremiah had hired a local studio, which in turn had to hire freelancers due to the size and nature of the job. The bikes and bikers would be spread out most of the day so that they would need photographers all over the place.

"Joci, is that you?"

Joci looked over and saw Molly Bates, an independent photographer she had met at a seminar.

"Molly! Yes. It's great to see you here. Let me introduce you to Jeremiah Sheppard. Jeremiah, this is Molly Bates, a friend I met a couple of years ago at a seminar for us 'artsy types,'" Joci said with air quotes.

Molly smiled and shook hands with Jeremiah.

"I've been looking forward to this for a long time."

"Good to hear. This is my pet project each year. Thank you for taking part."

"You're welcome. Joci, we should catch up. I have a couple of ideas I'm working on that you would be perfect for. How about lunch next week?"

"Sounds great. Email me a couple of days that work for you and we can plan on it. See you around today."

They waved goodbye and continued making the rounds. Gunnar was working with the other Sheppards in the parking lot. As Joci and Dog approached him, he smiled and met them halfway.

"I'm so damned excited for today. Mom, you're going to love this ride."

"I'm looking forward to it. Thanks again for introducing me to it."

"Sooo, what did you guys do last night?"

Joci's face turned bright red. Jeremiah snickered just as JT and Ryder came walking over. "We went back to my house and talked."

Gunnar looked over at the twins, and they all chuckled.

"'Talked?'" JT questioned with air quotes.

"Never mind, guys. If you don't have enough to do, I can find some things for you."

The boys all turned to go back to work, laughing at Jeremiah and Joci. She covered her face with her hands, but Jeremiah quickly pulled them away and kissed her forehead. "Hey. They're young men; they know what we were doing last night. For the record, I would love to shout it from the roof. Maybe I'll go do that right now."

Joci's eyes grew huge and she opened her mouth to tell him he had better not, but the first bikes had started rolling in.

Jeremiah slapped her ass. "Come on, babe; we have bikers to take care of." He grinned as he grabbed her hand and pulled her over to the sign-up tent.

For the next two and a half hours, it was a steady stream of bikers and passengers rolling in and signing up.

People came in groups and by themselves, hoping to meet up with friends. The weather was great, and by the looks of it, they were in for a record turnout. There are people of all shapes and sizes who ride motorcycles. You could see a thousand Harley shirts and not see the same one twice. Some people wore leather vests with patches and pins signifying their affiliation with a HOG Chapter or club or group of some sort. There were tall people, short people, heavy people, skinny people, doctors, lawyers, clerical workers, mill workers, presidents of companies and their employees, but they all had this ride in common.

Over the years, since Joci had learned to ride, she had participated in many such events. First, she felt good about supporting a cause. Second, she just loved to people-watch. The variations of people and their bikes were like no other. Third, she loved walking up and down the rows of bikes to look at all the different makes, models, colors, customizations, and doodads. Everyone had his or her little decorations or thingamajigs on the bikes based on taste and probably budget. It was nice seeing all of this, and yet in spite of their differences, all of them together were here at this special event. You could see people you hadn't seen in years. And she always met new people too.

Jeremiah enjoyed working with Joci. He was proud of her, and he was so happy she was sharing this with him. He had been a nervous wreck yesterday, not knowing how it would work out with her, but he knew he had to take a stand and let her know he wanted to be with her. He wasn't going to take no for an answer any longer.

That was more confident than he felt. He was thrilled beyond any words he had to describe the fact that they were together. Jeremiah heard Joci's sweet voice.

"Hi, Connor. How are you today?"

Connor reached over the table and hugged Joci. She looked over at Jeremiah and saw the scowl on his face.

She winked at him and leaned in and whispered, "The look on your face is priceless. It's probably what my face looked like this morning when LuAnn hugged you." Straightening, she addressed her friend, "Connor, you remember Jeremiah, don't you?"

Jeremiah held out his hand, and Connor shook it.

"Yes, of course, we've met several times. How are you, Dog?"

"I'm great, Connor. Glad you could make it today."

Jeremiah leaned down and kissed Joci on the temple, then gave her a little squeeze. Connor watched Joci while this was going on. He turned to start filling out his form for the ride.

As soon as Connor had his form filled out, he handed it back to Joci with his twenty dollars for the ride and asked, "So, you're with Dog now?"

Joci looked at Connor and smiled. "Yes."

Connor took a deep breath and nodded. "I'm going to go find Gunnar."

He turned and walked away.

12

VETERANS' RIDE

Soon, it was eleven-thirty and time to start the blessing of the bikes and thanking the veterans, and then it would be time to start riding.

Jeremiah kissed Joci and walked up to the stage. Through the PA system, he asked everyone for their attention and then introduced Father Ryan, one of the local Catholic priests. Father Ryan asked everyone to bow their heads and pray. He said a prayer for all those present today, for all those who couldn't be here, and for all those who had already gone to Heaven. He prayed for those serving their country and asked for blessings to be sent their way. He prayed for those who had already served the country and were struggling with issues. He asked for safe riding and blessings from the Lord for a safe, happy day. He ended the prayer by blessing the bikes and asking the Lord to keep the demons away. And everyone said, "Amen."

Jeremiah introduced some local veterans. They each spoke a little and then Jeremiah said, "The donations for this year are going to help a local man who has just come back from Afghanistan. He had one of his legs blown off by an IED. His house is not handicapped accessible, and it's difficult for him to use the stairs to go to bed. The money will help him build a first-floor bedroom and bathroom, along with some other repairs the house needs for him to be comfortable.

"Some other money will go to a couple of older vets who need repairs done on their houses. We get a group together in the fall to go and help with the repairs. Check out Rolling Thunder's website. My girlfriend, Joci, has a link set up to better explain the repairs that are needed and the dates we will be working on the houses. There is also a link to sign up or donate time or materials. If you want to help out, we can always use more people.

"Everyone, be courteous and ride safely. The ride will begin in fifteen minutes. Please start heading toward your bikes and get ready to ride out."

Joci started packing up the sign-up table and laptops. She thanked everyone who helped out at the table and began carrying everything into the store. Jeremiah caught up to her with the computers and a box of sign-up sheets and opened the door for her. They walked in together and set their respective items on the counter.

Joci grinned. "You're a natural on stage, Jeremiah. You didn't even look nervous."

He chuckled. "I guess I don't feel nervous. This is my thing. It's not like I'm trying to sing or something."

Joci nodded. That made sense. When she sang karaoke, she had to have at least three shots first.

After setting the laptops on the counter, Joci turned to Jeremiah. "Do you want to know how many bikes we have?"

She was rocking back and forth on her feet with a big smile on her face, waiting for him to guess. Jeremiah walked forward until he was right in front of her and crossed his arms. Being this close, his scent teased her nostrils and thoughts of last night came rushing back to her. How he felt, tasted, sounded.

He smiled back at her and took a stab at it. "I'm guessing by the look on your face it's a new record. I'm going to say, eight hundred fifty bikes."

Joci laughed. "Nope."

Jeremiah's brows raised and lowered right away.

"Hmmm, nine hundred bikes."

"Nope."

She was enjoying this. His smile grew wider.

"Nine fifty?"

Joci laughed out loud. "Nope!"

"Wow. Okay, spill."

She giggled and clapped her hands once. "Jeremiah, we've got one thousand and seven bikes!"

He leaned down and picked her up and spun her around.

"How many riders?"

Joci was still laughing.

"Eighteen hundred and three people altogether, with the bikers, passengers, car clubs, and veterans."

"Whoo!" Jeremiah yelled. "That's a huge record."

He fist pumped a few times and spun Joci around again. She hung on to his neck as he spun her. Being pushed tight to his chest made her nipples pucker.

"God, I'm so pumped. What a great turnout! Thank you so much for helping me out, sweetheart."

He kissed her, and she kissed him right back. They were locked together when the door opened.

"Seriously, you two need to get on a bike and get this show on the road."

Ryder stood in the doorway, looking at them with a goofy grin on his face.

Jeremiah laughed and grabbed Joci's hand. "Let's go, baby."

They walked out, locked the door, and headed to Jeremiah's bike. People were starting their bikes and the rumble from all the loud pipes vibrated through their bodies.

This was the exciting part. Everyone was fresh and excited to get rolling. The roaring of the bikes and the smiles on people's faces were intoxicating. Joci found herself shaking a little at the excitement. Jeremiah leaned back against her as they were waiting for the starting signal from one of the veterans to start the ride.

"Are you nervous, Joci?"

Joci smiled and replied, "No, I'm excited. This is my favorite part. Hearing all the bikes rumble and roar and getting ready to start riding. I love this."

Joci hugged Jeremiah, and he squeezed her arms as they came around him. He loved this, too.

Soon they were given the signal and started to roll. They rode through the lines of people who had gathered to wave them off. Local people lined the roads and waved and took pictures and videos of all the bikes. If a person had never experienced something like this, it's hard to understand the feelings.

The first leg of the ride was about 49 miles. Jeremiah and his guys had scoped out some beautiful back roads with twists and turns. Joci loved riding into corners because she could look back and see all the bikes behind them. Well, not all of them. With so many, she could only see a portion of them. But what a sight it was. She didn't get to look at that when she was driving. Riding along was fun—she had the opportunity to take a look around and see more.

Along the way, there were cranes and heavy machinery with people sitting or standing up to see from higher vantage points.

Some of the people who lived along the route allowed photographers to stand on their roofs to take video and pictures and memorialize the ride. Jeremiah had photo albums of all the rides. This year, Joci was going to make a video and put it to music for him, then put it on the website. She was excited to work on it for him.

It took about an hour and a half at the slower pace they were riding to get to the first stop, which was a large bar out in the country on the way to Green Bay. Since Rolling Thunder was between Green Bay and Appleton, it was easy to find roads between the two cities. This bar, appropriately named 'The Barn,' was out in the country and was an old barn converted into a bar. The upstairs had also been remodeled, so there was plenty of space for almost all of the bikers. However, since the weather was so nice, they also had several makeshift bars set up outside to hydrate all the riders. Once they had been parked, Jeremiah took Joci's hand.

"I want to introduce you to Kevin. He owns the bar, and we've been friends for years. I've told him about you a few times. He's dying to meet you."

Joci looked at Jeremiah with her head cocked to the side. "How does he know I'm here?"

Jeremiah smiled crookedly. "I texted him this morning to tell him. He has listened to me whine about you not going out with me for a long damn time. I couldn't wait to tell him you were riding with me today."

They walked into The Barn and strode to the far end. Jeremiah stood taller than most people in there, so he could see where they were going. Joci just hung on to his hand and followed along. She couldn't see anything but the backs and fronts of the people they were passing.

Soon Joci heard, "Dog, you son of a bitch, there you are."

Jeremiah pulled Joci to the end of the bar and then drew her behind the bar so she wouldn't get lost in the crowd. Jeremiah and Kevin hugged like guys do—arms wrapped around shoulders and a lot of backslapping. As soon as they were finished, Jeremiah reached for Joci and pulled her forward.

"Kevin, this is Joci. Joci, this is Kevin. We've been friends for about eighteen years."

Kevin leaned down and hugged Joci.

"I've heard quite a bit about you, Joci. It's great to meet you. And I'm thrilled you're finally with Dog."

He winked at her and looked at Dog. "What'll ya have? The usual?"

Jeremiah shook his head. "Water, one for each of us."

Kevin smirked and turned to get their drinks. When he returned, Jeremiah took both water bottles and opened the first one and handed it to Joci.

As he was opening the second one, he told Kevin, "I'll bring Joci out this week one night, and we'll sit and have a few. Today, I need to stay straight in case we have any issues."

Kevin nodded. "Sounds great. Come on Tuesday. For some reason, that's a slow night around here. I can knock off early, and we can sit here and drink without interruption."

Jeremiah looked at Joci. "Good with you?"

She smiled. "Sounds great."

Jeremiah looked at Kevin and smiled. He heard his intake of breath when she flashed that big smile. Who could resist the dimples in her cheeks? And, of course, those smoky gray eyes. Jeremiah had a difficult time not staring at her. As they stood there talking, Joci was suddenly pushed as LuAnn shoved herself into Jeremiah. LuAnn then elbowed her way past Joci and cut in front of her to throw herself at Kevin.

"How ya doin', Kev?" Kevin gave LuAnn a quick little hug and looked at Jeremiah with his brows furrowed.

Jeremiah wrapped his arms around Joci and whispered in her ear, "You okay, hon?"

She looked back at him. "Yes. Getting sick of this, though."

Jeremiah nodded at Kevin and grabbed Joci's hand. "Let's go see how the boys are doing."

They wove their way through the crowd and found Gunnar and Ryder talking to Connor. Jeremiah's stomach rolled at that scene, but he didn't want Joci to think he didn't like Connor.

He didn't dislike him; he just knew Connor was in love with Joci, even if she couldn't see it. He was worried that Connor knew her better than he did and maybe would step up his game to try to win her. He was also a little worried that Connor would try and get to Joci through Gunnar. He was going to keep his eyes on that. Luckily, Jeremiah worked with Gunnar every day. Sheesh, listen to him—he was jealous! Jeremiah had never been jealous in his life.

They walked up to the boys and Joci hugged each of them. Everyone was excitedly talking about the ride and asking Joci and Jeremiah how many bikes and riders there were. It was fun. After speaking with them for a little while, Jeremiah wanted to go and find his parents. He and Joci walked off to find Thomas and Emily.

"They'll probably be outside with the old car club, *The Good Times Roll*. There are about thirty old cars from that group. My dad chums along with some of those guys."

As they walked up and down the rows of old cars, Jeremiah found his mom and dad speaking to one of the guys from the club in front of an old truck. It was an orange 1937 Ford pickup with an oak box and oak box rails. It was beautiful.

Joci asked the owner a slew of questions. "Has this truck been in your family since it was new? Where did you find it? Did you refinish it? Do you take it out a lot? Is it easy to drive?" She was in love with that truck. The owner lifted the hood and showed Joci and the others the engine and explained all that he had done on the motor and lines.

He loved watching her excitement; her smile was bright and her giggle infectious. Emily caught his eye and winked. He was staring like a little school girl, but this was so new and fun.

Soon Jeremiah's family found them chatting and joined them. It was comfortable with his family. They were all very genuine people, Joci thought. Emily, Jeremiah's mom, had a great sense of humor and ribbed his dad quite a bit. She called him an old coot more than once, and he feigned hurt, but his laugh gave him away.

Soon enough, it was time to get rolling again, so they all started back to their bikes to get packed up and ready to ride. Joci and Jeremiah finished their waters, threw the bottles into the recycling bin, and walked arm in arm to his bike. When they got to the bike, Jeremiah pulled Joci in for a hug and kiss.

"I have competition, I see."

She looked up at him, her brows furrowed. "Really? Mind filling me in?"

Jeremiah laughed. God, he was handsome. His smile lit the whole sky. He had beautiful straight teeth, and his eyes sparkled when he laughed.

"The old guy couldn't talk to you enough. My mom noticed it, too. I saw her smiling, and at one point, she looked at me and winked. Not that I blame him, I'm pretty hung up on you too."

She hugged him and pulled back to look up in his eyes. "Just remember, if you leave me, I have options."

A smile spread across her face, and he leaned down and pecked her lips. He held her head in his hands and kissed her—long, slow, deep. She thought her toes were curling up in her boots. Crazy sensations zinged through her body, landing in her core. Her stomach flipped at this new affection and how demonstrative he was.

Jeremiah put his forehead on Joci's. "It's going to be painful riding with a raging hard-on. Look what you did to me!"

He ground himself against her a little so she could feel his hardness.

"That's not fair. You're making me wet," she whispered.

Jeremiah hugged her tight. "If I have to suffer, so do you. But, when we get home...don't expect any sleep tonight."

She moaned as her nipples pebbled into hard peaks, and her core throbbed just thinking about how he felt last night. It was dream-worthy.

"Seriously, you two need to get a room." Joci turned to see Sandi and Jon. Joci hadn't had a minute to talk to Sandi this morning.

"That's what I was just telling, Joci. How are you two?"

Jeremiah and Jon shook hands, and Joci hugged Sandi and then Jon. Joci and Jeremiah gave them the number of riders and bikers. They talked a little, and the whistle sounded that it was time to get ready to roll.

Sandi leaned in to hug Joci again. "Did you have a great time last night?"

Joci giggled. "God, yes. I can't wait to talk to you."

Sandi hugged her again. "I love you. I'm so happy for you. Let's talk at the next stop."

They parted, and Jeremiah jumped on his bike, kicked the kickstand up, and nodded to Joci to climb on. Once she was seated, she leaned forward and hugged him.

❧

"It's been a great day today. Thank you. I'm beginning to love riding on the back." Jeremiah leaned his head back on Joci's shoulder and looked back at her.

"It has been a great day." Joci tightened her arms around him. "And, for the record, you can ride on back anytime you want. I love having you back there."

She squeezed a little harder and kissed his neck. She wanted it to work out; she really did, but she was just so afraid to let herself believe it was going to last. The smorgasbord comment LuAnn made sure didn't make her feel any better.

The bikes started up, and they were on the road again. This next leg was only about 32 miles. Hills and curves created a mesmerizing ride. Some of the road was canopied by trees which sent a chill down her arms as the sun was hidden from them. Then the canopy would open, and the sun felt warmer than before. Joci was amazed at all the locals along the way waiting out by the roads or at the ends of their driveways to watch all the bikes ride past. Most of them waved American flags and cheered as the bikes rode by. Many of them had little canopies and coolers and whole driveways full of cars. They invited people over to watch the bikes and make it a party. Some people made signs thanking the veterans, and some of them had signs stating where they had served.

People were taking pictures and waving and yelling thank you. At one point, Joci teared up; she was so overwhelmed by the show of support for the veterans.

She leaned forward and hugged Jeremiah. "Does that make you feel good about serving, Jeremiah?"

He nodded, unable to speak. A couple of farmers had huge tractors with big cherry-picker baskets on them, and they parked them next to the road across from each other and strung a big banner between them over the road that said, "Thank You Veterans." Some people went all out for this. Now she understood why they mailed the fliers out to each home along the route.

The weather was just perfect. They didn't have to wear jackets or sweaters. The sun was shining, the roar of the bikes, Jeremiah in front of her, rubbing her leg and pushing his back into her so he could feel her. Life was made of fantastic moments like this. Joci would remember this for the rest of her life.

She hadn't been able to make this ride last year, but Gunnar had told her about it. It was why she agreed to help out with it this year. Gunnar talked about it all year. He was so excited about it; Joci wanted to see it for herself. She was very glad she had. First of all, she met Jeremiah. Second of all, this was amazing.

All too soon, they were pulling into the next stop. It was a resort just out of Mansfield, a small little town out in the country. The resort had plenty of parking and bars had been set up outside for people to buy drinks. Jeremiah and Joci were walking to one of the bars when Sandi and Jon caught up with them. They walked together to get drinks.

They stood talking and watching people mill about. Soon, JT and Ryder came over to say hello, and not long after that, Bryce and Angie stopped by.

Angie was very pretty, as were the other sisters-in-law. The Sheppards were a beautiful family. Angie had short blonde hair and light blue eyes. She was about Joci's height. Bryce was smaller than Jeremiah in height and weight. He had darker hair—a light brown where Jeremiah and Dayton had blond—and he had brown eyes. They were a striking couple.

Jeremiah leaned over to Joci. "I'd like to go in and say hello to the manager and thank him. Would you come with me?"

Joci smiled. "Sure, I'd like to use the restroom anyway."

Saying goodbye, they walked hand in hand into the resort. Once inside, Jeremiah maneuvered them to the bar and asked the bartender where he could find Smitty. The bartender nodded to a door at the other end of the bar, and Jeremiah waved two fingers in thanks and off they went, weaving their way in and out of people.

As soon as they were able to get to the door, Jeremiah knocked and was greeted with a terse, "Yeah."

Jeremiah opened the door laughing. "Hiding out?"

Smitty quickly stood up and shook hands with Jeremiah and nodded to Joci.

"This is my girlfriend, Joci. Joci, this is Smitty."

"We have over eighteen hundred people today, Smitty. Best turnout ever. Eighteen hundred and three!"

"Holy shit, Dog. This thing keeps growing, we're going to be too small for you. It brings a lot of money to us. The guests here just love looking at all the bikes and cars. The past couple of years, guests ask when the ride is going to be here because they want to come and see all the bikers."

"Great to hear. We'll manage with the numbers, no matter what. We need to run, but I wanted to stop by and thank you and introduce you to Joci. See ya around."

"Yeah. Nice to meet you, Joci. Ride safe."

They turned to leave the little office, and Jeremiah leaned down to Joci's ear. "The restrooms are right over there. I'll wait right here at the bar for you."

She made her way to the restroom and waited in line for a short while. She loved looking at all the women and their clothing and jewelry. She used the toilet and washed her hands. As she walked out of the restroom, she was making her way to where Jeremiah said he would be. Joci froze.

Jeremiah faced her direction. LuAnn stood between his legs with her arms wrapped around his neck, and they were kissing. Jeremiah looked up and saw Joci staring at them. She was frozen in place. She and Jeremiah stared at each other for what seemed like forever—though it couldn't have been more than a few seconds. Joci two finger saluted him and weaved her way in and out of people to get out of the bar. She would not cry, she would not cry, she would not cry. Tears threatened, but she refused to let them fall. She'd been down this road before. She could handle it.

Once she got to the door, she took in a deep breath and walked over to lose herself among the cars.

"Hey, what's up with you?"

Joci turned to see Sandi walking toward her. Joci couldn't help it—the tears started flowing.

"Oh, Sandi, I don't know what to do."

Sandi hugged Joci to her. "Tell me what happened."

"I walked out of the bathroom and saw Jeremiah and LuAnn kissing. I'm devastated, Sandi. I can't compete with LuAnn. She has everything a man like him wants. I don't. What am I going to do now? I'm stuck on the back of his bike until we get back to the shop."

"It probably wasn't what you saw, Joci. Did you ask him to explain?"

"No. I didn't want to cry in front of her. I just turned and walked away as quickly as I could."

Sandi grabbed Joci's hand and held it. "Maybe it's a good thing you have to ride with him. You'll have to talk to him. You at least owe him the opportunity to explain what you saw. And he owes you an explanation. From there, depending on the explanation, what you do will be clear. I love you no matter what and I doubt that Jeremiah is interested in that slut. I would bet she set it up for you to see. She's been dogging you guys all day, pardon the pun."

Both women giggled.

"Joci?" Jeremiah called. "I've been looking all over for you." She looked over to see him quickly walking toward them.

Sandi squeezed her hand and smiled. "I'm going to find Jon. Call my cell if you need me."

She kissed Joci on the cheek and began to leave. Sandi looked at Jeremiah with her brows up in the air as she walked away.

Jeremiah sighed loudly. "Joci, baby, I know it looked bad, but it wasn't what it looked like. I saw you coming out of the bathroom in the mirror behind the bar and turned to face you when LuAnn jumped in front of me and kissed me. I swear to you that's what you saw."

Joci was staring at the ground. "Have you slept with her before?"

Jeremiah put his fingers under her chin and turned her head, so she was looking at him.

"No, I haven't slept with her."

Joci's chin trembled as she moved to turn her head. Jeremiah leaned forward and held her face between his hands.

"Joci, I'm not interested in her. I don't want her. I want you. I'm only interested in you. Just you."

He moved in to kiss her, but she pulled away.

"No. You smell like her, and you still have her lipstick on your lips."

She turned away, swiping under her eyes and hoping her makeup wasn't a mess. Jeremiah rubbed the lipstick from his lips with his fingertips. He pulled his shirt out of his jeans and used the tail of his shirt to wipe his face.

"Joci, please look at me." He pulled his shirt off and threw it on the ground. He reached over and grabbed Joci and pulled her in for a hug.

"I swear to you, I don't want her. I've never wanted her."

Joci took a deep breath. "Why do you keep her at the store if she's like this all the time? Why would you tolerate this? She doesn't exactly give your store a great reputation. She dresses like a pole dancer. You must like it. And what about her comment that you like a smorgasbord? I don't know, Jeremiah. I can't go through this again. I just can't."

She pulled away, planted her hands on her hips and squared off.

His brows drew together as he searched for the right words. "I can't explain why I keep her around. Please believe me. She was just being bitchy with her smorgasbord comment."

They heard the whistle blow, and Joci closed her eyes. "We have to go."

She started walking toward their bike. She felt numb, not knowing what to think. He couldn't explain why he kept LuAnn. She wasn't exactly the sharpest tool in the shed. She was loud, obnoxious, and irritating. The only thing she had going for her was she was pretty. The guys all said she was hot.

Now, she was going to be a royal pain in Joci's side, one that Joci wasn't sure she was willing or able to handle on a daily basis. Jeremiah started walking with Joci. He grabbed her hand and pulled her over to the chaser truck. Joci tried pulling away, but he held on tight.

When they got to the truck, he threw his shirt in the back and opened a box and pulled a new shirt out and pulled it on. Once he had the new shirt on, he turned to Joci and grabbed her hard and hugged her tightly. He cupped the back of her head and wrapped his other arm around her waist. She could feel how tense he was, and his breathing was ragged.

"Joci, I need you to believe me. I know you have trust issues, and that sure didn't help, but I swear to you, I didn't initiate anything with LuAnn. I'll tell her to stop this behavior immediately. I don't want her, Joci—I only want you."

They stood that way for a few moments, and Thomas and Emily walked over to get into the truck.

"Hey, you two, you'd better get on your bike."

When Joci looked up, she smiled weakly and nodded. Thomas saw the look on her face and looked at Jeremiah with his brows furrowed. Jeremiah shook his head and pursed his lips. They started walking toward his bike. Silently.

When they got to the bike, people were catcalling and yelling at them.

"'Bout time. Making out in the back?"

Jeremiah climbed on the bike and kicked up the kickstand. He waited for Joci to get on. She leaned back against the backrest, not ready to lean into Jeremiah just yet. Her stomach was rolling and twisting.

J eremiah's gut felt like it was filled with stones. Fucking LuAnn. He knew Joci was having a hard time with this. With her trust issues, this was a real blow. He was going to have another long talk with LuAnn. He couldn't chance her pulling shit like this again. But right now, he had to get Joci to realize he wasn't cheating on her.

How to do that was a mystery. He had better think quickly since they only had about an hour before returning to Rolling Thunder. One thing he knew, Joci had the stubbornness of a fucking mule, so he'd better be on his A game.

The last leg of the ride began. He had 40 miles to figure this out and make sure she didn't get on her bike and ride off. He wasn't a game player, but he had work to do.

Jeremiah reached to the side and touched her leg. He wrapped his hand around her ankle and squeezed, just trying to keep contact with her.

Finally, they pulled into Rolling Thunder, and Jeremiah rode around to the back of the building. JT, Gunnar, and Ryder were right behind them.

Jeremiah didn't shut his bike off. He looked at the boys. "We're going home to get the truck. Be back in a few." He maneuvered the bike out of the back driveway.

J oci was surprised at this revelation. As soon as they pulled into his garage, he shut the bike off, closed the garage door, and got off. Before she could climb off, he was standing right there.

"We need to talk, Joci."

Joci looked at him and sighed. He held his hand out to help her off the bike. She looked into his eyes; her mouth turned down at the corners, but she took his hand and allowed him to help her off the bike. He held her hand and led her into the house. He led them to the sofa, then sat and pulled her down next to him.

He turned to face her. "Tell me what you need. I'm at a loss here. What you saw was not what it looked like."

Joci stared at him. "I can't give you the answer you want, Jeremiah. I don't have it. You know what I've been through. I just can't turn it off."

Her lip trembled, but she refused to cry. He leaned forward and lightly touched his lips to hers. Feathery light. She felt his lips tremble, and she softened, just a bit. Then it dawned on her that he was so worried, he had brought her home to his place while there were two thousand people at his shop partying and celebrating a great ride, listening to music, and having a few drinks, but he was here with her.

"Jeremiah, I'm sorry. I told you last night you might want to walk away." Joci took a deep breath then said, "We should get back to the shop."

Jeremiah slid his hand behind her head and held her close.

"I'm not leaving here until I know we're okay. I want to know that tonight; you're coming home with me, and I'm going to sleep with you in my arms. I need to know that you're not running from me."

Gray eyes met green. For several heartbeats, they sat that way.

Joci sighed. "I don't know, Jeremiah. It's too much. My stomach is in knots. I don't understand your connection with LuAnn and you don't seem to want to explain it. It's suspicious. I don't want to venture into this relationship any further to find out you've been lying to me. I just can't go through that again."

She swallowed the lump in her throat and slowly let out a long breath.

"Joci, LuAnn means nothing to me. I swear it. I owe her brother a favor, so I keep her employed to repay that favor. That's it. I swear it."

Jeremiah never looked away from her. She stood and took two steps away, turned and walked a few steps in the other direction. Placing her hands on her hips, she looked out the large window to the street and saw a younger couple walking their dog, while their child rode his bicycle in front of them. The flowers in the neighbor's yard were blooming, and the brilliance of the new spring grass made her think of fresh starts.

Joci sighed deep and long. She turned to see he had stood up, fingers tucked into his pockets, trying to look casual, but his rigid posture and shallow breathing proved him anything but. The shit of this whole thing was, she knew he was different than the men in her past, but she reacted badly to situations like the ones LuAnn insisted throwing her way. It didn't absolve LuAnn from her behavior, or Jeremiah for tolerating it and by ignoring it, allowing her to continue to behave as she had been.

Looking into his eyes, she pursed her lips briefly, then said, "I'm coming home with you tonight."

He took a step toward her. "But." He halted. "I will try to monitor my reactions to situations like today's. But you have to work on this too. It can't be one-sided."

13

DANCE THE NIGHT AWAY

They pulled into the parking lot and tried to find a place to park the truck. The place was packed. There were hundreds of cars, so either a lot of the bikers had gone home to get vehicles or more people had decided to come late, listen to music, and eat burgers and brats. Either way, it was good for the veterans and Rolling Thunder. Jeremiah drove around to the back and hit the garage door opener, then pulled into the back garage. There were many perks to owning the business—great parking being just one. He hit the garage door button again, and the door closed, but he made no move to get out of the truck.

Instead, he turned toward Joci. "Listen, I want you to know that I'm sorry about the way things went down today. We had a great day going, and I let it get ruined. I'm sorry, Joci."

Joci shrugged. "It's over now, so let's move on. But think about this. How would you feel if Connor pulled that shit on me? Would you like it if I just shrugged it off, or would you expect me to cut ties and keep him away from me?"

Jeremiah let out a long slow breath. "I would kick his ass, and there would be nothing left for you to cut ties with."

"I see, so that's what you want? You want me to physically kick the shit out of LuAnn?"

They stared each other down; testing, measuring. Joci knew if she continued to allow Jeremiah to have this kind of relationship with LuAnn, she wouldn't be able to tolerate it for long. She would become bitter, angry, and jealous. She would never be able to trust Jeremiah like she was going to need to if they were to have any kind of relationship. On top of that, he refused to explain to her why he put up with her flirting, other than a favor he owed her brother. The only conclusion she could come up with was that he liked it.

Jeremiah wasn't sure where to go from here. On one hand, it was good business, in a sense, to keep LuAnn around. If she stayed in the back where the bike parts were sold, she flirted with them, and they liked it. Plus, he felt he owed it to LuAnn to give her a job. What would she do if he fired her? She had no skills; she wasn't cut out for any work other than what he had for her at the store.

Despite owing Lance—LuAnn's brother—he wasn't going to let LuAnn chase Joci away from him. He had never felt like this before in his life, and dammit, he liked how he felt about Joci. It was scary to need someone so badly, but also, the way she made him feel was indescribable.

When she looked at him and smiled, he would do anything for her.

"No, I don't want you to kick the shit out of her or have to fight with her in any way. She's really harmless. She's always been very flirty with everyone. Since you've been coming around, she has gotten more...possessive, but I'm in no way interested in her. She works for me, and that's it."

Joci let out a determined breath. "Tell her to keep it that way, or you'll be able to spend ALL of your time with her...I won't be around."

Jeremiah leaned in and smiled at Joci. "I think you're jealous!"

Joci raised her eyebrows. "Perhaps. Wouldn't you be if the tables were turned?"

"Yes. Don't talk about that anymore. I hate hearing it."

Joci smirked. "So, here's the rub. I have trust issues, and it bothers me to see LuAnn hugging you, kissing you, and paying 'special' attention to you. You can't stand even talking or thinking about me with someone else in the same situation. So, tell me how we deal with this."

Jeremiah let out a long breath as he held her gaze.

Joci started to scoot over to the other side of the truck to get out, but he grabbed her and held her in place. He leaned forward and teased her lips with his tongue. He lightly touched his lips to hers. Her sigh was his cue that she was softening. His tongue danced along hers. Jeremiah's hand slid down to Joci's breast and pinched her nipple. A rush of air huffed out of her mouth. Yeah, he loved that. Her breasts were simply fantastic.

She reached over and covered his thickening length with her hand, and he involuntarily lifted his hips to add pressure. She fondled him through his jeans and his breath caught. The constriction was beginning to be too much.

He rasped out, "Jesus, Joci. Look what you've done to me."

Joci smiled against his lips. "You started it."

She continued to rub him until he pulled away abruptly.

He sat back. "Jesus, these jeans are incredibly tight right now. You'll cut my circulation off, causing an amputation here."

Joci pursed her lips. "That would be terrible. I would hate that. But, you do have an amazing tongue."

Her smile widened, and his mouth dropped open before he slammed it closed.

"You'll pay for that remark. Later."

Her smile stretched across her face which created those sexy dimples in her cheeks. He took in every inch of her face, committing it to memory for the hundredth time since he'd met her.

When she spoke, her voice was low and breathy. "I can't wait."

He had never had his heart so completely involved in sex. Every time he looked at Joci, he wanted to consume her, to be part of every minute of her every day. He wanted her body in every way he could have her. He wanted her to want him just as bad. And he wanted her to trust him, love him, and be with him through thick and thin.

"And for good measure, I'll show you just how good my tongue is too." She winked and raised her eyebrows while staring at him.

Every drop of blood in his body ran screaming to his cock. The swiftness of it made him light headed. He blinked a few times as he came back to reality. A lazy, sated smile formed on his lips.

"I don't know how you just did that with just your words, but I want more of it. And, I'm going to hold you to it."

He leaned forward and kissed her lips and laid his forehead against hers for a few moments.

His heart returned to its normal beat, and he softly said, "While we're out there talking to people, I want you thinking about how I'm going to lick your sweet little pussy as soon as I get you home. I'm going to slide my tongue into you. I'm going to lick it and suck your clit. I'm going to slide my cock inside of you after you come and I'm going to make you crazy for more."

She moaned and her heartbeat accelerated. "You know we could just go home now. It wouldn't be fair for me to walk around wet and ready."

Jeremiah fixed his clothing, adjusted his cock as the swelling started to subside and got out of the truck. He reached in and pulled her down out of the truck and hugged her for a long moment.

He chuckled. "Just make sure you don't go to the bathroom and take care of yourself. I promise I'll make it worth your while."

He kissed her forehead and took her hand and headed toward the door. As soon as they stepped out of the garage, they saw JT and Gunnar standing there.

"What took you so long? We were afraid to come in there and get you. We didn't know what we would see."

JT smirked; Gunnar did too, sort of. At the look on both Joci and Jeremiah's faces, they both started laughing.

"Oh, my God, you're fucking kidding me! Mom!"

Joci opened her mouth to say something, but Sandi and Jon walked up right at that moment. "Hey, what's going on?"

JT turned to Sandi. "Well..."

"Never mind, JT. Go somewhere...you, too, Gunnar," Jeremiah chided.

Jeremiah looked down at Joci and squeezed her shoulders. She was mortified, grunted an unintelligible word and rubbed her forehead with her fingers. God, what was she thinking. She knew both their kids were there. Crap. She assumed their kids would figure out that she and Jeremiah were having sex. It's quite another thing to be caught in the act or close to the act. She liked that he told her what he wanted, but she was acting like a silly teenage girl.

Yesterday, when he told her they were going to be together, she was so turned on she couldn't concentrate all day.

The boys walked away chuckling. Sandi looked at Joci and raised her eyebrows.

"Never mind...kid stuff." Jeremiah chuckled.

Sandi smiled at her and looked at Jon, who had a smirk on his face.

"Let's go get a drink, shall we?" Jeremiah told the group.

He grabbed Joci's hand and walked toward the drink tent.

As they walked, he leaned down and whispered in her ear, "They assumed anyway, Joci. Don't let it bother you."

She looked up at him and frowned. "I should be setting a better example."

Jeremiah laughed out loud. "Joci, you're a beautiful woman. Our boys know that, and they know how much I want you. Being boys, I think they have a clue as to how it works."

Sandi gasped at his words. "Did they just catch you two--?"

"Stop. No. God, Sandi, don't say it." Joci's face stained bright red.

"Oh. My. God. They did catch you!"

Jeremiah and Jon laughed. Joci covered her face with her hands. Jeremiah squeezed her shoulders and kissed the top of her head. "Not really, Sandi. They assumed, and the looks on our faces made them think it was more than it was."

They got their drinks and turned to listen to the fabulous local band that was playing. Joci was happy for the distraction.

As the night wore on, a steady stream of people came up to Jeremiah to tell him what a great turnout they thought today was and how much they enjoyed the ride. The veterans in attendance made sure to come by and thank Jeremiah for all of his help in bringing attention to the plight of so many veterans. They told him how much it meant to them. His face was a sight to behold. He looked so happy and proud. And he should be. What he had created here was amazing. It tugged at her heart that this day had almost been ruined for him.

Around ten o'clock, Jeremiah wrapped his arms around Joci and asked, "Are you ready to go?"

She nodded. "I was ready to go while we were still in the garage!"

He leaned down and whispered in her ear, "Are you wet, Joci? Have you been thinking about me?"

She chuckled and whispered, "I've been wet all night."

Jeremiah hissed out his breath. "Fuck, I'm hard as a rock. Let's get the hell out of here."

Her brows furrowed. "Don't you have to stay until the end?"

He shook his head. "That's another perk of being in charge. I can tell someone else to be the last man standing. Deacon is in charge of the final curtain."

He grabbed Joci's hand and pulled her toward the garage. LuAnn came running over just then. "Dog, I'm ready for the dance you promised me."

She shimmied for effect.

"LuAnn, I didn't promise to dance with you. I believe I've already told you this today, but let me tell you again. I'm with Joci. Only Joci. Do you understand?"

LuAnn shrugged and pushed her bottom lip out in a pout as she turned and walked away.

They kept on walking and LuAnn yelled out, "Enjoy it while you can, Joci."

Joci's steps halted briefly, but he kept pulling her along. As soon as they got to the building, Jeremiah unlocked the service door, and they quickly slipped inside. He turned to her and looked her straight in the eyes. "You will enjoy it; I promise you that."

He strode quickly to the truck, Joci at his side, and opened the door for her to slide inside. He slid in right behind her and quickly turned the key in the ignition.

Joci smirked at him. "You seem to be in a hurry, big guy."

He looked at her out of the corner of his eye and hit the garage door button. "When my woman is wet and ready, I'm not wasting any time. Besides, I've been hard as a rock all evening thinking about you naked."

She leaned back and looked at him. "Sheesh, it's scary how much we think alike."

After pulling into his garage, he turned the ignition off and twisted slightly in his seat. "Go inside and undress. Take a bubble bath and relax. But in half an hour, I want you kneeling in the middle of the bed and waiting for me."

She looked at him, her brows raised high into the bandana she still wore. He smirked, "Ahh, you like that?" He smoothed her cheek with the back of his fingers. "You are my woman in so many ways."

He hopped out of the truck and reached in to help her out.

As soon as she was on the ground, he swatted her on the ass. "Thirty minutes, Joci. Don't keep me waiting."

Joci walked quickly to the bedroom, pulling her shirt out of her jeans as she walked. She couldn't help but smile as she turned the water on in the tub. She looked around and found bath soap on the counter and squeezed some into the bath. She finished undressing while the tub filled.

As she slid into the warm, soothing, floral-scented water, the day floated over her. All in all, it had been a great day. She could have done without LuAnn. But he certainly didn't seem interested in her either, and yet, he seemed to have a connection to her. In some ways, it was a bit sad that LuAnn seemed so starved for attention. She was pretty. She'd be a knockout if she didn't trash herself up so much. There was a story there, she'd bet.

She finished her bath, dried off, and climbed into the middle of the bed with a smile on her face. This was so damned exciting. She read about foreplay like this but hadn't experienced it. The butterflies swarming in her stomach couldn't be eased by placing her hands on it and gently pressing in.

She heard Jeremiah walking down the hall toward her and her breathing sped up. She bit her bottom lip and squirmed.

The handle turned on the door, and her breath hitched. "Joci, you're so fucking beautiful. You take my breath away." He stood in the doorway—filled it, actually. His large arms were a sight to behold. The tattoos and the muscles wrapped around and created a myriad of places for her eyes to inspect. His shirt was still tucked into his jeans, but the zipper and button were undone as if he had opened them while walking down the hall toward the bedroom.

She licked her lips. "Actually, I was just thinking the same thing about you," her voice quivered.

He smirked. "Your voice is shaky. Are you excited, Joci?"

She nodded.

"Say it."

Joci licked her lips again. "I'm excited, Jeremiah." Her voice was breathy, but she couldn't help it. He was a force. Tall and broad.

Commanding. The way he looked at her took her breath away. Intense but...loving?

Jeremiah took a couple of steps closer and leaned across the bed until he was nose to nose with her.

"What are you excited for, Joci?" His smile grew. "I want to know what you want."

She took a deep breath and she squeaked. "I'm excited for you to touch me, to make me come, to slide inside of me."

Jeremiah hissed out a breath. "Yes, I'm going to do exactly that and more."

He stood and pulled his shirt out of his jeans. His eyes never left hers. He pulled his shirt off and tossed it to the floor. He pushed his jeans down his hips to fall on the floor. Her eyes focused on his rigid cock and she squirmed again.

"Look at you, Joci. Your nipples just beaded up looking at my cock. I think you're turned on. Are you?"

She sucked in a breath, and he smirked at her.

"Yes," she said, her voice barely audible.

"Turn around and come closer to the edge of the bed. Put your hands behind your back." His voice was soft, but it was issued as a command.

Joci turned around and scooted herself to the edge of the bed. She put her hands behind her back and held her breath. Jeremiah reached around and rolled her nipples between his thumbs and fingers. She groaned, and he pulled her against his hardness. Almost instantly her hands cupped around his balls, and Jeremiah sucked in a breath.

"Jesus." He pulled away and leaned down, so his mouth was next to her ear. "You're a little vixen, Joci. But we have some playing to do first."

His warm breath floated over her shoulder and her ear. She shivered. He chuckled. His scent wrapped around her, and she felt the wetness between her legs. Had she ever been this excited?

She felt something soft wrap around her wrists. Jeremiah tied both hands together with a soft cord or cloth.

"Now, turn back around and scoot to the middle of the bed." His voice was tight.

She scooted on her knees and moved to the center of the bed. She turned to face him and then sat on her legs. When she raised her eyes to look at him, he sucked in a breath.

"You're stunning, Joci. I can hardly believe you're finally here with me. All day today, I kept reminding myself it was real. I've waited so long for you and dreamed about you so much."

Joci had to blink back the tears. She was still amazed at the fact that he felt so strongly about her. That he was willing to voice those feelings was even more amazing.

He leaned forward and ran his fingers along her jaw. He slid his fingers into her hair at her temple and cupped the back of her head. He ran his thumb over her bottom lip and then let his hands fall to her breasts.

"Do you know what I like about you having your hands tied behind your back?"

"No." Her voice was so soft, her throat so dry watching him and listening to him, she couldn't even hear herself. She cleared her throat and licked her lips.

"No," she said a little louder.

"I like that your amazing breasts are thrust forward and just begging me to touch them, lick them. I like that I can do what I want to you, and you can't stop me with your hands, but you trust me enough to know that I won't hurt you. Do you know what that means to me, Joci?"

"No," she said again, softly.

He looked into her stormy eyes. For several seconds, they stared at each other. He didn't even know if he had the words to tell her what this sight did to him. He had to pick the time right to tell her how he felt. He didn't want to screw this up.

"I can't explain it. I've never been so speechless in my life. Right now, you render me speechless."

Joci's lips tilted up on the sides. Jeremiah leaned forward and sucked one of her breasts in his mouth. He reached a hand up and cupped the other breast while he suckled the first in his mouth. He sucked hard and nipped at her nipple. She closed her eyes and moaned. Jeremiah pinched her other nipple between his thumb and forefinger and rolled it until it was hard and pointed. Joci huffed out a breath and squirmed. He smiled against her breast while he sucked and licked.

"Do you like that, Joci?" He looked up at her. "Does that make you wet?"

She gazed at him and nodded. At the same time, she sighed, "Yes."

"Really? How wet are you, baby?"

Jeremiah trailed kisses down her belly all the way down to her curls. He dipped his tongue a little lower. He licked her seam and found her clit and sucked it into his mouth.

She groaned loudly. Her legs shook.

"Spread your legs wider for me, sweetheart. Show me your pretty pussy."

Joci moved her legs apart a little more.

"Oh, so pretty. And you taste so good."

Jeremiah slid his tongue along her opening and sucked her into his mouth. She panted. She'd been waiting all friggin' night. After she had sucked his cock in the garage and he told her what he would do to her, it was all she could think of. She wanted him in every way. He was like a drug to her. On some level, she felt like she shouldn't want this so bad; but on another, she couldn't stop herself.

This afternoon, when they came back to the house and she thought she would leave, she really couldn't bring herself to do it. All her bravado to Jeremiah that she would walk was just that. Bravado. She didn't know if she could walk away. She couldn't let him cheat on her, but walking away from him would be tantamount to cutting off a limb.

Jeremiah continued to pleasure her with his thick, strong fingers. He knew just how to use them on her. In and out, slowly while he sucked and nipped at her clit. The rhythm he used was intoxicating. His mouth and tongue were like heaven.

"Jeremiah, can I come? Please tell me I can come."

He looked up at her. "You never have to ask me if you can come, Joci. If I make you feel good enough to come, I want you to come. I want you to come on my face, on my fingers, on my cock. I want you to come everywhere."

She whimpered. Jeremiah went back to licking and sucking her, and then he slid a second finger inside of her channel, and that was it. Joci cried out his name as the orgasm hit.

"I love watching your face when you come. Gorgeous."

He reached around and untied her hands. He massaged them to bring the circulation back; then he gently pushed her until she was lying on her back. He grabbed her ankles and pulled her to the edge of the bed. He grabbed his cock and directed it to Joci's entrance. His eyes never left hers.

"Breathe, baby. I won't hurt you. I'll never hurt you."

She took a breath, but her eyes never left his.

"Watch me, Joci."

She lifted herself up on her elbows and watched him slide in. First, he pushed in just a little so that only the head of his cock was in her. He gave her a couple of seconds and pushed in a little more. He slid out of her to the head and slowly pushed back in a little more.

He pulled out and then slid in a little further. He leaned forward and lifted Joci's legs up and spread her knees open, so she was completely open to him.

"All the way, this time, baby," he said with a ragged breath. "Are you with me?"

She smiled up at him, and he sucked in a breath.

Her voice was breathy again as she replied, "I'm with you. You feel amazing, Jeremiah, and it looks hot as hell."

Jeremiah grunted, "Damn right it does."

He pushed himself into her all the way. Joci closed her eyes as a sigh escaped. He hit all her good spots. He wouldn't even have to move, and she could come again. She opened her eyes and watched him. He was so magnificent.

"I want you to come very fast, Joci, because I won't be able to hold off for long. I want to watch you come one more time and then I'll let go."

Jeremiah reached down and started rubbing her clit while he moved in and out of her. She watched as his cock disappeared inside of her and his fingers drove her wild. His skin became damp with sweat and the soft light from the hallway highlighted his muscles. Sexy.

He groaned out a breath. "Fast, Joci. Come fast for me."

She whimpered as she felt her orgasm build and then race through her body. He picked up his speed and added more pressure to her clit.

She cried out. "Jeremiah..." Her body stiffened as the effects of her orgasm spent itself. Finally over, her muscles relaxed. She opened her eyes to see him watching her, still inside but not moving.

He leaned down and kissed her.

"I will never get tired of watching your face when you come, Joci. So beautiful I don't even have words for it."

She reached up and dug her hands into his hair and fisted it in the back. She kissed him hard while holding him. He groaned loudly.

"Ride me, Jeremiah. Ride me hard and fast."

Fuck. She could make him come just by talking to him. He groaned again but didn't wait for her to say anything more. He slid an arm behind her back and pulled her up the bed so he could lie on top of her. He pounded into her, his need and passion exploding out of him. His breathing was labored and his muscles taut from exertion. He moved swiftly, the need to come almost unbearable.

Gritting his teeth, he managed, "Not. Long. Baby...Get there." His vision blurred. His cock was on fire.

She moaned very loudly. "Yes, Jeremiah...yes. God...so...good."

He felt her stiffen and gasp out his name. He was right there, draining himself into her, thrust after thrust. He thrust two more times, spilling into her. As he lay on top of her, he kept his arms under her, so he didn't crush her. After a minute or so he started to lift up, she wrapped her legs around his back, holding him in place.

Jeremiah cupped her head in his hands and kissed her temples, then her ears. When his breathing was steadier, he whispered in her ear, "Never thought I would find you, but I did."

He leaned down and kissed her, tenderly, gently. Their tongues mated just as their bodies had done, still joined, needing to stay close to each other. Joci ran her hands through his hair, kneading his scalp and holding him close to her. His heart felt content.

14

YOU'VE GOT A FRIEND

"Don't forget, we're going to The Barn tonight to have a couple drinks with Kevin."

Joci meet his gaze in the bathroom mirror as she dusted blush on her cheeks. "What time do you want me to be ready?"

He pulled his hair back into a ponytail and tied it with a rubber band. "What time do you want to go? Did you want to go out to eat first?"

"I can make something here if you'd like. Or maybe my place. I feel like I haven't been there in weeks. I probably have food going bad in the refrigerator."

Jeremiah chuckled and turned to lean against the counter. "Wow, you make that sound great. I'll have a helping of bad food, please."

She laughed. "Not what I meant. I just meant you're going to have to let me go home eventually. I played hooky with you yesterday. I have to go and work and clean my house. Let me make you supper there."

He frowned a bit. "I like you here. I don't want you getting used to being without me. Move in with me, Joci."

She packed her blush brush into her little makeup case and turned to face him.

"I can't, Jeremiah. It's too soon. I need office space to work. I have a house...full of stuff. What would I do with all of it? Where would I work?"

Jeremiah walked to her, looking into her eyes. "Those are simply excuses. You know all of that can be worked out."

He ran the backs of his fingers over her cheek. "I want you here. I want to wake up with you every day. I want to go to sleep with you every night. I want to see you in my space—our space—every time I look around. Will you think about it, please?"

He leaned down and kissed her tenderly.

She tucked her hands in his back pockets and gazed up at him. "Yes, I'll think about it."

Jeremiah nodded slightly. "Maybe one of the boys will want to live in your place rather than pay rent somewhere else."

She shrugged her shoulders. "It's a thought. It's also a big step."

She turned to pack up her toiletries and zipped the top closed.

Jeremiah crossed his massive arms over his broad chest. "Are you more comfortable making something for dinner at your place, Joci?"

She tucked her makeup bag under her arm and turned to face him.

"It's not about comfort. I feel oddly comfortable here with you." Joci took a deep breath. "It's scary, Jeremiah...I've never lived with a man before, except my son, and he doesn't count. I'm his mom. If it doesn't work out, then I have to find another place to live. And I work from home most of the time. My work would be disrupted, too."

She looked down at the counter. Her heart beat like it was trying to burst out of her body. She opened and closed her fists to relieve the building tension.

"Joci?" Jeremiah's voice was soft. "Look at me, baby." He sighed.

She looked into his eyes. He reached over and slid his hand in her hair at the temple and pulled her close to him.

"I would like for us to build a relationship looking forward. When Jackie and David moved in with each other, don't you think they had the same concerns? We'll have disagreements over time, and we'll have to work through those disagreements. I'm committed to that. Are you?"

Joci looked into his eyes. Those beautiful green eyes never wavered. She took a deep breath.

"Yes, I'm committed to making it work. I just worry about...everything. This is a big step." Her voice was soft and shaky.

Jeremiah pulled her to his body and wrapped his arms around her. She breathed deep and inhaled his scent, strength, and comfort.

After a few moments, Joci looked up at him. "I'm sorry, Jeremiah."

He shook his head. "No need, babe. I know it's scary for you. For me, I've thought about you moving in with me for months. I'm excited as hell for you to be here with me."

She took a breath. "How about I make us supper here tonight, and then we can head to The Barn later?"

Jeremiah kissed her lightly. "That sounds amazing, Joci. Thank you."

They walked together to the kitchen and made breakfast. Jeremiah had to go to the shop, and Joci had to go home and get some work done today. She would run through her cupboards and see what she had to bring here and stop at the store on her way back to Jeremiah's if she needed anything else. She thought she could stay at Jeremiah's the majority of the time and go home in the mornings to work. She wanted to try it that way for a while and see how that worked without making it a permanent move right away.

Jeremiah opened a drawer in the kitchen and handed her a garage door opener. "Keep this with you. Come and go as you like. I'll have a key made today. Your bike is fine at the shop. I'll run you home this morning on my way."

She smiled at him. "Thank you."

At 7:30 that evening, they were in Jeremiah's truck heading to The Barn. It had been a beautiful day, but still a little cool in the evening, so they opted for the truck instead of the bike. As soon as they walked into The Barn, Kevin waved at them as he was serving customers at the far end. Jeremiah held Joci's hand as they walked to the opposite end and took a seat. Kevin finished with his customers and headed their way. Jeremiah got up and walked behind the bar to 'man hug' Kevin. Kevin looked at Joci, a big smile on his face.

"How ya doin', Joci?"

She couldn't help but giggle. "I'm great, Kevin, how are you?"

Kevin held out his arms and looked up. "Livin' the dream, darling."

She giggled. Kevin got them their drinks. "At eight o'clock I have a bartender coming in so we can sit and shoot the shit. My girlfriend, Kathy, is coming in as well."

Joci smiled. "That's great. I'm looking forward to meeting her and chatting."

They sat at the bar talking, and suddenly Kevin's face lit up like a Christmas tree.

"Hey, baby, give me some lovin'." He stretched his arms wide as his smile lit up the room.

A beautiful redhead walked around the end of the bar and wrapped her arms around Kevin, and he swung her around. Jeremiah chuckled at Kevin's display. They were a fascinating couple.

Kevin turned toward Joci. "I want you to meet Kathy. Kathy, this is Joci James, Dog's girlfriend."

"Kevin's been excited all weekend that you were coming in to visit. It's very nice to meet you," she said.

Kathy reached over the bar and shook her hand, and Kevin pointed them all over to the corner of the bar where there were a fireplace and a couple of sofas.

They grabbed their drinks from the bar and made themselves comfortable on a sofa while Kevin and Kathy got drinks for themselves.

Kevin and Kathy joined them. Joci admired Kathy. She was beautiful, long red hair, bright blue eyes, vivacious and a killer body. But she was also genuinely sweet and pleasant to be around. She practically sat on top of Kevin.

Joci asked Kevin, "How did you and Jeremiah meet?"

Kevin laughed. "I met Dog years ago at another bar I was managing. He was on his bike, and it had started pouring rain outside. Dog stopped in to wait for the rain to stop and we struck up a conversation. From there, we became fast friends." Kevin inclined his head at Jeremiah.

Jeremiah tightened his jaw. He had picked up a woman in the bar that night. Something Joci didn't need to hear.

Kathy leaned forward, winked, and said, "They had to kiss a lot of frogs to find us, Joci."

Joci smirked. "I suppose you could look at it that way."

Jeremiah shot Kevin a look, and Kevin took the cue. "Dog, are you ready to shoot some pool?" Jeremiah leaned over and kissed Joci on the temple.

"If you're ready to have your ass kicked, I am," he said, laughing.

~

Kathy came over and sat on the sofa next to Joci. "Holy crap, Joci. I've never seen Dog so head-over-heels. How did you wrap him up so quickly?"

Joci sighed. "I don't know that I would say wrapped up. We've known each other for close to a year now. Just recently we moved into a relationship."

Kathy laughed out loud. "I would definitely say 'wrapped up.' He can't take his eyes off you. He's always touching you and the fact that he wanted us to meet you says a ton."

Joci turned to look at her new friend. "I'm trying not to get too caught up in all of this. With him. I don't have a great track record. You know?"

Kathy shook her head. "Baby, you have nothing to worry about. Dog has been with women—a few, not a ton. Kevin was a huge whore before he met me. I've only seen Dog with one or two women all the time I've known him, and that's been about four years now. And then, he barely paid them any attention. You could tell it was simply a booty call for him."

Joci sighed. "Yeah."

Kathy chuckled and put an arm around Joci. "Girl, don't you worry about that. The past is the past. You have to look forward. Think about what you have now and what you want in the future. If you live in the past, all you'll get is more of the past!"

Joci frowned. She wanted nothing to do with the past. She decided to change the subject and steered the conversation to other things.

"Tell me all about you, Kathy."

"Let's see. I have three children, all grown now. I met Kevin four years ago when I started working for him here as a bartender. We've been together ever since. Not always easy, after all. He used to be a manwhore; I had to overcome that. We've had a lot of rocky times, but we're doing well this past year and a half."

Joci and Kathy talked for a couple of hours while the guys shot pool and bullshitted.

Around 1 in the morning, Jeremiah and Joci pulled into his garage and closed the door. He got out of the truck and reached in to pull Joci out. She slid over and was about to step out when he scooped her up and carried her into the house. She wrapped her arms around his shoulders and nuzzled his neck and ears.

He carried her straight back to the bedroom and laid her carefully on the bed. He started to stand up but stopped and swept a lock of hair away from Joci's brow, softly, tenderly, sliding his fingers along her forehead and temple.

15

IT'S MORE THAN SEX

She was so amazing to him. Never in his life did he believe he would feel this way. Watching her with his friends tonight made his chest so tight; her smile and laugh—her everything —were a sight to behold. He couldn't process all these emotions. They were just so strong. The butterflies wouldn't stop flying around in his belly. This emotion of needing her, wanting her, just kept getting stronger and stronger the more time he spent with her.

He slid his hand to her temple, into her hair, and to the back of her head. He rested his thumb on her cheek and leaned in for a tender kiss.

She squeezed him hard, her breathing jerky.

"If I lose you, Jeremiah, it's going to leave a scar that won't go away," she whispered, her voice raspy.

He swallowed the lump in his throat. "Let's make sure that doesn't happen."

Jeremiah leaned down and tenderly touched his lips to hers. He was still holding her head in his left hand, keeping her where he needed her. With his right hand, he started undoing the button on his jeans. He began undressing while continuing to kiss her. As he got to a point that he needed to pull away, he gently rubbed her nose with his and pulled away to push his jeans to the floor. Joci shoved her panties down her legs and kicked them off, then sat up to pull her shirt off, leaving only her bra. She reached back and unhooked it and let it fall off her arms.

Jeremiah never took his eyes off her. He watched her remove her clothes while he removed his. As soon as they were both naked, he gently lay next to her on the bed and immediately rolled on top of her, holding himself up on his elbows so he wouldn't crush her. He nudged her legs open and kissed her, slowly.

He entered her while kissing her. As soon as he was all the way in, he groaned. He pulled away from her mouth and laid his forehead on Joci's.

"This feeling is overwhelming. You feel so good, Joci. I'm addicted to you," he whispered.

Joci's voice was soft as she replied, "Yes, I know the feeling."

Jeremiah lazily moved, in and out, making love to her slowly. He held her head in his hands and continued to kiss her lips while sliding into her. He could hear and feel her wetness. The tightness of her pussy gripping his cock as he entered her hot channel and molding herself to him made him breathless. The only reason he slid back out was so he could slide back in and feel it again.

"Joci." Jeremiah lifted his head to look into her eyes. His voice choked with emotion, he said, "Watch me make love to you. Can you feel how amazing this is? Do you understand what I'm doing to you here? Do you understand what you're doing to me?"

Her eyes brightened with tears. "Yes" was all she could say.

She wrapped her legs around his hips, and they slowly rocked together. The only sounds in the room were their ragged breathing and the slippery sounds of their lovemaking. The most beautiful sound in the world.

Joci whimpered his name as her body rocked with her orgasm. He pushed himself into her and held himself there as his release instantly followed hers. He could feel himself pulsing as his warm seed spilled into her, but his green eyes never left her gray ones, both bright with moisture.

16

CONNOR

"Hey, there. I'm glad you could make it," Mason said. Mason Wagner, Connor's son, was 28 years old and handsome, just like his father. Mason's eyes are dark blue, his hair slightly curly, though short. At six feet, he was an impressive man. Joci had known Mason most of his life.

Joci stepped forward to hug Mason. "Mason, this is Jeremiah. Jeremiah, this is Mason Wagner, Connor's son."

"Nice to meet you, Jeremiah. Thank you for coming. Abby has been beyond excited to see Joci and Gunnar today."

Just then, a little voice squealed, "Joci! Joci! I here."

Joci giggled and looked at the little bundle running toward her. Abby was Mason's daughter and today was her fourth birthday. She was dark like her father, though her hair was longer. She had her father's blue eyes and olive skin, a stunning little girl.

"Happy birthday, Abby. You look so beautiful." Joci clapped her hands together, her smile for the little girl stunning.

Abby was wearing a pink dress with purple sparkles on it. She had little pink shoes and a purple headband holding her riot of curls off her face.

"Abby. I want to introduce you to Jeremiah."

Jeremiah kneeled down to greet Abby. "Abby, it's very nice to meet you. I've heard a lot about you. Happy birthday."

Abby's head bobbed up and down. "I'm four today." She held up four fingers to show him.

Then she pouted. "Where's Gunnar?"

Joci chuckled. "He'll be here very soon. I promise."

Abby nodded and ran off to play with her cousins. Jeremiah, Mason, and Joci laughed as they watched her bounce out of view.

"Come on over. Dad and Betsy are waiting for you."

They walked over to a table where Betsy—Mason's wife—and Connor were sitting, talking with family. Connor stood when they approached and shook Jeremiah's hand while Joci hugged Betsy. Connor leaned over and hugged Joci. He introduced Betsy and Jeremiah.

Betsy beamed. "I'm very happy to meet you, Jeremiah. Thank you for coming. Joci, you're beautiful as always. Where's Gunnar?"

Joci laughed. "He'll be here soon. I spoke to him on our way over, and he was just pulling out of his driveway. And, thank you. You look beautiful also."

They were ushered over to the table holding the snacks and drinks and told to make themselves at home. The birthday party was held at Perkins Park in Green Bay. It was a beautiful park with many little pavilions nestled here and there, offering places to hide from the sun on warm days and shelter from the rain on wet. Today was a beautiful, warm day. People were sitting on lawn chairs and visiting at tables. Betsy had a large family, and they all gathered for occasions like this.

Just as they were grabbing their drinks out of the cooler, Joci and Jeremiah heard Abby squeal, "Gunnar!"

Joci turned to see Abby throw herself into Gunnar's arms. He was laughing and crouched down on his heels to catch her. Joci and Jeremiah stopped to watch the show, both chuckling at Abby's enthusiasm.

Joci leaned into Jeremiah and said, "She has loved Gunnar since she was old enough to know him. He has always loved her as well."

They walked over to Gunnar and Abby and sat on the ground with them. Abby was excited about her party and telling them about her new 'school.' Her school was day care, but to get her to go, Mason and Betsy called it school. Abby was four going on sixteen. She was animated as she talked and kept hugging Gunnar and Joci. So adorable.

"I have to go and play now." She took off as fast as she came over.

They stood. "I could use something to drink. What do they have?"

Jeremiah chuckled. "A little hair of the dog?"

Gunnar rolled his eyes. "You could say that. Long night. I look better than JT does; I can tell you that."

They got Gunnar a beer, then found a table. Connor walked over a while later and sat down with them, directly across from Joci. Joci watched Jeremiah assess Connor. His jaw tightened, his posture was rigid. He looked uncomfortable, to say the least. She reached under the table and held his hand. He glanced at her, and she winked. That seemed to relax him. A little.

Connor leaned forward on the table. "Did Betsy show you the photo album from years past?"

Joci smiled. "Oh, no. I would love to see it. Where is it? I'll go and get it."

"I'll be right back. I know where it is." Connor got up and walked away.

He was back within a few minutes, but instead of taking his seat, he stood just between Joci and Gunnar and placed the album on the table. He opened it up and started pointing to pictures.

Joci looked over at Jeremiah and squeezed his hand to include him. Jeremiah leaned over and kissed the side of Joci's face. Connor kept talking and pointing at pictures as they laughed at a few of them. There were many of Joci and Gunnar. They had been to all of Abby's parties. Just then, Abby ran over and climbed up on Joci's lap to look at pictures, too.

She giggled and laughed at the pictures of her as a baby. There was a picture of Gunnar sticking his tongue out at the camera, and Abby squealed in delight. They looked at a few more pictures, and Abby turned in Joci's lap to face her. She put her hands on Joci's face and with a serious look she said, "I love you, Joci."

Awww, how sweet. "I love you, too, Abby."

"Grandpa loves you, too."

Uh, oh. Joci froze. So did Jeremiah. Not realizing how uncomfortable she just made the situation, Abby continued. "Gunnar loves you, too."

"Yes, and we all love you, Abby." Joci smiled at her. Abby squeezed Joci's neck and scrambled off her lap to run and play again.

Connor took a seat across the table again, while Gunnar and Jeremiah made conversation about last night and the fun the boys had while they were out. Joci suddenly felt uncomfortable and sat quietly listening to their conversation.

She glanced up and saw Connor watching her. Actually, staring at her. She had never felt uncomfortable with him before, but today seemed different. He seemed different. Soon, Betsy clapped her hands and announced that Abby should come and open her presents.

All the kids gathered around the 'chair of honor' and watched as Abby's presents were placed before her. She squealed when she saw all of them. One by one, the gifts were opened and then discarded almost as quickly as the next gift appeared for her to open.

Joci's mind wandered. She had never given Connor any indication that she would be with him one day. A couple of years ago, a little while after he was divorced, he had asked her out and tried kissing her, but she just didn't feel it for him. He was handsome. He had dark hair like Mason, dark blue eyes, and a beautiful smile. He was about six feet tall. He was vice president at a manufacturing company in Green Bay, making good money. He was a good man, but when it came to that spark, there just wasn't one. She loved him as a friend. She thought Connor understood. Last year, he had introduced her to a couple of girlfriends. But today, something was different.

Betsy called out. "Okay, let's eat, shall we?"

Jeremiah, Joci, and Gunnar waited until everyone had gotten their food before venturing to the table themselves. Joci asked, "Should we sit in the sun and eat?"

Jeremiah inclined his head to a spot near the pavilion. "That looks like the perfect spot."

Gunnar gathered their empty plates. "I need a drink. You guys want anything?"

Joci smiled. "No, honey, you go ahead."

Gunnar nodded his head, looked at Jeremiah. "I'm good, Gunnar."

As Gunnar walked away, Jeremiah leaned forward and kissed Joci lightly on the lips. "I've been dying to do that for what seems like hours now."

Joci giggled. "What took you so long?"

Jeremiah looked back at the people gathered under the pavilion and then back at Joci. "It felt disrespectful for some reason. I feel like these people think of you as Connor's."

"Awww, sweetheart, I belong to you." She leaned forward and kissed Jeremiah on the lips. She smiled, "Whenever you're ready, we can go."

"I'll follow you, baby," he quickly replied.

Gunnar came back over and sat down. "How long do we have to stay, Mom?"

Joci burst out laughing. "Jeremiah and I were just talking about that. I think we're ready to leave. Did you want to follow us out?"

Gunnar nodded. He took a drink of his water. "Yeah, I'm ready."

They got up to say their goodbyes and thanks. Abby ran up to Gunnar and wrapped her little arms around his neck and sweetly told him thank you. When Gunnar set her down, she looked at Jeremiah. He was tall, so she had to look up pretty far. He saw her craning her neck and kneeled down.

She hugged him as well. "Thank you for coming."

Jeremiah smiled at her. "You're welcome. Thank you for letting me share this day with you."

Abby laughed. She hugged Joci then and ran off to play. Connor walked over to say goodbye to them. They started toward their vehicles, Connor walking with them.

When they got close, Connor asked, "Joci, may I have a word with you?"

Jeremiah looked at Connor and then at Joci. She nodded to him, letting him know it was okay. Jeremiah and Gunnar shook Connor's hand, and they walked the last few steps to their trucks. They stood talking to each other when Joci turned and looked at Connor.

"Is everything okay, Connor?"

Connor looked at Joci for a few seconds, and then he took a deep breath. "Is it serious with you and Jeremiah?"

Joci looked surprised, her brows furrowed and she said, "Yes, I think it is."

"Why?" Connor said.

"I don't understand. What do you mean, why?"

"Why him? Why not me?" Connor's voice cracked a little.

Okay, there it was. That's why he was different today.

"I don't know, Connor. I can't explain it. The first time I met Jeremiah, it was like getting hit by lightning. There was just something electric and powerful between us. It's not something you make happen, it just…is."

Connor swallowed and nodded slightly. They looked at each other for a long time. Connor took a deep breath. "I always thought we would end up together. But, I watch you with Jeremiah and I realize you will never be mine. I can see it in your eyes. I can see it in his. I hate it, but I see it."

Joci didn't know what to say. She wasn't expecting this. Never had she thought Connor felt that way.

Connor took a deep breath. "Can we still be friends?"

"Of course, Connor. You've been in my life for so long; I don't know how I could live it without you. Over the years, if it weren't for you, Gunnar and I would have had a hard time. I hope I've always thanked you for your help and willingness to step in."

Connor shook his head and looked away. He stared off into space for a long time and sighed.

"I did it because I love you. I love both of you. I would do it all over again if I had to."

Joci stepped forward and hugged Connor. "Thank you. I love you, and so does Gunnar."

"Yes, but you're not in love with me."

Joci's voice was so soft it was hard to hear. "No, I'm not in love with you."

A tear slipped down Joci's cheek. She didn't want to hurt him. He had done so much for her and Gunnar over the years. She always thought he had taken on Keith's guilt as his own. He had once told her he felt guilty that he hadn't tried harder to make Keith see the error of his ways. Then, he felt guilty for maintaining a friendship with Keith, because of Joci and Gunnar.

Connor sighed and scraped his hand through his hair. He swallowed hard. "Okay. Well, I just needed to know. I'll talk to you later."

He turned and walked away. Joci watched for a few steps, and the tears started rolling faster down her cheeks. She took a deep breath and wiped her eyes with her fingers. She turned and walked toward Gunnar and Jeremiah. They both had worried looks on their faces.

"You okay, Mom? What happened?"

"I'm okay. It's nothing." Joci smiled weakly.

Jeremiah took a deep breath and let it out slowly. He looked at Gunnar and then back at Joci. Gunnar's brows were furrowed in worry. He glanced at Jeremiah and then back at his mom.

Jeremiah put his arm around Joci's shoulders. "He's in love with you."

Joci nodded slightly. Gunnar looked at Jeremiah again with his brows furrowed.

"You mean...as in *in love*...in love?" Gunnar asked, disbelief in his voice.

She nodded and hugged Gunnar. "Have a great rest of your day, baby. I'll talk to you tomorrow."

Joci turned to get into Jeremiah's truck. Gunnar got into his own pickup. He looked back at Joci and Jeremiah, the confusion on his face. Jeremiah slid in beside Joci and started his truck. He took a deep breath and let it out slowly.

"Do you love him, Joci?"

A lone tear traveled down Joci's cheek. "Yes." Her voice cracked.

Jeremiah sucked in a deep breath. "Jesus."

"But, I'm not *in* love with him. Jeremiah, I'm in love with you," Joci said.

Jeremiah and Joci sat in his truck, looking into each other's eyes for what felt like an eternity. Joci's heart raced in her chest; she thought it would burst right out of her body, the beating so erratic and hard it made her body move with it.

Slowly, Jeremiah touched Joci's cheek with his left hand, running the backs of his fingers along her cheek to her jaw. His eyes never left hers. She saw him swallow twice then clear his throat. "I love you, Joci James...I love you."

His fingers curled into her nape and pulled her head to his as he kissed her softly. His full lips lightly moved over Joci's, needing the contact. It meant more than any other moment in time for him, her declaration of love. He had never been in love before and never had a woman he loved declare love to him. So, this was the big fuss. He understood it now.

As their kiss ended, Jeremiah pulled back and looked into Joci's eyes. "Are you okay? I mean...Connor. Are you okay with that?"

Joci took a deep breath. "That was hard, and I wasn't expecting it. It caught me off guard."

Yeah, he felt sorry for the bastard, but he wasn't sorry in the least. Now Connor knew the score on this front and Jeremiah hoped that would be the end of his having to worry about him. Jeremiah leaned over and hugged her to him, then kissed the top of her head.

"Sorry it was hard for you, but I'm glad he knows. I'm so damned in love with you."

17

MOVE IN WITH ME

Joci walked into Jeremiah's around 5:15 p.m. on Wednesday. He was there, putting something together for supper.

"Sorry I'm late getting home. I was in the middle of a project and lost track of time."

He stopped what he was doing, turned and smiled at her.

"You just said you were late getting 'home.' You think of this as home."

He walked toward her. Stalked was more like it, with a smile on his face.

"Move in. Live with me, Joci."

He watched her reaction and held his breath. Joci saw him come closer and held his gaze. She did feel like this was home now. It was a Freudian slip that she called it home. But, that was a sign, wasn't it? She took a deep breath.

"It's been four weeks. We've been playing this game—you running to your place during the day and coming back here in the evening.

You're practically living here. I want you here. You want to be here, don't you?"

Joci took a deep breath. "I suppose you have all the logistics worked out in your head?"

"I do."

She smirked. "Tell me about it."

Jeremiah smiled and touched her face. He kissed the tip of her nose and then her lips.

"There's room here for us. Plenty of room. The spare bedrooms can certainly be rearranged, or the furniture can be removed for any of your furniture that you want here. One of the rooms can be converted to an office for the time being. But, I have an office space at Rolling Thunder you can use. That way you can meet with clients there. You told me once that sometimes you had to look for a space to have meetings because you were uncomfortable having people at your house during the day when you were there by yourself. You can use my conference room. You can have the office set up any way you like. I can see you all day. I can talk to you and be with you."

Jeremiah took a deep breath and continued, "If there is furniture here you don't like or would like to replace with yours, just let me know; we can switch it out. One of the boys would probably need some of the furniture, too. It can work, Joci. And, if after all of that, you aren't happy here, we'll buy another place. I don't care where we live, as long as we're together."

Jeremiah stared at her, willing her to say yes. Joci took a deep breath. This was big.

"Say yes, Joci. You're here most of the time anyway. Say yes."

She swallowed. Giving up her home, starting over at another place, living permanently with Jeremiah. Joci's voice was soft, barely a whisper. "Yes."

Jeremiah whooped, lifted her up and spun her around. When her feet were firmly on the ground, he planted his lips on hers in a toe-curling, consuming kiss that had her light headed and dizzy.

"I'm so happy, Joci. You won't regret this. I promise."

As they finished making supper, they discussed the logistics of making this move.

Joci began. "The first thing I need to do is talk to Gunnar and see if he wants to move into the house. His apartment is small and kind of crappy. Now that he's been working for a couple of years and making good money, he might want a bigger place."

"You should sell him the house."

"Jeremiah, can you slow down? I want to keep it. For a while anyway. I'll rent it to cover the mortgage payment. If Gunnar isn't interested in the house, we can ask JT and Ryder if they might like to rent before I put an ad in the paper."

"I'm not thrilled that you won't sell the house. I still feel like I'm pushing a giant boulder uphill with you, Joci." Joci opened her mouth to argue, but Jeremiah held his hand up.

"I'm trying, babe. I'm trying to be patient. It's probably the hardest thing I've ever had to do."

Joci's face softened. "I know. Thank you. I really do appreciate it."

"Okay, so we better get going. We have tonight's shop ride starting in about twenty minutes and it's Gunnar's turn to lead. A couple of other riders are coming too—not just staff. He's been skipping around, pumped up all day." Jeremiah shook his head with a smirk on his face.

"Also, we have our own private Rolling Thunder shop ride this weekend. I found a house for us to rent on Lake Pentenwell. But LuAnn will probably be along. You good?"

Joci rolled her eyes. "I don't have a choice, do I?"

Jeremiah pulled his hair back into a band at the nape of his neck. He looked at Joci, and she stood with her hands in her jeans pockets, her hip against the kitchen counter.

"Babe...she's nothing to me. Why can't you understand that?"

"But you seem to be a lot to her. Does she still touch you every chance she gets? Does she still shove her boobs in your face and show off most of her body to you?"

Jeremiah crossed his arms over his chest. "Me and everyone else. She's an attention whore. I can't change that. I don't want to expend the energy."

Joci huffed out a deep breath. *Fuck.*

Walking toward her, Jeremiah gripped her shoulders in his big hands. "I want you to move in with me before this weekend."

"Jeremiah, that's only two days away!"

"We'll get it done. Tomorrow night after work, I'll get the boys and my brothers over there to move what you're moving here. You can talk to Gunnar tonight. I'm not negotiating on this."

He grabbed her hand and pulled her to the garage door before she could say anything.

18

ROLL ME AWAY

By Friday afternoon, they had finished moving all of Joci's clothes and the furniture she was bringing with her into Jeremiah's house. They had to pack quickly and get to the shop to leave for Lake Pentenwell for the weekend. It was about a two-and-a-half-hour ride. Luckily, Gunnar and JT weren't moving in for a week or so, so she could get over there and clean next week.

Joci quickly packed and strapped her bag on her bike when Jeremiah came out to the garage carrying his bag and placed it on his bike. He was taking the bike he and his sons had built.

"Do you need to put anything on my bike, babe?"

Joci smiled at him. "No, I think I've got it."

"What are you smiling at?" Jeremiah asked, grinning back at her.

"I love that you call me 'babe' and 'darling' and 'sweetheart.'"

He finished strapping his bag on his bike, walked over and hugged her tight. "I'm glad you like it. I don't plan on stopping."

He kissed her and hugged her again. Then he teasingly slapped her ass.

"Gotta get going, babe. We're going to be late."

He winked at her and went back into the house to check everything over one last time.

Soon, they were on the road heading for the shop. They pulled in around 5 and most of the employees were pulling in at the same time. They had signs up on the doors all week letting customers know that they would be closed this weekend. It was the only weekend of the year the shop was closed.

Together, Jeremiah and Joci walked into the garage, and the employees who were there were standing around talking excitedly. Joci was introduced to Deacon's wife, Julie. She was sweet. Dark like Deacon and had tattoos all over her body. She was a tattoo artist, which explained why Deacon had so many tattoos.

Joci was also introduced to Angel's husband, Ray. Angel was the clothing manager at Rolling Thunder.

Janice was there, and she rode her own bike. JT, Ryder, and Gunnar were there as well, each riding alone. Chase showed up, and he seemed to be in a pissy mood. No LuAnn. Perhaps that had something to do with Chase's mood. Usually, when there was a shop event, LuAnn rode with Chase.

Joey was a bike designer. He rode alone. Ricky and Bear were in parts sales at Rolling Thunder. Ricky was riding alone, and Bear had his girlfriend, Ashley, there.

Frog was a mechanic at the shop, and he was riding alone, too. That left LuAnn, who, so far, hadn't arrived. Joci hoped that meant she wasn't coming along this weekend. Jeremiah looked at his watch. "It's five-thirty, let's ride." He glanced around to make sure the lights were turned off. "Go on out and I'll lock up."

As they were getting on their bikes, a bike pulled into the parking lot. *LuAnn was coming after all.* She was riding with someone on a ratty-looking older bike that needed a lot of attention. It was spitting and sputtering and coughing. Of course, LuAnn was wearing short shorts and knee-high, black high-heeled boots, a bra top, and a ton of jewelry. Her messy blonde hair was blowing around like a whirlwind.

She jumped off the bike as soon as he stopped so everyone could get a good look. She shimmied around and yelled as loud as she could. "I'm glad we aren't late. We were...kind of busy."

JT was the first to say anything at all. "Get on the bike, LuAnn. We were just leaving."

She shrugged her shoulders and climbed back on the bike, without ever introducing her 'date' to anyone.

Jeremiah climbed on his bike and motioned for JT to take off since he was leading. Soon they were on the road. Joci ended up in the back of the pack, which she didn't mind at all. She could watch everyone riding up ahead of her. Directly in front of her were Jeremiah and Gunnar. She could ride behind him any day. It gave her a chance to look at his strong arms gripping the handlebars, his hair blowing around. Though he pulled it back into a ponytail, little tendrils made their escape. His massive shoulders tapered down to that fabulous ass of his. Yeah, great view.

About an hour into their ride, an older Ford Mustang pulled up behind Joci. It was way too close. Joci watched the car in her mirrors and became uncomfortable with how close the car was to her. Soon, the Mustang pulled into the left lane and drew up alongside her.

"Hey baby, you wanna ride me?" The other guys in the car laughed hysterically.

The guy in the back seat leaned out of the car and yelled, "Hey, sugar, wanna fuck?"

Jeremiah and Gunnar were watching this go on. Jeremiah pulled out into the left lane in front of the Mustang, and Gunnar followed. They slowed down, so the car had to slow down. Joci pulled ahead, and Jeremiah motioned for her to move up in front of him and over to the inside of the lane. She moved and Jeremiah slid into the lane next to her. Gunnar stayed behind her. The group up front picked up the speed.

The guys in the Mustang yelled out to Jeremiah, "Fuck you, buddy. We're just having a little fun with the hottie."

Frog and Bear, with Ashley on back, pulled out into the left lane then, to slow the Mustang down and the rest of the group pulled ahead quickly. As soon as the group had made some tracks down the road, Frog and Bear pulled back into the right lane and increased their speed to catch up. The guys in the Mustang were not to be swayed and tried keeping up with the bikes, but the bikes were faster and eventually, the Mustang was caught behind some traffic, which the bikes were able to weave in and out of.

Joci's heart raced. This shit happens once in a while, but she never got used to it. It was so dangerous when cars got so close. One wrong move, one big pothole in the road, and it could be deadly. Idiots.

JT pulled into a gas station about twenty miles up the road and they each went to available pumps to fill up. Joci dropped her kickstand and stood on shaky legs.

"Are you okay, baby?" Jeremiah asked.

Joci smiled at him. "I'm good. They're just idiots."

"I know, but that could have been bad. You're a good rider, Joci. You knew just what to do when I pulled over."

She wrapped her arms around Jeremiah's waist and soaked up his strength. He kissed the top of her head and held her tight.

After they had filled their tanks, Jeremiah and Joci moved their bikes off to the side as the rest of the group filled up. Once they had their tanks full, they came over and joined Jeremiah and Joci. LuAnn's 'date' pulled up last and shut his bike off. LuAnn was adjusting her clothing and trying to get anyone to notice her.

Finally, Chase said, "What the fuck is your problem, LuAnn? Aren't you getting enough attention?"

LuAnn gave him the finger. She turned to the guy she was riding with and winked.

"This is Boyd."

Boyd's chin jerked up which seemed to be his hello.

Jeremiah looked at the group and said, "Listen up. For the rest of this ride, Joci is not to be last in the group. I want all of you to make sure she has a spot in the middle of the pack. I don't want any more bullshit like we just encountered back there. For that matter, Janice and Julie should not be at the end of the group either. No woman should ride in the back. As we saw, men can be pigs."

Jeremiah smirked. Everyone nodded and mumbled that they agreed with that.

Gunnar looked at his mom. "Are you okay, Mom?"

Joci smiled at him. "Yes, I'm fine. Thank you for helping Jeremiah move me forward; I appreciate it."

Gunnar hugged Joci. "Always."

LuAnn gave a loud, "Geez, you act like she was in danger or something."

She was largely ignored, but Joci got the feeling this might be a long weekend.

When they got back on the road, Jeremiah and Joci rode in the middle of the pack. The weather was beautiful and enjoyable. As they got close to the lake, the humidity in the air increased, making it very comfortable riding. They pulled up the driveway of their rented house, and JT opened the garage door so the riders could pull their bikes in out of the weather. It was after 8:30 and the sun had just gone down below the horizon. They had worked out all the sleeping arrangements at the shop. The house had six bedrooms. Jeremiah and Joci got the master bedroom, which was amazing. It had its own bathroom with a big garden tub in it.

The other five bedrooms had multiple beds in them. Two of the bedrooms had a set of bunk beds and a double bed. Everyone was able to sleep in a bed. There was a gorgeous kitchen and two other bathrooms in the house.

"Okay, listen up. Since it's after eight o'clock, we can either find a bar to hit or go buy some drinks and stay here at the house. What does everyone want to do?"

"I want to go out and shake it," LuAnn piped up.

Joci spoke up, "I think it would be better if we stayed and drank here, so no one is driving after drinking. I'm happy to go and pick up the drinks."

"I think that sounds great. I'll go, Mom. Why don't you unpack—again." Gunnar smirked.

"What does that mean, 'again'?" LuAnn sniped, using air quotes.

Gunnar turned so he was facing LuAnn head on. "It means that my mom just moved in with Dog, and she's been unpacking the last couple of days." He smiled at the look on LuAnn's face.

LuAnn's eyes narrowed as she looked past Gunnar right at Joci.

Chase burst out laughing. "Careful, LuAnn, your face will stay that way."

Jeremiah pulled Joci to the master bedroom while Gunnar and Ryder took drink orders and headed to the nearest store.

As they walked into the master bedroom, Jeremiah hugged Joci and picked her up and laid her on the bed. He stretched out next to her and kissed her.

"I thought I was going to go out of my mind when those assholes got so close to you, Joci. I couldn't stand it if anything happened to you."

She wrapped her arms around his neck and pulled him to her for a kiss.

"I'm fine, babe. Thank you for worrying."

Jeremiah's smile grew across his face.

"You called me 'babe.' That's the first time you used an endearment for me. I love the way it sounds coming from your lips. Let's make out."

Joci laughed, but they heard Gunnar and Ryder coming back into the house. "Okay, we'll finish this later. Now, think about that for the rest of the night," he whispered in her ear.

The boys came in and were carrying their packages and putting beer and wine coolers in the refrigerator as Joci and Jeremiah walked into the kitchen.

Deacon's wife, Julie, and Janice started mixing drinks and playing bartender. The kitchen had a breakfast bar, and they used that as a bar. As soon as everyone had drinks, JT proposed a toast to a great weekend. Everyone cheered and sipped at their drinks. The boys had also bought snacks and dips, and those were spread out on the kitchen table.

Joci began talking to some of the girls and trying to get to know them. Julie was an artist with a vividly creative mind. Janice was very sweet and closer to Joci in age. Joci knew her already, but they hadn't had the time to get to know each other.

Jeremiah sat on the sofa and patted his knee for Joci to come and sit on his lap. Suddenly, LuAnn jumped in and sat on his lap first. She wrapped her arms around his neck and tried to kiss him, but he pulled his head back as soon as he saw what was happening.

His jaw tight, he growled, "Get the fuck off my lap, LuAnn."

She acted pouty and said, "Dog, you know you want me."

Jeremiah put his hands on her hips and picked her off his lap. When she was standing, he gave her a little shove.

"I've told you this is inappropriate. Enough."

Jeremiah stood up quickly and walked over to Joci and grabbed her hand and pulled her out on the deck. Once they were outside, he turned to her and framed her face with his hands, holding her in place.

"I love you, Joci. I did have a talk with her. I swear it."

"I believe you, baby." Joci sighed heavily and wrapped her arms around Jeremiah.

"You don't sound sure."

He pulled away and looked at her. She closed her eyes and sighed again.

"I just hate having to deal with her every time we do something with your employees. How much temptation can you handle?"

"She's not a temptation to me. I couldn't give a shit. You're the only woman I want. You're the only woman I will ever love. Ever."

Just then, the door opened up, and JT, Ryder, and Gunnar walked out onto the deck.

"Everything okay out here?"

Joci and Jeremiah smiled at them.

"Yes, everything is fine. How about in there?" Joci said with a smile.

Gunnar was the first to make a comment. "I would like to wrap my hands around her throat. She is such a piece of trash, and I hate how awful she is to you. When Chase said she wasn't riding with him, I had hoped she wasn't coming at all. Then she showed up with Boyd, a guy she met in a bar last night."

Joci looked at Gunnar and then JT and Ryder. "I'm okay. I don't like it either, but it is what it is at this point, so we have to suck it up and deal with it. Only Jeremiah can change the situation."

Ouch, that stung. Talk about being sucker-punched. But she was right. He just felt like he owed it to Lance to make sure LuAnn had a job. Never in his life did he think he would find a woman like Joci and have a woman like LuAnn try to fuck it up for him. He would never try to harm another person's relationship—ever. It was beyond him that someone would do this to him.

"I'll take care of it. Right now, let's try to enjoy the weekend and not let one person ruin it. If we all stick together, we can have a great time," Jeremiah said.

JT nodded. "How about we talk about the house then?"

A grin grew across his face. He looked at Gunnar, who smiled.

"We're excited to move in. Now that I know the house is available, I can hardly stand to stay in my shitty apartment," Gunnar stated.

Joci said, "Jeremiah and I finished moving today. I'll go over next week and clean so it's ready for you guys. You can move in any time after that. If you don't want the furniture I left there, we can get a storage unit and move it there."

JT let out a whoop, then high-fived Gunnar. People started filtering out on the deck to see what was going on. Gunnar and JT told them they were moving into Joci's house next week, and they were excited.

They talked excitedly when LuAnn had to get her two cents' worth in.

"Can't you afford to live on your own anymore, Joci?"

Joci looked at LuAnn and took a deep breath. "I certainly can. After all, I have a house that I bought on my own. What do you have?"

LuAnn lived with her sister in her sister's basement. She turned and walked back into the house to make herself another drink. JT smirked and high-fived Joci.

Conversation resumed and the mood lifted. They were going to be okay. They were okay. The remainder of the evening, everyone had a great time. LuAnn was quiet and drank heavily, to the point that Boyd had to carry her to bed around ten o'clock.

Joci seemed to enjoy herself, which helped Jeremiah enjoy himself. Later in the evening, Jeremiah sat in a big brown leather chair and winked at Joci as he patted his lap, knowing the little joke was not lost on her. She gladly climbed on his lap and wrapped her arms around his neck. She leaned into him and whispered in his ear.

"Dog, you know you want me."

Jeremiah squeezed her tight and kissed her on the lips. "You're right about that. More than I can get my mind around."

19

LAST CHANCE

On Saturday morning, Joci woke up to Jeremiah sliding into her. She was lying on her back, with her arms over her head. She felt him push himself into her and she moaned. He kissed her neck and nibbled her earlobe.

He swirled his tongue around the shell of her ear and whispered, "Good morning, gorgeous. I love waking up with you."

She wrapped her arms around his neck and kissed his jaw.

She nibbled her way to his ear and whispered, "I love waking up with you in me."

He hissed out a breath. "God, Joci, you could make me come just by talking to me."

She moaned at the feeling once he was completely inside of her. As he started moving, she made little sounds that drove him wild.

"Hmm, you feel like heaven inside of me."

Jeremiah loved making love to her, with her. He loved that she had moved in with him. He loved how he felt about her.

"Joci...get there, baby...fast."

She smiled. He rode her hard and fast, the way she liked it. He massaged her inside, filling and stretching her completely. It never took him long to bring her to orgasm. He ground his hips against her a few times, and she felt her orgasm growing fast and furious. Her body heated, starting at her feet and moving up. Her nipples were hard little peaks. Her breathing was ragged as she tightened her arms around him. Her vision grew blurry, and she knew she was close, so close.

"Jeremiah...I love you."

She stiffened when her orgasm hit her. She sighed as she came. He pumped one more time and floated over the edge with her. They lay there for a while, floating off to sleep again, wrapped in each other, still joined at their most intimate parts.

When Jeremiah woke up about a half hour later, he kissed Joci on the neck and nibbled her shoulder. He breathed in deep.

"I love the way you smell after we've made love. I love the way you feel. I love you."

Joci smiled. She wrapped her arms around him tighter and kissed his neck.

He pulled out of her and went into the bathroom to get a wet cloth to clean them up. "I think someone's up. I can smell coffee. Do you want some?"

"Yes, I'll get up with you. We can sit out there and talk to whoever is up."

She got up and threw on some yoga pants and a bra and t-shirt while Jeremiah pulled on his jeans and a t-shirt. They walked into the kitchen together, holding hands. Bear and Ashley were sitting at the table talking and drinking coffee. Joci went to the coffee pot, got two cups from the cupboard, and poured them coffee. She turned with the pot in her hand and motioned to Bear and Ashley. They both shook their heads no. She replaced the coffee pot and sat next to Jeremiah at the table.

"Dog, we've been looking at the map, and here's a nice route we can take today." Bear motioned on the map in front of him.

"Looks great. Why don't you lead today? I'm fine with anywhere we ride today. The weather looks good. Go for it."

Bear's broad grin grew. "Thanks, Dog."

Deacon and Julie came in, and so did Janice, Angel, and Ray. "Guys, check this out." Bear pointed to the map.

"Looks like a great route, Bear," Deacon said.

As they sat with their coffee, Jeremiah said, "Is there a little town where we can eat along the way, Bear? That way no one has to cook or clean."

They all bowed their heads over the map on the table, and Bear pointed to a little town. An agreement was made to be ready in an hour.

Gunnar told Joci that LuAnn had slept with Chase on many occasions, usually because she knew he was the only one who would let her ride on his bike when she had no one else. "Ass for Gas" was the saying. Joci thought that was rather crude, but when it came to LuAnn, she wasn't at all surprised that was her lifestyle.

They saddled up when LuAnn, in very few clothes, made her appearance and climbed on the back of Boyd's bike. As they took off, Jeremiah nodded to Joci to go ahead of him, and he pulled out right behind her. After they ate, they would gas up and then head north a little for the day.

They rode to a little town just outside of Wisconsin Rapids for breakfast. Jeremiah sat at one end of the long table, and Bear sat at the other. Everyone else filled in where they wanted. Joci sat to Jeremiah's left, and JT sat to his right. Boyd and LuAnn sat down toward the other end of the table on the same side as Joci, which meant she didn't have to look at LuAnn. That eased Jeremiah's mind a bit.

As soon as they had finished eating, they rode next door to a gas station to fill up before heading off on Bear's route. Afterward, Jeremiah and Joci rode to the edge of the parking lot and waited for everyone else. Jeremiah grabbed Joci and hugged her tight. "It's going to be a great day, babe."

Joci laughed. "I think so, too."

"Okay, saddle up." Jeremiah swatted Joci's butt and swung his leg over his bike, then winked at her as he started it up. Joci smiled and shook her head as she swung her leg over her own bike and started it up. The group started pulling out of the gas station. Jeremiah took off, thinking Joci was with him. Just as Joci started pulling out, Boyd cut her off and drove in front of her, with LuAnn giving Joci the finger and laughing.

~

Joci's heart thudded in her chest. She could have dumped her bike there. What the fuck is going on with those two?

They got out on the road, and Jeremiah looked back at Joci. She gave him the thumbs up, and he nodded at her, but she could tell he was pissed. She was pissed, too, and it left Joci at the back of the group again, which Jeremiah had specifically told everyone not to do.

Jeremiah slowed down until he was alongside Joci in the inside lane. They were on a two-lane road, but there wasn't any traffic at this time of day, still early Saturday morning. Jeremiah nodded his head to Joci to follow him, and he took off, passing Boyd, Frog, and Janice, and then Gunnar and Ryder. Joci looked up the road and still saw no traffic, so she followed Jeremiah. Gunnar and Ryder slowed down to give them room to come into the lane. They safely slid into formation in front of Gunnar and Ryder. Joci gave them the thumbs up as she moved in front of them.

The roads were curvy, and the weather was warming up. It was beautiful riding weather. The sun started warming the day; traffic was still light. It was late June and the temperature today was supposed to be in the low 90s, perfect for Joci.

About an hour and a half into their ride, they were looking for a gas station to gas up again. Bear found one on the outskirts of a little town near Tomah. They pulled in, but there were only two pumps, which meant most of them had to wait for others to finish up. Joci got off her bike, and so did Jeremiah. The others got off their bikes as well for a leg stretch and to get gas. Jeremiah walked over to Joci and hugged her.

"Are you okay, baby?"

Joci smiled. "Yes, I'm fine. But, what the fuck?"

"Exactly. I've had enough." Jeremiah stalked over to Boyd and before even stopping in front of him, he punched him in the mouth. Boyd went down hard. LuAnn screamed, and everyone came running over to see what was going on.

Jeremiah stood over Boyd and glared at him. "I told you, Joci was not to be left at the back of the group. Not only that, but you cut her off. She could have dumped her bike, you ignorant fuck. Get the fuck out of here. You're not welcome."

"Fuck, man, I didn't know it meant today, too. LuAnn said it didn't matter."

"It does matter. It matters a hell of a lot. When I give an order, I expect it to be followed. Even if that hadn't been an order, you never, ever cut anyone in my group off. Get out."

LuAnn stood with her hands on her hips. "Dog, that's bullshit. Joci shouldn't be riding if she can't handle it."

Jeremiah glared at LuAnn. "Since you don't fucking ride yourself, you shouldn't open your fucking mouth. Get the fuck out of here, both of you. Now!"

Boyd got up off the ground and walked over to his bike, rubbing his jaw. He nodded for LuAnn to get on, but she stood with her arms crossed.

"Get out, LuAnn; you have no one else to ride with, and you're not welcome anymore."

LuAnn started with the waterworks. "Dog, please let me stay. I can ride with Chase."

Chase spoke up. "No, you can't, LuAnn. I asked you last week, and you said no. Now I don't want you on with me."

LuAnn walked over to Boyd's bike with tears in her eyes. She looked back at Jeremiah. "I don't have a key to get my stuff."

Jeremiah shook his head. "Someone will bring it back to the shop. You're not welcome at the house. Especially when there isn't anyone there to watch you."

Jeremiah turned his back on LuAnn and walked toward Joci, hugging her to him. Joci could feel him shaking and breathing hard. She wrapped her arms around him and hugged him tight. "Thank you for sticking up for me."

Jeremiah looked down at Joci and slowly shook his head. "I'll always stick up for you; don't you understand?"

20

TONIGHT WE PLAY

LuAnn and Boyd took off, and the rest of the group continued to gas up and talk. The rest of the day went along smoothly. The ride was fabulous, and the weather was even better. Jeremiah watched Joci ride, and his heart swelled. She was amazing. Most women would have freaked out yesterday when those assholes got so close to her, but she kept her cool and knew what to do when he pulled over. She was a great rider. Today was the same. Boyd had cut her off, and she hadn't bitched or made a scene. She just fell in line where she could and rode along.

She looked fantastic on her bike, too. She rode a Harley Davidson Fat Boy. She had it custom painted, pearl white with gold ghost flames. She sat with a small lean forward and looked sexy as hell. He couldn't blame the guys for admiring her yesterday. Jeremiah had a hard time taking his eyes off her. He was a lucky man.

Joci looked over and saw him watching her. She smiled at him, and his heart skipped a beat. She winked and looked back at the road. This was without a doubt the woman he wanted to spend the rest of his life with.

They pulled in the driveway at the house around 5:45and everyone rolled their bikes into the garage.

J oci got off her bike and said, "If someone wants to go to the store and pick up some chicken and potatoes, I'll be happy to cook."

"Joci, I don't want you to have to do that. We should be relaxing," said Jeremiah.

Joci smiled. "Not having LuAnn here is relaxing. Besides, we can have drinks and no one has to drive."

"I'll go," Ryder volunteered. Frog piped up, too. "I'll go with you."

Joci and Janice gave them a shopping list and decided to take their showers while the guys were shopping. Then, while they were cooking, the guys could clean up.

Joci went to the bathroom and turned on the shower to warm up. As she was pulling her clothes out of her bag, Jeremiah walked in and locked the door. He had made her a drink and brought it in with him.

He handed it to her with a wink and she took a sip and licked her lips and said, "Mmmmm. Thank you."

He snatched the glass from her hand and set it on the dresser. He grabbed her around the waist and pulled her close to him.

"You set my blood on fire, Jocelyn James. I can't stop looking at you. I can't stop thinking about you. I can't stop dreaming about you. I can't and won't ever stop wanting you."

Joci smiled at him and sighed. She shook her head and looked up at him.

"It took me a long time to find you, Jeremiah. It took me a long time to admit my feelings for you. But I'm such a lucky woman. You were definitely worth the wait."

They kissed, exploring each other's mouths with their tongues. Nipping lips, tongues mating, like they were starving for each other.

"Take your clothes off, Joci. I want to watch you."

Joci smiled at him and began removing her clothes. She pulled her shirt off and threw it on the bed. Then her jeans came off and hit the bed. She pushed her panties down her legs, and they went in the same direction. She reached back and unhooked her bra and sent that sailing to the rest of her clothes. When she was completely naked, she walked forward and looked at Jeremiah.

"What do you want me to do now, babe?"

Jeremiah hissed out a breath.

"Get in the shower and wait for me."

Joci smiled and walked into the bathroom. She was turned on like crazy, loving the way he loved her. She stepped into the shower and started lathering up her hair. She soaped up her body, and as she was rinsing out her hair, she felt Jeremiah grab her ass in both of his hands. He quickly wrapped his arms around her from behind and pushed her against the wall.

"Spread your legs, baby. Open yourself up for me."

Joci spread her legs. She felt him slip a finger inside of her, and she gasped at the feel of him. She put her forehead on the shower wall and groaned.

"Feel how tight your little pussy is? It feels amazing wrapped around my cock. Wet and hot and fisting me like a glove. It sucks me right in and holds me so fucking tight. I can't get enough of how you feel, Joci."

He moved his fingers in and out of her. Slowly...agonizingly slow. With his other hand, he reached around and rubbed her clit. Joci hissed out, "Jeremiah. That feels amazing."

"Not nearly as amazing as you feel."

He bent his knees to position himself at her entrance. He pushed, and Joci let out a sigh. Jeremiah pulled out again and pushed in all the way.

"Joci, you feel like heaven. I want to live just like this inside of you. You drive me wild with want and need."

Joci didn't have words for how she felt with him inside of her. Full, so full. Like nothing else in this world. He made her come so fast. But also because she loved being with him. He made her feel complete. She was as addicted to him as much as he was addicted to her.

Jeremiah started moving in and out of her. Joci put her hands above her head and hung on to the wall for support. Jeremiah wrapped his arms around Joci's waist so he wouldn't push her over.

"Are you ready, baby? I need to push into you hard now, or I'm going to lose my mind."

"Yes, Jeremiah. Make me come."

He pushed into her, moved in and out several times. He kissed her neck and the top of her head.

"Jeremiah, don't be gentle. I need to feel your passion."

He hissed out a breath and tightened his hold on her. He began thrusting into her.

"Baby, you always have my passion."

He squeezed her waist tighter and began wildly pumping into her. Joci whimpered and fisted her hands against the wall. Her orgasm was building quickly. She felt hot all over, and there was an edginess within her that needed to be released. Jeremiah circled her clit again and thrust into her as she moaned his name and came. The walls of her pussy pulsed and milked him, which threw Jeremiah over the edge. He came hard with a groan. He held her tight and pushed up into her as hard as he could.

"Joci...Fuck...You feel so damn good." He kept his arm around her and moved backward to sit on the bench in the shower. Joci sat on Jeremiah; he was still inside of her, and he wrapped both of his arms around her, pulling her back onto him. She laid her head back against his shoulder and moved her arm to reach back and cup his head. Her heart hammered in her chest, and she was still breathing hard. She felt amazing. She loved the way Jeremiah made love to her. He knew what she needed, and he gave it to her every time.

An hour later, the women were cooking in the kitchen. The guys were either on the deck or in the living room bullshitting. As the girls enjoyed a couple of drinks and were talking, they were having fun making grilled chicken, stir-fried veggies, and grilled parmesan potatoes.

Ashley finally asked, "Joci, are you feeling better now that the skank LuAnn is gone?"

Joci smiled at her. "I hate to say that I'm happy she's gone, but I am. I can't figure out what Jeremiah sees in her to keep her, and it bothers the shit out of me, but I feel great that he kicked her to the curb today."

Janice nudged Joci. "Babe, you have nothing to worry about when it comes to Dog. He is one thousand percent in love with you. We can all see it. LuAnn can see it, too. That's why she has gotten so awful."

Joci looked at Janice for a moment and shook her head. "I can't figure out what her hold is over him that he tolerates it when it messes with my head so much."

Ashley smiled at her. "Darlin', I wish Bear was half as crazy about me as Dog is about you. Seriously, as far as that bitch goes, who gives a shit?"

The girls giggled. If everyone felt this way, why did Jeremiah keep her around? Just then, he walked into the kitchen and saw them all laughing.

Joci turned and saw him watching her. She pointed her beautiful, dimpled smile right at him. "Hey, you. What's up?"

"Not much. Just came in to see if you needed help."

Joci glided over and slid her arms around him and squeezed.

"Thank you for checking, but we're doing great. Anything I can get you?"

"No, baby. I'll just go bullshit with the guys. Can I get you another drink?"

Joci laughed. "Not if you want a tasty supper. I should wait until I'm finished cooking."

~

Jeremiah looked over at Janice and Ashley, who were both watching and smiling. Janice held her glass up and nodded at Jeremiah to go ahead and make Joci another drink. She would probably be cute as hell drunk. Jeremiah smiled and squeezed Joci again, then turned to leave. He was back in minutes with another drink. He walked over to Joci and held the glass to her lips.

"Drink up, baby. Tonight, we play!"

"I won't be able to ride tomorrow, babe. I can't."

Jeremiah kissed her quickly on the lips. "If that's the case, I'll take care of you. I want to watch you let go of yourself. Let me see it, Joci. Have fun with me."

Joci's eyes grew big as Jeremiah held the drink to her lips and smiled at her.

"I'll take care of you, always."

Joci took the drink and sipped it. He smiled at her while Janice, Julie, and Ashley giggled behind her.

He kissed her quickly and left the kitchen. The girls were still giggling when Joci turned around. Janice put her arm around Joci's shoulders and hugged her. "He wants to see you drunk, Joci. Haven't you gotten drunk in front of him before?"

Joci smiled at her. "No, I don't drink much. I've always been alone and had to get myself home and take care of Gunnar."

"Ah, so that's it. He wants you to know you aren't alone anymore. Drink up, Joci. Tonight's going to be fun!" Ashley stated.

They ate a great meal, and Joci was feeling no pain. The boys laughed at her silliness.

"Mom, too bad the Golden Girls aren't here," Gunnar said.

Joci rolled her eyes. "The Golden Girls haven't been together in a while, Gunnar."

Jeremiah looked at Joci. "Who are the Golden Girls?"

Joci grinned at him and shook her head.

Gunnar laughed. "Mom, Jackie, and Sandi are the Golden Girls. They used to go out on 'girl's night' and sing Karaoke. Mom can sing like crazy. Their signature song is 'Lady Marmalade.' You should hear her, Dog. She blows the room away when she sings it."

Jeremiah looked at Joci, and her face flamed up bright red.

"Really? Sing for me, sweetheart."

Joci shook her head no. "I can't sing without my girls."

She had a goofy grin on her face. Jeremiah leaned over and hugged her. "Then we're going to go out with your girls soon. I want to hear you sing."

Joci leaned her head into Jeremiah and closed her eyes. She whispered, "Guess I'm a cheap date."

He kissed the top of her head. "I love you, Joci." Then he whispered, "I'll take care of you."

Joci closed her eyes and let herself believe that was true. Only time would tell.

21

TWO STEPS FORWARD

Sunday was a long day. Joci had a headache but refused to ride behind Jeremiah and let everyone think she couldn't take it. But she was suffering. She remembered laughing and having so much fun, actually everyone was having fun. When she looked around, it looked like a lot of them were hung-over, so she wasn't the only one. Even Jeremiah looked kind of worse for the wear. Deacon and Julie were the only ones who didn't look tired and drawn. Joci couldn't wait to get home and take a nap.

They stopped for gas and Joci pulled to the edge of the parking lot to drink a Gatorade. Jeremiah walked over to her but didn't say anything. He kissed the top of her head and laid his head on top of hers. They stood together like that for several heartbeats.

"Are you okay, sweetheart?" he whispered.

Joci chuckled a little. "I'm good. How about you?"

Jeremiah snickered. "I'm good. However, I want to get home and take a nap with you."

She nodded her head. "I was just thinking the same thing."

When Joci woke up from her nap, she had a dry mouth and a slight headache. Jeremiah was nowhere to be found. Hmm. She got up and went to the bathroom, took a couple of aspirin, and looked in the mirror. Oh, well. She walked out to the living room to find her man. Nope, not there.

She walked out to the garage and there he was, removing their bags from the bikes. He smiled at her when she walked out.

"Hey, gorgeous. How are you feeling?"

Joci laughed. She had just seen herself in the mirror.

"If you're talking to me, I'm okay. If you're talking to someone else, never mind."

He grabbed their bags from the bikes and walked up to her and kissed the top of her head. "You're the only woman in the world I think is gorgeous. So, yeah, I'm talking to you."

She shrugged. "Okay. You?"

He shrugged too. "Been better. But totally worth it. You're a very cute drunk."

Joci groaned. She didn't want to know. He put his arm around her and walked into the house. He looked around at the boxes of Joci's stuff stacked everywhere, looked at her and smiled.

"I think we are going to need a bigger house after all. Where are we going to put the kids?"

Joci's eyes got huge. *Did he just say that? No, no, no, no, no.*

"Jeremiah...we...I...no." Joci shook her head.

He squeezed her and turned to wrap his arms around her.

"Joci, don't get scared. I want to have babies with you. It'll be different this time. We'll both be able to enjoy the whole process, including raising a beautiful little girl or boy. We'll do it together."

She shook her head. She tried to pull away, but he wouldn't let her go. No, she couldn't go there. She didn't know what would happen in the future, but she couldn't think about babies when they had only been with each other for a couple of months. No, she didn't want to do that unless she was married. She didn't want to be a single mom again.

Joci's body tightened, and she could feel her pulse thrumming through her body. Her head still ached from last night, and now he wanted to have babies.

Jeremiah tightened his arms around her. He rocked her back and forth for a little while.

He took a deep breath. "Don't be nervous; I won't push. I just can't help myself. When I look at you, think about you...I just want the whole package."

She trembled. Of course, not feeling well didn't help things at all, but this wasn't a conversation she wanted to have. She decided to change the subject.

"Are you hungry, Jeremiah? I can throw something together for us to eat."

She still wasn't even sure she could still have babies. But if she were ever going to have another baby, it would certainly be with him.

Jeremiah squeezed her a little. "I don't want you to have to do that. Why don't we order a pizza?"

"Mmm, that sounds awesome."

He kissed the top of her head and pulled out his phone. Joci began digging through boxes. She had to work tomorrow, and she wanted to get her office set up so she could get right to it. The photographer from the Veteran's Ride had sent her all the pictures from the day, and she wanted to start working on the video. She didn't tell Jeremiah because she wanted to surprise him with it.

Joci had gotten a few boxes unpacked when the pizza delivery person knocked at the door, announcing supper. Jeremiah paid the guy and brought the pizza into the living room. Joci washed her hands and grabbed them each a bottle of water from the refrigerator. They sat on the sofa to eat and watch the news.

Jeremiah looked over at Joci. He took a deep breath and said, "I didn't mean to scare you before. I'm sorry."

She caught his gaze and saw the love in his eyes. She leaned forward and grabbed his hand. "I know, baby. I'm sorry I got weird. Being hung-over doesn't help. I don't want to be a single mom again, Jeremiah. It's important to me. I don't want to bring another child into the world without both parents being right there for him or her."

"I'm here, Joci. You're here. We're together, and I'm not gonna let anything change that. I won't push you. Well, I'll try not to push you. But I'm committed to being with you forever."

She nodded her head. What more could she say? For now, he wouldn't push, and she could see how things worked out between them.

Around nine p.m., Joci and Jeremiah crawled into bed, exhausted. Drinking sure takes its toll on a person.

The next morning, as Jeremiah was getting ready to leave for work, his phone rang.

As he answered, he looked at Joci with a smile and mouthed, "My mom."

She smiled. They had eaten dinner with his parents last week. She enjoyed spending time with them. Emily had a great sense of humor and teased her husband and Jeremiah endlessly. She seemed to have a very comfortable relationship with all her men.

Jeremiah hung up the phone and looked at Joci. "Why do you have that little smirk on your face?"

"I was just thinking about your mom teasing you and your dad last week at dinner. She's funny."

Jeremiah smirked too. "Always has been. Anyway, she called because Thursday is Eli's graduation. She wanted to make sure you and Gunnar would be there also."

Joci nodded. "Absolutely. Can you remind the boys at work today?"

"Yeah, I'll make sure they all remember. I would love it if you asked the rest of the Golden Girls to go out with us the Saturday after we get together with my Marine buddies. I want to hear you sing, Joci."

She groaned. *He just didn't let anything go, did he?* She didn't respond right away. Jeremiah stood back a little and looked down at her.

"Hey. Don't you want to sing for me?"

Joci smiled. "I'm really not that good, Jeremiah. After a couple of drinks, I just think I'm good. There's a difference."

He crossed his arms over his chest and stared, and she sighed. "I'll see if they want to go out. Sandi just mentioned something about that at lunch last week, so I would bet unless they have plans, she's in."

"Perfect. See you at lunch."

Joci cocked her head to the side. "Do we have lunch plans?"

Jeremiah slapped her on the ass. "Now that you live here with me, I'm coming home for lunch. Do you have a full workload today?"

"Not too bad." Joci smiled.

"Great. Meet me in the bedroom at noon, with nothing on. Lie on the bed, on your back, with your head toward the door. And be ready for me."

He kissed her on the lips and walked out the door.

Joci smiled all the way to the back bedroom/office. She was turned on already, so being ready for him at noon wasn't going to be a problem. As a matter of fact, it was going to be a long morning for her, thinking about him coming home for a nooner. She giggled as she thought about it. She was forty-four years old and was about to have her first nooner.

She worked on the video until eleven. She was organizing the pictures in an order she thought would work well. She was going to set the whole thing to music and was running songs through her mind. She stood up, stretched, and decided to take a quick shower before Jeremiah got home. She giggled as she walked into the bathroom and turned the water on.

She took a nice long shower and made sure she was shaved and soaped—everywhere. She put body butter all over herself, so her skin was smooth, and dried her hair. She looked at the clock and noticed she still had about fifteen minutes. She walked to the kitchen to grab a bottle of water and strutted back to the bedroom, humming a song to herself.

She put the bottle of water on the bedside table and took her robe off. She stretched out across the bed like Jeremiah had asked her to do, on her back, and hummed while she waited for him. Soon, she heard the door open and heard his footsteps walking toward her down the hall. The bedroom door opened, and she heard a soft whistle.

She looked up to see Jeremiah devouring her with his eyes.

"You are...without a doubt...the sexiest woman I've ever laid eyes on. And you're mine."

Joci smiled from ear to ear. He walked toward her and touched her cheek. He ran his hand down her cheek to her jaw and under her chin. Softly but forcefully, he pulled her chin up. He reached under her arms with both hands and pulled her to the edge of the bed, so her head slightly hung over the edge. He ran a finger down her throat and over to her breasts. He palmed a breast in each hand and massaged them. He pinched each nipple and made them hard peaks, straining for his mouth. He chuckled. "I could play with you all day."

S lowly he unzipped his jeans and let them fall to the floor. His boxer briefs followed. He pulled his t-shirt up over his head. In record time, and he was standing at her head, completely naked. He stroked his hard cock up and down a few times while watching her. She squirmed, watching him pleasure himself, and he smiled at her.

"Do you like watching me, Joci? Does that turn you on?"

Joci licked her lips. "Yes, I like watching you. You're beautiful. Watching you touch yourself is sexy as hell."

"Is it now? Let me see. Touch yourself. I want to watch you."

She reached down with her right hand and slipped her fingers into her soft folds. She moaned a little.

Hissing out a breath, he said, "You're right, that is sexy. Keep touching yourself, Joci; I want to watch you and hear you."

He grabbed his cock and touched her lips with it. She opened her mouth, and Jeremiah slid himself inside. He knew she couldn't take him all the way, so he kept his hand on the base of his cock so he wouldn't get excited and forget how little she was.

She tightened her lips around his length and let her tongue slide along the underside of it when Jeremiah pulled out and slid back in. He hissed out a breath. He'd thought about this all morning, and still, he was amazed at the feeling of her mouth and watching her touch herself. Shit, there was nothing like it. Joci slid her tongue along the vein on the underside of his cock and he groaned.

"Joci...geez...fucking amazing," He panted.

She wiggled around her fingers working furiously. He watched her squirm and knew she was having trouble making herself come. Fine with him. He would rather help her anyway. He leaned down and ran his tongue around her swollen, sensitive little bud while pushing in and pulling out of her mouth. Joci moaned again and lifted her hips to intensify the pressure from his mouth.

He licked her clit again and sucked it into his mouth. She reached up and cupped his balls in one hand, and put her other hand on the base of his cock. Jeremiah used the opportunity to slide a finger into Joci's wet little pussy. Two pumps and her orgasm started racing, her body warming and her breathing ragged. He added pressure on her clit with his tongue, at the same time pushing two fingers into her wet channel, and she exploded. She pulsed and clenched.

She continued to rub Jeremiah while working her mouth along his length. She licked his balls, and they sucked up inside of him. Gently sliding back into her mouth, Jeremiah let go. Joci swallowed quickly to drink all of him down. He laid his forehead on her belly, giving them both a little time to catch their breath. She licked his cock as it fell from her mouth and he groaned again. He stood up as soon as he could, climbed onto the bed next to her, and pulled her into his arms. Joci wrapped her arm around his waist and kissed his chest.

They lay quietly a few minutes, and Jeremiah kissed the top of her head.

"Sorry, baby, I meant that to last longer. Sometimes you make me come so fast my head spins."

Joci smiled. "It isn't about the amount of time. It's about the quality. That...was high quality."

Jeremiah squeezed her shoulders again and sighed, contented and happy.

"I suppose I should feed you before you have to run back to the shop. What would you like?"

"Why don't we finish up the pizza from last night?"

Joci nodded. "Sounds good. Give me about ten minutes."

She got up and put her robe on. He watched her and smiled.

"You're a sexy woman, Joci."

She smiled at him. "And you're a sexy man."

Joci walked out to the kitchen and started warming up the pizza. She set the table and got two bottles of water out of the refrigerator. Just as the microwave dinged, Jeremiah walked into the kitchen. He was pulling his shirt on over this head. He looked delicious; really, she was a lucky woman. As she watched him, his head poked through the top of his t-shirt.

He looked at her and smirked. "I do have a brain, you know."

Joci burst out laughing. "Yes, you do, but you also have that smoking hot bod. I love looking at you."

He sat down, and they ate lunch. Joci was dying to know, so she asked. "How did this morning go with LuAnn?"

Jeremiah shrugged his shoulders. "I guess okay. She acted contrite and she's been pretty quiet. Janice said she hasn't asked anything about the rest of the weekend at all, which is kind of weird. LuAnn always wants to know what she missed. Honey, all I care about is that she's good. I won't tolerate anyone hurting you, ever."

Joci looked over at him. "Thank you," she said softly.

He chuckled. "You don't have to thank me, honey. I mean it."

She nodded. She wished she could get over this niggling little feeling that LuAnn was about to drop a bomb or something. Jeremiah was right. It wasn't like LuAnn not to want to know what she missed, especially when it came to Jeremiah.

He broke the silence. "Did you call Jackie and Sandi this morning?"

Joci shook her head. "I never call Jackie before noon. Yikes, she's crabby in the morning. Sandi worked this morning, so I'll call her after two. Are you afraid I won't do it?"

She smiled as she asked. Jeremiah was a great guy. He was a good person, but when he made up his mind, he would move heaven and earth to get what he wanted. Right now, he wanted to hear Joci sing, and he wanted babies. How was she going to get around that?

Jeremiah wiped his mouth with his napkin. "I can't help it that I want to know the things about you that others know. I want to know everything there is to know."

He never looked away from her, which she had quickly learned was his way of letting her know that he intended to get his way.

"I feel the same way, but you keep things from me."

Jeremiah's head jerked up. He furrowed his brows and stared into her eyes. "I haven't kept anything from you."

"Really? Why won't you tell me why you keep LuAnn around? You said you couldn't explain it." Joci's voice got quiet. "Are you committed to her in some way? Did you once have feelings for her... or do you still?"

Jeremiah stood up and walked around the table. He leaned down and pulled Joci to her feet. He wrapped his arms around her and squeezed her tight. She could feel his heart beating a rapid rhythm.

"I have never loved anyone, Joci. Not until you. You're it for me, babe. I need you to believe that."

Jeremiah pulled back just enough so he could kiss her. It was gentle and sweet. A kiss that curled her toes just as much as one of his passionate kisses did.

When he ended their kiss, he moved his hands into her hair and cupped her nape in his hand. With his other hand, he ran his fingers down the side of her face.

"You are so perfect, Joci. I still can't believe that God brought you into my life. I'm not like those other fuckers who treated you like shit. You need to start believing that."

Joci smiled at him and looked into his eyes. She believed that he loved her, but once again, he was avoiding answering her question. She nodded and stepped back a little. She turned and started clearing the table.

Jeremiah knew he was going to have to tell her about LuAnn; he just couldn't do it yet. He hated the wall she just erected between them. It made him feel cold and alone again.

He watched Joci move around the kitchen. He was at a loss for words. He decided to go back to the shop and let her have some time to herself. He kissed her on top of her head and told her he would be home at five o'clockish and left the house.

Joci didn't know what she wanted to do. She had lost her enthusiasm for finishing the video for the Veteran's Ride. She didn't feel like unpacking boxes. Quite frankly, right now she felt like packing up and going back home. Maybe that's what she would do—go home.

F ive hours later, Joci's phone rang. She wiped her hands on a towel and picked it up without looking at who was calling.

"Hello?"

"Where are you?" Jeremiah's voice was tight.

"I'm at home."

There was a long silence. "No, you aren't. I'm here—and you aren't. It doesn't look like you've been here all afternoon. Where are you?"

She could tell he was trying to keep it light, but the tightness in his voice was a dead giveaway.

Joci sighed. "After you left for the shop, I decided to come home and clean up a little." Her voice grew soft. "I didn't feel like staying there any longer."

Jeremiah sucked in a big breath. There was silence on the other end of the line while he tried to control himself. Joci looked at her kitchen, which was as clean as a whistle right now, and leaned against the counter.

With as much lightness in his voice as he could muster around the fear and tightness, Jeremiah said, "This is your home now, Joci."

Joci closed her eyes. She couldn't say anything.

"Are you coming home, baby?" Jeremiah was on the verge of smashing something. He hated that just when he thought they had moved so far forward they were moving backward again. He was going to have to tell her about LuAnn. He could hear Joci sniffling over the phone. Goddammit. "I'll come and get you," he said around a tightness he thought would choke him right off.

"No...I'll be there in a few minutes." Her voice was so soft he barely heard her.

22

TRUST

Joci pulled into the driveway. The garage door was open, and Jeremiah was pacing. He turned and moved aside as she pulled in. He ran over, opened the door for her, and pulled her out of the car. Without saying anything, he took her hand and walked into the house. As soon as they were inside, he slapped the button on the wall to close the garage door and then drew her into the living room. He sat on the sofa and pulled her down next to him. He looked into her eyes for an impossible amount of time, trying to gauge her reactions.

"Tell me what was going on today. With you. With why you felt the need to leave here."

She grimaced, unsure how she should answer. She licked her lips, trying to form the thoughts to answer that question.

"Were you leaving me?" His voice cracked.

Softly, so softly, he almost didn't hear her, she murmured, "No. I needed space from you. I didn't want to unpack anything else because that felt permanent. I wasn't feeling very permanent after you walked out. You know if I can't trust you, it will never work. If you can't talk to me, I can't trust you. We have a real problem here."

Jeremiah closed his eyes for a moment and pinched the bridge of his nose. He swallowed hard and opened his eyes to look at her.

"Yeah. That's what I thought. Not at first. At first, I thought you left me. But you didn't take anything with you, so then I figured you needed some space."

He got up and went to get a beer from the refrigerator. He looked at Joci to see if she wanted anything; she shook her head no. He walked back into the living room and sat next to her on the sofa and turned to look at her.

"LuAnn's brother, Lance, was my best friend. We went to high school together. We went into the Marines together. We were inseparable. We managed to keep ourselves stationed together and then deployed together. I loved him like I love Dayton, Tommy, and Bryce."

His voice cracked. Joci's heart swelled for him. She figured there was going to be a sad end to this story. She reached forward and took his hand in hers.

"Lance's parents died when LuAnn and Linda—their sister—were young. A lot like you and Jackie. Lance looked after them. Made sure they were safe. But he wanted to be a Marine so damn bad; we both did. So, he told them he had to go, but he would be back. An aunt and uncle watched over the girls. They were already in high school by that time, so it wasn't like he was abandoning them. But he always knew when we were finished in the Marines, he would come back and finish taking care of them. He sent his checks home to them and called them all the time. He really loved them. By that time, Barbara was pregnant with the boys. Lance and I knew that, at least for me, my time in the Marines was almost over. I was coming home. Then we were deployed to Iraq."

Jeremiah took a long pull off his beer. His chest heaved as he drew in a deep breath.

"We were under fire. It was horrible. It was chaotic, and we couldn't see anything. The sand was always blowing, and the buildings are the same color as the sand. We couldn't see shit, and we couldn't hear shit because of all of the gun and mortar fire. My unit huddled behind an overturned vehicle to reload our weapons. We were mapping out our plan when Lance heard an incoming grenade. He threw me down on the ground and then lay over me to protect me."

Jeremiah's eyes welled with tears. He took a deep breath. His voice was very quiet. "He didn't make it," he choked.

Joci leaned forward and hugged him tight. She rubbed his back and held him while he composed himself. He wrapped his arms around her and let the tears flow. They sat that way for a very long time. She rubbed her hands over his back and through his hair, anything to soothe. Finally, he pulled away and wiped his eyes.

"I don't love LuAnn; I never have. But I feel that because of me, she doesn't have Lance anymore. She doesn't have anyone to take care of her. She always was wild and unfocused. Where will she work if I don't keep her at the shop? I owe it to Lance to make sure she has a paycheck, that she's somehow taken care of."

Joci didn't know what to say. She sure hadn't expected this. Now she felt like crap. She swallowed and placed her hand on his jaw, looking deep into the green orbs she loved so much.

"Jeremiah..." she said, "Lance wasn't asked to save you. He loved you and wanted to protect you. You don't owe him. There is no way you can repay him, except to live a good life and be good to people. You have the Veteran's Ride every year to help give back to people just like yourself and Lance. You can't live your life trying to pay back a debt that isn't payable."

She looked into his eyes, seeking, searching for words to comfort.

She took a deep breath. "That being said...I understand why you would want to try. I do understand it."

She continued rubbing his back. "We have to find some way to make LuAnn understand that you love me and that she can't keep interfering."

Jeremiah nodded. "I know, and believe me, I've been wracking my brain. She's always sought a certain amount of attention from men. But she's been especially nasty since you've been coming around. Maybe she's afraid of losing the bit of security she has at Rolling Thunder because she views you as a threat to that." They leaned back into the sofa and sat staring straight ahead for long moments.

Their hands were linked, and she absently rubbed circles with her thumb. "Thank you for telling me, Jeremiah. I needed to know what it was."

He kissed the top of her head and took a deep breath.

His voice was raspy when he said, "It feels like a weight has been lifted...talking about it. I've never told anyone that before."

Joci looked over and furrowed her brows. "Really?"

Jeremiah shook his head. "Really. It's just too personal...and I feel guilty."

"LuAnn and Linda don't know?"

Jeremiah sighed. "They know I was with him when he was hit. They don't know that he saved my life."

Joci wrapped her arms around him. "I'm very glad he did."

"I need you, Joci," he whispered.

Without a word, she stood and took his hand, pulling him to the bedroom. Once inside, she urged him to lie on the bed. She began unbuttoning his jeans while he consumed her lips, her tongue. She enjoyed running her hands over him. Feeling his heated skin under her fingers was a thrill. It was like running her hands over freshly laundered cotton. A bit of texture, warm from the dryer and the scent one she wanted to inhale.

Her lips kissed and licked up his chest, paying special attention to each nipple. She pushed his arms up over his head so she could slide his shirt off. Gently running her hands over his body, feeling the plains and ridges of his muscles, watching them quiver under her touch, she met his eyes. "You're a good-looking man, Jeremiah Sheppard."

She stepped back long enough to divest him of his jeans and boxers. She admired him lying across their bed, naked, aroused, and allowing her to do as she wanted to him. A light shiver winged through her body. Goosebumps grew on her arms, and her nipples puckered tight. She pulled the remainder of her clothing off and slid her hands up his massive thighs as she stood between them.

Her hands roamed his body, enjoying the feel of his skin on hers. She bent down and licked his balls as her hands found his thick erection and massaged him root to tip. Jeremiah hissed out a breath. She smiled against his balls, placed a few light kisses and stood. She reached over to the nightstand and pulled out some massage oil, squirted some in her palms and rubbed them together to warm it.

Jeremiah's eyes never left hers. He reached over and grabbed a pillow to prop his head. She smiled as she wrapped her fingers around his thickness and began to pump him up and down, the oil making his cock so silky and smooth under her fingers.

"Jesus," Jeremiah husked out.

She smiled again at the coarseness in his voice. Her tongue darted out to lick her lips, and his cock jerked in her hands. She smiled again. "I want to make you come with my hands, Jeremiah."

"Jesus."

Joci increased the pressure and speed of her manipulations. She alternated between watching his cock slip through her fingers and watching his face. He was beautiful, this man of hers. She wanted to make him come without him having to do anything for her.

She slid one of her hands over his balls, and they pulled up inside of him. As she reached the tip of his cock, she ran her thumb over the head, causing pre-cum to form. Jeremiah's breathing grew choppy, his chest rising and falling rapidly. He fisted the comforter on the bed and threw his head back as his muscles tightened. "Joci...fuck...baby."

She watched the ropes of semen spurt from him as she slowed her manipulations. His cock pulsed as he groaned. Once he had emptied himself, she gently massaged him as he softened. She walked to the bathroom to wet a cloth so she could wipe him up as he regulated his breathing. Softly she swiped the warm cloth across his abdomen, cleaning him. She tossed it into the bathroom hamper and slid into bed beside him.

He quickly wrapped her in his arms and kissed the top of her head. He swallowed a few times. "I've never done that before. Fucking amazing."

Joci smirked. "I've never done that before, either. Fucking amazing is right."

23

FAMILY

Thursday night found Jeremiah and Joci sitting in his parents' living room, celebrating Eli's, Bryce and Angie's youngest, graduation. The whole family was there, including Gunnar.

Gunnar nudged Joci's arm. "I invited JT, Ryder, and Connor to listen to the Golden Girls on Saturday."

"It appears the crowd is growing. I'm going to need to practice; we haven't done this for a long while." She would tell Jeremiah as soon as they had a minute alone with each other. They hadn't seen Connor since the birthday party. "What made you decide to ask Connor?"

Gunnar looked into her eyes. "He called me the other day to talk. I feel sorry for him. He said he didn't mean to make things weird; he just feels the way he feels." He shrugged and looked across the room to Jeremiah talking with his brothers. "I'll catch ya later." He walked outside where Ryder and JT were sitting on the deck drinking beer.

Staci sat down next to Joci and patted her on the knee.

"Looks like you and Jeremiah are doing well. How are you?"

Joci smiled. "I think we're good."

She looked over at Jeremiah talking to his brothers. He glanced at her and winked. Her smile grew. "We're really good."

She blushed. Staci giggled and nudged her. "We're thrilled, you know. He has never, in all the years I've known him, looked so happy. Whatever you're doing, keep it up."

Angie joined them and soon so did Erin. They talked about kids and Joci moving in with Jeremiah, family and all that was going on.

J eremiah glanced at his mom and saw that she was watching him. She smiled, and he smiled back. She walked over and hugged him. "I can see you're crazy for that girl. I love the look on your face when you look at her. You look happy."

Jeremiah snickered. "God, Ma, I'm so happy I could bust."

Emily looked over at Joci with her daughters-in-law and nodded her head. "What are you going to do about it?"

Jeremiah leaned down close to her ear, and said, "Mom, I'm going to marry her. I'd like to have babies with her, but..." He shrugged.

His mom glanced at him, then back to her daughters in law. "Does she know that?"

Jeremiah's brows drew together. "About the marriage, not yet. I don't think she wants to have another baby. I've brought it up a couple of times, and she gets scared and changes the subject."

Emily shook her head. "Don't you think that's because she doesn't want to be a single mother again? Even if you would marry her if she got pregnant, she may not want you to marry her because you have to. She would more than likely only want to get married because you wanted to marry her. The baby could—and should—come after." Emily stared into his eyes and raised her eyebrows.

He took in his mother's expression. "You're a smart woman, Mom. I didn't think of it that way."

She became slightly exasperated. "Jeremiah, you're my son, and I love you to death, but you're such a...man. Treat that girl right and you'll have a happy life."

His gaze slid over to Joci and his sisters-in-law. "Thanks, Mom." He took a step towards the women and turned back to his mom. "Just so you know..." A sly smile creased his face. "One of the things I think she loves about me is that I'm a man." He smirked and winked at her and started toward the lady in his life.

He felt his phone vibrate and pulled it from his pocket. He swiped his thumb across the screen and tapped the text message. He began reading and then froze. His brows furrowed. His heart raced like he was flying down the highway at midnight with no headlight. Sweat beaded on his forehead. His eyes darted to Joci. The icy dread that filled his stomach almost brought him to his knees when his eyes met hers.

She stood and walked to him. "Are you okay? Your face just drained of color, and you look like you're going to be sick. Come on and sit down." She led him to a chair in the kitchen and immediately touched his forehead. She frowned, turned toward the sink and wet some paper towel with cool water. She placed the towels on his forehead as she knelt before him. "Are you going to be sick, Jeremiah?"

The concern in her eyes made his stomach roil. He took the towel from her hand and laid it on the table. "I'm okay, babe. Just dizzy for a minute. Don't fuss."

She clucked. "Get used to it. If you're sick, I'm going to take care of you."

He pulled her up to his lap and lay his head on her shoulder. "Just give me a minute. I need to let my heart slow down."

She held him, her arm around his large shoulders, her other hand gently soothing his face. He'd grown a beard, and the hair now felt soft and silky where before the stubble had felt like sandpaper to her skin. He was warm, and his heart was still pounding away against her ribs. She'd make sure he went to the doctor first thing tomorrow.

Emily walked into the kitchen and caught Joci's eye. "Everything okay in here? Jeremiah?"

He lifted his head and looked at his mom. "Yes, I'm fine. I just got a little dizzy—it's nothing."

"People don't just get dizzy. Has this happened before? When was the last time you went to the doctor and had a check-up?"

Jeremiah inhaled deeply. He picked Joci off his lap and stood her next to him. He rose from the chair and said, "It hasn't happened before. I can't remember my last appointment with Dr. Jerzak, but I will call him tomorrow. I'm fine, really." He dropped his phone into his pocket and took Joci's hand. "Do you mind if we go home?"

Joci looked in his eyes. "No. Of course not. I'll drive." She smiled as she held her hand out for the keys to his truck. He frowned for a minute and then reached into his pocket and handed them to her.

"I don't need to go to the doctor, I'm fine. I had a couple of beers in a short amount of time, and it hit me." He finished pulling his hair into his signature ponytail and looked at Joci in the mirror. He saw her lips turn down into a frown, and he felt bad. Stepping closer to her, he whispered close to her ear, "You're stuck with me for a good long time."

She smiled sweetly, her dimples winking at him as she lifted one shoulder. "I'm counting on it." She swiped the lip gloss across her lips, and he had the powerful urge to immediately lick it off. The light reflected on her perfectly shaped lips, and he balled his fists together. "You told your mom you'd call Dr. Jerzak today."

He frowned. "I'll deal with my mom."

His phone chirped, and he grabbed it as he stepped out of the bathroom. Tapping the screen a few times he entered the password for his voicemail.

"Dog, it's Deborah. You didn't respond to my text last night. We need to talk about this. I don't know what to do. I'm stopping by Rolling Thunder later to talk. Bye."

There it was again, that icy cold dread planting itself in his stomach. His heart began racing, and he broke out in a sweat. He walked to the sliding patio doors and opened them. Sucking in the fresh air, he leaned against the door frame trying to figure out what to do.

"Are you feeling sick again?"

He swung around and plastered on a fake smile. His face felt wooden and just smiling took a huge effort. "No." His voice cracked. He cleared his throat again and with more air than he felt he had in his lungs, he said, "No. Just checking the weather."

Joci's brows drew together; she glanced outside and then into his eyes. She raised her brows. "Really?"

He nodded and pulled the door closed. Flipping the lock, he stepped into the kitchen. "I don't have time to eat anything, so I'll see you later, okay?"

He walked toward the door to the garage, but Joci stopped him.

"Jeremiah?"

He quietly took a deep breath. He turned to face her. "Yeah?"

"What's going on?" She crossed her arms in front of her and stood directly in front of him. His eyes searched her face, and his stomach twisted a bit tighter.

"Nothing. I have an issue with Chase to deal with this morning, and I almost forgot about it. I need to get there before the day gets busy."

He leaned forward and pecked her on the lips, then quickly turned and left.

24

THIS IS BAD

"I don't know what to think, Sandi. His behavior was weird this morning. I'm trying not to let my mind wander, but shit—the feeling in the pit of my stomach isn't good."

Sandi reached across the lunch table and squeezed Joci's hand. She smiled her brightest smile, which made Joci worry more. The fake smile was never good.

"Don't read too much into this. He runs a growing company, and there are bound to be times when he is preoccupied or busy." She released Joci's hand and picked up her menu. "What are you having for lunch? I'm starving."

Hmm, changing the subject wasn't good either.

Joci walked into Rolling Thunder from the garage entrance. Gunnar was working on a bike at his station, so she headed over to him. "Hey there, how's your day going?"

Gunnar turned and smiled brightly. He wrapped his arm around her shoulders, without touching her with his dirty hand. "Hi. What brings you here?"

Joci looked around the garage. She didn't want to seem like a stalker, but she couldn't shake the niggling feeling that something was wrong. "I just stopped to see Jeremiah. Is he in his office?"

Gunnar nodded. He reached forward and picked up a grease rag and wiped his fingers. "Yeah. He's been up there most of the day. Go on up."

She leaned forward and kissed his cheek. "Thanks, honey. You doing okay?"

He smirked. "Yeah. You?"

She looked toward the door to the store. Absently, she responded, "Yeah. I'm good. Talk to you later, okay?"

She walked toward the store, her stomach a little queasy. The door from the garage into the shop opened directly to the parts counter and just beyond that were the parts shelves, to the left the sales floor and to the right, the clothing. There were several customers milling about. JT was helping a customer at a desk on the sales floor. Janice was speaking to a customer in clothing. LuAnn was speaking to a tall brunette with short spiky hair and a protruding baby bump. When she saw Joci, she nodded her head toward Joci and the brunette turned and smiled at her then quickly turned to LuAnn. They whispered to each other, and as Joci walked past them, they giggled loudly.

Heaving out a breath to keep herself calm, she refused to look at them again. Climbing the stairs was difficult as her knees felt weak. Today was weird—she'd like a do-over.

Jeremiah's door was open, and he sat staring out the window that looked out over the parking lot. He looked sad. Lost in thought. But he was still the sexiest man she'd ever known. His broad shoulders seemed to slump forward, and his hands were at his sides, balled into fists.

"You look pensive."

He swung around, his eyes large and shocked. It took him a moment to compose himself, but she saw the shutter close in his eyes. He cleared his throat, but when he spoke, his voice was gravelly. "Hey. What brings you here?"

Joci's brows furrowed. She stepped into his office, and he didn't move toward her. That was the first time he held himself back. Wait. Nope, it was the second time; the first was this morning when he left. She swallowed the large lump in her throat. Softly she said, "I just had lunch with Sandi, and I wanted to see you. You seemed preoccupied this morning, and I was worried." She looked into his eyes, noted his jaw clench and tighten, and his hands flexed open then closed again.

"I'm fine, Joci. Just busy." He walked toward her and kissed the top of her head before he turned and sat at his desk. Tears sprang to her eyes. This was it. She shouldn't have moved in with him; it was too soon.

25

THE GOLDEN GIRLS

J oci stood in the closet trying to decide what to wear. She was as nervous as a cat tonight. She had gone out plenty of times with Jackie and Sandi to sing Karaoke, but it had always been impromptu. This felt staged and planned, and she had butter-flies beyond belief. She had even gotten together for lunch with the girls today to practice. They thought she was being silly, but she didn't want to embarrass herself or Jeremiah. Now, what to wear?

"There you are. What's up?"

Joci turned to look at Jeremiah standing in the doorway of the closet. Did he always have to look perfect?

"I don't know what to wear. I'm nervous," she said softly.

Jeremiah walked toward her and slid his hand in her hair. As he cupped her head, he leaned down and kissed her softly.

Looking intently into her eyes, he husked out, "You could wear a sack and still look perfect, babe. But maybe I can help."

He walked past her to the closet and pulled a little package off a top shelf. He handed it to her with a smile on his face.

"I bought this for you."

She opened the package and pulled out a beautiful gray blouse. Its capped sleeves and crystals decorating the front were beautiful, the crystal buttons ended, creating a low V. The material felt silky and soft in her hands and sliding through her fingers.

She looked up at Jeremiah and smiled. "Thank you. It's just beautiful."

She stepped forward and wrapped her arms around his neck. She kissed his lips softly and tenderly, and she shivered when he wrapped his arms around her waist and pulled her close.

"I don't know when you had time to shop for me; you've been preoccupied this week, but thank you."

He squeezed her one more time and pulled his head back to look into her eyes.

"I think about you all the time, Joci. You're always in my thoughts. And, I'm sorry I've been a bit in the clouds this week. Just a lot on my mind."

She squeezed him again and turned to head toward the bathroom for a shower. She placed her hand over her tummy to quell the fluttering.

At eight-thirty, they were walking into Purcell's to meet their friends.

Sandi jumped up and hugged Joci when she saw them. Saying hello to Jeremiah, she pulled Joci forward to a group of tables she had pulled together to accommodate their large group. Sandi and Jon, Jackie and David, Gunnar, JT, and Ryder were already there. Joci looked back at Jeremiah and saw his scowl. She followed his line of sight to Connor as he walked in. She tightened her lips as she caught his eye. He sheepishly nodded once and joined her at the table.

A waitress came and took their drink order as the first Karaoke singer went up on stage, and the show started. Joci blew out a long breath and said, "I'm going to need a few drinks before I can get up there."

"Dog? God, that *is* you. How are you, darling?" a seductive, smoky voice purred.

Joci turned to see the tall brunette from Rolling Thunder the other day, standing next to them. Jeremiah's jaw tightened. "Deborah. What are you doing here?"

Deborah leaned forward and took Joci's hand in hers, pumping once. "Hi. I'm Deborah. I believe I saw you at Rolling Thunder the other day." She ran her hand slowly over her baby bump, and a sickening feeling hit Joci.

Deborah's eyes slid to Jeremiah. "Have you told her yet?"

Joci looked at him and saw how pale he'd become. His chest rose and fell, and she could see the sweat bead up on his forehead.

"Told me what?" Though at this point she wasn't at all sure she wanted to know.

Deborah's smile crept across her face. "Dog is about to be a da—"

"No," he barked out. "No, I'm not. It's not mine. I've told you until you agree to a paternity test, I refuse to claim it."

Joci's world began tumbling out of control. Her vision dimmed as the voices around her faded to the sound of the thrumming of her blood through her veins. Her knees threatened to give out, and she swayed. Strong arms wrapped around her and picked her up. The last thing she remembered was seeing the ceiling rush past her line of sight and the scent of Jeremiah.

"**F**uck. Fuck. Fuck." He eased Joci into the seat of his truck and reached across to buckle her in. She turned her head toward him, and her eyes slowly came open. She stared at him, though he didn't think she was seeing him.

He heard the voices of their families walking toward them. Jackie, Joci's sister, came running.

"Joci. Baby, wake up. Are you okay?" Jackie pushed him out of the way and patted Joci's cheeks—her forehead furrowed in concern, her voice near panic.

Joci's eyes focused on her sister. "Jackie. Did you hear that?" She sobbed. Then the tears gushed out. "Did you hear?" She openly cried. "He's having a ba...ba...by—with someone else." Joci's arms snaked around her sister's shoulders as she sobbed into Jackie's neck.

Jackie patted her sister lovingly, smoothing her hand over Joci's hair and whispering soft words of comfort in her ear.

Hearing Joci's anguished cries, Jeremiah turned and emptied the contents of his stomach on the parking lot. His back was so tight the retching hurt, but he didn't care. He wanted the pain right now. He wanted to feel so much pain—anything to block out the sound of Joci's crying because of him.

26

IS IT YOUR BABY?

"I can walk myself." She slapped Jeremiah's hands away as he tried helping her from the truck. She'd eventually calmed down, thrown up, and then went into a state of disbelief.

Jeremiah blew out a breath and stood to the side of the truck, waiting for her to jump out. She stepped down then pulled her shirt down. The very shirt he had lovingly given her just a few short hours ago, while knowing he was lying to her. She numbly walked around the front of the truck and to the door leading into the house. His house. Not hers. Not anymore.

She stepped to the cupboard above the sink, pulled a glass from the shelf and filled it with water, watching the water bubble and spin as it filled her glass. These stupid mundane thoughts kept her sane. She had been so careful all these years not to fall in love, not to get hurt. This was why. The pain was unbearable. She felt numb.

"We should talk." His voice was raspy. Weary even. He wanted to talk.

She raised the glass to her lips, almost in slow motion, and drank. The cool water slid down her warm throat, cooling her from the inside. She enjoyed the feeling of...feeling—for just a moment.

Setting the empty glass on the counter, she sucked in a deep breath and slowly let it out. Turning to face him for the first time since 'the news,' she looked into his eyes. The sadness and pain she saw there threatened her equilibrium. It was dizzying dealing with all these emotions. Seeing them written on his face was almost devastating.

Her voice barely above a whisper, she asked, "How long have you known?"

He took a step forward, and she swiftly held her hand up to halt him. She never took her eyes from his. "How. Long?"

He released a shaky breath. "Since Wednesday at Mom and Dad's."

She nodded her head. "So, you weren't dizzy or sick?"

He raised a hand palm up then let it drop like a hot rock. "I was dizzy and sick. She...Deborah..."

At the sound of her name, Joci turned to look at the picture she had just this morning hung on the wall of her and Jeremiah at the Veteran's Ride. How happy they looked, holding hands as they spoke to friends. But she was finished with tears.

"Texted me. When I saw the text, I felt physically ill." He turned and grabbed a beer from the refrigerator, twisted the cap and tossed it on the counter. He gulped down the majority of it before leveling his eyes on hers.

"She was at the shop because I didn't return her text or her voicemail. She wanted to talk about the ba...." He swallowed. "Her pregnancy." He finished off his beer, set the empty bottle on the counter and briskly strode to the patio doors. Wrenching them open, he sucked in several deep breaths.

"Why didn't you say anything to me?" Joci crossed her arms in front of her, her jaw set. She hated lying more than she hated anything else. Now that the shock was wearing off, she was pissed.

He turned toward her, hooked his thumbs in his jeans and set his jaw. "I wanted to be sure before I knew anything. For the record, I don't think it's mine. I did have sex…" He faltered as she turned her head. She turned back to him and looked into his eyes and waited.

"I had sex with her. Once. Many months ago. I've been trying to remember, but honestly, it just didn't mean that much. I just wanted to get laid. You wouldn't go out with me."

Joci flew into a rage. "Don't. You. Dare." Each word punctuated with a finger jab. Her eyes shrunk as she squinted at him, she was nearly yelling. "Don't you dare blame this on me. If you had kept your cock in your pants, we wouldn't be dealing with this now."

He looked down and quickly back up. "Jesus. I wasn't blaming you. I'm trying to explain. If you can't stand here and listen, don't ask me the fucking questions." His voice grew louder with each word. He turned and stalked to the living room and then swiftly came back. Still in a state, he finished, his voice a bit calmer, "You wouldn't let me touch you. I was horny. Deal with it. But that was probably eight months ago. She's not eight months' pregnant." He slammed his fist on the top of the counter. "I don't know what her game is, but that kid isn't mine." He stalked back to the living room.

Joci followed him, saw him standing at the picture window and flopped on the sofa. She pulled her legs up to her chest and hugged them. Resting her chin on her knees, she stared at the blank television screen, a faint reflection of herself staring back. She felt the sofa dip. His scent floated over her, and she closed her eyes.

Softly, she said, "Why would she do this? Why would she say it's yours if it isn't? Did she ask for money?"

He shook his head but didn't say anything. They sat quietly for long moments.

Taking a deep breath, she said, "LuAnn." She turned toward him. "Deborah is friends with LuAnn. I saw them talking when I walked in the shop the other day, and they giggled when I walked past them."

Jeremiah turned his head and stared. When she met his gaze, her lips thinned, then turned down. He flung himself back against the sofa and let out a string of curses that would make the devil himself blush.

27

THE EXES

Sunday morning, Joci woke to Jeremiah kissing her head. Her eyes slowly opened. Jeremiah was on his back with his right arm wrapped around her. She was on her side, with her right leg thrown over his legs, her right arm thrown over his waist, and her head cradled on his shoulder. They had gone to bed without saying a word after sitting in the living room for what felt like hours. Joci was too weary to keep her eyes open. She laid as far to her side of the bed as she could, and he on his. Not even a good night was spoken, both of them raw and bloodied from the extraction of emotions. She must have rolled toward him in her sleep.

"Sorry. I didn't mean to crowd your space," she said as she lifted to glance at the clock.

He sighed and when he spoke his voice was hoarse. "I love you, Joci. We'll get over this and work it out. I haven't cheated on you; I never will."

She glanced at him for the first time. His eyes sought hers, hungry for reassurance.

She sat up, raked her hands through her hair and let out a breath. "Yeah." She scooted to her side and slid from the bed, still wearing the gray t-shirt she had hastily thrown on with the silky black shorts. It was the first time she hadn't slept nude with him.

"I can't have this conversation again right now. I need coffee and some time to process it all." She walked to the kitchen, rubbing her gritty eyes. She absently reached into the cupboard for two cups and poured one for each of them. Turning to the refrigerator, her stomach rolled at the thought of food. She immediately closed the door and picked up her phone from the counter. Several missed calls. She tapped Gunnar's missed call first.

"Are you okay, Mom?" He sounded as if he had been awake for some time. She glanced at the clock on the stove.

"Yes. I'm fine. What gets you up so early on a Sunday?"

She heard him hesitate. "Do you want to talk? Are you sure you're fine?"

She chuckled. "I'm fine. It's going to take some time, and we have things to work through, but..." She couldn't finish. She didn't know what would happen next.

She heard him clear his throat. "Okay. Well, Connor asked if he could speak with us today. He wouldn't say what it was, but he wanted us both to be there. Are you feeling up to talking with him this morning?"

Joci closed her eyes. What could he possibly need to speak with them about? She couldn't handle much today; she felt weak and exhausted. Letting out a deep breath, she said, "Let's just pull the Band-Aid off quickly and get it over with. What time do you want to come over?"

She threw away Jeremiah's beer bottle and cap from last night and wiped the sticky ring from the counter. She walked to the bedroom with their coffee cups and saw that Jeremiah had gotten up, and she heard the shower running. She pulled clothing from the closet and sat on the edge of the bed. She'd never hesitated to go into the bathroom when he was in showering before; now, she felt different. Distant.

The shower shut off, and she listened as he sighed heavily. He was apparently feeling it too. He opened the door and froze when he saw her sitting on the bed facing the door. "You could've come in," he said, a bit terse.

She nodded once. "I brought you coffee." She retrieved the cup from the nightstand and handed it to him. Their fingers brushed, and she looked into his eyes. He reached forward with his other hand and cupped her chin.

"I love you. We need to move forward and figure this out." She caressed his arm; her eyes welled with tears. Stepping forward, she wrapped her arms around his waist and buried her face in his massive bare chest. The hairs tickled her nose and eyelashes; his skin smelled heavenly. As he wrapped his big arms around her shoulders and waist, she felt cocooned and safe from the spoils of the world around them.

She reluctantly pulled away and looked into those green orbs she loved so much. "I love you too. We'll have to figure this out later, though. Gunnar and Connor are on their way over. Connor has something he needs to talk to us about."

Jeremiah groaned. "I'll bet he does."

Joci turned the water on in the shower. "I don't think it has anything to do with Deb—with you." She took a deep breath. She'd have to say her name eventually.

Gunnar walked in the back door from the garage. He had a bakery box in his hand and a coffee cup in the other. Jeremiah stood from the table, and eyed him warily. Gunnar nodded and set the box in the center of the table. "Morning. Where's Mom?"

"Taking a shower. She'll be out in a minute."

Gunnar took a drink of his coffee, set the cup on the table and took a seat. "Everything okay?" he asked cautiously.

Jeremiah sat across from him, folded his hands together and heaved out a sigh. "Look, Gunnar, I didn't cheat on her—I never would. And that's not my kid. I don't know what game she's playing at, but it's not mine."

Gunnar nodded. "Then we'll need to find out what her game is." He leaned forward and placed his forearms on the table. "But you won't get another chance if you hurt my mom; she's been through enough."

"What's this, you're protecting my virtue?" Joci strolled into the kitchen, her hair still damp from her shower, no makeup on and she was still the most beautiful woman he'd ever laid eyes on. She took his breath away. This setback was just that: a setback. But they would get through it. He'd move heaven and earth if he needed to.

Gunnar stood and hugged his mom. "Not necessarily your virtue, just wanting the air to be clear."

"Hmm." Joci glanced at him, and Jeremiah smiled at her. He stood and walked to her, kissed the top of her head and pointed to the table. "Sit. I'll warm up your coffee." He proceeded to the coffee pot when the doorbell rang.

"Okay, let's find out what this important meeting is all about," Joci said as she stood to open the door for Connor.

As soon as the stiff pleasantries were exchanged, Jeremiah sat at the table to Joci's left. Then he had an uncomfortable feeling that this might be private, and he shouldn't be involved. "Would you like me to go in the other room?"

"No," both Joci and Gunnar said at the same time.

Jeremiah smiled at both of them. Relief washed over him like the shower water had this morning. He glanced at Gunnar, and he nodded. He turned his head to Joci, and she reached over and took his hand on the table and gently squeezed. Baby steps.

Connor finally cleared his throat. "I know this is going to be difficult to hear, but I wanted to let you know that Keith is back in town. He and Dianna and the boys moved back last week. They're living at Keith's parents' house."

Joci looked at Gunnar to see how he was taking this. Her son's jaw was tight, and she could see him grinding his teeth together. He looked at her and then back at Connor.

Connor continued, "He wants to see you. Both of you."

Gunnar slapped his hand on the top of the table, hard, making Joci jump. He stood suddenly, knocking over his chair. "Tell him to go and fuck himself. I sure as fuck don't want to see him."

Her eyes grew large as she watched Gunnar, and even though she felt the same way, she was surprised that he didn't want to see Keith. Glancing at Jeremiah to see his reaction, she saw his jaw clamped like a vise; his lips pressed together in a narrow line, and his hands were balled into fists on the table.

Connor took a deep breath and looked at Joci. "How do you feel about it, Joci?"

She snapped her head to look at Gunnar again and then at Connor. "I don't have anything to say to him. He left us twenty-five years ago with no word, no contact in any way, shape, or form. No forwarding address, no way to reach him if Gunnar needed him. I can't possibly imagine why he would think either of us would want to see him now."

Connor nodded. He looked at Gunnar again. "He's your father, Gunnar. Don't you want to meet him?"

Gunnar exploded. "He isn't my father. He's a fucking sperm donor. He has a lot of nerve asking to see me after all this time. Up until now, my fathers were you and Uncle David. Now I have Dog. He's the only father I want."

Joci's mouth dropped open and tears sprang to her eyes. She knew Gunnar liked Jeremiah. She had no idea he felt like Jeremiah was a father to him. She looked at Jeremiah, whose eyes were red and glistening. He got up out of his chair and walked over to Gunnar and wrapped him in a strong embrace. They held on to each other for a long time.

Joci's gaze was fixed on the two most important men in her life. Her heart was so full of love right now she struggled to breathe. She swallowed several times rapidly and blinked furiously to keep the tears from flowing.

When Jeremiah and Gunnar pulled away from each other, both had red eyes. Jeremiah held Gunnar's head in both of his hands and kissed the top of Gunnar's head.

Once they were able to compose themselves, they sat down again. Jeremiah reached over and took Joci's hand. She squeezed and looked into his eyes. The house was eerily silent. Joci cleared her throat as she looked over to Connor.

He reached over and laid a hand on top of the hand she had on the table. Jeremiah leaned forward as if he was going to object, but Connor spoke up.

"Joci, I love you and Gunnar. I always have. I wanted to be there for you both when Keith left. I know this is hard for you—both of you."

He looked over at Gunnar, and then back at Joci. "Keith is dying, Joci. He has stage four lung cancer. He realizes what he did was wrong. He wants to apologize for his behavior."

Joci slowly pulled her hand away from Connor. Now she was mad. She closed her eyes for a long moment, shook her head and looked at Connor. Softly as she could, she said, "How long are you going to do his dirty work? When he left, you stepped in and picked up some of the brunt. You were doing what he should have done. Now he's dying and wants to absolve himself of his wrongdoing, and once again, he sends you here to do his dirty work. How dare he want to see us when he is dying? He isn't thinking of us; he isn't thinking of Gunnar. He's worried that he won't get into heaven without asking for forgiveness. It has nothing to do with us!"

She stood up. "You go tell him that, Connor. He has no right to ask this of us. He has no right to try and use his final days to disturb our lives to ease his guilt."

Joci started to walk outside when she heard Connor say, "You'll regret this, Joci. I know you. You're the one always saying to step up and be the better person. If you let him die without seeing you, you'll always wonder if you should have given him the chance to apologize."

Joci spun around to yell at Connor, but Gunnar punched him in the face first. Connor flew back and fell off his chair. Gunnar went to lunge at him again when Jeremiah stepped in and grabbed him.

"Son, it isn't Connor's fault Keith is a coward. If you hurt him, you'll feel bad about it. Let's just let it go. Please."

Gunnar looked at Jeremiah for a few beats then nodded his head. He walked out past Joci and into the backyard. She followed him out, not wanting him riding his bike when he was pissed. She caught up to him and asked him to sit with her on the swing she'd brought from her house. She used to swing with Gunnar on it in the evening while they read books. Later, when Gunnar was older, they would sit in the swing most evenings and talk about what had happened during the day. Gunnar would tell Joci about school, and Joci would tell Gunnar about her latest project at work.

She started to move the swing back and forth—slowly—to help calm them both down. Neither said anything for a long time. They just let the soft calming motion soothe them as they collected their thoughts.

Finally, Gunnar took in a shaky breath. "I'm sorry, Mom. I don't want to see him. Are you mad at me?"

Joci pulled Gunnar to her for a hug. He rested his head on her shoulder like he used to as a kid, though now he had to hunch over to do it, and she rubbed his back.

"I'm not mad at you, baby. I don't want to see him either. I can't even process what's going on." After a short silence, she said, "I had no idea you loved Jeremiah like a father. You've never said."

Gunnar smiled. "Didn't you wonder why I always tried to get you to go out with him? There was something about him right away. I was drawn to him in a way I couldn't explain. He's been so patient and kind to me. Always teaching me things, just like his boys. Never yells, just corrects and explains, and we move on. Just like I always dreamed my father would be.

"Mom, when you finally started dating him, I was so fucking happy. I thought I would finally get my family. I don't mean to make you feel bad, but I always wanted a dad. You're a great mom and Uncle David has been great over the years. But, I wanted a dad. My dad and not Keith. A dad who loves me."

Joci had no idea. Tears slid down her face and into Gunnar's hair. She didn't care; she let them flow. What a weekend. Never had she been on such a roller coaster ride. And as the universe has its way of putting things in your way to change your direction, here was another one. She loved Jeremiah, and she'd do what it took to work this thing out with Deborah. If the baby was his, Joci would find a way to be a good parent to it. Though she hoped Jeremiah was right, and it wasn't his.

They sat and swung for quite a while, each lost in thought.

Gunnar raised his head and looked into her eyes. "Are you and Dog okay?"

Her lips turned down. She looked away from the hopeful look in Gunnar's eyes and stared at the bright pink polish on her toenails. "It will be. Last night was quite a shock and more than anything I'm pissed that he's been hiding it from me. It doesn't help me to trust him."

Gunnar sighed. "I know. But you'll be able to. Right?"

Joci lightly pushed his shoulder and chuckled. "Yeah. You better not be ganging up on me, though."

Gunnar laughed. "Naw. I won't do that."

She nodded, then a tall figure cast a shadow on them where the sun had just been shining.

"May I join you?"

Joci and Gunnar both looked up into Jeremiah's beautiful face. She smiled and scooted over to make room for him. He wrapped his arm around her shoulders and rested his hand on Gunnar's.

"I take it Connor left," Joci said.

"Yes, quite a while ago. I cleaned up the table and wanted to give you two some time to talk. But I was spying on you. I sat at the table and watched you two sit and swing out here for a long time. I got jealous and decided to come and join you."

He looked at her so lovingly her heart melted. She leaned up and kissed him. "You're always welcome to join us. You should never feel like you can't." It had been the first time since last night. She saw his eyes grow moist, the edges red and knew he realized it too.

Gunnar nodded. "Agreed." He looked around Joci. "Is Connor okay?"

"Well, he has a sore jaw, but nothing's broken. He feels bad. He said you had a point, Joci, about his doing Keith's dirty work. He had never looked at it that way. He wanted me to tell you both he's sorry he came here to ask you to see Keith."

They sat quietly for a while.

Jeremiah said. "My mom called and wanted to know if we would like to go to Pamperin Park for a barbecue this afternoon. How do you guys feel about that?"

"Nothing I would like more than to be with my family," Gunnar said. Jeremiah smiled and nodded at him. He squeezed Joci's shoulders.

"You good with that?"

She nodded. Tears slid down her cheeks again. Stupid emotions.

"Yes, that sounds like a fabulous way to spend the day."

Joci had been working on the plans with Jeremiah for the employee party for the past few weeks. She had also worked hard on the video from the Veteran's Ride. Even with their setbacks this past couple of weeks, life was slowly getting back to their normal--what they'd become accustomed to. Since she'd met Jeremiah, the new normal still had to show itself. Today, she was meeting him for lunch at Rolling Thunder to discuss preparations for the annual staff dinner.

She walked into the shop, and Janice greeted her with a huge smile. "Hi, Joci. How are you?"

Happy to see her, Joci greeted her warmly. They spoke for a few minutes, and Joci walked upstairs to the offices. Jeremiah's office door was open, and she walked in to find him reading something. She walked over and kissed the top of his head.

He looked up and smiled while pulling her down on his lap. She giggled and wrapped her arms around his neck and kissed his lips.

Kissing him was something close to heaven. His lips always molded to hers. Soft and supple while commanding her in ways she would never tell him lest he use it against her.

A gravelly voice from the doorway said, "Well, well, well. What do we have here?"

Jeremiah touched his forehead to hers and hissed, "Fuck."

Joci turned to see a woman who looked like an older version of LuAnn. Oh. My. God. Bleached blonde hair. Tattoos everywhere. A ton of jewelry. Over-tanned skin. Dark eye makeup. She looked like someone had dragged her behind a bike.

Jeremiah stood, holding on to Joci. "Barbara, what brings you here?"

Barbara? *This* was Barbara? She looked like LuAnn's mother...or grandmother.

"Aren't you going to introduce me to your plaything of the day?" Barbara smirked.

Jeremiah took a deep calming breath. "Barbara, first of all, she's not my 'plaything of the day.' This is Jocelyn James, my girlfriend, and I won't allow you to disrespect her."

"Joci, this is Barbara, JT and Ryder's mother."

Joci cleared her throat. "It's nice to meet you, Barbara."

Barbara sneered. "Sure."

"I need to speak with you, Dog..." She looked at Joci and raised her brows. "Privately."

"Tough. If you have anything to speak with me about, you'll say it in front of Joci," Jeremiah ground out.

Barbara sauntered in and flopped onto the chair across the room like she owned the place. "Suit yourself."

Jeremiah sat in his desk chair; Joci leaned against the desk, hands on either side, bracing herself. Joci glanced at Jeremiah, trying to gauge his mood.

"Go ahead, Barbara. Spit it out. We're on our lunch break here."

"Yes, I saw what you were eating," she snorted. "I need money, Dog. I've kind of fallen on hard times."

Jeremiah huffed out a breath. "Tough. JT told you last year, and I'm telling you this year, no. If you need money, get a fucking job like everyone else."

"I bet your little 'girlfriend' gets all the money she needs from you."

Joci opened her mouth to say something. Barbara's little air quotes as she said girlfriend was the last straw. Before she could say anything, Jeremiah jumped up and pointed to the door.

"Get the fuck out. For your fucking information, Joci works. She's always worked for a living. Something you wouldn't know anything about. I told you I wasn't going to let you disrespect her, and you've done it again. Get the fuck out."

Barbara smirked as she got out of her chair. She walked to the door and looked over at Joci. "See how he treats the woman who bore him children?"

She walked out. Jeremiah picked up the phone and barked at someone on the other end. "Barbara's on her way down. Make sure she doesn't grab anything and make sure she walks straight out the door."

He hung up and rubbed his forehead. "I'm sorry you had to endure that. She's a crass bitch. Always has been."

"So, that was Barbara."

"Hey, you know she was just trying to get to you. Don't let her."

She looked up into his handsome face. Worry etched his brow; his mouth, moments ago so soft and demanding, now took on a hard line. "You good?"

She swallowed. "It's not her comment as much as it is how she looks. LuAnn looks just like her. Clearly that's the look you go for."

He let out a pent-up breath. "When I hooked up with Barbara twenty-seven years ago, I just wanted to get laid. She looked like someone who wouldn't want anything more than that. I told you, no commitments, just fucking. LuAnn dresses like she dresses, I don't know why. What I like...*love* is this beautiful woman standing right here in front of me, with sandy brown hair and eyes like a stormy sky. I think you're the most beautiful woman in the world."

She ran her hands over her face. An effort to wipe away the worry. "I'm sorry." She smiled at him. "Are we finished dealing with shit this week, because, honestly, I'm not sure I can handle anymore."

He kissed the top of her head and hugged her close. "I sure hope so."

Jeremiah pulled back and smiled. "The best part about Barbara coming around is that it's usually only once a year. We won't have to see her for another year now."

Joci giggled.

"Okay, come on. I was just reading the menu the restaurant emailed over. Let's get this ironed out and go for some lunch."

They finished up the plans for the staff party. The menu was set, the DJ selected, and the gifts were taken care of. Jeremiah gave each employee a bonus every year, based on his or her performance and the shop's numbers. This year, the bonuses were very generous. He had also put a little extra in the checks for Deacon, Gunnar, JT, and Ryder for all of the additional work they'd done on the Veteran's Ride.

After they ordered their meals, and while they waited, Jeremiah took a deep breath.

"Joci, don't make any plans this weekend. I just want to spend the weekend alone with you. Just the two of us. Maybe we'll tell everyone we're going somewhere, so they don't come over."

Joci sighed. "That sounds fantastic."

"Let's just tuck in at home and hide."

She smiled. "I would love that."

He chuckled. "Great. I was worried you wouldn't want to. Friday too. Three days, just us. I think we need it."

Joci giggled. "You can see how hard it was to talk me into it. I'm looking forward to not having to share you with anyone for a few days, no exes, no pretend baby mommas, no one."

28

EATING IN

Friday morning came slowly. They were lying in bed, enjoying a cup of coffee, when he said, "Today, no clothes. Just you and me naked all day, okay?"

Joci laughed. "Really? What if someone comes over?"

"No one's coming over. The boys think we flew out this morning for a weekend getaway, and everyone else is busy with their own lives. It's just us, alone here, all weekend." He leaned over and touched his lips to hers. Kissing her was tantamount to making love to her in so many ways. The prelude, the beginning of good things.

She hummed, and his heart soared. "Okay. No clothes." She giggled.

He smirked. "Okay, now stay right here. I'll be back in a few minutes." He slid out of bed and walked out to the kitchen.

They needed this—time together to heal their wounded hearts. A weekend alone wouldn't fix everything they needed to sort out with Deborah being the black cloud hanging over their heads. He had to resolve that issue but was at a loss as to how since she was refusing a paternity test.

He prepared a tray of breakfast foods: sliced strawberries, cheeses, Danishes, coffee, and yogurt. Carrying the tray back to the bedroom, he shook the dark thoughts from his mind and thought only of the life he was making with Joci. Entering the bedroom, he said, "Breakfast in bed."

He slid in beside her and set the tray between them.

Joci's brows raised. "When did you find the time to pick this up?" She bit into a strawberry and closed her eyes as she hummed appreciation.

"On my way home last night. I left work a little early, so I could shop. Wait till you see what I got us for dinner tonight." He waggled his eyebrows.

"Wow, Jeremiah. You're going to spoil me rotten. Then I'm going to be awful to live with."

"I doubt that, but I want to spoil you."

She finished her Danish and noticed that Jeremiah wasn't eating anything. She frowned at him, her eyebrows dropping down. "What's wrong? Aren't you hungry?"

He turned slightly to face her, his eyes hungry. "When you're finished eating, I'll eat. Off of you."

Joci froze as what he said registered. Then a smile grew across her face, so big it nearly flattened him. "Really?"

He picked the tray off the bed and set it on the nightstand beside him. He grabbed a plate with a cut-up Danish on it and set it down next to Joci. "Roll over onto your tummy."

Joci rolled over, resting on her elbows. "Down, all the way. Lie flat on the bed, hands above your head."

She moved the pillow and did as he asked. He began placing little pieces of the cut-up Danish down the center of her back, on her butt cheeks, down the seam of her butt, tucking a few at the juncture of her thighs. He moved to straddle her legs and began kissing her shoulders. He kissed the back of her neck, licking and nipping. He moved down and snagged a piece of Danish and ate it while he continued pressing kisses down her back. He kissed and nibbled all the way down to her ass, nipping and biting as he did. The lower he got, the more aggressive his kissing became.

She hummed.

He ate the Danish from the seam of her ass, licking and dipping his tongue in as far as he could go. A sigh escaped Joci's lips as he continued this sweet assault on her body. Best meal ever.

After he had eaten the last bite from deep between her thighs, he lifted slightly, his voice husky, he said, "Roll over, baby. I'm still hungry."

She rolled over and the look in her beautiful gray eyes was a sight to behold. He began placing sliced strawberries across her chest, on her nipples, between her breasts, down the center of her tummy. As he got lower, his nostrils flared as he looked at her, "So fucking beautiful."

He placed two slices of strawberry over her clit and took a whole strawberry and gently placed it between the lips of her pussy. He leaned forward and kissed her lips, gently. He licked across her bottom lip and pulled it into his mouth and sucked on it. She slid her hands into his hair and held his head.

"Jeremiah. Holy shit, this is...it's great, but...I need you."

"You have me, Joci. Always." He kissed her neck, across the top of her chest, eating his strawberries and licking and nipping at her skin as he went. When he reached her nipples, he placed his mouth over her breast and sucked the strawberry and her nipple into his mouth. Sucking and pulling and teasing her until she began squirming.

"Don't knock my breakfast off, Joci."

She blew out a breath.

He did the same to her other breast as she moaned. He smiled against her skin as he continued to kiss and eat his way down her tummy. Finally, he made it to her clit. He ate the strawberry slices from her and sucked it into his mouth. He was still straddling her, so she couldn't open her legs and let him in. He sucked her clit into his mouth and flicked his tongue over it. Her skin became clammy and her breathing heavy as he pulled away and slid down her legs. He pulled her knees up and gently spread her legs open to him.

"Now this...this is a sight to behold." Before she could say anything, he dipped down and sucked the strawberry from her opening. As he chewed, he slid two fingers into her channel and smiled up at her. "Joci, you're so wet, baby. I think you like feeding me breakfast."

"Jeremiah...please." He chuckled as he swiped his tongue down the seam of her pussy and began moving his fingers. She whimpered, and he felt her grow wetter. He sucked her clit into his mouth, and she exploded.

He pulled his fingers out and thrust his tongue inside to taste her. He continued to lap at her until her orgasm subsided. He crawled back up her body as he said, "That was the best breakfast I've ever had. Now, dessert."

He swiftly plunged into her and began riding her hard. She slammed her hands into his hair and wrapped her legs around his waist and rode with him. Too soon, Jeremiah thrust hard into her, and she cried out his name as he released himself into her. He held himself inside of her for several moments, letting his heart slow. "Jesus. What you do to me is mind-blowing."

29

THE FUTURE

They spent the day lounging in bed, watching movies and talking. Around five o'clock, Jeremiah said, "Okay, we have a problem here."

She looked across the sofa where he was sitting and frowned. "We do?"

"Yeah. I wanted to grill dinner and forgot about that when I issued the no clothing rule. I'm not afraid for people to see me naked, but I don't want the neighbors calling the cops on me. So, just for dinner, we can wear clothes. Okay?"

Joci scrunched her face. "I don't know. A rule is a rule."

He jumped on her and began tickling her. "My rules, so I can change them."

She squirmed and squealed, "Okay. Okay."

He kissed her lightly on the lips and stood up. He reached his hand down for her and pulled her to him. "I loved spending the day with you."

She smiled up at him. "I loved spending the day with you, too. I've never, and I mean never, lounged around the house naked before. It's kind of...freeing. But, now I'm going to get dressed." He swatted her bare butt, and she giggled as she strode down the hall, happy again after last weekend.

An hour and a half later, Joci walked out of the bathroom, ready for dinner. She wore a white sundress, no shoes. Jeremiah was working at the kitchen counter on a salad. He whistled and walked over to her and spun her around.

"You look so beautiful."

She hugged him to her and kissed his temple.

"You look pretty hot yourself."

He was wearing light tan khaki shorts and a light green shirt, which made his eyes look even more amazing than usual.

"Ready?"

She nodded. He held out his arm for her with a grin on his face. She slipped her arm through his, and they walked out the patio doors where a table had been set with candles all around it and all over the patio. She was mesmerized by the flickering lights.

She looked up at Jeremiah, and her breath caught at the love in his eyes. Walking her to the table, he pulled out a chair for her to sit down. He sat across from her and poured them each a glass of champagne. He handed Joci her glass; then he picked up his.

"I want to toast. Here's to us, Joci. I love you."

He tapped his glass to hers.

"I love you, too."

They sipped their champagne and set their glasses down.

She smiled. "This reminds me of the first night we spent together. You had these candles all over the house. You said you didn't know anything about being romantic, but you do. Here you are doing it again."

He looked into her eyes. "Well, you'll have to pardon me for repeating a good move, but after the no clothing rule was lifted and I came out to start the grill, I realized how nice it is out here, so I thought we could come outside and play."

He got up and opened the grill, placed two lobster tails on a plate surrounded by vegetables and set it in the middle of the table. Joci looked up at him as a smile slid across her face. "Lobster? You truly spoil me."

"Good. I'm glad you feel spoiled."

They ate their meal and sipped their champagne in comfortable silence. A light breeze blew across the patio, making the candles flicker. Joci sighed loudly and sat back in her chair. "Bliss. This is bliss."

He stood and walked around the table to her. He bent down on one knee. "Joci. I'm so sorry things went dark on us last weekend. Please know that I would never willingly hurt you. Ever." He brushed the backs of his fingers along her cheek. "When I look at you, I see my future. I see my life with you and Gunnar, JT, and Ryder. I see us playing with children and grandchildren. I can't picture my life without you in it. I don't want a future without you. Joci, will you marry me?"

She stared into his eyes. She had no idea he had planned to propose this weekend. It hadn't occurred to her with everything else going on.

"Jeremiah." Her eyes filled with tears and she had to shallow the emotions riding in her throat. When she could speak, she softly said. "Yes, I'll marry you."

He jumped up and pulled her with him. He hugged her tight and kissed her lips. When they needed air, he gently set her on her feet and pulled a ring from his pocket. The candlelight flickered on the stone, making it dance and gleam. He slid it on her finger, and she gasped. A three-karat, princess-cut diamond solitaire—the most beautiful ring she'd ever seen in her life. Tears welled up in her eyes.

She whispered, "Jeremiah, it's so beautiful."

"Joci, I'm so happy right now I can barely catch my breath. I was so worried you would say no."

She glanced back up at him, then back to the sparkler on her hand. "A couple of weeks ago, I might have. But this past weekend, when Gunnar told you he loved you, and you told him you loved him back, something happened inside of me. For the first time, I felt like there was a future for us. You love my son, and it suddenly seemed real for me like nothing ever has. I was so afraid to think long-term about us because I didn't want my heart to get broken. I was holding back. But watching you and Gunnar with each other made me realize you were committed to our family. It isn't just sex—you love us both."

He wrapped her in his arms and held her for long moments.

"I've been in love with you for so damned long. It was never about sex. I met you, and I knew you were special. I worked with you this past year and fell in love with you more and more every day. In some ways, it was great you keeping me at arm's length. We got to know each other slowly, even though I would have given anything for it to be different. I wanted you so badly. Waiting was the hardest thing I've ever done."

She wiped her eyes with shaking fingers and giggled.

"I asked Gunnar's permission to marry you. The first time we spoke about it was last Friday. He asked me if I was going to marry you. After the fiasco with Deborah, I asked him again yesterday morning. I needed to make sure he was still okay with us."

"Thank you for that. I bet it meant a lot to him that you asked." She squeezed his hand.

"I told the boys I was asking you to marry me this weekend, too. They're excited as hell. They love you, Joci. Ryder especially. It's been a little harder for him, being so shy. But I'd watch him stare at the door on ride meeting nights, waiting for you. My heart swelled."

"I love them, too. You've raised amazing young men, Jeremiah."

"Yes, I did." He held her hand as he pulled her inside. Turning just inside the door, he scooped her up in his arms. "I want to get married soon. Can we get married in the fall? It'll be beautiful with the trees in full color."

She laughed at his request. "Clearly you have no idea about all the planning that needs to happen for a wedding. "

30

MILWAUKEE

They got busy calling family and friends. The boys were happy for them but weren't surprised. Jeremiah's parents were elated. So were his brothers and sisters-in-law. Joci called Jackie and Sandi too.

"Jackie, I'm going to need help planning a wedding for the end of September or early October."

"What year?" Her tone flat.

"This year."

Jackie burst out laughing. "He doesn't want much, does he?"

The remainder of the weekend they discussed the future and the upcoming rally to Milwaukee. They had quite a crew going. Most of the employees from the shop were coming along, as well as Jeremiah's brothers, Jackie and David, Jon, Sandi, and Connor.

At four, they were standing in front of the shop talking to the large group of rally riders. Spirits were high. Joci was thrilled that Jackie and Sandi were coming along, as well as all of Jeremiah's sisters-in-law. They might even get some wedding planning done.

"Okay, let's roll," Jeremiah yelled over all the talking. He walked over to Joci and gave her a hug and kiss. "Ride safe, baby."

"Same to you."

The rumble of a bike caused them both to turn. Chase pulled in with LuAnn on back. *Another weekend with LuAnn.* Joci looked over at her sister, and Jackie shook her head. Okay, at least she felt she had support. With her lips pulled into a thin line, Joci climbed on her bike. Jeremiah looked back at her and winked.

He mouthed, "I love you" and started his bike. Everyone else followed suit. Jeremiah nodded at JT and Gunnar to lead them out. He made sure she was riding alongside him the whole way down.

The weather was fantastic, high eighties and no wind. The scent of fresh cut hay from farms along the highway caused her to smile. Flowers along the road and in yards they passed brightly decorated their respective homes. Her heart felt happy and light. They met so many bikes as they rode. Thousands of people were headed their way to the rally and the excited butterflies in her stomach took flight each time they met a new group of riders. She'd been excited about the rally for months now.

Their group behaved and stayed together on the ride, something she appreciated and knew made Jeremiah very happy. They stopped for gas in Fond du Lac, which left them only around an hour to go before they reached their hotel. They gassed up, talked a little, and got back on the road. Surprisingly, LuAnn was quiet. Fine by Joci; she was sick of the drama.

They checked into their hotel rooms around seven p.m., the sun still high in the sky. When their bikes were unpacked, they checked into their rooms, then headed back down to the parking lot to discuss what they would do from here.

≈

"So, listen up. Joci and I, and anyone who wants to join us are heading down to the Summerfest grounds. We'll grab a bite to eat there and listen to music. There are several bands around the grounds, with many different types of music, something for everyone. If you want to go a different direction, just be careful, please. There are thousands of people pulling in that aren't from around here and may not be looking at where they're going." He probably didn't have to sound like everyone's dad, but if something happened he'd feel guilty. So, better safe than sorry.

Walking from the parking lot to the grounds, he looked back at Joci and smiled as he pointed to an old truck parked in the lot. As soon as she saw it, her smile grew wide.

He walked back to where she stood. "Do you want to go and take a closer look?"

"Oh, I really would if no one else minds. Do you mind?"

"Of course, I don't." He chuckled.

They headed in that direction and continued looking at bikes along the way.

He watched her eyes as she looked at the truck. Her face was so expressive; her smile lit up his whole world. He would do anything in his power to make sure she was happy. "Hey, maybe we should find the owner of the orange truck from the Veterans Ride and see if we can use it for the wedding. Would you like that, Joci?"

She looked at him and squealed, her eyes bright. "I would love that! Really?" She clapped her hands together, her smile bigger than the sun.

He chuckled. "Of course. I'd love that, too."

Chatter turned to the wedding. Nothing had been decided, except the date—September twenty-eighth—which was only five weeks away. He was happy to stay out of most of the planning. His head began to spin when the women started talking about all of the meals, drinks, flowers, location. It was more than he cared about. He just wanted to get married. All that other stuff could sit for all he cared.

Staci's voice rose in a gasp, and he looked over at her. Her eyes were wide when they turned on him. "You don't have anything planned? Are you kidding?"

"We've been so busy with everything else we haven't had time for wedding planning," he said a bit defensively.

"When we get back home, we'll get everyone together to make plans," Joci said, trying to soothe ruffled feathers.

Jackie asked, "Do you think you should wait until next year, so we have time to pull everything together?"

"No," he said, emphatically.

He leaned down and kissed Joci's forehead. She smiled, looked at Jackie and shrugged. He grinned; she was coming around to the idea of a fall wedding. She had worried out loud to him at first.

The next morning, the Rolling Thunder group met for breakfast at the hotel. The local dealerships all had bands, vendors, food, and events going on. The whole gang decided to check out the action. At the first dealership, they pulled some picnic tables together to sit and listen to music for a couple of hours.

Later in the afternoon, the group headed to another dealership. The band played fabulous rock and roll, despite the heat. The crowd shifted as people came and went. He was proud of his group for sticking together and acting responsibly.

By seven that night, he was tired. "Okay, listen up." He looked around to see who they were missing: Frog, Chase, LuAnn, and Ryder. "I'd like to head back to the hotel. If you want to stay, that's great, but Joci and I..." he locked eyes with hers. She smiled and nodded. "...are taking off. Not sure what we'll do this evening, but I think the hotel has a band playing."

JT looked around, then addressed his dad. "We have a few missing right now. Can you hang around until they come back? I'll text Ryder now."

"Yeah. No problem." He leaned down close to Joci's ear, breathed in the scent of her perfume and closed his eyes; even now, it stirred him. "You okay with waiting a few more minutes?"

"Of course. The music is good, and I'm with my fiancé." She giggled, "Honestly at my age you'd think that word wouldn't send a thrill through me, but it does. Every time."

He kissed her lips softly. "I know exactly what you mean. But the word wife is so much better."

She giggled again; he could listen to that sound over and over.

Half an hour later, Frog and Ryder came walking back, practically carrying LuAnn. Ryder walked over to Jeremiah, Dayton, JT, Gunnar, and Joci. His brows were furrowed and his lips pressed into a thin line. "LuAnn's wasted and Chase left."

"What the fuck happened?" Jeremiah asked.

Ryder looked a little sheepishly at Joci. "She kept on whining and whining about how much she loves you and can't stand the fact that you and Joci are getting married. She continued to drink, and Chase got pissed and left. He has feelings for her."

Jeremiah pulled Joci close and squeezed her shoulders as everyone else floated over. He looked over at LuAnn. She could barely stand up, let alone hang on to anyone on the back of a bike. His jaw tightened, and his body grew rigid. Too good to be true.

"Let's go," he barked out. He grabbed Joci's hand and started toward the bikes.

Frog grew tired of trying to get LuAnn to walk, so he threw her over his shoulder and carried her back to the bikes like a sack of potatoes. When they reached the bikes, he set LuAnn down, and she promptly slumped to the ground. Janice leaned down and tried talking to her to see if she was even conscious. With darkness starting to set in, they needed to figure out what to do with a very inebriated LuAnn.

Jeremiah's voice was tight. "She'll have to ride on back with me. I'm the only one who has a seat she won't fall out of."

Joci sucked in a breath. "Wait! LuAnn just spent the afternoon whining about how much she loves you and doesn't want us to get married, and now you want to put her on the back of your bike and take her back to the hotel? Jeremiah, you'd better be joking." She planted her hands on her hips and widened her stance.

He turned to look at her. "I don't know what else to do, Joci."

Joci stepped back. "Don't do it, Jeremiah. I mean it. Don't."

"Joci, what else am I supposed to do? We have to do the right thing here."

"Fuck the right thing. Why do I always have to do the right thing? Do the right thing for Keith. Do the right thing for LuAnn. They both have done nothing but shit on me. Now, after a whole afternoon of her professing her love for you, I'm the one who has to do the right thing?"

He scrubbed his hands through his hair. "I don't know what else to do, honey."

She backed up and walked toward her bike. She threw her hands up. "I have nothing else to say."

"Joci, baby, please talk to me about this."

"No fucking way, Jeremiah. I've had enough of this bitch and your catering to her. Enjoy your fucking ride back."

Joci jumped on her bike. Jackie came over and stood next to Joci. "Joci, please don't take off like this. Ride with the group. We need to be safe out there."

"Fuck," Jeremiah swore. "Get that piece of shit on my bike." He looked at Frog and Ryder.

Joci nodded slightly but refused to watch the guys load a wasted LuAnn onto the back of Jeremiah's bike. There was something sacred about allowing someone on the back of your bike. Thinking about LuAnn getting her way and riding with Jeremiah stuck in Joci's throat like a dry rag.

Jeremiah took a deep breath. "Someone stay alongside and behind me and make sure it doesn't look like she's going to fall off. When we get back to the hotel, Frog, you take her upstairs to your room and tell Chase to get his ass downstairs, immediately."

Frog nodded and got on his bike. Everyone else saddled up, and they were off.

Jeremiah's gut was in turmoil. He was so frustrated by this mess. They had been having a fantastic weekend. Now, once again, because of LuAnn, here they were. Joci was right—why did she constantly have to be the one to do right by everyone else? How was he going to fix this? The first thing he was going to do is kick Chase's ass for leaving LuAnn. The new motto at the shop is going to be: *You bring her, you take care of her.*

On the ride back to the hotel, LuAnn stirred a couple of times. Jeremiah could feel her moving around on the back. He looked over at Gunnar, who was riding alongside him and Gunnar shook his head. When they were within two miles from the hotel, LuAnn woke up and slid her arms around Jeremiah's waist.

"I knew you would take care of me. I think you love me." She rested her head on his shoulder.

He stiffened. He didn't want this bitch touching him, let alone hanging on to him like she was. She started moving her hands down to his crotch, and he grabbed her hand and squeezed hard.

"Don't!" was all he would say.

"Oh Dog, don't be mad at me. I love you so much," she slurred.

He didn't say anything. He wasn't going to have this conversation with her when she was drunk, but they were going to have a serious talk. He had already told her that he was with Joci and that he wouldn't tolerate LuAnn making snide comments, jumping at him and kissing him, and trying to pull the little shenanigans she had been. Apparently, he needed to be clearer. He didn't tell her not to get wasted and expect everyone else to take care of her.

Pulling into the parking lot at the hotel, she moved off her bike and started pulling her things out of her bags. Jackie and Sandi walked over to her and waited patiently for her to be ready to talk to them.

"There's a swing out back nestled in the landscaping. Would you like to come and swing with us?" Jackie asked hopefully.

She turned and saw them standing there, and her shoulders slumped. The tears started flowing like crazy. Jackie walked forward and hugged her little sister. Then she whispered softly in Joci's ear, "It's okay, baby. It'll all be fine. Come and sit with us, please."

Joci nodded, and they all walked toward the swing at the back of the hotel. Jackie looked back at David, who nodded at her and started walking upstairs to their room.

As soon as the girls reached the swing, Joci turned and flopped down in the middle. Jackie and Sandi each took a seat next to her. They sat for a long time, slowly rocking back and forth. The silence and rocking were a balm to her frazzled nerves. This past few weeks, just when it seemed things are going well, another bomb dropped in her lap. She took a deep breath and scraped her hands through her hair.

"I'm so tired of all of this. I'm tired of LuAnn and her bullshit. I'm tired of Jeremiah letting her pull it. I'm tired of worrying about Deborah, and I'm just plain tired."

"Honey, you've handled all this bullshit like a champion. What LuAnn's been pulling and keeps pulling is absolute bullshit. Jeremiah is going to have to deal with it and her, finally. I think you got your point across by telling him off today. You wouldn't have hit him harder if you had kicked him in the balls." Jackie smiled.

Joci giggled and rubbed under her eyes.

Sandi chuckled. "You should have seen the look on his face, Joci. It was a look I've never seen on anyone before. Like he was pissed and hurt and confused at the same time... It was kind of funny."

Jackie laughed, and then Joci couldn't help herself; she started laughing, too.

She laid her head back against the swing and closed her eyes. She was exhausted.

31

ENOUGH

As soon as Jeremiah pulled into the parking lot, he dropped the kickstand down. Frog immediately hopped off his bike and reached over to grab LuAnn. She pushed him away, but he pulled again. She wrapped her arms around Jeremiah tighter.

"Get your fucking hands off me this minute." His jaw was so tight he had a hard time getting the words out.

"But, Dog. I love you," LuAnn whined.

He pried her hands away from his waist and jumped off his bike. He looked at Frog and Frog nodded. Jeremiah turned and saw Joci walking to the back of the hotel with Jackie and Sandi.

He started walking toward Joci and her girls. Gunnar took a breath. "Dad, let them talk a little while. It'll help her."

He stopped and looked at him. His eyes welled with unshed tears. He took the few steps forward and hugged Gunnar tight. They held each other for a long time. Jeremiah swallowed around the lump in his throat several times.

"That is the best thing you could ever call me, son."

Gunnar squeezed tighter. When Gunnar pulled away from Jeremiah, he reached forward and opened his arms for all the boys.

"Thanks, I needed this right now. I'm scared shitless if you know what I mean. Joci's a little thing, but she scares the shit out of me."

The boys' laughter succeeded in alleviating some of his anxiety. He wasn't kidding; he was scared shitless. He had no idea what he would say or how he would make this better, but he was going to try.

"Um, Dog. You wanted to see me?" Chase's voice was soft.

Jeremiah turned around and looked at him. Jabbing a finger into his chest, he clipped, "From this point forward, if you bring her, you take care of her. I'm not going to ever, ever do that again; you got it?"

Chase stammered, but Jeremiah put his hand up to stop him.

"Tomorrow morning, you and LuAnn are leaving. I don't want to see you for the rest of the weekend. Next week at work, I don't want to see you. If you see me, you better turn and walk the other way. If you ever pull a bullshit stunt like this again, you will be out on your ass, got it?"

Chase nodded but didn't say anything. *Smart boy.* He waited for a beat, then backed up a few steps, turned and walked back to the hotel.

Watching Chase leave, he took a deep breath. Now, he needed to talk to Joci. He nodded at the boys and turned to walk to the back of the hotel. When he got back there, the swing was empty, but still moving slightly, so they must have just left.

He turned and walked back to the hotel. He took the stairs to give himself a bit more time. He knew he was stalling slightly, but he still didn't have the words. He unlocked the door to their room and heard the shower. Thank God she was in here. He tried the bathroom door, but it was locked. She never locked the door, so he was still in trouble. *Shit.* He kicked his boots off and pulled a beer from the refrigerator. He sat in the armchair by the window and waited for her to finish.

He had swallowed his whole beer before the bathroom door opened. She stepped out in yoga pants and a t-shirt. When she rounded the corner, she stopped in her tracks and stared at him. She took a deep breath and continued walking to the dresser, where she set her toiletry bag down.

He watched her, trying to gauge her mood.

"Can we talk?" he whispered.

She shook her head no. She didn't look at him, just turned and walked over to the bed and climbed in. She pulled the covers up to her chin and closed her eyes.

He stood and padded to the bed, leaned over her, softly crooning in her ear. "Honey, I don't want to go to bed mad at each other. Please, let's talk."

She opened her eyes and looked at him. She waited.

He took a deep breath. "I'm sorry. You were right about you always having to suck it up and do the right thing. I hadn't thought about it before, but you're right. I've asked an awful lot of you these past few months. I can see how tired you've been lately, and I realize how all of this is affecting you. The fact that I own Rolling Thunder makes me responsible for my employees. Even though this isn't an employee event, I still always feel responsible." He took another breath while raking his hands through his hair. "But that being said, I could have done things differently. I should have had Frog or someone take my bike with LuAnn, and I could have taken his. I was pissed and not thinking clearly. I'm sorry."

She didn't say anything. He waited for a little while and then lay down next to her and wrapped his arms around her. "I'm not leaving you, and I'm not letting you leave me. You may as well talk to me."

She sighed. "I just can't do it anymore, Jeremiah. I just can't. I thought I could, knowing why she's around. But..."

He slid an arm behind her head and pulled her tightly to his body. He kissed her temple and the top of her head.

"You won't have to, baby. I told Chase to leave with LuAnn in the morning. The new rule at the shop is 'if you bring her, you take care of her.'"

Joci snorted and tried to pull away. He held on to her. His brows furrowed. "Hey, what?"

"You're such a fucking man. Big, fucking deal your big 'If you bring her, you take care of her' bullshit." She used finger quotes. "She's still going to be working there, with you, every day. She'll just be trying to hatch out another plan of attack. She spent the whole fucking afternoon whining about how much she loves you and doesn't want us to get married. How fucking dense are you?"

She pulled away and slipped out of bed. She walked over to the window and stared out at the night sky. He rubbed his forehead and stared at the ceiling. After a few moments, she walked over and climbed back in bed. She turned her back to Jeremiah and closed her eyes.

Jeremiah rubbed his eyes and got up to get undressed. He jumped in the shower to wash this day away. He quietly padded back to bed and slipped in without waking Joci. He wasn't going to get a lot of sleep tonight. Fucking LuAnn.

The next morning, Joci woke up hot and sweaty. She couldn't breathe. She opened her eyes and looked around. She was in the hotel. She looked down, and Jeremiah was practically lying on top of her. His head was on her chest; his arm wrapped around her, and he was lying on one of her legs. She tried to take a deep breath and was able to get half a breath in. She closed her eyes and attempted to clear her head. She hadn't wanted to go to bed mad last night. She was just so damn sick of this shit. This morning, her eyes felt all puffy and swollen from crying in the shower and lack of sleep. Great.

She had to pee, but when she struggled to get up, his arm wrapped around her tighter. She pulled an arm from under the covers and pushed gently on his shoulder.

"Jeremiah, please get off me. I've got to pee."

He squeezed her tighter and mumbled. She pushed at him again, and he opened his eyes.

"I have to pee," she said, slightly exasperated.

"Sorry, babe." He rolled over onto his back.

She rolled out of bed and went to the bathroom. A short while later, she walked into the room and started pulling clothes out of her bag to wear for the day.

"We need to talk, Joci."

Her shoulders sagged. He was right, but she wasn't going to tell him that. She slowly turned to look at him.

"Okay," she whispered.

He pushed himself up against the headboard and patted the mattress. "Come sit here with me."

She walked over and perched herself on the edge of the mattress, her back rigid. He leaned forward and wrapped his arms around her and pulled her back against him.

"I'm sorry. About everything. If I could change it, I would. I can't. It won't happen again. What more can I say to you?"

She closed her eyes. "Okay. Is that it?"

He let out a snort. "'Okay, is that it?' You don't have anything else?"

"I simply don't know what to say, Jeremiah. I feel like we've been down this road, but nothing seems to change. I've just had enough of it. LuAnn pulls crap. You apologize and tell me it won't happen again. It happens again, you apologize and tell me it won't happen again and on and on. What do you want me to say?"

She could feel his chest rise with the induction of air and slowly release. He squeezed her and placed his head on hers. They sat quietly. Not knowing what else to say, he chuckled. "Gunnar called me Dad last night."

Joci closed her eyes and let a tear fall. Gunnar. It wasn't just about her and Jeremiah; Gunnar was also involved. Ryder and JT, too. Shit.

She wiped her eyes and started to pull away. She pushed her hands through her hair and held them there.

"I just can't do this anymore. I've reached my limit. I don't want a life of constantly having to deal with a woman who thinks she's in love with my husband. Especially when my husband won't do anything to change the situation. It's really that simple."

"Please give me another chance, Joci. I mean it. LuAnn will be made to learn that she can never bother us again."

"Why, Jeremiah? Why do you keep putting me through this?"

She got up and began dressing, put on a little makeup and threw a bandana on her head to protect her forehead.

He lifted himself out of bed and dressed as well. As soon as they were ready to go down for breakfast, Jeremiah walked up to her and hugged her.

"I love you, Joci. I love you crazy. This hurts so badly right now. This distance. I hate it."

"I don't know what else to do, Jeremiah. I keep getting hurt. I don't want to hurt anymore."

He tightened his arms around her and stood with her in his arms, swaying back and forth. She heard him swallow a lump in his throat and take a deep breath.

"I won't hurt you anymore. I'm so fucking sorry I ever did. You're the last person I want to hurt, ever."

She stepped back and looked into his eyes, not as green today as usual, and filled with sadness. With a heavy sigh, she said, "I know you don't mean to. But you do."

She turned and walked out the door. He followed her down the hall to the elevator. They rode in silence to the lobby and walked to the room where the continental breakfast was served without saying a word to one another. The others were all sitting around tables pushed together, talking and laughing. The only people missing were Chase and LuAnn.

Joci walked over to the table. "Have you eaten yet?"

"No, we were waiting for you two," Sandi said.

"Okay, well, let's eat, shall we?" She walked to the buffet and began filling her plate. She wasn't hungry at all, but she was going to do her best not to ruin anyone else's weekend.

While they ate, the conversation went on around them. She nodded once in a while and pushed her food around her plate. They talked about where they wanted to go today, and plans were made to head downtown to party on the streets.

Once downtown, they found spots to park along the street and found a nice little bar where a local band was playing. They pulled tables together and listened to the music for a while. Joci found a seat and plopped down. Jackie and Sandi sat on either side of her, and they were quiet for a long time.

"Joci, honey, are you okay? You look so sad and lost. You're breaking my heart," Sandi said, rubbing Joci's shoulder.

"I don't know, Sandi. I just can't snap out of this funk. I feel broken or something. It's like it was the last straw for me. I'm so sick of dealing with LuAnn and her bullshit. It drives me crazy that Jeremiah hangs on to her for some ridiculous, perceived obligation. He would never tolerate the same situation in the reverse. And on top of her, we have Deborah still hanging out there, too."

Jackie put her arm around Joci and sat there for a while. Staci, Erin, and Angie came over and joined them. Joci was grateful for the camaraderie and change in topic.

After they had eaten dinner, they went back to the hotel and sat by the pool. The boys entertained them most of the evening by playing a mean game of water volleyball and then acting silly when a group of hot babes started paying attention to them.

The Rolling Thunder group headed home late Monday morning. The weekend had been a turning point in their relationship. Which way the turns went, Joci wasn't sure.

"I love you, Jeremiah, but we have to do something about this. I know some of my frustration with this situation is from my past. That said, I also know it isn't healthy for you to feel this responsibility to LuAnn when all she wants is what's best for her, not you."

He pulled her in for a hug and kneaded his fingers into her tense shoulders. For the first time in a day and a half, she let Jeremiah kiss her. God, she missed his touch, his lips, his warmth. She couldn't help the tears that leaked out of her eyes. She hoped this was the last time she had to spend time away from this man—emotionally and physically.

32

THE VIDEO

"My bike isn't running right, Jeremiah. It was sputtering a lot yesterday. Do you think Gunnar can take a look at it? Probably the plugs, but I'm not sure. Since we won't be riding this weekend because of the staff party, this will be a good week to have it at the shop. Do you mind?" Joci asked.

"Of course, I don't mind. One of the perks of owning a bike shop is you can have your bike worked on anytime you want."

She chuckled. "I don't own a bike shop; I just sleep with a man who does."

"Once we're married, you'll be part owner of a bike shop."

She leaned back and looked into his eyes, her brows furrowed. "Jeremiah, I don't want to take anything away from JT and Ryder. They are the rightful owners after you."

"It's my business. They're fine. But while we're on the subject, what do you think of me adopting Gunnar? He would legally be my son. He could change his name if he wanted, and for all intents and purposes, be entitled to anything JT and Ryder were entitled to. I want us all to be a family, with the same last name. What do you think?" He had been thinking about this for a while, but it seemed silly until he'd spoken to his attorney and found out you can adopt anyone you want. As long as they are competent to make the decision on their own.

"I think it's amazing! I don't know what he'll say." She wrapped her arms around his shoulders. "Thank you, Jeremiah."

He squeezed her tight, and she felt perfect against him. She was soft and pliable and molded to him in a way that soothed him. "No need to thank me," he whispered. "I've been thinking about it for a while, but the other night, when he called me Dad, it cemented the whole idea."

Clicking the *save* button, Joci smiled and sat back in her desk chair. The two songs she chose to add to the slide show were *Roll Me Away* by Bob Seger and *Let's Ride* by Kid Rock. Her slideshow turned out amazing. She tried to get pictures of everyone who had participated in the Veteran's Ride, especially the men and women who worked at Rolling Thunder. She was stunned at the number of pictures of her and Jeremiah. She wasn't even aware of the photographers around them. There were a few pictures of LuAnn, most of them crude, with her sticking her tongue out or holding up her breasts or pulling her shirt down to show maximum cleavage. She really had zero class.

Nevertheless, there were two pictures of LuAnn, which had been taken when she wasn't aware of the photographer, and they were nice photos of her, so Joci used them. One of the two was a picture of LuAnn looking over the crowd at Jeremiah with what she would call longing in her eyes. Joci cropped out Jeremiah and just showed

LuAnn looking off into space over the crowd. She didn't want Jeremiah and LuAnn in the same picture if she could help it. Yes, it was immature, but so what?

There were great pictures of the boys and Jeremiah's family. There was a cool picture of all of them standing at Rolling Thunder together before the ride. Her favorite picture, though, was the one she used to end the video. It was of Joci leaning against a wall at The Barn. Jeremiah had his left forearm leaning against the wall above her head. His right hand was on her chin, and they were staring into each other's eyes. Both had soft smiles on their face. It was a beautiful, sweet picture of them. When she looked back at it now, she could see the love in her eyes for him. The look in Jeremiah's eyes reflected the same thing. She couldn't wait for him to see it.

She pulled the thumb drive from her computer and called Sandi.

"Hey, there. I'm leaving for the restaurant now. Do you need directions?"

"No, I looked it up on the Internet. I'll be walking out the door in five. See you then."

Joci put the thumb drive into the computer they would be using to show the video on a large screen in the back party room tomorrow night.

"I want you to be honest with me, Sandi. I haven't shown this to anyone yet. I'm so nervous. I want it to be perfect for him."

"Okay. Start it up; I'm ready to critique." She reached for her iced tea and sat back.

When it was over, Sandi's eyes were bright with moisture. "Wow, Joci...that's beautiful."

Joci smiled at her and grabbed her best friend's hand.

"It's going to be a surprise for tomorrow night. He doesn't even know I have the pictures."

Sandi's eyes got big, and she raised her eyebrows. "Oh. My. God. I would love to see the look on his face when he sees this. It's really fantastic, Joci. You're great at all this stuff. Now let's talk about the wedding."

They planned and talked all through lunch. Just four weeks away now. According to the *Farmer's Almanac*, the trees were going to turn colors early this year because there had been a drought last year.

"After lunch, I'm going shopping for a dress for tomorrow night. Do you want to join me? We can do some preliminary wedding shopping for you and Jackie, too."

That evening, Joci and Jeremiah stayed home. Lying on the sofa, wrapped up in each other, listening to music, they heard someone in the garage around eight o'clock, and Jeremiah jumped up. "Stay put until I know what's going on." She smiled at her alpha fiancé, but worry creased her brow.

Soon she heard JT, Ryder, and Gunnar laughing. And apparently, they had been drinking.

"You boys scared the shit out of us," she heard Jeremiah admonish. "Come on in. Mom's in the living room."

They sat around for the remainder of the evening. She and Jeremiah giggled at the boys' goofy antics. Then, she made them spend the night because they didn't want them driving after they had been drinking.

As she slipped into bed, she giggled. "You know, they're all cute together. I can see why the girls were paying attention to them in Milwaukee. What a handsome group of boys we have."

He chuckled. "Yeah. Good boys, too. They work hard, they're polite, smart, and loving. We're lucky, yeah?"

"Yeah." She sighed.

33

THE EMPLOYEE APPRECIATION PARTY

Joci closed her eyes as the warm water caressed her body. She took a long nap again today. Seemed to be a habit lately. Her body was achy, and she'd not felt like herself for a few days. All this bullshit in her life was messing with her physically as well as emotionally. She needed to get herself in a place where she could handle the baggage that seemed to follow Jeremiah. One thing she knew for sure, however; he was worth it. Her thoughts and the water washing away her worries caused her to moan as relief swirled down the drain.

"I love listening to you moan, but usually, I'm inside of you somewhere."

She opened her eyes and smiled at the strong, virile man standing before her. A smile parted her lips. "I vaguely remember something like that."

"Vaguely?" He stepped farther into the shower and wrapped his hands around hers. Slowly, he lifted her hands and kissed the back of each before pulling them up over her head. He pushed his body against hers and backed her up against the shower wall. His eyes blazed with sexual tension as he hooked her hands over the ledge in the wall above her head. "Keep your hands up there on the ledge. Don't let go. Okay?"

Looking into those green eyes she loved so much, she whispered, "Yeah."

He bowed his head and lightly pressed his lips to hers. His palms slid down her body, stopping at her breasts. He gently squeezed, then his hands continued their descent. His palms gliding easily over her wet skin, he cupped her ass and pulled her into his erection.

"You are my everything, Jocelyn James. You are the air I breathe. You're the food that sustains me. You're the liquid that quenches me. My heart beats for you."

She whispered, "Jeremiah."

Sliding his right palm along her thigh, he lifted her leg and pulled it around his waist.

"Don't let go, baby." Feather-light kisses rained down across Joci's forehead, her cheeks, and across her lips as his rigid length slid inside of her.

"Oh."

Holding her bottom in his hands, he began driving into her.

She hung on to the ledge with all her might. She wanted nothing more than to wrap her arms around his shoulders and hold him tightly to her. Her orgasm built like a tsunami, rolling in fast and furious. The leg she stood on began to shake.

"Jeremiah...please."

"Come for me, Joci. Jesus, you feel so fucking good. Your tight little pussy feels like heaven," he husked out.

She cried out his name as her orgasm crashed through her body. When he spoke to her like that, she reacted instinctively.

"I'm with you, babe." Two more thrusts and he poured himself into her.

An hour later, Joci walked out of the bedroom and into the living room. He was sitting on the sofa, but her perfume tickled his nostrils, and the sound of her dress swishing caught his attention. He looked over his laptop and froze. His eyes slowly traveled the length of her body. A low whistle slipped from his lips.

"I say we stay in tonight. I'm not going to be able to think of anything but getting you out of that dress."

She smiled as he continued to stare at the slinky, red dress with a short front and a long back, a black leather yoke, and keyholes above her perfect breasts. It hugged her curves like it was painted on. The black strappy heels showed off her ankle tattoo and shaped her legs to perfection. If he hadn't just made love to her, he'd already be ripping it from her shapely body as he pulled it over her stunning head.

She caught his eyes with hers and smirked. "I'll be thinking about taking your clothes off, as well. I love what's underneath so much more."

He set his laptop aside and rose from the sofa. He took her hand and placed it on his swollen cock.

"See what you do to me?"

He ground against her as she rubbed up and down. She moved her hand and pressed her pussy against him. He groaned and slid his hand down to her ass, held her close and kissed her temple.

"God, I love you crazy, baby."

Joci giggled. "I love you crazy, too."

A while later, they stood around greeting the employees and their spouses or significant others. Jeremiah had worried about this event all week. LuAnn had been better at work, sufficiently chastised for her drunken behavior, but, as usual, that never lasted long. She liked making a scene, and this would be the perfect venue for a scene.

As soon as he thought it, she walked in with Chase. She wore a very tight black dress that barely covered her ass and ridiculously high heels that she seemed to be having a hard time walking in. Her hair was some blonde frenzied, big, wild mess, her eyes glassy, and she stumbled just a bit. Chase took her hand, and they made their way to him and Joci. LuAnn leaned in to give him a kiss on the cheek and, of course, to rub her breasts against his arm. He stepped back quickly and put his arm around Joci and nodded at Chase. Understanding the silent message, Chase quickly steered LuAnn to a group by the bar. Jeremiah looked down at Joci and whispered, "Sorry."

Joci looked into his eyes, her mouth tightly pinched closed and simply raised her brows. The manager approached them and mentioned they could go into the private room and be seated.

After their group had been seated, he stood and cleared his throat. "I'd like to thank each one of you for all of your hard work this year. Our company is growing, and your continued help and outstanding customer service will keep it that way." He reached into his shirt pocket and pulled out envelopes. He walked around the room and handed each employee a bonus and said 'thank you.' He enjoyed being able to make them smile and show his appreciation. At the shop, he was always occupied with what he needed to accomplish next. One of the things he needed to do better was show appreciation. He returned to his table and Joci stood. He enjoyed watching her sensuous body rise from the chair. It conjured up memories of them together and gave him ideas for more activities in the future.

Her full lips parted in a soft smile, the light kissing the shine in the most seductive way. "I have a little surprise."

He looked into her eyes, enjoying the gray tones shining back at him. Turning to his employees, he said, "Joci has a little surprise, and I'm a bit nervous because I have no idea what it could be." She giggled, kissed his cheek, and stepped to the computer. She tapped a few keys, and a slideshow popped up on the screen. His eyes followed her as she stepped to the light switch and dimmed the lights. The sway in her dress tantalized him. The cheers and whistles caught his attention as he turned to the screen and saw Rolling Thunder Motorcycles, Inc. splashed across the screen. Then the strains of Kid Rock filled the room, and his heart beat with the timing of the music. She resumed her position next to him and took his hand, but he was mesmerized by the photographs floating across the screen. The room filled with cheers and whistles as pictures of themselves or people they knew flashed onto the screen.

He leaned forward at one point and whispered in her ear, "I love it, Joci. It's the perfect surprise."

She looked at him and kissed his cheek. A few moments later, the last picture showed on the screen. He did a quick intake of breath. Everyone grew quiet in the room, and someone got up and turned the lights back up. She turned her head toward him, but the tears in his eyes made her waver and glimmer. He reached forward and hugged her tight.

"Thank you, baby. That was beyond anything I have words for."

She smiled at him, and the room broke out in applause. She blushed, her beautiful cheeks tinted pink as she ducked her head. He leaned forward and kissed her lips, which brought on a few whistles.

LuAnn was sullen after the video had played. She pushed her food around and ordered two drinks from the waitress as she brought their dinners out. Joci felt sorry for her but honestly didn't know how to reach out. She wouldn't carry on a conversation to save her life. So, the hope of ever handing her an olive branch was long gone.

After dinner, they headed out to the bar for a drink and then she and Jeremiah would go home. As nice as the evening had been, she was still a bit uneasy with LuAnn around. Even though nothing had happened other than her trying to kiss Jeremiah, it still made Joci quite uncomfortable.

She excused herself and quickly walked to the bathroom. Her nausea reared up again, and the last few steps were at a trot. She threw up once and heard the door open. She closed her eyes and waited for the sickness to end. As soon as she was able, she walked out of her stall. LuAnn sat on the counter waiting for her. She sucked in a deep breath and waited for what LuAnn had to say while she rinsed her mouth and washed her hands.

"You know he's going to get tired of you, right? I mean, look at you. Sure, you're kind of pretty, but he likes this." She gestured at herself and her body. "If you've seen Barbara, you know I'm right. I've been giving him some time to get over you, but you're a pesky little gnat, hanging on so tight. So, I thought I would just let you know that Jeremiah will get married, but it will be to me, not a little plain Jane like you."

Joci smirked. She didn't know why she thought that was funny, but she did. Then, she couldn't help herself and burst out laughing.

As soon as she composed herself, she said, "I could almost take you seriously except for the fact that you can barely speak because you're wasted. But also, what you don't see is, while I might be plain compared to you, I'm original. You're a carbon copy of the loose, classless piece of biker trash who got herself knocked up and took off after having her twins. She rolls through town once a year begging for money and then leaves. Jeremiah doesn't look for her, wait for her, or in any way want anything to do with her when she comes to town. What you did to yourself was make him steer clear of you because of your silly little-girl imitation of what he doesn't want."

She turned and walked out the bathroom door with a smile on her face. Damn that felt good.

She walked back to the bar where Jeremiah and the boys were talking. She caught his eye as she walked back. A soft smile appeared on her face when she looked at her stunning man. Big and strong, lean muscle and the best part, an enormous heart. Her shoulders felt like a weight had been lifted. As she sidled up next to him, he snaked his arm around her and leaned down to kiss her forehead. He pulled back and looked at her with his brows furrowed.

"Honey, you're very warm. Are you okay? Did LuAnn…"

"I'm okay. I don't want to cut your night short. If I start feeling too bad, I'll go take a nap in the truck."

"No, you won't. I did what I needed to do here tonight, Joci. There's nothing more important than making sure you're okay. Let's go."

They said their goodbyes to everyone, and Joci hugged the boys. When she hugged Gunnar, he looked at her with alarm in his eyes.

"Mom?"

Jeremiah spoke before she could, "She's not feeling well, Gunnar. I'm taking her home. We'll talk to you tomorrow."

He hugged each of the boys and took her hand.

As soon as they got in the truck, she began shivering. The air outside just felt so cool to her skin. The drive home wasn't far, but the rocking in the truck made her stomach lurch. "Baby, pull over, please. Real fast."

He jerked the truck to the edge of the road; she had her hand on the door handle and opened it before they came to a complete stop. She tripped stepping out and caught herself, then kneeled down and emptied anything that may have been left in her stomach. Jeremiah ran around the truck and knelt alongside her. He rubbed her back as she retched, even though her stomach was already empty. She shivered.

He reached into the truck, grabbed a couple of tissues, and handed them to her. After she had finished wiping her mouth, he picked her up and set her down in the truck.

"Joci, I'm taking you to the hospital."

"No. I just want to go home. I must have the flu."

"Joci, people don't get the flu in August."

Joci leaned her head back against the seat. "There isn't actually a flu season." She couldn't even argue about this.

He leaned over and grabbed her hand. "Honey. Let me take you to the hospital. I just want to make sure you're okay."

"I'm just tired and need something like tea in my tummy. I'll be fine tomorrow."

She closed her eyes and leaned her head back, but the motion of the truck made her tummy roll. Opening her eyes, she watched the road and noticed Jeremiah frequently looking at her. She rested her hand on her tummy when it felt queasy and by shear will, she made it home without vomiting again.

She made her way to the bedroom with Jeremiah's assistance. He gently took her dress and shoes off. He left her underwear on and tucked her under the covers. "Relax, sweetheart. I'll make you some tea." She smiled weakly and closed her eyes.

J eremiah pulled his phone from his pocket and tapped his mom's number as he walked to the kitchen. "Mom, sorry, I know it's late. I don't know what to do. Joci's sick. What should I do for her?"

"Tell me what's going on with her."

"She's been warm all day. She took a two-hour nap this afternoon and then some aspirin before we went to the employee dinner. She threw up while we were there and again on the way home. She's hot now and so pale, and she's sweating and shivering at the same time."

"Make her some weak tea and bring her some crackers, and I'll be there in a few minutes."

"Mom, you don't have to come over, it's late."

"Nonsense, I'm just sitting here in my chair watching your father nod off anyway. We're so close, it won't take me long to get there. Go make tea."

He took the tea and some crackers into the bedroom. "Joci, honey, can you sit up?"

She nodded and pushed herself up. He pulled one of his t-shirts out of the drawer. "Mom is coming over to help. Let's cover you up."

She weakly pulled the t-shirt over her head and leaned back against the headboard. He handed her the cup of tea, and she put it to her lips and took a little sip. He gave her a cracker and sat alongside her on the bed. He plumped a pillow and tucked it behind her. He rubbed his hand along her leg, trying to soothe both of them. He watched as she took a couple of nibbles of the cracker and leaned her head against the pillow.

A light knock at the door signaled his mom's arrival. He squeezed Joci's hand. "Mom's here. I'll be right back."

He opened the door to see his mom, her hair a bit mussed, shorts and shirt slightly wrinkled, but a smile on her face.

He stood back for her to walk into the house. He motioned to the bedroom and they began walking to Joci.

"So glad to see you. I've never been good with sickness and I guess I just wanted some reassurance." He said a bit sheepishly as they stepped through the door.

"How are you doing, dear?" Emily asked Joci softly.

She opened her eyes and smiled at Emily. "I'm sorry you felt you had to come over. I just think I have the flu."

"How long have you felt bad, Joci?" Emily asked solicitously.

She shrugged. "Off and on, a couple of weeks. Today was the worst."

Emily looked at Jeremiah with her brows raised. He shook his head. She had never said anything to him. While they had been at the rally in Milwaukee, she had been tired and didn't eat much, but that could have been the bullshit with LuAnn.

"Baby, why didn't you tell me you weren't feeling well?"

"I didn't want to worry you. Just when I thought I should go to the doctor, I started feeling better, so I didn't go. Today is the worst. Before this, I've just been tired and a little warm. I thought it had to do with him switching my birth control."

Emily walked over and touched Joci's forehead. "You're not very warm now. Are you starting to feel better?"

Joci nodded and took a deep breath. "A little. Still a little queasy."

Emily looked at Joci and then at Jeremiah.

"Joci, could you be pregnant?"

Her eyes flew open. She shook her head slowly.

"Are you sure, honey?"

"When I switched birth control they did a pregnancy test."

"How long ago was that?" Emily asked.

Joci slowly opened her eyes. "About five weeks or so."

Emily cocked her head to the side and watched Joci's eyes. She smiled softly at Joci, "Get some rest, dear." Emily kissed Joci's forehead, took her empty tea cup and walked out of the bedroom.

Jeremiah followed her to the kitchen. He watched his mom refill the pan with water and set it on the stove. She pulled tea bags from the pantry and added some ginger to the water. He sat at the breakfast bar not saying anything.

Emily turned and glanced at him. She smiled as she mixed her tea. When she had a moment, she looked at him and sighed.

"Any other symptoms?"

He shook his head. "She's been emotional. I thought she was just working too hard."

Emily smiled and nodded.

"You think she's pregnant, don't you, Mom?"

"Well, I'm not a doctor, but I do think it's a possibility. She needs to go to the doctor and make sure one way or the other. If she isn't pregnant, there's something going on for her to be so tired and now sick. Usually, the flu only lasts a day or two at most. The change in her birth control could be messing with her."

Jeremiah locked eyes with his mom. They stared at each other for a few moments, and then a broad smile spread across his face.

"I want her to be pregnant, Mom. I want it bad. Since I first met her, I just knew she was the one for me."

Emily smiled at him. "Don't get too excited until we know for sure."

He nodded. She was right, of course. But, he couldn't help himself. He wanted to have babies with Joci.

Emily finished making her tea, and he followed his mom as she carried it to Joci. She was still sitting up, her head dipping into the pillow, her eyes closed. Emily walked around the bed and set the tea on the bedside table and touched Joci's forehead.

"I brought you some ginger tea. It'll help calm your tummy. Will you try it?"

She nodded and Emily handed her the tea and sat on the edge of the bed. Joci scooted over to make room for her. She sipped the tea and smiled. "This is good."

Jeremiah smiled as he watched his mom tend to Joci. The two most important women in his life were a sight to behold. His heart fluttered and felt so full. He reclined on the bed, propping himself up with his arm.

Emily folded her hands in her lap. "You need to go to the doctor, Joci. If you're pregnant, you'll need to take proper care of yourself and the baby. If you're not pregnant, there might be something else wrong." She looked over at him and smiled. "Jeremiah worries about you like crazy. We all do."

Joci smiled. "I don't want to worry anyone. I'm on birth control because I haven't had a regular period in a few years. It's common in my family."

Emily patted her hand. They sat quietly for a few moments. Then Emily said, "Jeremiah won't leave you, Joci. He loves you. He told me that very thing a while ago."

A tear silently slid down Joci's cheek. He reached over and took her small hand in his and squeezed. She set her cup on the bedside table and swiped under her eye. She looked into his eyes and smiled. He saw her swallow a couple of times, and his heart constricted.

Watching her struggle with her emotions was difficult, but she needed to work through this.

Emily broke the silence. "Okay, if you're feeling better, I'll go home. But, promise me you'll call the doctor first thing Monday morning."

Joci blinked and looked at Emily. "Yes, actually, my stomach feels much better. Your tea is a miracle cure. And I promise to call my doctor."

Emily smiled again, looked over at Jeremiah and winked.

"You need to get some sleep. Goodnight, honey. Call if you need anything."

She stood and walked around the bed. Jeremiah winked at Joci and got up to walk his mom to her car. When she got in her car, he leaned down and kissed her temple.

"Thanks, Mom. I appreciate you coming over to help. I was scared shitless. I didn't know what to do."

Emily smiled at him. "You may have a few months to get it right if she's pregnant. I left more tea in the fridge. If her tummy starts acting up again, just warm some up for her. I'll see you tomorrow."

He closed her door and walked back into the house. He felt happier than the day Joci agreed to marry him. He turned off the lights in the kitchen and living room and softly walked to the bedroom. She was sound asleep, hugging his pillow. He put his hand on his chest. If his heart got any bigger, there wouldn't be any more room in there. He undressed and quietly climbed into bed. He slid over to Joci and pulled her into his arms. He laid his hand on her belly and closed his eyes.

34

ONE STEP BACK

Joci woke up feeling better. She had slept through the night without waking. She felt rested and had no fever, but Jeremiah wasn't in bed with her. She looked at the clock—it was nine o'clock. Holy crap, she had slept late. She got out of bed and went to the bathroom before walking out to find Jeremiah. As she walked down the hall, she heard Emily and Thomas' voices. Good thing she had thrown some clothes on—that could've been embarrassing.

"Good morning," Emily said.

"Good morning," Joci echoed.

Jeremiah jumped up and hugged her. He cradled her head against his chest. She loved the strong, solid beat of his heart. Of course, the sinewy muscle and strong arms wrapped around her were amazing, too. After a few moments, he pulled back and cradled her head in his strong hands. He looked into her eyes.

"Are you feeling better?"

"Yes, actually, I feel pretty good this morning. It feels like my fever is gone."

She smiled at him, and he leaned down and kissed her gently on the lips.

"Sit down, baby. Do you want coffee or more tea?"

Joci smiled. "The coffee smells good."

Joci looked at Thomas. "Good morning."

"Morning, Joci. Glad you're feeling better."

She sat at the table. "What brings you guys here this morning?"

Emily patted Joci's hand. "We were on our way home from church and wanted to see how you were doing."

Joci smiled warmly. "Thank you, Emily."

After making comfortable small talk and assuring themselves that Joci was okay, Emily and Thomas left. As soon as the door closed, Jeremiah picked her up in his arms. She squealed and wrapped her arms around his neck to hang on. "I'm sorry I ruined your night last night, Jeremiah."

He walked with Joci in his arms into the living room, reclined on the sofa with her lying on top of him.

"I told you—everything I needed to do, I did last night. You didn't ruin anything. And I didn't properly thank you for the video. You did a fabulous job putting that together, Joci. Blew me away. I want a copy of the last picture for my office and my computer and my phone."

She giggled. "Is that all?" She sat up and tucked her hair behind her ears. "They're your pictures. I have the video and the pictures on a zip drive for you to load on your computer. Let me know what else you need."

Then she took a deep breath before confessing, "I have to tell you, I cropped a few of them to make them look nicer. And I cropped you out of one because LuAnn was looking at you like she wanted to eat you."

He sat up and cradled her in his arms. He took a deep, shaky breath.

"You have nothing to worry about with her, honey. I saw her follow you to the bathroom. What did she say to you?"

"Just more of the same. You'll get sick of me. I'm plain compared to her, won't be able to keep you happy for long. The usual."

He took a deep breath and let it out slow. "It's not true. None of it."

"I know." Joci sighed. "It hit me last night while I was talking to her." She turned to face him. "I know. It's freeing."

He squeezed her and kissed her temple.

"Do you think you might be pregnant, Joci?"

She took a deep breath.

"Joci. We need to talk about this. Do you think you might be?"

"I don't know, Jeremiah. I've never missed a day of my birth control pills. This is so different than when I was pregnant with Gunnar. I had morning sickness until about the end of my third month. I was tired but not so emotional. My periods have been different, which is why I went back to the doctor. She just thought I had been on the same pills for too long and that sometimes that happens. She switched my prescription. I thought she did a pregnancy test. I'll call tomorrow and find out."

"If you're pregnant, I don't want to wait until the end of September to get married. I want to do it right away. I don't want to risk anything happening."

"Jeremiah, let's wait until we know for sure."

"I want to be your husband. I want you to be my wife. Dammit, I don't want to wait. And if you're carrying my child, I want it legal that you're both mine. And I don't want you to have too many stresses while you're expecting. It should be a happy time for you to grow a happy, healthy baby. I can't even process all the emotions. I have to marry you, because if I don't, my life will be empty and meaningless."

She turned in his arms and straddled him. Her tummy growled, and she giggled.

"Let's go and get you two something to eat," he said.

"Jeremiah. Don't get too emotionally attached until we know for sure. I would hate for you to be let down."

"Too late. I already feel it. Mom does, too. That's why they stopped by this morning. You know the ginger tea she made you last night was the same tea she made all of her daughters-in-law when they were pregnant. It's helped them with their morning, or evening, sickness. It has to be, Joci. All of your symptoms lead right to you carrying my child."

"At my age, having a baby will be difficult. Losing the weight after-ward will be impossible. Jeremiah, you don't understand the toll this will take on me and us. We're at a point in our lives where our kids are self-sufficient. We can come and go as we want when we want. With a baby, we'll be starting all over again."

"Yes. We'll start over together. We have my sisters-in-law, my mom, Jackie, all of the nieces and nephews, and three strong, loving boys. Plenty of babysitters and help."

He pressed his lips to hers. "You worry too much, Joci. I'll love you no matter what. The little things, a few pounds, being tired—those are all meaningless in the whole scheme of things. What matters is that we're together. I've never been happier." He chuckled. "If you need me to gain a few pounds to make you feel better, you got it."

She burst out laughing.

35

TRAGEDY

Monday morning, Joci called her doctor. The nurse took the information and said one of them would call her back. She tried to work, but her mind kept tossing things around. She called Jackie and talked to her about her symptoms along with her thoughts and her fears.

Jackie laughed at her. "Joci, it's different this time. You're in a great relationship, and you're getting married. It isn't like last time. Try and enjoy this time for you two. You didn't get to when you were pregnant for Gunnar. If Jeremiah wants to get married right away, we'll all pull together and get everything done for you. To be honest, I'm pretty excited to be an aunt again. What does Gunnar think about having a little brother or sister?"

"I haven't said anything to him yet. I don't want to until I know for sure. He called this morning to tell me my bike is ready, and it was hard not to say anything. I'm waiting for Doctor Wan to call back. I'm on pins and needles."

They finished their conversation, and Joci tried getting a few things done around the house. Jeremiah called three times to see if Dr. Wan had called back. He was nervous and excited. She hoped he wouldn't be disappointed.

Finally, at three thirty, Dr. Wan's office called and asked if Joci could come in for a pregnancy test. She called Jackie to come with her then Jackie could drop her by the shop so she could bring her bike home. Nothing could clear Joci's head like a great motorcycle ride.

After the doctor visit, the two sisters were headed to the shop. The ride seemed endless, she was nervous about the whole thing. Jackie chattered all the way about everything, which gave Joci a headache.

Pulling up to the back door, Jackie turned to her sister. "Call me when you get home. I want to hear all about it."

"I will. Wish me luck." Without waiting, she turned and walked into the shop.

She said hello to Janice and Angel and walked up the stairs to Jeremiah's office. She opened the door to see LuAnn sitting in a chair in Jeremiah's office, crying. "Well, look, Joci's here to gloat," she spat.

"What are you talking about?" Joci looked at Jeremiah, her brows furrowed.

Jeremiah stood. "LuAnn is just leaving. For good."

Joci held his eyes with hers for several heartbeats.

"You two piss me the fuck off," LuAnn exclaimed as she rammed Joci with her shoulder and stormed out the door.

"You fired her?"

"Yes. You've had enough; I've had enough. If we're going to have a baby, I don't want her anywhere near you. Speaking…"

A loud crash sounded down in the shop, and somebody screamed. Jeremiah ran to the door, Joci following close behind. As they landed on the bottom step, Jeremiah ran across the shop just as LuAnn grabbed one of the bikes on the floor and pushed it over.

"Goddammit, LuAnn, what the fuck are you doing? Get out. Get the fuck out now," he roared.

LuAnn flipped him off and headed to the shelves and began throwing the stock onto the floor. She picked up an oil can and flung it toward Joci. She had moved out of the way before it hit her. Jeremiah grabbed LuAnn's arm before she threw another can of oil, getting hit in the arm himself. He pulled both of her hands behind her back. Everyone else in the shop scrambled around.

LuAnn screamed, while leveling her eyes at Joci. "You fucking bitch; you ruined everything."

She kicked back at Jeremiah, who held her hands tighter while trying to dodge her feet.

"I hate you, you bitch. I hate you! I hope you die," she shrieked.

Jeremiah yelled to Joci, "Go home, okay? I'll be there as soon as I finish here. I don't want you to get hurt."

Jeremiah's gaze held Joci's. LuAnn's heel landed on the top of Jeremiah's shin, and he bellowed and hopped to the other foot, "Fuck, LuAnn. Knock it off. "

Chase ran from the back to see what was happening. "LuAnn, what the fuck? Cool it, for crying out loud."

"This fucker fired me. Can you fucking believe that? His girlfriend is jealous as hell, so he fires ME!" she yelled and squirmed trying to get away from Jeremiah.

Chase walked closer, never taking his eyes off of LuAnn. "LuAnn, honey, please calm down." His hands held out in front of him, imploring her to calm down.

Deacon had been getting ready to leave for home, but he rushed in and picked up the bike LuAnn had pushed to the floor. He turned towards Jeremiah. "Deac, get Joci out of here."

Jeremiah's eyes flicked over to Joci. He jerked his head toward the back door; she nodded and backed out of the shop toward the garage. Deacon followed her out.

Joci glanced back and saw JT and Ryder each grab one of LuAnn's arms to help Jeremiah.

As she zipped up her jacket, her hands shook. She had never seen anyone lose it like that.

"You okay, Joci?"

"Yeah. That was disturbing, though."

"Yeah. She's one fucked-up bitch. Can you ride?"

She took a deep breath. "Yeah. That'll help me clear my head."

They saddled up, and Deacon nodded his head to her. She rolled on the throttle and headed toward the front of the building, Deacon following her out.

Several minutes later, two police officers came into the shop and relieved JT and Ryder of their burden. Jeremiah, out of breath, walked over to where the boys stood when his phone rang. He tapped the answer icon and barked into the phone. "What?"

"Dog, you have to come now. Joci's been in an accident," Deacon huffed, out of breath.

His heart sank. "Where?" His voice cracked, his head began to spin, and the contents of his stomach began to rebel against him.

"We're at the end of the road by Benson's Bend. Fuck, Jeremiah, Joci flew into the corner. She didn't even hit the brakes. She slammed into the tree at the end of the road. It's bad. You've got to get here."

Jeremiah took off toward his truck, yelling at the boys. "We have to go. Joci's bike went down." He shoved his phone into his pocket as he headed to the door. Speaking to the cops, "I'll come to the station later and deal with this." He glanced at JT and Ryder, and they waved him on.

Gunnar jumped into the truck with him and raced down the road. They arrived as the ambulance sped toward them. Jeremiah's heart sank when he saw the wreckage. Joci's bike was in pieces all over the road. There was a huge mark in the tree about three feet off the ground where she must have flown into it. He groaned as the fear and panic threatened to choke his oxygen off.

They jumped out of the truck and ran over to where Deacon crouched down alongside Joci in the ditch. She was lying on the ground, not moving. He was holding her hand with tears in his eyes. Deacon looked up when he saw Jeremiah and Gunnar. He scooted away to allow them room.

Deacon shook as he spoke. "I'm sorry. So sorry, Dog...Gunnar. I was behind her, but she came into the corner. It looked like she hadn't slowed enough. She's a good driver, so I didn't worry. She wasn't speeding. But she never hit the brakes. I don't know why. She tried turning on it, but she couldn't get low enough. She flew off the corner into the air and hit the tree. When I got here, she wasn't conscious. I couldn't feel a heartbeat. I was shaking so bad. I called 911, and then I called you. I'm so sorry." He babbled.

Jeremiah leaned down close to Joci's head. "Baby, please don't leave me. Joci, baby, please wake up. Please." He touched her forehead. There was blood everywhere. Her right arm was laying at a weird angle. The right side of her head was bloody and raw where it had hit something—the tree or the road. Her jeans were ripped open at the hip, and there was blood running from the tear.

The rescue workers moved in with equipment. "Excuse us, sir; we need to get to the patient."

"Joci. Her name is Joci," Jeremiah croaked. His lip trembled as he tried not to think the worst.

"Are you her husband?"

"Yes."

In his mind, he certainly was. The rest was a technicality. Gunnar knelt with Jeremiah. Tears streamed down his face. The EMTs quickly put a brace around her neck. They promptly assessed all of her injuries, vitals, pupils.

"Is she allergic to anything?"

Gunnar and Jeremiah both shook their heads no.

"She's pregnant," Jeremiah hissed. The EMTs, Gunnar, and Deacon all looked at Jeremiah with stunned expressions.

"She might be. I'm not sure yet."

The rescue workers started shouting about her possible pregnancy and what they could and couldn't give her. They loaded her onto a gurney and ran with her to the ambulance. Jeremiah wanted to come with her, but they said they couldn't allow him in. They shut the door on his protests and headed out, lights flashing and sirens wailing.

"Deacon, take care of having Joci's bike brought to the shop after the police have finished with it. Lock it up." Jeremiah and Gunnar jumped in the truck and flew to the hospital.

He watched from the corner of his eye as Gunnar pulled his phone from his pocket. His hands shook, but he swiped and found the number he was looking for.

"Aunt Jackie." His voice cracked and he swallowed. "Mom's been in a bad accident. We're..." A strangled cry escaped as he ran his hand down his face. "Dad and I are on our way to the hospital." He sniffed loudly, his voice still shaky, he asked, "Can you come?"

Jeremiah watched as Gunnar listened to his aunt. He struggled to stay sane enough to follow the ambulance. He flew along the road, navigating the corners a bit faster than he should, but not wanting to lose sight of the vehicle carrying Joci to help.

Gunnar's splintered voice broke into his thoughts. "I know. Dad just said, well, he said he wasn't sure."

Gunnar tapped his phone and dropped it into his lap. He glanced at Jeremiah. "What the fuck?"

Jeremiah flicked his gaze quickly at Gunnar and then back to the road. "Well, you know about LuAnn. I fired her. She didn't take it well. We thought that your mom might be pregnant on Saturday night. She went to see the doctor this afternoon. She was coming to tell me the results. We didn't get the chance to talk about it." His eyes welled with tears. He blinked rapidly to keep them from spilling over. He ran his thumb across one eye, then the other. He let out a deep breath as he continued to navigate the road and calm his fears.

"Aunt Jackie said she was pregnant," Gunnar said in a quiet voice.

They sat in silence for a few minutes. Jeremiah sucked in a breath, "Is."

Gunnar slowly turned his head toward Jeremiah, his brows furrowed. "What?"

Jeremiah's voice softened. "Is. She *is* pregnant. She isn't dying, and neither is our baby."

Gunnar turned his head and watched out the window of the truck.

J eremiah, Gunnar, and the others waited in the emergency room visitor's area for what seemed like hours. Every time a nurse, orderly, hospital worker, even someone from housekeeping, walked into the room, Jeremiah hit them with questions. All they knew so far was that Joci had been taken into surgery. Her right arm was broken. Her right shoulder and collarbone were broken. Her hip was damaged but not broken. Apparently, the way she hit the tree had been a "good" way, if there was one.

The bike had taken the brunt of the hit. She'd been leaning the bike away from the corner to try and make it. That meant the bottom of the bike probably hit first. The seat hit before her hip, which helped. Her head slammed into the tree, giving her a concussion. It could have been worse. Right now, Joci was in surgery to repair her arm, her collarbone, and her shoulder. No one could tell them if she would miscarry. The doctor told them that their priority had to be Joci, but they would do whatever they could not to harm the baby.

36

HEALING

During the several hours Jeremiah and Gunnar had been anxiously waiting, other family members had gathered at the hospital. He looked around, grateful for their support as they all waited to hear about Joci. She had so many people who wanted her to get well. God needed to hear their prayers. Thomas had led them in prayer when he and Emily had arrived; Jeremiah kept praying.

Finally, the doctor walked into the visitor's waiting room. "Mr. Sheppard?"

"Yes." Jeremiah stood. Gunnar followed.

The doctor walked over to them and shook their hands. "I'm Dr. Jerzek."

Dr. Jerzek motioned for them to sit down. He took a seat right in front of Jeremiah.

"Ms. James has come through surgery fine. We found no internal injuries. We put four pins in her right arm. Her shoulder was broken, but we were able to set it. Her collarbone was broken and has been set. Her hip was not broken; however, her skin was split open in several places. We stitched her up. She has deep bruising, which is going to cause her quite a bit of pain for a while. She should be out of recovery in about an hour then she will be taken to a room close to the nurse's station so they can watch her."

"What about the baby?" Jeremiah asked in a hoarse whisper.

Dr. Jerzek looked closely at Jeremiah. "We'll have to wait and see. She's badly injured, Mr. Sheppard. With her trauma and her age, there's a good chance she will miscarry. Only time will tell."

Jeremiah dropped his head in his hands and prayed again that both Joci and the baby would be okay. They just had to be.

Gunnar wiped at his eyes. He got up and walked over to Jackie.

She reached out her arms and pulled her nephew in for a hug.

"She has to be okay, Aunt Jackie." Jackie and David both swiped at the tears in their eyes.

"She will be, baby. She will be. We all know how strong she is."

They sat and waited until a nurse finally walked in to let them know Joci had been taken to a private room. The nurse led them down the hall and stepped into Joci's room. At Jeremiah's huge intake of breath, the nurse explained, "She's pale because she's just come out of surgery and hasn't been moving around. Her legs are elevated because of the baby. She woke up for a few minutes in recovery and was able to answer simple questions. She'll be going in and out for a while due to the anesthesia and her body trying to heal itself. The best thing that can happen right now is that she gets plenty of rest."

Jeremiah nodded. He stepped into the room and quietly pulled a chair to the side of the bed, turning it, so he faced Joci. He bent down so he could kiss her forehead. He touched her hair and kissed her lips lightly.

"I love you, Joci. Please know that."

He sat in the chair next to her and watched. She was pale everywhere except under her eyes. There, it was bluish gray where her lashes rested on her cheeks. The right side of her face was swollen, and a few cuts and bruises were visible on her right temple and cheek. Her right arm and shoulder were thickly bandaged. They looked huge compared to her slight frame. The rest of her looked small. So incredibly small and fragile. Three different IVs led into one line in her arm. He reached over and laid his hand on her belly. Then he rested his head on the edge of the bed, next to her left hand.

Gunnar walked over and touched Joci on the forehead. He touched her hair and whispered, "Mom, I love you. We all do. We'll be here as long as you need us."

Everyone else took turns stopping in and watching and processing what happened. They counted ceiling tiles, floor tiles, and even the beeps from the heart monitor. Jeremiah listened to the seconds ticking by on the clock until he thought his jaw would break from the tightness.

The nurse walked in and saw them sitting and watching Joci. No one was talking. She checked the IVs and felt Joci's forehead to gauge her temperature.

"Ms. James, can you wake up please?" she asked her a few times in a kind voice. The nurse rubbed Joci's left arm and moved her left hand up and down to get her to wake up. Finally, the nurse put her hand on the top of Joci's head to gently rub the uninjured side of her face. "Ms. James, can you wake up for me?"

J oci opened her eyes and closed them right away.

"That's it. Take your time and open your eyes," said the nurse.

She tried again. She tried to lift her hand to shield her eyes. The nurse leaned forward and adjusted the overhead light.

"Here. Now give it a try. I turned the lights down."

She slowly opened her eyes again, and was able to get them to stay open. She looked at the nurse, trying to comprehend what was going on.

"Your family is here for you. But before you can visit, I need to take your temperature."

The nurse stuck a thermometer in Joci's mouth and took her pulse. Joci looked around the room, seeing her family there, and her brow furrowed until it dawned on her. She'd had an accident. She gasped and sobbed at the same time. She immediately reached for her tummy. She found a hand already there—Jeremiah's. The nurse quickly pulled the thermometer out of her mouth so she wouldn't bite into it. Tears spilled out of her eyes.

"Baby?"

The nurse smiled at her and touched her cheek. "You're still pregnant. We're watching you closely. Have faith, sugar."

The nurse grabbed a tissue off the table next to the bed and handed it to Joci. She took it in her left hand and wiped at her tears. The nurse turned and walked out of the room. Joci looked down and saw Jeremiah sitting next to her. He was still, very still. The tears threatened again as she choked out, "I'm so sorry." Her lip trembled.

Jeremiah leaned forward. "Shh, honey don't make it worse. Try and relax, okay?"

"Mom, how do you feel?"

Joci turned her head toward Gunnar. She weakly smiled at her son.

"Well, I guess I've been better."

"Mom, what happened? Deacon said you didn't brake."

She looked at Gunnar and her eyes filled with confusion.

"I did. I tried. The brakes didn't work. There wasn't anything there."

Gunnar sucked in a deep breath. "I checked everything myself. I took it for a test drive before I called you to tell you it was all good. I swear it."

Joci's swallowed. "I believe you, baby."

Jeremiah eyed Gunnar. "When?"

Gunnar frowned. "I don't know. I worked on it Thursday morning. It ran great. Ryder took it for a ride, too, because we were adjusting the belt and he helped me with it."

Gunnar looked at Ryder, and he nodded, "I did. It was fine. After we had adjusted the belt, I took it for a ride and everything was working great."

Joci sobbed. She looked at Jeremiah. "I'm not lying. The brakes didn't work. They were squishy, both hand and foot. There wasn't anything there. I tried to lean into the corner, but I was too fast for it."

Jeremiah touched Joci's hair and tenderly stroked her head. He stood up, leaned down and kissed her forehead.

"Don't cry, honey. We'll figure it out. I'll be right back." He walked out of the room. Everyone watched him leave—his jaw tight, his back ramrod straight.

Jackie came to Joci's side and rubbed her left shoulder. "Joci, honey, don't get too worked up. It's not good for you or the baby."

She glanced at Jackie and nodded. "I didn't try to hurt the baby, Jackie. I didn't."

The room was quiet, each person processing his or her thoughts on the matter.

"Honey, I know you didn't. I know you never would. Jeremiah knows that, too."

Joci calmed herself as much as she could. She placed her hand on her belly again. Everything just had to be okay. She was doing her best to remember everything that had happened, but she was still groggy.

I n the hospital hallway, Jeremiah's mind whirled. *Fuck! Joci's bike had been sitting at the shop for about a week. Anyone could have done something to it. Something could have fallen against it and damaged it. She said she didn't try to hurt herself or the baby.* He believed her. Pulling out his cell phone, Jeremiah called Deacon. "Deacon, where are you?"

"I just got home. How's Joci?"

"She just came around. She said she tried her brakes, but there wasn't anything there. Are you sure you didn't see her brake lights?"

Deacon let out a breath. "I'm positive, Dog. I kept waiting for her brake lights, knowing she was heading into the corner."

"Where's her bike now?"

"I have it at the shop, in the back storeroom. The door is locked, just like you asked."

Fuck! Jeremiah walked back into Joci's room. He looked around the room and found his brother, Tommy. "I need to speak with you."

Tommy looked at Erin, stood up, and walked into the hall with Jeremiah. When he stepped into the hallway, he and Jeremiah walked a few feet away from the door.

"I just got off the phone with Deacon. He has Joci's bike locked in our back storeroom at the shop. He swears Joci never hit the brakes."

Tommy rubbed his forehead. "I'm starting to think the worst here. I watched her face. I don't think she's lying."

Jeremiah looked like he wanted to hit something. "Of course, she isn't lying. Fuck, Tommy!"

"Hey. Ease up, man. We have to look at everything. I'll call my chief. We'll have officers go over and look at it with a mechanic. Gunnar shouldn't be the mechanic."

Jeremiah was enraged "Gunnar would never do anything to hurt Joci."

"Hey, I didn't mean to make it sound that way. But if he was the last one to work on the bike, he shouldn't be the mechanic to work with the police on the findings. We need an official report."

Jeremiah let out a breath. "Find out when someone can get over there. I'll call Frog."

Within a couple of hours, two officers, Frog, Tommy, and Jeremiah were at the shop looking at Joci's bike. It was a mess. Jeremiah's stomach turned looking at the wreckage. The largest part of her bike was standing up on a trailer. The handlebars were twisted and scratched. One of the mirrors listed on the side of the handlebar, the other mirror lay on the floor of the trailer. The parts that had flown off when she crashed had also been placed on the floor of the trailer, scattered here and there. Some pieces had been broken into tiny pieces. Others were scuffed from sliding across the road or from the impact. They were so damn lucky she hadn't been killed.

"Fuck!" Frog swore.

"What?" Jeremiah quickly asked.

Frog pulled his hands out of the bike wreckage. "Her brake lines were cut."

Jeremiah looked at Frog with disbelief on his face. One of the officers looked at the bike where Frog had been working.

"Show me why you think that," he said.

Frog reached his hand into the mangled mess and pointed to the brake lines. The officer shined his flashlight into the area. Cuts could clearly be seen across the top of each line. Frog cleared his throat.

"When the tops of the lines are cut, the fluid leaks out slowly and drips down the top of the lines. It falls into the bike somewhere and doesn't leave a big mess on the floor."

The officer then pointed with his index finger, following the path the brake lines took and showed them spots on the bike frame and other parts where older, hardened brake fluid had settled.

Frog went on. "It has likely been slowly leaking over the past few days. We had the bike here at the shop and moved it around out of the way a couple of times. No one started it up to move it; we just pushed it around. But we would have used the brakes to stop it when we got it in place. Each time the brakes were pushed, fluid leaked out and dripped down the lines. The brakes would have worked for a little while."

Jeremiah's stunned face found his brother's. His voice cracked. "Someone cut her brake lines?" Everyone here loved Joci—except LuAnn. She had been enraged the day she found out Jeremiah and Joci had gotten engaged. "Deacon told me he sent LuAnn home from work the day our engagement was announced because she was throwing things around and being a bitch to everyone. Then the Milwaukee fiasco."

Tommy cleared his throat. "You have a video here in the shop, don't you, bro?"

Jeremiah slowly nodded his head. "I can take you to my office and show you the backup."

Numb was the only word Jeremiah could come up with to explain his feelings right now. It had to have been LuAnn. No one else there hated Joci. LuAnn wouldn't have known that Joci was pregnant. No one suspected except his parents, Jackie, Joci, and himself.

Tommy, Jeremiah, and one of the officers walked into Jeremiah's office. He unlocked the closet where the computer system was housed and showed it to them.

The officer whistled. "Wow, you have a great system here."

"My brother Dayton is a computer geek. He set me up with this system a couple of years ago. An employee was stealing from me. It backs up to the cloud, so I don't have to change tapes. It saves perpetually."

Jeremiah walked over to his computer, booted it up and logged onto the Internet, then called up his cloud surveillance backup for the past week. Based on Gunnar and Ryder's conversation earlier, Jeremiah pulled up the backup video beginning with last Thursday. They all sat and watched in silence. Jeremiah focused on Joci's bike.

Based on the time stamp, it had been around 8:30 in the morning when Gunnar had taken off on the bike to test it. He and Ryder then looked at it. Ryder took off the belt cover and loosened up the tension bolts on the back tire, then adjusted the tension on the belt. He tightened the bolts on the back tire and put the belt cover back on. Ryder left the shop on the bike. When he returned, they set the bike over to the side. Around eleven thirty, the guys in the shop all went to lunch.

At eleven fifty-one, LuAnn walked up to the bike. She looked around, leaned in with a knife and sliced the lines. She stood up with a smirk on her face and walked away.

Jeremiah sucked in a breath. "Goddammit, I'll kill that fucking bitch."

Tommy put a hand on Jeremiah's shoulder. "Easy, bro, don't make threats."

They went back and re-watched the recording. The officer wrote down the times on the video.

"We'll need access to this video," he said.

Jeremiah nodded. He couldn't look away. That smirk on LuAnn's face enraged him. How fucking dare she? She hurt the one person in the world he loved the most. She had hurt Joci time and again. Why couldn't he have seen it? Now, he might lose his baby—*their* baby—because of that fucking bitch.

Tommy put his hand on Jeremiah's shoulder. "Watching it over and over isn't going to help, Jeremiah."

Jeremiah scrubbed his face with his hands. He stood up and paced around the room a few times.

"How could I not see her escalating to this point? Jesus, I'm just as guilty for allowing that bitch to be within a thousand feet of Joci. God, I should have seen it."

Jeremiah broke down. He had been holding back for so many hours. He was worried about Joci and the baby. He was worried about everything. He dropped into a chair, put his head in his hands and cried.

Tommy walked over to Jeremiah and put his hand on his shoulders.

"It's not your fault, Jeremiah. You can't think you're responsible for the actions of anyone else. LuAnn is responsible for herself."

The other officer got on his phone and called the station. "Is LuAnn Mason still in custody? Then we'll need a warrant for her arrest. I have a video of her cutting the brake lines on Joci James' bike, which resulted in Ms. James being injured in an accident earlier today."

37

BABY

Joci laid back in her hospital bed. Everyone had left a couple of hours ago. According to the clock on the wall, it was near two in the morning. A nurse had just left her room and would be coming back with pain medication.

Her shoulder and arm hurt. The throbbing wouldn't stop, and she couldn't sleep with the pain. She didn't want to put the baby in any more danger than she already had. The nurse told her that if she couldn't get any rest because of the pain, that was worse for the baby than taking a mild pain reliever. After that, she finally agreed to take something.

She hadn't heard from Jeremiah since he left the hospital hours ago. Her heart hurt more than her arm and shoulder. On top of that, she might lose the baby. She broke down in a hard cry. It hurt, but then, everything hurt right now.

"Hey. Aww, baby, don't cry. I'm here now," Jeremiah's voice cracked.

She looked up at him and tried to compose herself. "I don't want to lose the baby. I don't."

"I know you don't, honey. Please don't cry."

He leaned down and laid his forehead against hers. He placed his hand on her belly and lightly rubbed back and forth, then leaned down and kissed the place where his baby rested, fighting to live. Joci sobbed.

The nurse walked in with a syringe and injected something into Joci's IV line. In a calm voice, she said, "Okay, sweetheart, you have to settle down. This should help calm you. I promise it won't hurt the baby. You're doing well, you know. It's been several hours now, and you're still pregnant. Every hour that passes means a better chance for your baby. Try and stay positive; okay, honey?"

Joci nodded and calmed as the medication hit her veins and made her feel drowsy. She closed her eyes and drifted off to sleep. The nurse looked at Jeremiah and raised her brows.

∾

"I'm staying," was all he said.

The nurse nodded, then turned and left the room. He pulled the recliner next to the bed and sat down, holding Joci's hand in his. His mind reeled over the day's events, and he prayed that God wouldn't let them get pregnant only to take the baby away. That would be worse than never being able to have another baby. Having one so close, only to be lost, would be unbearable. He drifted off to sleep about a half hour later, still holding her hand.

He jerked awake at the sound of a nurse coming in to check on Joci but he didn't open his eyes all the way. He looked to see who was in the room and then closed his eyes again. He listened to the nurse monitor the IVs. She checked Joci's vitals, straightened the blankets on the bed, and left. Then he realized that someone, at some time during the night, had put a blanket over him. He fell quickly asleep.

Joci awoke to see Jeremiah sleeping alongside her bed. She took in his beautiful face and saw the lines that had formed over the past day. *Poor man, she must have given him a fright.* Dark circles had taken residence under his eyes, and he was still wearing clothes with her blood on them. A blanket covered his lower chest and legs.

She closed her eyes and sighed. Relationships were hard. She had never had a normal relationship with a man one on one. Keith had been distant and obviously otherwise involved. Derrick had been in a band and traveled around a lot to be where money could be made. He hadn't known how to do a one-on-one relationship either. He had a different woman in every city. Joci found out after a few weeks with him. She looked back on it now and thought about what an idiot she had been.

Jeremiah was the very first man she had been in an honest and close relationship with. She had a lot to learn.

She rubbed her hand over her belly and looked at the spot where their baby was resting. She glanced at Jeremiah and froze. His eyes were open, watching her. "I love you." He spoke softly.

She took a deep breath. "Jeremiah...I'm so sorry."

"Don't be sorry, honey. We'll get through this."

After a moment of silence, she grinned. "So, I came to tell you, I'm pregnant."

He looked at her and smiled. "I'm thrilled beyond belief. I already knew it before you went to the doctor. I just knew we were having a baby."

She nodded. She took a huge breath.

"Jeremiah. What happened after I left yesterday?"

Jeremiah leaned forward and grabbed Joci's hand.

"You know, I thought LuAnn would adjust and realize how much I love you and leave us alone. I wanted to honor Lance by giving her a chance, but now I know I'm not responsible for Lance's decisions. You made me realize that. I'm so sorry, honey." He scratched at the hair on his chin. "After you left, Chase came in and tried talking her down. She was beginning to listen to him; then the cops came in. Janice had called them when LuAnn started screaming and yelling. She knew I was going to fire LuAnn and was on alert that it might not go well. They arrested LuAnn for the damage she did in the shop and took her in. They released her a few hours later."

Jeremiah stood up and kissed Joci gently on the lips. He touched her hair and her jaw. He gently touched where she was bruised on the right side of her face.

"How do you feel this morning, baby?"

"Sore. Tired. Hurt." She smiled at his handsome face. "And unbelievably lucky."

He sat back down, never letting go of her hand. He took a deep breath and looked at her.

"Joci, I need to explain what happened. Do you think you can deal with that now without getting too upset? I don't want you to hurt yourself or the baby. But the police may be coming in to speak with you, and you need to know everything."

She swallowed hard, her brow furrowed; she tried to adjust herself and gasped at the pain that shot through her arm and hip as she moved. She looked down at her hip and noticed the bulge of bandages there.

"I don't even know what my injuries are. Can you tell me that, too?"

"I can tell you in layman's terms. The doctor will need to tell you the medical version."

～

He listed her injuries and sat still, waiting to see how she would react to that news before he continued. What he was going to tell her next was going to be more unnerving than her health update. He watched her eyes, needing to make sure she was okay. What he saw took his breath away. His brave woman sat stoically listening and taking it all with a grain of salt. He took a deep breath. "It appears that the reason your brakes didn't work was that LuAnn cut your brake lines."

Joci sucked in a breath and closed her eyes.

Softly she asked, "How do you know? Let's get it out and move on."

"Deacon swore he didn't see you touch your brakes. Your brake lights never went on. He was behind you the whole time. He saw that you were coming into Benson's Bend, and he kept waiting for you to hit your brakes. When you didn't and hit the tree, he freaked out."

"I did...I tried to brake. Nothing was there."

"Yes. I went back to the shop with Tommy, Frog, and two police officers. The officers watched Frog examine the bike. He showed them where the brake lines had been cut on the top. That kept the brake fluid from dripping out completely and leaving evidence on the floor. We checked the video footage and clearly saw LuAnn cutting the brake lines on your bike. It was Thursday morning.

"Deacon told me he had sent LuAnn home the day we told everyone we were engaged. The boys had gone to the shop and told everyone the news, and she didn't take it well. She was acting terrible, throwing things, being bitchy to everyone. Then, of course, Milwaukee. I had words with her when we got back. I told her that was it. One more incident and she was gone. Thursday afternoon, all the guys were taking a lunch break. That's when she did it."

Joci sat staring at him. Telling her this was difficult; his voice cracked, and his lungs felt constricted. He watched her eyes for signs of distress; her lips trembled slightly, and her hand balled into the blankets around her.

"Are you okay, honey?"

She nodded once. "Just trying to process all of this." Her voice was soft. He knew what she meant. He had spent yesterday trying to grasp everything that had happened in such a short period of time. It was never easy finding out someone deliberately tried to hurt you.

"Are *you* okay?" she asked.

He blew out a breath. "Even during Desert Storm, I didn't feel as murderous as I felt yesterday. If she walked in this door right now, I would strangle her with my bare hands and smile as I watched the life leave her body. She tried to kill you. That almost killed the baby. Our baby. I will never forgive her for that."

Joci nodded and swallowed. "Where is she now?"

"I'm hoping in jail. I was going to call Tommy before you woke up. I left Tommy and the police after we straightened out the video exchange. I wanted to get back here to you. They were arranging the arrest warrant and then going to pick her up."

Joci slowly nodded her head. She licked her lips and glanced at the bedside tray where a pitcher of water sat. Jeremiah instinctively poured water into a cup, opened a straw and set it in the cup. "The nurse said you can only sip."

She sipped and closed her eyes.

He set the cup on the table. "Are you okay while I call Tommy?"

She nodded. "I need some more pain medication and some rest," she told Jeremiah. He stepped out into the hall and found a nurse to take care of her. He watched as the nurse tended to her needs, adjusted the bedding, checked bandages, then injected pain meds into her IV. Joci faded off to sleep a few minutes later.

When she woke up, Gunnar, Jackie, Emily, and Thomas were in her room, along with Jeremiah, talking softly. Joci immediately found Jeremiah looking at her. She smiled softly, and he got up and walked to her bedside. He leaned down and kissed her softly on the lips. He had a hand resting on the top of her head and one resting on their baby.

"How do you feel, Mom?"

Joci looked over at Gunnar. "Better. Thank you. How are you doing?"

He looked worried and tight. His body language was something she could always read.

"I'm trying to process everything. I'm worried about you. Are you sure you're all right? How about my little brother?" Gunnar smiled.

"Sister." They all had puzzled expressions as they looked at Jeremiah.

"We're having a little girl."

Joci giggled. "When did you become a fortune teller?"

Jeremiah smiled. "There are a lot of things you don't know about me, darling. If you ask anyone in my family," he gestured wide towards his family sitting around the room, "you will hear that I have correctly determined the sex of each of my brothers' babies before they were born."

Joci and Gunnar looked at Thomas and Emily for confirmation. Thomas nodded, and Emily smiled.

"He currently holds the Sheppard record for the most correct guesses, although we still argue over Bryce and Angie's Daniel. Jeremiah wavered back and forth on that one."

Jeremiah shrugged. Jackie walked in and touched Joci's feet. "I would love a little niece to spoil. All I got was boys."

When she and David married and had babies, they had two boys: Jeremy and Dean. Jackie leaned over and hugged Gunnar with one arm.

"But they're great boys." She smiled at Gunnar, and he bowed his head, his cheeks tinted pink.

"Did they put LuAnn in jail?" Joci needed to know.

Jeremiah took a deep breath and looked at Gunnar and then back to Joci.

"Not yet. They're looking for her. She must have heard about the accident and then took off. Police are looking everywhere for her."

David walked in just then. "Hey there, girl. You feeling better?"

Joci smiled at him. "I'm better. How about you?"

David laughed. "Well, you made my hair grayer. My wife is now married to an old man."

He kissed Jackie on the temple and hugged Gunnar with one arm. "What about you, Gunnar?"

Gunnar grinned. "I'm going to have a little sister."

David looked at Joci and Jeremiah, his brows high into his hairline.

Joci giggled. "Jeremiah thinks he's the baby whisperer."

"Hey, I know some things," Jeremiah said with a grin and a fake defensive tone.

As the group quietly chatted, Joci drifted off to sleep. Some time later, she woke to David's voice, low and menacing. "Get out."

Joci opened her eyes to see Connor and an older man standing in her room. Jeremiah looked at David and then at Joci. Gunnar was watching David, as well. Jackie's mouth had dropped open, but not a sound came out.

"I said *get out*," David said again as he stood up.

Connor stepped forward and looked at Joci. "Joci, he demanded I bring him here when he heard about your accident."

Joci looked at the older man again and then gasped. It was Keith. He looked horrible—like he was twenty years older than he was.

Jeremiah looked at Joci with a question in his eyes.

"Keith," was all Joci could say.

Jeremiah stood to his full height. "Now, *I'll* tell you. Get the fuck out."

Keith looked at Gunnar. Gunnar stared at him for a long moment.

Keith turned toward Joci. He stepped forward and Jeremiah moved to block him from getting any closer. Keith stopped and looked at Jeremiah and then Joci.

Keith's voice was barely above a whisper, but he said, "I just needed to say I'm sorry." He took a few moments to catch his breath. "I didn't know how badly you were injured. I'm sorry about your accident. But in case you didn't make it out of the hospital before I died, I really wanted to say I'm sorry. That's it."

Keith's voice was barely audible; he struggled to breathe. It must have been hard for him to make it here today. He was clearly very sick. His skin was ashy and gray.

Keith looked at Gunnar and nodded slightly.

"Why?" Gunnar asked.

Keith glanced at him. "Connor told me what your mom said." Keith looked over at Joci. "It isn't true, Joci. I'm not worried about my mortality. I'm ready for any punishment God thinks I deserve. I wanted you to know that I do realize how badly I treated you...and Gunnar."

His eyes flicked to Gunnar and back to her. In a soft, breathy voice, he said, "I've thought about it so many times over the years. Dianna encouraged me to try and touch base on several occasions, but I was scared. When I was diagnosed with cancer, I worried that I wouldn't get the chance to tell you."

Keith took a short, trembling breath, then went on. "You were a wonderful girlfriend, Joci. Connor has kept me up to date with you and Gunnar all these years. I'm sorry I was such a dickhead." He slightly chuckled as he rested to fill his lungs. "I have no excuse for my horrible behavior. I hope someday you'll be able to forgive me. I treated you terribly, for no reason whatsoever. I really am sorry."

Keith looked at Gunnar. "I'm sorry, Gunnar. I really am."

Gunnar bobbed his head once and held Keith's gaze.

"I hope, with my whole heart, that you're happy, Gunnar." Keith rested his hand over his heart.

Gunnar stood tall. "I am. Dog is my dad. I now have brothers." He nodded to JT and Ryder sitting across the room with them. "I have a great mom and a great life."

Keith nodded, tears glistening in his eyes. "Good."

He turned to leave, and Connor helped him out the door. That was it. He just said what he needed to say.

Connor looked back at Joci. "I'll call you later." And they left.

They were all quiet for a long time. Things just couldn't get any more surreal than this week.

Joci looked at Gunnar. "Gunnar?"

He looked at his mom. "Yeah, I'm good, Mom. I don't feel anything really, other than sorry for him. He looks like hell...how about you?"

Joci shrugged her left shoulder a little. "I would say I'm stunned."

David walked over and put his arm around Gunnar. "I'm sorry, Gunnar."

Gunnar shrugged. Joci watched him very closely. She would have given anything for that meeting not to have happened on the heels of her accident. Poor guy had enough to deal with.

Gunnar looked at Joci again. "I'm okay, Mom. Please don't worry about me."

Then Jeremiah walked over to Gunnar and wrapped him in a hug.

Joci leaned her head back against the pillow and closed her eyes. She was tired again. Her arm and shoulder hurt. She was grateful, though. For some strange, weird reason, it did help to hear Keith say she hadn't done anything to make him cheat on her. For so many years now, she thought maybe she wasn't good enough—in bed, out of bed, it didn't matter—to keep a man happy. It was one of her biggest fears with Jeremiah. How could she make him happy when she didn't know what she had done to make Keith unhappy? Now, she knew it wasn't anything she had done or hadn't done. It was him. It felt good to know that.

The nurse walked in. Joci opened her eyes when the nurse asked her to open her mouth so she could take Joci's temperature. She chuckled a little, and the nurse looked at her with a funny expression on her face.

"I just thought you must be psychic. I hurt again and in you walk. You and Jeremiah must both have crystal balls hidden somewhere."

The nurse looked at Jeremiah with a funny look on her face.

Jeremiah smiled. "We're having a baby girl."

The nurse nodded. She gave Joci something for pain and Joci floated off to fairyland one more time.

38

IT'S ALL GOOD

The next time Joci woke up, she heard female voices speaking softly. She opened her eyes to see Staci, Jackie, Sandi, and Emily sitting in her room talking. Sandi looked up and noticed that Joci was awake. She got up and walked over to the left side of the bed. She leaned down and kissed Joci's forehead.

Sandi started crying. "God, Joci, I was so scared when I heard you had an accident. They wouldn't let me come last night. Are you okay? How are you? You're going to have a baby!"

Sandi's blubbering and prattling on without giving Joci the chance to speak made her giggle. The other women began laughing at Sandi. Jackie stood and came over next to Sandi, then put her arm around Sandi's shoulders.

"Sorry, Joci. She promised she wouldn't cry again."

Jackie smiled. Sandi tended to get emotional over things, especially something this big. Joci smiled and reached for Sandi's hand.

"Hey, it's okay. I'm going to be fine. Jeremiah thinks we're having a girl." Joci smiled.

Stiffly, she looked around for Jeremiah. Staci piped up then.

"We sent him home to change clothes. He was still wearing his bloody clothes from yesterday. He was going to shower and change and be right back."

Joci smiled and nodded slightly. It hurt to move her head more than a little.

Jackie spoke up next. "We were just talking about babies. Do you realize that Staci's grandchild and your baby will be just a few months apart in age? Jeremiah's daughter and his niece or nephew will be the same age." She smiled. "Emily and Thomas will have a grandchild and great-grandchild in the same year. Christmases will be fun."

The girls giggled and talked about babies again when the nurse walked in a few minutes later.

"We have to get you up today, Joci. How are you feeling?"

"Wait. No. We have to wait for Jeremiah. He'll be pissed if he misses that," Staci said. She looked at Joci and shrugged. "We have strict orders that he wants to be here when you get out of bed the first time."

Staci looked at the nurse. "Can we wait a few more minutes?"

The nurse glance at Joci. "Can you wait a few minutes, honey?"

Joci smiled. "Yes. I don't want Jeremiah to worry that every time he leaves here, I'll hit some milestone he wants to be here for." To Joci, this did feel like a milestone.

The nurse smiled and went on. "We aren't going far with you, Joci. We just want to get you sitting up in the chair for a little while so your lungs can work better. We don't want pneumonia setting in. I'll change your sheets. Then we'll get a new gown on you and get you back to bed. I'll have pain medication right here for you for afterward."

She nodded. She could do that. A few minutes later, Jeremiah walked in. God, he looked so good. He had showered and shaved and pulled his hair back into a ponytail. He looked yummy in his fresh shirt and clean jeans. She could look at him all day. It made her feel better to see him not so tired and dragged out. And dang, he smelled heavenly.

Jackie said, "You're just in time. They want to get Joci up."

He walked quickly over to the side of the bed on Joci's left. He leaned down and kissed her and put his hand on the baby. He did that every time now.

"Are you up for that?"

She looked at him with a bit of a shrug. "I guess it's better for me to move around a little."

"But is it going to hurt?" He worried.

"Like hell, I think. But I want to get better fast. So, I need to do what they ask of me."

Jeremiah's jaw tightened. Joci watched him process this. "Hey, if you can't handle it, Jackie can stay with me."

Jeremiah shook his head no. "If you can take it, I can."

"Good to hear," the nurse said from the doorway.

She looked at the rest of the girls. "She might be uncomfortable with a big audience. Can I encourage you all to wait in the family room?"

The girls stood to leave. They said they would be back shortly and then walked down the hall. The nurse closed the door.

She held up a syringe. "When we're done, it'll help you with the pain. Are you ready for this?"

Joci swallowed. Here goes. She nodded.

The nurse bustled around, getting the chair ready so Joci wouldn't have to go far. Her hip was going to be very sore. The nurse explained to them what needed to happen. Jeremiah could stand close by, but she would help Joci. She reminded Joci about all the places she had stitches as if she weren't aware. It would hurt like hell, but Joci should try and breathe through it. It was important. The nurse moved the IV pole and then it was time for Joci to move as well.

She took a deep breath while the nurse raised the head of the bed and lowered it so her feet could touch the floor without having to drop down. When the bed was set, she instructed Joci on how to turn toward her and scoot forward. Joci did as she was told. More than once, she gasped in pain. She breathed through it and kept moving. By the time she reached the chair, she was sweating and panting, and tears slid down her face. The nurse got her situated, covered her up with a blanket, and began changing the sheets.

Jeremiah kneeled down next to Joci. His eyes were bright with moisture. "That was pure torture watching you in so much pain."

She gasped. "Should've been me."

His voice hoarse, he said, "I'm so proud of you, Joci. You did so good, baby."

She smiled weakly. Whew, that had been hard. Before long, the nurse finished with the sheets and told Joci it was time to move back to the bed. Tears slid down Joci's face. She wiped them off and nodded. She was still a bit shaky from moving to the chair, but she was so tired that all she wanted to do was get back to bed and sleep.

She took a deep breath, and they moved her back to bed. She felt as helpless as a baby. True to her word, the nurse gave her a shot of something to manage the pain and told Jeremiah she would let the girls know it was okay to come back in. She looked at Joci and said, "After that, labor will seem like nothing."

Joci groaned. She couldn't even think about labor right now.

Jeremiah's hands shook as he caressed her face and smoothed her hair.

"I love you so much, Joci. God, I'm so proud of you."

39

GOT HER

The next morning, Joci woke up feeling better. Jeremiah couldn't be swayed to leave her alone at the hospital, so he slept in the recliner next to her bed, holding her hand.

The night before, Jackie had asked if there was anything she needed and Joci asked her to bring something else to wear besides these hospital gowns. The doctor had said they were taking the catheter out today, and she would have to start venturing all the way across the room to the bathroom. She wasn't sure how she was going to do that, but at least she wanted to have something that fit a bit better and wasn't so baggy. She thought a pair of yoga pants and a tank top would be great and was oddly excited about the prospect of wearing real clothes again.

She looked over at Jeremiah. He still slept in the chair. His breathing was steady and strong. His beautiful face was relaxed in sleep. Their baby was going to be beautiful, whether it was a boy or girl. She couldn't blame LuAnn for wanting him. What normal, red-blooded woman could look at Jeremiah and not want him?

She reached down and touched her belly where their baby rested. It had been three days now. The doctors were feeling more and more positive that she wouldn't miscarry. She had been trying not to get too excited about having another baby. If she did miscarry, it would be heartbreaking.

While she laid here in the hospital, she found herself dreaming about their lives together. Having the girls around chatting about the baby increased her excitement. Now she found that she couldn't think of the future without thinking about the baby.

She whispered as she caressed her tummy, "Please be okay, little one."

Jeremiah opened his eyes. "I love watching you talk to her." He smiled and leaned forward.

She looked into his eyes and grinned. "I love that you place your hand on my tummy every time you kiss me as if you're telling her hello as well."

"I am. I can't wait to hold her in my arms and kiss her."

She sighed. She was still sore, but she was happy.

"You know it could be a boy, right? I don't want you to be disappointed."

Jeremiah laughed. "Baby, I could never be disappointed with a child we made together...but it's a girl. I've dreamed about her."

She giggled. "You know we have a lot of work to do at the house, right? We aren't exactly set up for a baby. I was getting overwhelmed listening to the girls talk about it yesterday. So many things to buy, so much stuff to get. God, I forgot about all the stuff!"

He put his hand on her tummy. "We'll be fine, sweetheart. Whatever we need, our families will have it in a snap. We're fortunate this time. Money isn't an issue like before." He leaned up and kissed her tummy. "Good morning, little one."

Then he looked at Joci, leaned in and kissed her good morning. "Good morning, little one. How are you feeling this morning?"

"I feel better. I'm excited over getting to put clothes on. Simple little things like that and it was the first thing I thought of this morning— although the prospect of trekking to the bathroom has me practically hyperventilating."

"I hate that you have to go through this. I would take it myself in a second if I could. I'm here for as long as it takes. I hope you know that."

She smiled. She knew.

There was a knock on the door. "Glad you're awake. I have clothes." Jackie's smile could light the sky. "I knew you couldn't wait to get dressed. So, I got up early and picked up some of your things." She walked in and set a bag on the bed near Joci's feet. "How are you this morning?"

"I'm better today. Thank you so much for bringing me real clothes." Joci giggled.

"You're welcome. How are we going to do this?"

Joci tried adjusting herself in the bed. "I think I have to wait for the nurse to remove the catheter before I can put pants on."

Jackie nodded. "I had forgotten about the catheter."

The nurse rounded the door just then. "I saw a bag of clothing walk through the door. I bet you're ready to take off that designer gown you've been wearing."

Joci nodded.

"Okay, the first thing is to remove the catheter. Then we can work on getting you dressed. If you still have some strength, we'll take a trial run to the bathroom."

The nurse looked at Jackie as if to say, "You need to leave." Jackie got the message, raised her hands in the air. "I'll be out in the hall."

Then the nurse looked at Jeremiah. "I'm not leaving."

It was a statement that brooked no argument. The nurse looked at Joci, and she smirked. "Pick your battles." Once the catheter was removed, it was now time to get dressed. The nurse helped remove Joci's hospital gown, and Jeremiah gasped at all the bruises and marks on her body.

"God, Joci. Oh, honey, I'm so damned sorry."

She looked at him and touched his face. "Please don't worry. They'll heal."

They wrestled with her clothing. Jeremiah helped where he could. The nurse cut the right strap of her tank top and then slid the right side of the tank top up under her arm and over her breast. Then she pulled the straps back up over her shoulder and with a couple of safety pins, fastened them together. They laughed—it wasn't designer, but it would keep her from showing her visitors anything they shouldn't see.

"Do you feel like trying to get to the bathroom?" the nurse asked.

She nodded. "I need to know I can do it. Dreading it won't help. I need to try."

Jeremiah stood close to Joci. "I want to help her."

The nurse nodded and instructed him on how to be of the most assistance. She was cut and bruised everywhere. Joci slowly stood and grabbed Jeremiah's arm. She shook from head to toe.

"We don't have to do this, honey."

She shook her head. "Yes, we do. I need to do this."

She took a tentative step. Then another. With long pauses between each step, it took them forever to get to there. Once they made it, Joci was exhausted. She wanted to brush her teeth and wash up a little. Jeremiah insisted on helping her. They filled the sink with water, and he grabbed a washcloth. He wet the cloth and added soap. Gingerly, Joci sat on the edge of the toilet and washed her face, then her underarms. After the two of them wrestled her yoga pants down, she finally washed her lower region. It wasn't great, but it felt better to feel a little cleaner.

"I never would have dreamed you would have to help me take a sponge bath. It's embarrassing."

"Joci, there isn't a part of you I haven't already seen. Besides, do you know how impossibly useless I feel not being able to help you? This at least makes me feel like I'm of some use."

"Okay. I'm sorry. I have no idea what you must be feeling. But I can guess."

"Ready?" he asked.

She took a deep breath and nodded. He held out his arm, and she grabbed it and hoisted herself up. She cried out a little at the pain, but it wasn't as bad as yesterday. They slowly made their way back to the bed, and she eased her exhausted self into it. She shook and sweated from the exertion. But she felt great that she had accomplished what she had.

He leaned down and kissed her. "I'm very proud of you. You are one tough cookie."

Joci smiled. "You better believe it."

Jackie came back in and saw how pale Joci looked. "God, Joci. Are you okay?"

She opened her eyes. "I went to the bathroom."

Jackie looked at her sister, her brows furrowed. "Ooooookay."

Jeremiah laughed. "She means she walked to the bathroom."

"Ohhhhh. How great. How did it go?"

"Well, I'm exhausted now. So I guess I'm still pretty helpless," Joci quipped.

Jackie smiled. "But yesterday, you wouldn't have been able to do that much, so you did great."

Joci closed her eyes and quickly fell asleep.

People floated in and out all day. She took catnaps between visitors. She just couldn't help it. Jeremiah never left. Around 6:30 that evening, Jeremiah's phone rang. Most of the family was there visiting. He looked at his phone. "Tommy. Hopefully, he has some news."

He answered his phone and took Joci's hand in his. "Tommy, what's up? When?"

Jeremiah looked at Joci and watched her face.

"That's bullshit. You saw the recording. She knew exactly what she was doing... Okay. I know...sorry. Thanks, Tommy."

Jeremiah put his phone back in his pocket. "They have LuAnn. They found her in Upper Michigan hiding in a run-down motel. She's claiming she didn't know what she was doing with the bike; she was just mad at Joci."

Gunnar jumped up. "That's fucking bullshit."

Jeremiah held his hand up. "I didn't say it was true, Gunnar. I was simply repeating what Tommy said. We have the video of her cutting the brake lines. We could clearly see the look on her face. She'll go to jail."

40

MOVING ALONG

Joci spent the next week in the hospital. She was healing and still pregnant. Things were looking up. She could now make it to the bathroom on her own. She had made the trek by herself yesterday while Jeremiah was on the phone dealing with shop business. He was irritated with her for trying to do it on her own, but she needed to know what she could do in case she was home alone and needed to use the toilet. She was excited as hell to be able to go home today. It felt like weeks since she'd been there.

Jeremiah and the boys walked back into her room. They had taken all the flowers and gifts down to her car.

"Are you ready to come home with me?" Jeremiah asked as he walked back into the room, smiling when he saw her sitting up.

"Yes. I can't wait to get home." Joci sat in the chair that Jeremiah had slept in for the past week and a half. She was dressed in a clean pair of yoga pants and a new tank top, decorated with surgical tape. She was ready, just waiting for the doctor to come in and release her. Jeremiah and the boys sat in the other chairs in the room while they waited. Joci looked up when Dr. Wan, her OB-GYN, walked into the room.

"Good morning. I hear you're being released today."

Joci smiled. "Yes, I can't wait to get home. Dr. Wan, I would like you to meet Jeremiah and my sons Gunnar, JT, and Ryder. This is Dr. Wan."

Jeremiah and the boys stood up and shook hands with the petite Asian woman in the white coat. They exchanged pleasantries, and Dr. Wan glanced at Joci, a smile on her face.

"Joci, before you go, may I listen to your tummy and check on the baby?"

Joci nodded and slowly stood up. She felt a little out of balance with her arm in a cast and her shoulder in a cumbersome corset-type thing to keep it from moving. But if she moved slowly, it wasn't too bad.

Jeremiah and the boys shot up to help her, but Joci shook her head no. She needed to do this. She limped over to the bed and sat on the edge. She pushed herself back and slowly turned into the raised head of the bed. She grabbed the controller and lowered the head down so she was lying flatter.

Jeremiah and the boys hovered nearby. Dr. Wan smiled as she pulled her stethoscope out.

Dr. Wan winked at Joci. "I probably won't be able to hear the heartbeat, but I would like to do a sonogram to make sure everything is okay. We might be able to see the baby's heartbeat on the sonogram. If you're at least six weeks pregnant, we'll be able to hear it. Do you mind if we do it right now before you leave?"

"No, I don't mind. I want to know that she's okay." Joci glanced at Jeremiah, and he nodded in agreement.

"'She?'" Dr. Wan smiled.

Gunnar spoke up. "Dad knows the baby's a girl. I'm going to have a little sister." His smile lit up the room.

Dr. Wan smiled and nodded. "I'll go out and have the technicians bring the machine in, and we'll take a look. Stay right where you are, Joci."

She left, and Joci winked at Jeremiah. He had a huge grin plastered on his face.

Within half an hour, the technician was in the room hooking up the sonogram machine and preparing Joci. When Joci had been pregnant with Gunnar, she hadn't done this. The technician pulled up Joci's shirt and tucked towels around her clothing, so nothing got full of gel. They dimmed the lights. Dr. Wan and the technician were to Joci's right, and Jeremiah and the boys were to her left, watching the screen on the sonogram machine.

The tech started pushing the probe around Joci's tummy and stopped on a little blurb. It didn't look like anything but a blob. The tech took a few pictures and kept moving the probe around. After a few minutes, she moved the probe around, then stopped and went back.

"Oh, well, look at that. I think I see the heartbeat. Dr. Wan, what do you think?"

Dr. Wan looked closely at the screen. The tech put a little more pressure on Joci's tummy and there it was! You could see movement within the little blurb. It was very faint, but there was a little flutter.

"Yes, I believe that's her heartbeat," Dr. Wan said.

Jeremiah grabbed Joci's hand. "Amazing," was all he could say.

Gunnar said, "Cool."

Ryder whispered, "I'll be damned."

Joci just stared. The baby was alive. She was going to live. Her eyes sparkled with moisture; she was so relieved. She hadn't even realized how scared she'd been. Jeremiah leaned down and kissed her forehead.

"Don't cry, baby. Look, she's healthy."

Joci tried to control herself. "I know. I'm so relieved. I can't believe she made it through."

Dr. Wan touched Joci's leg and patted it. "Looks like you have a strong little girl there."

The technician spoke up. "We can't tell the sex yet."

Jeremiah informed the tech that he knew it was a little girl. He had dreamed about her. The technician just nodded her head.

A few more pictures were taken, and the technician packed up the machine and made her way out the door. Dr. Wan told Joci she would see her at her scheduled appointment in a couple of weeks, and she left. The attending physician came in a while later and released Joci to go home.

It took a while to get her into the car and then into the house. She let out a huge sigh of relief, it was great to be home. "I need to lie down. I hope you don't mind. Will you all be here or are you leaving?"

Jeremiah chuckled. "We're staying. JT and Ryder are running out to get lunch in a little while." He kissed her lightly on the lips.

"Then do you mind if I sleep on the sofa? That way I can hear you as I fall asleep."

JT shrugged. "Will you be comfortable on the sofa, Mom?"

She stared at JT and swallowed the knot in her throat. That was the first time he had called her Mom. She smiled. "It makes me feel better to hear people talking." As she walked by him, she gave him a brief hug. He gently wrapped his arm around her, afraid to squeeze her.

Jeremiah patted JT on the shoulder, his eyes growing moist, then walked into the living room with Joci.

She sat on the sofa. He plumped some pillows behind her back and gently pulled her feet up. Gunnar ran and got her a blanket and threw it over her. She smiled and drifted off to sleep right away.

"Ryder, you'll have to climb out of your shell eventually," JT laughed.

"Fuck you, JT. It might be easy for you to come on to women; it's not for me," Ryder muttered.

Joci opened her eyes and looked around the room. Ryder leaned forward and smiled at her.

"How are you feeling?"

Joci smiled at him, "I'm feeling pretty good. How are you doing? Are they picking on you?"

Ryder shrugged. "They're assholes. I'm sorry, Mom. I feel bad that you're going through this."

"Thank you, Ryder. I don't want you to worry. I'm just fine, getting stronger every day." Joci smiled and held his gaze.

He leaned forward and kissed her forehead. Her eyes glistened at the sudden show of emotion. Ryder...the shy boy.

When he sat back, JT piped up. "Are you hungry? We put some stuff together for a quick dinner."

She nodded, noticing for the first time that she was feeling a bit like eating. Gunnar and Jeremiah jumped up to bring the food into the living room.

She turned herself on the sofa, so her legs were on the floor. She struggled to sit up with only one hand free. With her bandages, she felt out of balance. Ryder and JT both jumped up to help her.

Joci looked up and smiled. "If I could just hold onto one of you, I should be able to leverage myself around."

Ryder leaned down and held his hand out for her. She grabbed his hand with her left and pulled herself to the edge of the sofa. Just that little movement caused pain to shoot up her right arm. She winced and yelped. Ryder leaned down closer and looked into her eyes to assess her.

She smiled weakly and took a deep breath. "I'm sorry. Sometimes I move wrong, and it hurts. But it hurts less today than yesterday. Tomorrow will be better still."

Ryder nodded and took a deep breath. "I love you, Mom."

Joci couldn't help herself. Tears sprang to her eyes, and a small sob escaped her throat. She reached her left hand up and cupped the back of Ryder's head, pulling him down for a little hug. Shaking from the exertion and emotion, she said, "I love you, too, Ryder."

When he sat back, she looked over at JT. His eyes were glistening as he watched them. "JT, I love you, too." He nodded and opened his mouth to say something but closed it quickly.

Just then, Jeremiah and Gunnar walked back into the room with a couple of trays.

Jeremiah looked at Joci, his brows furrowed. "Are you okay, honey?"

She smiled and nodded. "I'm better than ever."

"I wasn't sure how your tummy was doing. It's getting close to evening now, and I thought warm soup and crackers would be good for you. Mom left some ginger tea for you as well."

"Thank you for remembering, Jeremiah. While I was in the hospital, they gave me some anti-nausea medicine in the evening so I wouldn't have to go through that. But I don't have any now. I'll just sip my soup and tea and nibble on my crackers until I know."

He handed her a cup of soup, while the boys began eating. She sipped as her men sat and talked and ate. She conserved her energy as much as she could. She wanted to enjoy this for a while.

"Did Dad tell you about Deborah?" Gunnar asked.

Joci froze at Deborah's name. She'd almost forgotten about that can of worms. She slowly focused on Jeremiah, who turned toward her. Joci's voice felt small. "She's not pregnant?"

He leaned back. "Oh, she's pregnant. But, it's her boyfriend's kid." His jaw tightened and his lips thinned.

"You're not happy about that?"

His brows drew together then he leaned forward and gently took her hand in his. "I don't give a shit whose baby she has. I'm pissed that she tried causing trouble with us." He scratched his beard. "You were right; LuAnn put her up to it." He let out a long breath.

Joci stared into his eyes for a long time. The green was back. She'd been sad that the darkness had seeped in for a while. His sparkle was vibrant again; his light was shining through. "How did you find out?"

He sat back and lifted up his backside as he pulled his phone from his pocket. He swiped across the screen and pulled up a text.

"*Dog. Sorry to hear about Joci's accident. I need to tell the truth. I'm not expecting your baby. It's my boyfriend, Daniel's. We're going to get married this weekend. Hope all will be right with you. Deb.*"

Joci handed his phone back and shook her head. "So many people just love causing trouble for others. I don't get it."

He set his phone on the coffee table. "I don't either. LuAnn must have put her up to it. I don't know how they know each other. I don't care actually. But I'm just glad she felt the need to confess." He took a bite of sandwich and chewed. "She was probably worried she'd be implicated in your accident in some way and wanted to come clean."

Joci nodded and sipped at her soup.

JT was the first to bring up the wedding. "So, are you still getting married on the 28th?"

"No," Jeremiah replied.

Joci looked at him, startled. Had he changed his mind? The boys were very, very quiet.

Jeremiah looked at Joci. "I don't want to wait. I want to get married tomorrow."

Joci let out the breath she was holding and started shaking her head no. "For the rest of our lives, we'll look at the pictures of the day we got married. I don't want to see them with me all bandaged and bruised."

"But, I...""

"No, Jeremiah. Please don't fight me on this. I've never been married. I will only marry once. At least give me this. Don't let LuAnn take that away from me."

He closed his eyes. How could he deny her this after what she'd been through? He just wanted her to be his—legally. He was terrified that something else would happen to her.

"It's only three and a half weeks away Jeremiah. The doctor said he could have most of the bandages off by then. I'll find a dress to cover the rest of them up. I won't be one-hundred percent, but the pictures won't show that."

He turned to look at her, searching her eyes. He nodded very slightly. "Okay. But no later than that."

They had finished eating and were chatting. Suddenly, Joci sat forward. She looked panicked, and Jeremiah stood quickly and went to her side.

"Honey, are you going to be sick?"

She looked at him with tears in her eyes. He kneeled down, so he was eye level with her. He searched her eyes and saw the tears fall.

"Baby," was all she could say. Her left hand wrapped around her stomach and a sob broke loose. God, she was losing the baby. It had been nine days since her accident. She had gotten comfortable with the thought that she wouldn't lose the baby. But, right now she was experiencing severe cramps.

Jeremiah stood up, reached over, and grabbed his phone. He called Dr. Wan's number. When she answered, Jeremiah jumped in, "Dr. Wan, this is Jeremiah Sheppard. Joci is having sharp cramps."

"Okay, Jeremiah. Is she spotting or bleeding?"

"Joci, are you spotting or bleeding?"

"I don't know."

"Okay, Jeremiah, listen to me. Stay calm, please, for Joci's sake. Have her go and check if she's bleeding. Call me back as soon as you know."

Jeremiah squatted down in front of Joci. "Shh, baby, don't cry. We're all here with you." He wrapped his big hands around her small ones and squeezed. "Can you make it to the bathroom, baby? You need to check and make sure you aren't bleeding. Then I'll call Dr. Wan back. Okay? Can you do that for me?"

Joci gasped at another sharp pain. She breathed through it and then nodded.

41

FAMILY

"Mom, can we stay here tonight?" JT asked.

"You boys never have to ask to stay here. Of course, you can."

The men all fussed over her, brought chairs into the bedroom, and sat around talking. Joci nodded in and out of sleep, loving the sound of her men's voices.

At one point, she woke up, and the room was dark. Jeremiah was next to her, sleeping soundly. Joci looked at the clock on the dresser—it was two eighteen a.m. She slept so much that she didn't have a schedule anymore. And she had to pee.

It took her forever to maneuver herself around so she could get out of bed. She had started slowly walking to the bathroom when Jeremiah jumped out of bed, "What are you doing, Joci?"

"I have to pee. Go back to sleep. I'll be fine." She continued on.

When she finished, she opened the bathroom door, and Jeremiah was standing there, waiting for her.

She chuckled. "Did you listen the whole time? There's something wrong with that."

"No, but I heard you washing your hands, and I got up to help you. There's nothing wrong with me. I just wanted to make sure you were okay." He kissed her temple and held her left hand as she hobbled to her side of the bed and wrestled herself back under the covers. Once she was situated, she laid back against the soft pillows and let out a big sigh.

He walked around and slid into the bed behind her. Very gently, he pulled her to him so her back was pressed against his stomach. She sighed when she felt his arms slowly coming around her. "I missed this. I missed you holding me. I missed sleeping with you."

Jeremiah kissed the back of her head. "I missed this, too, and you so much. I'm so sorry I let this happen."

She let out a breath. "You didn't cause it to happen, Jeremiah. You didn't allow it to happen. LuAnn is the only one to blame there."

"Stop it. A long time ago, you asked me to take care of the LuAnn situation, and I only went so far as talking to her. I should have fired her and removed her from our lives. That's on me. Because I didn't, and now you're suffering."

She sighed. "Well, we could beat each other and ourselves up, and it won't change anything. So, we need to move on. Okay?"

He took a deep breath and let it out slowly. He kissed Joci's temple and pulled her in tighter.

"Will we have to sit through a trial, Jeremiah?" Her voice was small and soft.

"I'm afraid so, honey. But, I'll be with you every step of the way. I want her in jail. I want her away from us. I want her punished for what she's caused you."

Joci was quiet. She wanted LuAnn punished, too. But she was nervous about the trial and what she would have to hear throughout that process. LuAnn no doubt would make herself seem pathetic. She loved Jeremiah, and she lost her mind over him. Poor thing.

"Tonight, the boys called me Mom and told me they loved me." Joci smiled.

"I know. My chest has been tight all night, watching them with you. Did that make you feel good?"

"Yes. I guess I hadn't thought about the fact that they never had anyone to call Mom before. It makes it even more special to me that they think of me that way. If anything good is coming out of all of this mess, it's just that it brought us all closer together."

"How typical of you to look at the silver lining. It's one of the many things I love about you."

Joci smiled.

"Get some sleep, baby. Tomorrow everyone is coming over to plan a wedding. You aren't going to do anything but answer questions. You're going to marry me in three and a half weeks. I won't postpone it, not for anything. I don't even want to wait that long."

She drifted off to sleep, thanking God for giving her Jeremiah, the boys, and this little baby she was carrying. They had had a little scare, but it turned out to be just cramps. Dr. Wan talked them through it and said it was probably from all the trauma. Joci was to try and relax and keep tabs on herself. If the cramps started again, she was to call Dr. Wan.

42

AT LAST

J oci sat on a chair in front of a tall mirror, watching Sandi put the finishing touches on her makeup. A few more strokes of a brush and Sandi stepped back and looked at Joci.

"You look so beautiful. You always do; but today, you look even more beautiful. Being pregnant agrees with you," Sandi said.

Joci smirked. "Well, it does now that I'm not puking every day. Gawd, I hate that."

Jackie chuckled from behind her. "You were a puker with Gunnar, too; do you remember? I woke up every morning to you throwing up in the bathroom. At the time, I thought I would never get pregnant if I had to throw up every day. But less than a year later, I was puking in the bathroom, too."

They laughed at the memory. Emily and Erin walked into the room smiling.

"Glad everyone is so cheerful," Emily said, her cheeks pink with excitement.

"We were just reminiscing about how much we both threw up while we were pregnant. I'm glad Joci is going through it this time and not me." Jackie winked at Joci.

Emily looked at Joci and smiled warmly. "How are you feeling, sweetheart?"

"I feel great. I haven't thrown up in three days. It must be over, finally."

"You look beautiful. Jeremiah won't be able to take his eyes off you." Erin smiled.

Just then, Angie and Staci walked into the room. Staci whistled. "You look beautiful, Joci. Hubba-hubba."

Joci laughed. "Thank you. I guess it's time to wrestle me into this dress."

Jackie walked over to the closet where Joci's wedding dress hung. She pulled the gorgeous ivory dress off its hanger and cradled it in her arms as she carried it to Joci.

Joci's hard cast had been removed. She had to wear a soft cast for another few weeks, but today, she didn't have it on. She had had a few words with her doctor and Jeremiah about it, but Joci could be stubborn when she really wanted something too. And today, she didn't want any reminder of her accident or the person behind it.

The skin on her arm and shoulder looked nasty from being in a cast, but she had been exfoliating and moisturizing over the past few days to make it look better. She was going to start physical therapy in a week. Right now, she couldn't lift her arm very high. There were scars where the doctors had inserted the screws, but she had been told that the scars would gradually fade away.

Jackie held Joci's dress open as Sandi helped her out of her robe. She stepped into her wedding dress. Her baby bump was beginning to show, but it was almost unnoticeable. She was ten weeks pregnant now.

Emily, her future mother-in-law, held out her hand to support Joci. She smiled and grasped the older woman's hand, mostly so Emily would feel like she was helping. The main thing Joci learned over her rehabilitation was that everyone wanted to feel like they were helping in some way, no matter how small. Joci had to learn to let them so they would feel better. She had been so used to doing everything on her own; she didn't realize how helpless the people who loved her felt.

Sandi, Staci, and Erin zipped her up and started arranging the train. Sandi placed the beautiful wide ivory band with Swarovski crystals displayed in a floral pattern on Joci's head.

Her dress was simply stunning. It was a soft organza mermaid gown with hand-sewn Swarovski crystal and diamante beading encrusted on the neckline and dropped waist. The full skirt had dramatic layers of organza that flowed full to the floor. Joci had asked the seamstress to alter the dress to add sleeves to cover her scars and bruises. They were light and lacey, and even though you could see through them, the lace and beading camouflaged her scars. The add-on sleeves matched perfectly, and it would have been impossible to tell the dress hadn't initially been designed that way.

The back of the gown was open with lace trim trailing to a V that stopped at her waist. A deep gray satin sash went around her waist and tied in a perfect bow in the back and trailed to the bottom of the dress. There was an intricate lace detail at the bottom of the dress, highlighted by the gray sash.

It was stunning. And Joci felt fabulous in it. She turned to look at the other women in the room. They were quiet for a few beats.

Emily sobbed and raised her hand to her mouth. Tears formed in her eyes. "You look so beautiful, Joci. That dress is perfect, just perfect."

Joci smiled at her. "Thank you. It feels perfect."

Everyone else burst into excited compliments. Then there was a knock on the door, and Molly Bates, the photographer, walked into the room.

"Hi, can I come in and take pictures?"

"Sure, Molly. Come on in and meet everyone," Joci said.

"Molly, this is Emily, Jeremiah's mom. Staci, Angie, and Erin are Jeremiah's sisters-in-law. You know Jackie and Sandi, of course. Everyone, this is Molly. I met her a while back at a class, and then again on the Veteran's Ride. She was one of the photographers. She freelances and I am thrilled she could come today."

Molly grinned and said, "Hello, everyone; it's great to meet you. Okay, let's start getting some pictures, shall we? Then, while you're putting on the finishing touches, I'll go up and take pictures of the guys."

For the next forty-five minutes, they proceeded to snap various pictures in different groupings and poses.

Molly walked down the hall and knocked on the half-open door of the guys' dressing room. She peeked in, catching Jeremiah's eye. He quickly waved her in, then walked over and gave her a hug. "Thank you for being our wedding photographer today, Molly. Joci's ecstatic you were available."

Molly smiled. "I'm happy beyond belief to be here. I love Joci."

Jeremiah smiled. "Everyone, this is Molly Bates. Molly, let me introduce you to everyone here." He introduced his Marine buddies, then the family. "My father, Thomas. Joci's brother-in-law, David; and my sons, Gunnar, JT, and Ryder."

Ryder and Molly stared at each other for a few beats longer than everyone else. Jeremiah smiled, cleared his throat, and Molly looked at him, her cheeks tinted pink.

"Okay. Ummm, let's start over here." She pointed to an area in the corner.

Emily Ann, Dayton and Staci's daughter, knocked on the door. "Time to get married, Joci," she smiled.

The girls giggled and cheered. It was time. Erin opened the boxes with the flowers in them and handed Jackie and Sandi their bouquets. "Oh, so pretty, Joci. You did an amazing job on the colors," Sandi beamed.

"When you said we were carrying orange flowers with accents of silvery-gray Dusty Miller in them, I thought you were crazy, but this works," Jackie added.

The bridesmaids were wearing gray dresses to match Joci's sash with ivory sashes around their waists. Joci's bouquet consisted of long-stemmed silver roses with a few orange flowers tucked here and there. The corsages were pinned on, and they started down the hall.

Those not in the wedding party walked into the church and sat down.

Jackie hugged Joci. "I love you, Sis. I'm thrilled for you."

"Thank you, Jackie. For everything you've done for me over the years. I love you."

"Thank you for letting me be a part of this. I couldn't be happier for you," Sandi said.

Joci laughed. "I couldn't get married without you. I love you, too. Okay, let's go. I'm excited."

Gunnar came walking down the hall and stopped in front of her. He looked amazing. The guys were all wearing gray to match the girl's dresses. With Gunnar's dark hair and bright blue eyes, he looked gorgeous in the tuxedo.

"Wow, Mom. You look amazing. Jeremiah's going to shit when he sees you."

Joci laughed. "Not the reaction I'm hoping for, but I think I know what you mean. You look pretty handsome yourself, Gunnar. You clean up good."

Everyone chuckled, and Jackie opened the door to the church. Sandi started walking down the aisle. Jackie was next. As soon as she had made it all the way down the aisle, the processional music for the bride started. Then Joci and Gunnar began walking down the aisle.

The gasps and sighs as she walked by made her so happy. She felt like a princess. She felt beautiful. But all she could see was Jeremiah. He was stunning in his ivory tuxedo, ivory vest, and an ivory cravat with thin gray stripes in it. His hair was pulled back into a ponytail. He looked perfect.

Jeremiah sucked in his breath at his first look at Joci. She had refused to let him see her dress or know anything about what it looked like. It had driven him crazy not knowing. Now, he was glad she made him wait—again. She was amazingly beautiful. Jesus, he was a lucky man. He couldn't take his eyes off her.

Dayton chuckled next to him, and Jeremiah smirked. When they reached Jeremiah, Gunnar shook his hand and then grabbed Jeremiah in a hug. At the same time, JT and Ryder came up and hugged Joci. The boys sat down, and Jeremiah held his arm out.

She held on to his arm, and they walked up the three steps to the altar.

He looked down at her and smiled. "You are stunning, Joci. You take my breath away."

She smiled as she looked into his eyes. "I was thinking the same thing about you." She winked and the minister began talking.

A short time later, the minister said, "You may kiss your bride."

Jeremiah leaned down and pulled Joci into his arms. He turned his head so his mouth fit over hers and kissed her until her toes curled. Right in church! People whistled and clapped. Still he kissed her. When he finally pulled away, he leaned his forehead against hers for a few seconds.

"I'm the happiest man in the world right now, Mrs. Sheppard."

Joci laughed. "Good to know. I'm the happiest woman in the world right now. I love you crazy."

"I love you crazy."

"Ladies and gentlemen, I would like to introduce you to Mr. and Mrs. Jeremiah Sheppard."

The recessional began, and Jeremiah and Joci walked down the aisle together as husband and wife amid clapping and cheering from the congregation. They stood in the reception line, greeting all who came through. Molly walked up to them as the last few well-wishers hugged the bride and groom to ask for a few more pictures.

They needed to take family pictures and more pictures of the bride and groom.

Jeremiah leaned down and chuckled. "I think Molly and Ryder are attracted to each other. You should have seen the sparks fly when they met."

Joci looked up at Jeremiah. "Really? Very interesting. He's so shy. Will he approach her?"

Jeremiah shrugged. "Time will tell."

The remainder of the night was a blur. They went through all the motions and spoke to everyone who came to celebrate with them.

They left the reception around eleven p.m., neither of them able to wait another minute to make love.

43

MR. & MRS

As soon as the door closed in their hotel room, Jeremiah lifted Joci and carried her to the bed. "Jesus, I can't wait another minute to be in you."

"Jeremiah," Joci whispered.

Cupping her face in his hands, he looked deeply into her eyes. "I love you crazy, Mrs. Sheppard. Always have, always will."

She held his eyes in hers. "I love you crazy, Mr. Sheppard."

He fit his lips over hers and mated his tongue with hers. Slow, sensual, loving. He reached around her and unzipped her dress. He gently pulled the dress from her shoulders and down her arms. He stepped back to help her step out of it. Holding her left hand, she smirked at him as she lifted her left foot slowly out of her dress.

His breath caught. "Joci...I don't have words," his voice cracked.

He continued to stare at her foot while swallowing back the emotion.

"Do you like it?" Her voice was soft.

"Jesus. Joci, it's beautiful. I'm...stunned...honored. I'm speechless."

She'd had her tattoo finished by Julie, Deacon's wife. Where once had been a bud without a flower on the top of her foot, was a beautiful, gray flower with blue detailing and edging.

He bent down and lifted Joci onto the bed. He sat on the edge and pulled her foot onto his lap. He looked at the tattoo. It was still fresh, but so beautiful, the coloring perfect. His two favorite colors. He touched it and ran his finger around the little flower. He looked up at Joci and tears slid down his cheeks. Joci smiled and wiped the tears away from his face.

"I love you crazy."

"God, I love you, too. Thank you so very much for trusting me. For marrying me. For having my baby."

He leaned in and kissed her very tenderly. He framed her face with his hands and looked into her eyes. It was hard to speak with all the emotions clogging his throat. "What's this, Joci?"

Her voice cracked. "It's my family."

Jeremiah raised his eyebrows in question. Joci swallowed to wet her throat. "We are all bound by a tenuous little vine, which, if not nurtured, can wither and die. The vine is only as strong as the people who take care of it. The flowers are the fruit of that labor of taking care of each other. Each flower is one of the people in my family who help me nurture this vine. Each flower is the person's favorite color."

Jeremiah touched the little white violet on Joci's ankle and asked her about each flower.

"How about this new little orange flower?"

"JT."

"And this green flower?"

"Ryder."

Trailing his finger down the vine to the top of Joci's foot to a beautiful gray flower with blue edges, he asked, "And this?"

Her voice was full of emotion when she spoke, "That's the one man who loves me completely, doesn't let me down, doesn't betray me, keeps me safe, holds me when I'm sad, shares my happiness, and wants me and no other."

"Yes, it is," Jeremiah said, his voice husky.

He leaned over and kissed her, deeply and with the utmost tenderness. In unison, they worked at their clothing. Jeremiah positioned himself on top of her, gently sliding his forearms under her shoulders and holding her close. "This is without a doubt the best day of my life. Yeah?"

"Yeah. Mine, too." Never looking away, Joci slid her hand into Jeremiah's hair at the nape and squeezed.

"I'm coming in, baby. Open up for me."

She smiled as she wrapped her legs around him. He tilted his hips and pushed himself inside, causing each of them to groan.

She closed her eyes at the feeling of him sliding into her. There was no other feeling on earth like this. "Open your eyes, Joci. Watch me make love to you."

Opening her eyes, she met green eyes, full of love. "Yes. What a beautiful idea."

He slowly moved in and out of her. Loving her like this was sensual. Staring into her beautiful eyes, he continued the easy rhythm.

"Your hot little pussy is always so wet and ready for me, Joci. Do you know what that does to me?"

"All I know is when I see you, touch you, even hear your voice, my body responds."

Their breathing grew ragged. "What do you need, Joci? I need you to come."

"You. All of your passion. Give that to me, Jeremiah."

With a groan, he began his sweet assault on her body. Pushing into her, his rhythm increased, his breathing labored. His body tightened, and he implored, "Joci. Now."

She tilted her hips forward, feeling all of him as he plunged into her. Rocking her hips with his, the feel of him sliding into her was quickly pushing her to the edge. She whimpered as her core tightened. He pushed into her with more force. "Jeremiah…I…"

She cried out as her orgasm hit her. He pushed into her and held as his cock throbbed and pulsed with his release. He rested his head on her shoulder, waiting for his breathing to slow. She began gently massaging his head; her hand still tangled in his hair.

She lay in Jeremiah's strong, warm arms. Her three boys were happy and thriving, and her baby was sleeping in her tummy. Life had a way of breaking people apart and bringing them together. It was strong, this family unit. Joci's last thought before falling asleep was, "Thank you, God, for bringing me so much joy."

Moving to Hope is up next. Find out how Ryder and Molly find love -

Get book #2 Moving to Hope now.

Keep in touch and learn about new releases, sales, recipes, and other fun things by signing up for my newsletter - https://www.subscribepage.com/PJsReadersClub_copy

ENJOY THIS BOOK? YOU CAN MAKE A BIG DIFFERENCE

Reviews are the most powerful tools in my arsenal when it comes to getting attention for my books. As mush as I'd like to, I don't have the financial muscle of a New Your publisher. I can't take out full page ads in the newspaper or put posters on the subway.

(Not yet, anyway.)

But I do have something much more powerful and effective than that, and it's something that those big publishers would die to get their hands on.

A committed and loyal bunch of readers.

Honest reviews of my books help bring them to the attention of other readers.

If you've enjoyed this book I would be so grateful to you if you could spend just five minutes leaving a review (it can be as short as you like) on the book's vendor page. You can jump right to the page of your choice by clicking below.

Thank you so very much.

ALSO BY PJ FIALA

To see a list of all of my books with the blurbs go to: https://www.pjfiala.com/bibliography-pj-fiala/

You can find all of my books at https://pjfiala.com/books

Romantic Suspense

Rolling Thunder Series

Moving to Love, Book 1

Moving to Hope, Book 2

Moving to Forever, Book 3

Moving to Desire, Book 4

Moving to You, Book 5

Moving Home, Book 6

Moving On, Book 7

Rolling Thunder Boxset, Books 1-3

Military Romantic Suspense

MEET PJ

Writing has been a desire my whole life. Once I found the courage to write, life changed for me in the most profound way. Bringing stories to readers that I'd enjoy reading and creating characters that are flawed, but lovable is such a joy.

When not writing, I'm with my family doing something fun. My husband, Gene, and I are bikers and enjoy riding to new locations, meeting new people and generally enjoying this fabulous country we live in.

I come from a family of veterans. My grandfather, father, brother, two sons, and one daughter-in-law are all veterans. Needless to say, I am proud to be an American and proud of the service my amazing family has given.

My online home is https://www.pjfiala.com.
You can connect with me on Facebook at https://www.facebook.com/PJFialaı,
and
Instagram at https://www.Instagram.com/PJFiala.
If you prefer to email, go ahead, I'll respond - pjfiala@pjfiala.com.